Suit up in Scrubs

Also by Charles Clark

"Trails to Dos Encinos"

SUIT UP IN SCRUBS

Suit Up: *to put on an athletic uniform, spacesuit, etc. in preparation for a particular activity* (*Webster's New World College Dictionary* **FOURTH EDITION.**)

a novel by
Charles Clark

iUniverse, Inc.
New York Lincoln Shanghai

Suit up in Scrubs

All Rights Reserved © 2004 by Charles Clark

No part of this book may be reproduced or transmitted in any form or by any means, graphic, electronic, or mechanical, including photocopying, recording, taping, or by any information storage retrieval system, without the written permission of the publisher.

iUniverse, Inc.

For information address:
iUniverse, Inc.
2021 Pine Lake Road, Suite 100
Lincoln, NE 68512
www.iuniverse.com

ISBN: 0-595-31414-7 (pbk)
ISBN: 0-595-66310-9 (cloth)

Printed in the United States of America

For Joyce, my wife and partner

Acknowledgements

Devorah Fox for her wisdom, advice, and support

Kay Clark for another incredible cover design

Bob Hawkins for his patience in producing the cover photo

Chapter 1

▼

Westlake, Texas May, 2003

Josh Lehman flung his arm aimlessly toward the nightstand. "It can't be time…it can't be," he groaned as he groped for the alarm clock, only to find that the annoying sound was not coming from the clock at all. He tried to ignore the clamor, but to no avail.

He finally reached the phone and removed the receiver. The sleep-shattering noise that rudely awakened him abruptly ceased, but the shouting voice from the dangling hand piece kept him from drifting back into his peaceful slumber.

"Josh…damn it, wake up!"

Again, he tried to ignore what he heard and replaced the receiver. Immediately, the ringing started again. He couldn't ignore it any longer and made up his mind ahead of time that he was going to be plenty pissed off at this intrusion. He was sure it was Luke's voice that he heard before he hung up the phone. He picked up the phone and screamed.

"Luke, what in the hell do you want? It's three o'clock!"

"Josh, get your ass out of bed. I need you here…now!" said Luke. "I'm sending an ambulance for you…should be there any minute."

"What the hell for?" he asked.

"We've got major chest trauma here…probably a ruptured pulmonary artery. I'm fighting every minute to keep him alive."

"Herrington has taken over surgery call," Josh said. "I just finished my last case less than two hours ago. Call Herrington!"

"He's here now, jerk!" Luke yelled. "He can't handle it. You know that."

"Look, man, I'm wiped out. I couldn't even shave myself safely."

"I don't give a crap about how tired you are," said Luke. "This guy is dying and you are the only one who can turn this around. The old man is on my ass to get something done."

"What old man?"

"Bradford, dammit!" Luke answered. "It's his son…it's Donnie. He crashed his new BMW convertible into a brick wall." *Why did he have to ask?* thought Luke.

"Let the son-of-a-bitch die," said Josh. "I'm going back to sleep."

"Josh, damn it," pleaded Luke, "do this for me. I know how you feel, but this is me begging." There was a long pause. "Josh!" he yelled.

"I'm moving, Luke," he said, "but my heart is not in it."

"Thanks, Josh. Race to your front door and climb into the ambulance. Don't take time to dress. Go in your skivvies. They'll make a 'red light' run. As soon as you're in the ambulance, put on a scrub suit. When you hit the dock you'll be wheeled up here by chariot…straight to the operating room. Herrington will be scrubbed in to assist by the time you get here."

"You're going to owe me, Luke."

"We'll talk about it."

* * * *

The wailing of the siren in the distance, the flashes of red light across the ceiling and walls of his bedroom, then the sound of the ambulance coming to a screeching halt in front of his condo shocked Josh into the reality that he had to move fast. His mind rapidly cleared—a ruptured pulmonary artery! What chance did he have of getting it repaired quickly enough to save Donnie's life? Not very great. He hit the deck, barefoot and wearing only shorts, and flew down the stairs, hardly touching every third or fourth step.

No sooner had he climbed into the back of the ambulance than the door slammed shut and they were in flight toward the hospital. He donned a scrub suit, operating room gown, and shoe covers—even though there were no shoes to cover. *This will be a first,* he thought, as a faint smile crossed his face, *doing an operative procedure barefoot. Dr. Dubonet would have a good laugh if he knew.*

The few minutes before they arrived at the Emergency Room entrance gave Josh time to organize his thoughts. First, he mapped out in his mind the approach he would use for the major undertaking he would face in the operating room—identifying the torn artery and stopping the bleeding as quickly as possible. And what other injuries would he find when he opened Donnie's chest? A

CT scan, which he was sure had already been done, gave only a limited indication of the severity of any chest injury. He wouldn't know the entire extent until he got the chest opened and had a firsthand look. Thank God that Luke would be giving the anesthetic!

The constant screaming of the sirens had a mesmerizing effect on Josh as the ambulance weaved around the few cars on the streets at that early hour. He thought of the many times he and Luke had faced crucial moments—in the operating room, on the football field, and even in their personal lives. Being there together, supporting each other, was the driving force that so often led to some form of victory during those crises.

Josh grabbed for a handrail to keep from being thrown to the floor as the ambulance came to an abrupt halt. The doors swung open and he jumped out—literally—into the arms of the two massive attendants who plopped him into a waiting wheelchair. *Fortunately, at this hour only a few people will notice how embarrassed I must appear,* he thought. They raced down the hospital corridors at breakneck speed. The elevator door was being held open for them and soon they were at the doors to the operating room suite.

Josh ripped off the gown he had grabbed in the ambulance just before being enveloped in a sterile one, plus gloves that came from somewhere. He took his place at the operating table across from Herrington and immediately assumed control. He turned to Luke, who was busily adjusting dials on his anesthetic machine.

"What is his status?"

"Surprisingly stable," answered Luke. "We have a chest tube in place and we're re-infusing his own blood almost as fast as he's losing it. I'm fairly certain we've managed to keep his brain oxygenated."

"What brain?" asked Josh, sarcasm oozing from his every word.

"Josh…cool it!" Luke admonished.

"I apologize," he replied, as he adjusted the drapes in preparation to open Donnie's chest cavity.

Josh glanced over the drapes at the pale face of Donnie Bradford and again felt his anger beginning to boil. This creep had ruined his life, and now Josh was expected to use the skills he had acquired from years of training—years of sacrifice—to save his life? The thought crossed his mind: *Why even try?*

Josh shook his head, as if to clear the nagging bitterness he felt. *I have got to erase the identity of this patient from my mind. He is a dying man who needs me to put into use every bit of my training and passion to help. I've been trained to heal, regardless of my opinion of any person—whether beggar or rich playboy—regardless of my personal animosity toward that person.*

Josh became at once the skilled cardiothoracic surgeon—brought on stage for his unique ability to perform a difficult procedure. He would rise to the occasion and tackle the problem lying before him with the dexterity of a well-oiled, fine-tuned machine—a "robot" of sorts, programmed to save lives.

With scalpel in hand, held over the very center of Donnie's chest, he paused for an agonizing moment. He looked at Luke and Luke nodded reassuringly as if to say "Go ahead!" With lightening-like speed, Josh made a clean mid-line incision through the skin and soft tissue until he felt the grating sensation of the blade against the bone. He carried the slice well below the breast bone, then reached for the bone saw. He had a job to do.

Chapter 2

▼

Westlake, Texas, September 1987

The knock on the door jolted Josh Lehman away from his concentration on his homework—lessons he should have completed the night before. He glanced at the clock on the kitchen wall. *Must be Luke,* he thought. His dad had just come in from the night shift at the Westlake Refinery and was busy preparing breakfast before waking Josh's mom. She always seemed to be in her soundest sleep in the early morning, so his dad wouldn't disturb her for awhile.

"I'll get it, Dad," said Josh. "Probably Luke…almost time to leave for school."

"Bring him in…bet he hasn't had breakfast."

"It's late," said Josh, moving toward the front of the house. "We may not have time."

"Stayed up too late, didn't you?" asked Mr. Lehman, laughing.

"Guess so…good movie. Come on in, Luke!" Josh yelled through the door.

"Hi, Carrot-top," teased Mr. Lehman. "Just in time for breakfast. Have you eaten?"

"Nah," replied Luke. "Mom overslept…had to rush to work. The café owner said that if she missed that early morning breakfast crowd one more time, he'd have to let her go."

"I don't think he'll do that," said Mr. Lehman. "She has too many regular customers that come in there just because they want her to wait on them."

"Hope you're right," said Luke. "We live on what she makes…tips and all."

"How about your dad, Luke?" asked Josh, as he set the table and poured juice for everyone. "You haven't mentioned him lately."

"Haven't seen him in months," he replied. "When he does show, he just parks his eighteen-wheeler out front, sleeps overnight, and then he's gone again. It worries me that Mom goes out at night so much. You know, what if my dad came home while she was out?"

"Don't even think about it," said Josh.

"Yeah, you're right," said Luke, "but sometimes I wish it was different."

"All right, you boys, enough of that talk. Breakfast is ready," said Mr. Lehman. "Josh, how'd your mother do last night?"

"Fine, Dad," Josh replied. "She called once for me to help her to the bathroom, and again to check her oxygen. I think the tank's getting pretty low. There's not as much pressure."

"I'll take care of it," he said. "Josh, I have a chance to pick up some overtime this weekend. Can you hang around Saturday afternoon?"

"Sure, Dad," said Josh, as he and Luke wolfed down their food.

"Thanks, Josh. I can't miss a chance like that…need the money for home nursing visits," said Mr. Lehman. "You guys made any decisions yet about football?"

"Yeah, we're gonna try out for the freshman team this week," replied Luke.

"I'll bet you both make it. Right now you better get moving or I'll be getting a call from the principal."

"Thanks for the breakfast, Mr. Lehman," said Luke while Josh gathered his books and papers.

"Anytime, Luke," he said. "And Luke, don't get too close to those curtains in the school rooms with that flaming head of hair; you'll burn down the school house."

"Hey, not a bad idea," laughed Luke.

"Dad, if we make the team I'll still have time to run home to check on Mom before football practice," said Josh. "I won't disturb you."

"Thanks, Josh," he replied.

Josh and Luke raced for the door, jumped on their bikes, and headed for school.

* * * *

Josh Lehman and Luke Sanders grew up in Westlake and lived within a couple of blocks of each other. As kids they were always together—daylight to dark—playing, walking to school or riding their bikes, or just hanging out.

About the time the hormones kicked in they both became enamored with the same flirtatious twelve-year old. Her daily routine was to find a group of boys gathered on the school campus, saunter in front of them, undulating her precociously developed anatomy, then turn and walk away with all the guys—Josh and Luke included—lustfully staring at her tight-fitting jeans.

She managed to get Josh and Luke, plus a few others, to follow her around school like a pack of pups, each seeking some clue that he was her favorite. Josh and Luke's friendship was put to a crucial test when she kept teasing each, trying to turn one against the other.

It all ended the day Josh and Luke met behind the maintenance building and fought until they were both exhausted, neither to be declared winner by the crowd of spectators that included the girl.

"Dammit, Luke!" said Josh, loud enough for all to hear. "You can have her! She ain't worth all this shit!"

"Hell, I don't want her!" laughed Luke.

The crowd dispersed and the little vamp, after hearing the boy's remarks, turned her attention elsewhere. Josh and Luke walked off, arms around each other, toward the restroom, to get cleaned up before going in to class.

"Think she taught us a lesson, Luke?" asked Josh as they walked away.

"Yeah, she's probably laughing her head off at us right now," he replied.

"Maybe you'll quit having those dreams," Josh said with a chuckle.

"My mom will be glad. I think she's tired of washing my sheets and underwear every day."

"Hell, you ought to have your 'dreams' in the bathroom before you go to bed." Josh teased and stepped back.

"Damn you, Josh, I'm going to whip your ass again," Luke said with a laugh, faking an attack. "I thought you'd had enough."

"You ain't whipped me once yet, lover boy."

They kept walking, laughing, and chuckling all the way to the wash room, agreeing that the entire fiasco was a learning experience for both of them. Their friendship survived the test!

*   *   *   *

Josh and Luke went out for the freshman football team at Westlake High School and both made the team. With after-school practice every day, they had little time for anything else. No sooner did they finish scrimmage sessions than the coach sent all the team running a lap around the track. Both boys were breathless as they trotted to the gym to shower and change clothes. After securing their back-packs, filled with books, they took off toward Luke's house.

"Man, that Coach Staggs doesn't know when to stop, does he?" said Luke.

"Maybe he's just testing us...see if we can take it," replied Josh.

"You think we can stay with it?" asked Luke.

"Hell, it's got to get a lot worse than this before we quit," said Josh. "Agree?"

"Yeah, I agree," answered Luke. "Let's go to the house."

"Think your mom's home yet?" asked Josh. "Hope she brought some of that good banana pudding like we had last week."

"You know she's gonna bring something," said Luke. "I'm getting hungry."

"So am I," said Josh. "Do you think her boss minds that she brings food home for us?"

"She says he doesn't...says they have to throw it away after two days," said Luke. "Got much homework?"

"Yeah, I do. I'm not even gonna turn TV on tonight," replied Josh. "How about you?"

"Same here," said Luke. "Guess we oughta study together before you have to go home."

"Good idea," said Josh. "I need to get home about seven, after Dad goes to work. Luke, your mom is super to let me hang out here after school."

"She likes us to stay here...knows we're not getting into trouble."

"Hell, after football practice we're too tired to get in trouble," Josh said with a laugh.

Luke lived with his mother in a small two-bedroom cottage close to the school. It became a convenient after-school hang-out for Josh and Luke—even before football practice. Each day, as soon as school was out, Josh raced home to check on his mom. Luke usually went with him, but they left right away so as not to disturb Mr. Lehman's sleep before he had to leave for his night shift, then it was back to Luke's house.

✳ ✳ ✳ ✳

Scrimmage sessions with Coach Staggs were grueling. He seemed to have eyes in the back of his head. He never missed anything and he never let up on his drive to improve Josh and Luke's play. Josh was showing skill as a quarterback, and Luke, with his speed, managed more times than not to get in position to receive one of Josh's passes.

"Practice! Practice! Practice!" Coach Staggs yelled at them. "You gotta learn to place that ball where Luke's gonna be, Josh, not where he was when you threw it!"

"How do I know where he's gonna be, Coach?"

"Read the damn play book, Josh!" the coach answered. "When you call a play in that huddle, you know where he's gonna be. He damn well better be there."

"I'll try to do better, Coach."

The coach's constant hammering kept Josh and Luke focused. Every minute they could spare from study, they practiced. Josh threw long passes, short passes, floating passes, with Luke scrambling to be in the right positions to catch the ball.

In practice games, the coach put two linebackers guarding Luke. When Luke caught one of Josh's bullet passes, the two players crumpled him to the turf before he could take a step. No sooner did he climb from beneath their smothering weight than he was met with the coach's admonishment.

"Luke!" yelled Coach Staggs from the sideline. "Dammit, when you catch the ball, the play ain't over! You don't just quit! You gotta try to make a few more yards!"

"I'll try to do better, Coach," Luke replied, adjusting his shoulder pads that had been almost pulled over his head in the melee.

The coach then turned, walked out on the playing field, and screamed at Josh.

"Josh! When you're rushed, back up and throw! Get rid of the damn ball! Back-run! Back-run! You gotta learn to back-run fast or they'll kill ya!"

"Hell, they kill me anyway, Coach," said Josh.

"That's just part of the game, Josh,"

Both boys could have given up. The constant grilling and yelling from the coach was wearing them down. If they made a good play and came to the sideline, thinking they would hear some complimentary word, all they heard were words of criticism.

"Josh, where in the hell did you learn that play?" the coach asked.

"I don't know, Coach," replied Josh.

"Who's coaching this team?"

"You are, Coach," answered Josh.

"Then why in the hell do you and Luke make up your own goddamn plays? Stick to the book! You both can read, can't you?"

"Yes sir," they answered.

"Then, stick to the book!"

"We'll try to do better, Coach," said Josh.

"You and Luke always give me the same answer," he said. "Dammit, then do better!"

"Coach, we're trying as hard as we can," said Josh, a distressed look on his face. "We do everything you tell us. We get to bed early, we run the track, we do push-ups, we practice every minute we can. We don't want to quit, Coach. Do we, Luke?"

"We're not quitters, Coach!" said Luke, joining in on Josh and the coach's talk. "You think we should quit?" he asked the coach, a tone in his voice that bordered on being indignant.

The coach put his arm around both of them.

"OK, you guys come over here," he said as he led them away from the other players.

He squatted on the grassy field, picked up a sprig of grass to chew on, and motioned for the boys to sit in front of him.

"I've worked both of you hard because I know what you can do," said the coach. "I'm testing you…see how much you can take; see what we can expect from you next year. You're both good. I drive you hard because I know you're good, and I like you. Now, get up, run one lap and go home."

They stuck it out, consoled each other after practice each day, with eagerness talked about the next day, and then collapsed in bed from fatigue, but hearing the coach's words and telling each other that they were improving turned it into a pleasant fatigue. By the time the freshman year was over, there was no doubt that they would be "varsity team" the sophomore year.

Chapter 3

▼

Jackson Crain, the veteran star quarterback, was starting his last Westlake High football season at the same time Josh and Luke were starting their sophomore year. Something of a hero after two previous winning seasons, he paraded through the school corridors accompanied by his entourage of "worshipers," who always seemed eager to fluff up his already inflated ego.

Crain never missed the chance to malign Josh in some way—derogatory remarks in the dressing room, as if it were his intent to undermine Josh's self-confidence. The closer they came to starting the season, the more he escalated his attacks.

Josh was determined not to let it bother him. *"Surely he doesn't look upon me as a threat,"* he thought. The crowning blow came one day while Josh was dressing in an aisle in the gym behind the row of lockers from Crain and out of his sight. Crain was sounding off to some of his cronies and was unaware that Luke was dressing just a few lockers away.

"What the hell is happening to this school? A Jew-boy on varsity! I've never known a kike that could play football. Have you?"

There was no time for an answer to his question before Luke jumped him. First, a right hook to the left side of his head that staggered him, then a stranglehold around his neck, which Luke held while Crain pleaded for help. His buddies didn't move.

"You son-of-a-bitch!" yelled Luke, his eyes on fire and his flaming red hair, now wet from a recent shower, plastered to his head. "I'm gonna mop this fuckin' floor with you and all the rest of you bastards if you try to stop me. I don't know where Josh is right now, but when you find him you'll apologize or I'll beat the shit out of you every day until you do."

"Ok, Ok!" he cried. "Just turn me loose!"

"I'm not sure I will—yet," replied Luke. "Say what you are going to do, shit-ass! Say it in front of your friends!" he added. He tightened his hold.

"Apologize to Josh," he uttered, barely audible.

"One more thing," said Luke, loosening his strangle a bit. "Don't ever belittle Josh again in any way."

"Ok, Ok!" he said.

Josh rounded the corner and took in the scene.

"Let him go, Luke!"

Luke dropped his arms and turned away, still pale from anger.

*   *   *   *

Although they were on the varsity squad, Josh and Luke spent most of the sophomore year season on the bench. Occasionally, if the team was comfortably ahead, they were put in to play for a few minutes just to get the feel for what it was like to play in a real, scheduled game. It was invaluable experience that would prep them for their junior year. It was an exhilarating experience—being 'on stage,' hearing the roar of the crowd, being treated like warriors going into battle.

Westlake had not done well during the season. Without Jackson Crain to spark the offense and with a new quarterback who turned out to be a disappointment to Coach Staggs, they had lost more games than they had won. The loss of the last three games in a row had eroded the support and attendance of the school's football fans. It was the last game of the season, to be played against the unbeaten Grover High School team. If Westlake could win, possibly they could recapture some of their community backing.

In the last quarter, with only two minutes to play, the Grover High team scored a touchdown, putting them three points ahead. The after-touchdown kick into the end zone placed the ball in Westlake's possession on the twenty yard line. On the first play the quarterback was sacked, went to the ground, and didn't get up. The coach and the team doctor trotted out onto the field. The boy was able to stand, and although wobbly, was able to walk with assistance to the sideline. Coach Staggs nodded to Josh.

"Get out there, Josh!" he said.

"Yes, sir," Josh replied, his heart pounding as he jumped to his feet and adjusted his helmet. "Come on, Luke, let's go."

"No, Josh...just you," said the coach and directed his attention back to the injured quarterback.

Josh stopped, turned back toward Luke, and just stood motionless for a moment.

Coach Staggs glanced up at the two boys, a broad grin crossed his face.

"You too, Luke!"

On the second down, ten yards still needed for a first down, Josh called for a pass play. With the Grover defense blitz, the ball never left Josh's hand; he was smothered for a two yard loss. It was now third down, only two minutes left to play—he had to complete a pass. They could not possibly win if they lost the ball to Grover this near the end of the game.

The ball snapped, and again Josh went down from the blitz even before he could throw the ball away—another two yard loss. Josh looked for and found Coach Staggs on the sideline. He knew what the signal would be. A fourth down punt was out of the question. The coach, standing in a relaxed posture, a confident expression on his face, grinned affectionately at Josh and gave him a thumbs-up hand gesture.

Josh held the fixed gaze for a few seconds and smiled back at the coach. *He thinks we can do it!* thought Josh. Luke trotted back to the huddle, looked at Josh's face, and knew what they had to do.

"They're bringing their linebackers in closer," said Josh. "We can still win this game if you guys can keep them off me for a couple of seconds. Luke, play number 34A...from the book," he added with a laugh. "You know what to do. Let's make a first down. Hurry back to line up. We'll have time for one, maybe two, more plays."

With the snap, Josh took the ball, faked a right end run, stopped, turned back to the left, and released a bullet pass to Luke—clear and open exactly where he was supposed to be—for a first down. The Westlake players raced back to the line without huddling; Josh stood well behind the line.

On cue the center passed the ball squarely into Josh's waiting hands. Luke ran wide down-field, near the sideline, with the defensive linemen surrounding him. He turned abruptly and ran across the field just as Josh let go with a long, high pass. With a last second burst of speed, Luke managed to get directly under the football as it floated down near mid-field. He grabbed the ball, sidestepped pursuing linebackers, was caught by one player and almost went down, but swiveled and rotated to free himself and made an unobstructed fifty-yard dash across the goal line.

The crowd went wild. Josh shoved his way through the Westlake players surrounding Luke. The two boys hugged each other and walked off the field, each with arms around the other. The Lehman-Sanders Axis was born.

*　　＊　　＊　　＊　　＊*

During their junior year, Josh and Luke were first team starters. The season ended with an impressive record of wins, largely through Josh and Luke's efforts. They were already getting vibes of interest from major universities. The media labeled them the "Lehman-Sanders Axis," a reputation that they carried into the start of their senior year.

On a rare occasion, welcomed by the team, practice and "skull" sessions were terminated early because of rain and a sudden drop in temperature. Josh had already made his trip home to check on his mom and didn't want to return early for fear of waking his dad. He and Luke were lounging at Luke's house, munching on some snacks that Luke's mom had placed before them.

"Hey, we're starting our senior year soon, man!" said Josh. "Can you believe it? Whatta you gonna do after we graduate?"

"I don't know. Like to go to college," he replied. "One thing for sure…I'm not gonna to be a truck driver."

"The coach says we can get football scholarships," said Josh.

"That's the only way I can go—with a scholarship. My mom can just barely keep the day-to-day expenses paid," said Luke.

"Likewise with me," replied Josh. "My dad has so much expense with my mom being sick, needing visiting nurses and lots of medicines. I couldn't ask him for help."

"Whatta you wanna be, Josh? I see how you pitch in and help take care of your mom. You wanna be a doctor?"

"I sure think about it a lot. I've seen her so sick for so long. I tell myself sometimes that if I was a doctor I could do something to help her. She's so pitiful, Luke."

"You could do it, man. You oughta work at it."

"You know, all my life I've heard my mom talk about Mrs. Minsky, who lives across the street," said Josh, laughing. "She'll say, 'I saw Mrs. Minsky in the deli, her son's a doctor, you know' and look straight at me. And even now that mom's bedridden, she'll say, 'Mrs. Minsky came by to visit; her son's a doctor, you know.' And she always turns and looks at me when she says that."

"Sounds like she wants you to be a doctor," laughed Luke.

"I guess you're right," said Josh. "I think I'll take pre-med courses, if we do get into college, just in case I want to go that way. How about you, Luke? Ever thought of going to medical school?"

"I don't think I could ever be a doctor," he replied. "I even get sick when I go to the clinic for shots or something. I can't stand the smell. I used to go with my mother to the nursing home to see my grandmother before she died. What an ugly place! Just a smelly pit! All these old people parked around in wheelchairs, calling to you or pulling at you when you walk by. The last few times we went, my grandmother had to ask my mother who I was."

"There are other things doctors do besides taking care of old nursing home patients," said Josh.

"If you mean operating on people, count me out! When I see blood I feel like I'm gonna pass out."

"You've always liked chemistry and physics and courses like that. Same ones you take for pre-med," said Josh. "How about trying pre-med? You might surprise yourself and get interested in medical school. You can always change your mind."

"Hey, here we are, talking about courses we'll take, and neither of us have any idea how we will be able to go to college," laughed Luke.

"Maybe we can go to the same college. Take some of the same courses, even study together," said Josh. "Let's work at it. We can do it."

"Good enough," said Luke. "If we can put up with Coach Staggs and his nagging and still make our grades, what could be worse?"

"It could be harder, you know," laughed Josh.

"We can do anything if we set our minds to it, jerk."

"Be careful with your words, swivel hips, or I'll get Jackson Crain to come protect me," Josh retorted with a chuckle.

"One thing I'd like to avoid is going to the same college that son-of-a-bitch goes to."

"I'll bet he changed when he got into the big league."

"Josh, why in the hell do you always find something good about everybody? He's a horses ass anyway you turn him. He's a revolving horses ass."

They laughed, ate some still-warm Mexican food Luke's mother had brought home for them, wished for a forbidden beer, relaxed, and took a nap.

Chapter 4

Westlake High won every district and bi-district game during Josh and Luke's senior year—their last season to play high school football. The team just couldn't be beat. Every time they were backed against the wall, Josh and Luke would come up with some winning maneuver that put the team ahead.

They were going for State Championship!

The atmosphere at the school was charged with excitement. There were rallies by the school student body and hype by the news media like the community had never before experienced. Westlake had never won a state championship.

During the week before the state championship game, Josh and Luke were invited to the Westlake Rotary Club luncheon meeting to be interviewed as part of the club's weekly program. They were given guest seats at the head table. After lunch, which they scarcely touched, the program started with the moderator's addressing the audience and presenting Josh and Luke.

"We have two honored guests with us today," he said. "Let me introduce you to two members of the Westlake High School football team. As most of you know, Westlake will be competing for state championship this year. We have with us today Josh Lehman, team quarterback, and Luke Sanders, wide receiver." Both boys stood as the group applauded.

"Let me ask you boys a couple of questions," he said. "Are you nervous about this game?"

Josh and Luke looked at each other, both smiling as if in a quandary as to how to answer. Josh spoke.

"Well, sir, we get a little nervous before every game."

"But this is the big one."

"We are favored to win," said Luke, "but we know it will be a hard battle and we feel a lot of responsibility toward the players and the coach."

"Now, you two are known as the 'Lehman-Sanders Axis.' What is meant by that?" the moderator asked.

"We've played together for a long time and we know what to expect from each other," said Josh. "We have a good record for completing passes. I guess that's why they call it an axis."

"Do you think you will win?"

"Absolutely," said both boys at the same time.

"Thanks for coming," said the moderator, "and good luck in the game."

"Thank you, sir," said Josh. Loud applause followed as they left the podium.

∗   ∗   ∗   ∗

The day of the championship game arrived. They would be playing against their archrival, Reagan High School of Houston. They had faced Reagan many times before, but had always been beaten. This was going to be the year! Josh and Luke were looked upon as the keys to make it happen.

The game would be played in the giant University of Texas stadium in Austin. The size alone was overwhelming, notwithstanding the forty-thousand spectators in the stands, waving their school colors and keeping time with the school band playing favorite school songs. The din from the stadium penetrated the basement dressing rooms where the team was gathered for the coach's final instructions and words of encouragement.

"Look, guys," Coach Staggs yelled, trying to be heard above the clamor from the bleachers. "Don't let the size of the stadium and the size of the crowd get to you. Just remember: more than half of those people out there are pulling for you. You've done a beautiful job this year and whatever happens today I want you to know I'm proud of every one of you. Oh…there's someone outside who wants to say a word."

At Coach Stagg's signal, Jackson Crain, widely acclaimed as the leading quarterback for the University of Texas Longhorns, walked in. He stood before the boys for a few moments before speaking. Luke turned to Josh, "He's still a horse's ass."

"Shut up, Luke!" Josh replied.

"I want to tell you this," said Crain. "You can beat that team! It only takes the kind of teamwork that Coach Staggs has been teaching you for four years. You have what it takes, now go use it! I am proud to be a Westlake High alumnus. It means a lot to me and every day I reflect back on what I learned from Coach at Westlake."

Then he turned and looked straight at Josh and Luke.

"And one thing I learned at Westlake was humility," he said. "I made a mistake that day, Josh and Luke. I just have to live with it now. I was wrong and I apologize. Good luck, you guys! You can do it!"

* * * *

Both teams played their hearts out. First one team was ahead, then the other. At half time the score was tied. After a much needed rest, and after the bands and cheerleader groups did their thing, the teams resumed their positions on the field for the second half of play.

The score vacillated back and forth during the third quarter and well into the fourth quarter. Reagan made a touchdown and the extra point. Westlake now was one point behind with one minute left to play. Westlake had the ball and had penetrated deep into Reagan territory. Time was running out. Reagan had beefed up their defense in anticipation of pass plays.

Reagan backfield players had been double guarding Luke for the entire game. With the rush of defensive linemen, it had been doubly hard for Josh to get a pass off and on target. On every play, one of the Reagan defensive linebackers raced ahead of Luke while another covered him from behind, uncomfortably close.

To win this game, with only seconds left to play, Westlake had to move the ball down into field-goal range. On the third down, with the ball near the opponent's forty-yard line, Luke was racing down-field when he looked back and saw the ball leave Josh's hand.

A perfect pass, straight as an arrow, synchronized with his speed, and targeted to hit right in his hands. The defense player that was racing ahead of him slowed to glance back at the approaching football. Luke did not notice the player ahead in time and crashed into him, hitting the turf before he could grasp the ball.

All three players rolled and entangled themselves into a chaotic muddle. Luke was at the bottom of the pile with his knee twisted under him. He had to be carried off the field. Howls of rage and protest from the sidelines and the bleachers erupted when the referee ruled "no pass interference" and the game ended. It was a sad day for Westlake!

* * * *

The torn cartilage in Luke's knee required arthroscopic surgery. However, the orthopedist assured Josh and Luke that the outcome would be favorable and with physical therapy, Luke would be back to his usual performance level. The season became history. Despite the loss, scouts from major universities in the state were hammering at Josh's door almost daily.

* * * *

Josh was outside waiting when Luke came out of the physical therapist's office. Luke carried his crutches in his hand and walked with a slight limp.

"Use the crutches, dumb-ass!" Josh admonished.

"They get in my way," said Luke.

"Come on, Luke," said Josh. "The doc said crutches for two weeks, the brace for six."

"He doesn't have to put up with this shit."

"Look, I've got an appointment with that recruiter from Northwestern to talk about football scholarships for us. You've gotta take care of your goddamn knee. We've got a lot of football to play for the next four years."

"What the hell would he say if he saw me on crutches?"

"OK, I'll go talk to him alone," said Josh. "We might get to go to college if I can cut a deal with him. Northwestern OK with you?"

"Go for it, but don't be so fuckin' nice to the guy."

"Trust me!" said Josh, as he helped his buddy down the clinic's stairs.

* * * *

"What can we do to get you to come with us, Josh?" the recruiter from Texas Northwestern University asked after he presented the recruitment package to Josh. Josh studied the offer carefully before answering. *If we make our grades at Northwestern, Luke and I should get accepted to any medical school in the state if we still want to go to medical school.* thought Josh.

"I'll tell you what I need to do first," he replied, "I need to run this by Luke to see if he agrees with your offer."

"Uh...Josh," said the recruiter. "This offer is just for you. We haven't made an offer to Luke."

"What do you mean, no offer to Luke?"

"Look, Josh," he said. "This is not high school football. We look at statistics. We look at what we need. We don't need wide receivers. For every good quarterback there are twenty or more receivers out there. Luke has been injured once. He will probably be injured again. We can't afford to sign-on an injured lineman."

"I'm sorry," said Josh. "Luke and I are a team. I'm not interested in any offer that doesn't include Luke on equal terms."

"Josh, don't throw away your future like this."

"Thank you very much," he said. "I hope I haven't inconvenienced you." He stood up and walked toward the door.

"Wait, Josh," the recruiter called out, as Josh reached for the door handle. Josh paused for a moment. "We can sign Luke for one season on a trial basis," he said. "What do you say to that? If he proves himself we can extend the contract."

"I guess I didn't make myself clear," said Josh, and again turned his back to leave.

He strode down the hall, quite bitter about the refusal to offer Luke the same contract. Luke had worked hard with his physical therapy. He was back to a normal range of motion following his arthroscopic surgery to repair the torn cartilage.

I am not going to abandon Luke under these circumstances, vowed Josh, remembering the time Luke fought Jackson Crain because of an anti-Semitic slur. *Luke would protect me the same way if the tables were turned.*

He pushed the button for the elevator and was about to enter when he heard the recruiter running toward him. He still had his cell phone in his hand. *He probably called someone after I left,* Josh thought.

"OK, Josh, you've got you're deal!"

"One more thing," said Josh. "Luke is never to know how this came about."

"You've got it," said the recruiter. "You drive a hard bargain, Josh."

"That's because I'm good and I know it," he laughed.

Chapter 5

▼

Northwestern University, Plainville, Texas…1991

Josh and Luke stepped off the bus, backpacks in hand, to be met by the sting of wind-driven sand. The sky was so dark from one of the frequent dust storms that blew across the north Texas plains that visibility was practically zero. To avoid the cost of a taxi, they trekked the three miles to the university campus and found Ryan Hall.

Ryan Hall was the athletic dormitory. It was located close enough to the stadium and the sports arena to be convenient for the athletes and close enough to the classroom buildings to portray the image that the jocks were interested also in higher education. Someone had placed a hand-written sign on the entrance door that said, "Welcome to Jock Jungle."

The large glass double doors opened automatically as the boys shook the sand off their clothes and cautiously approached the entrance. Once inside, the place seemed eerily quiet, with no sign of activity. They wandered about the spacious lobby, taking in the elaborate furnishings. Over-stuffed leather chairs were placed in groups around glass-topped tables covered with a scattering of neatly arranged sports magazines.

One wall was completely covered with towering bookshelves, housing what appeared to be reference books as well as novels. Glistening sliding glass doors covered the shelves. Josh and Luke were studying the trophy cases and the portraits of famous players and alumni on still another wall when they became aware of someone standing behind them. They turned to look into the broadest welcome smile ever to be encountered.

Dressed in custodian attire, the smiling man wore a starched, spotless white jacket over a white shirt and a tie that reflected a pattern of the university logo in school colors.

"Yo boys checkin' in?" he asked.

"Yes, sir," replied Josh and Luke simultaneously.

"Name's Sam," he said. His smile seemed to broaden. *Sir, they says...two fine boys,* he thought.

"Where is yo boys from?" Sam asked, as he helped them carry their backpacks to the elevator on the way to their rooms.

"We're from Westlake," replied Josh.

"Yo both is heah for football?"

"Yes, sir," both boys nodded and answered. The smile broadened again as if to confirm that they had made a hit with Sam. *Sir...they says, twice! These heah is both fine boys,* he said to himself.

"Yo boys wanna room together?"

"They told us that it was the policy in the dorm for boys from the same school to have separate rooms," said Josh.

"Well, sometimes dey runs outta rooms and has to put yo boys wherevah dey can," he said with a twinkle in his eyes. "I think dey has just done run out," he added in mock sincerity, as he placed their bags in the same room.

"Thank you, Mr..."

"Just call me Sam," he said, grinning from ear to ear. *I likes these two,* he told himself. "This heah is the third floor where all yo first year boys is placed. The dining room is on the first floor. I 'spect you'll find dat when yo gets hungry 'nough," he laughed. "If yo needs anything, Ise always around somewheres."

Josh and Luke were busily unpacking their bags and exploring the features of their room when there was a knock on the door. Josh opened the door and stood face-to-face with the tallest person he had ever seen.

"Hi," he said, ducking to step through the door. "I'm Walt Wasson. Welcome to Ryan Hall! I'm the dorm manager. Thought I'd show you guys around."

Josh and Luke introduced themselves.

"That would be great," said Josh.

"I see you have already met Sam," he laughed. "Sam is an institution around here. You'll get used to him. He either likes you or he doesn't. But you can't tell right off, 'cause he never stops smiling. You'll know in time."

"He's been very helpful," said Josh.

"That's a good sign," he replied. "Sam has his own way of demanding respect."

They followed Walt as he led them back to the elevators. He walked with a decided limp and didn't seem to have good use of his right arm. When he became aware that he was being watched, he said, "Neck injury from a basketball game. Disabled ever since. Lucky to have this job."

They took the elevator to the basement.

"This is the work-out gym," said Walt. "All kinds of exercise machines, weights, racquetball courts, saunas, Olympic size swimming pool—everything you need. There are trainers here all of the time. I spent a lot of time here after my injury."

They went back up to the first floor and to the dining room—a tremendous hall with tables set for the next meal.

"Meals are at seven, twelve, and six. If you have any special orders or special times, it can be arranged. Guest day is Sunday," explained Walt. "Some people think that athletes should be stuffed with second and third helpings of everything, that overfed athletes perform better. I don't agree," he added with a laugh.

Walt showed them around the lobby and the lounge area.

"This is Sam's realm," said Walt. "Nobody challenges Sam about anything. He even decides whose portraits should have preferential placement. Whatever you say about Sam, he's always cheerful. Anytime the players come in all sweaty and grimy and plop down in one of these chairs, you'll see Sam right behind them after they leave with his deodorizing spray, cleaning and polishing until the locker-room smell is gone. He never complains, just works and smiles. He keeps this place spotless."

They walked through the lobby, passing several computer cubicles, into the sound-proof music and television lounge. A library of CDs and videotapes filled a cabinet on one wall.

"This is a great place to relax," said Walt. "You'll need that. You're football, aren't you?"

"Yeah," they both replied.

"Make sure you replace CDs and tapes. Sam watches this place like a hawk. He somehow knows who comes and goes through here. He likes to keep things orderly."

"How long has Sam been here?" asked Luke.

"Gosh, I don't know," he said. "Even before this building was here...probably over thirty years. He's never worked anywhere else. He's seen a lot of athletes and would-be athletes come through here."

Next stop was the telephone switchboard room.

"This is one person you have to know," said Walt, as he introduced them to Lola, who looked up and waved while she had a non-stop conversation going. "Lola and Sam are the two most important people on this campus. Even though we are in the technology age, we still use a live operator. She can usually tell you what's going on, what's on the menu, and where everybody is at any given moment.

"Looks like the sand storm has let up, so if you would like to we can ride around the campus and I'll show you the stadium and some of the buildings where your classes will be held," said Walt. "Have you guys ever been here before?"

"No, we haven't," replied Josh.

They climbed into the golf cart that was parked at the entrance. With Walt at the wheel, they traveled along the winding roads through the campus—first past the football stadium and the giant sports gymnasium and then past the ivy-covered classroom and laboratory buildings. Each structure carried some family name, like Littleton, Broughton, Summerfield.

"These buildings are all named after well-known patrons of the school, or sometimes noteworthy individuals who have contributed to society in some way. If you are interested, you'll find a plaque at the front of each building that tells the story of the benefactor. You guys are from Westlake, aren't you?"

"Yeah," they both responded.

"We're now going past the Bradford Building," said Walt. "The Bradford family is from Westlake. You know any of them?"

"Hardly. We don't run with that pack," laughed Josh.

"From some of the things I've heard, you're probably better off. The family wealth had its beginning with old John Bradford, a pioneer Texas wildcatter. Every hole he drilled in the ground struck oil. He never attended school a day in his life."

"What was his connection with Northwestern?" asked Luke. "Why did he donate to a university if he had no interest in education?"

"I think that probably, in spite of his wealth, he must have felt inferior because of his lack of formal education," Walt replied. "When he died, all of his estate passed into the Bradford Foundation that has since funded many programs here at Northwestern such as research projects, scholarships, and fellowships.

"Sadly, I've been told that the foundation has dwindled to practically nothing due to mismanagement by John's only son, Don, who has been the administrator of the foundation."

"I know very little about the family," said Josh. "There was a Donnie Bradford a couple of years behind us in school—probably a grandson of John's. The kid always stayed to himself, very few friends. I always thought he was just another snooty rich kid."

"Don Bradford, John's son that I was telling you about, went to school here years ago. He even lived at Ryan Hall for a short while—a very short while," Walt said with a chuckle. "You want to hear the story?"

They stopped by the spacious brick pavilion in front of the Bradford Building—in the shade provided by the strategically placed giant elm trees.

"Yeah, if you have time," Josh replied.

"Since you're from Westlake and since you have met Sam, I think you'll find it interesting," he said. "There are cokes and bottled water in the ice chest there. We can sit here in the shade for a while."

They climbed out of the cart and, with drinks in hand, sat at one of the many concrete tables and benches not already occupied by the flock of other students taking advantage of the shade and respite from the blowing sand. Walt started his narration:

"Don Bradford, Sr., John's son, played basketball for Westlake High School years ago, and with his father's influence managed to wrangle admission to the Northwestern U. athletic program with housing in Ryan Hall.

"So I'm told, Don lasted only a few weeks before it became obvious that he shouldn't have ever been in the program, or living in Ryan, in the first place. I think he was disliked by the other players, and by the coach as well.

"As the story goes, he faked a fall and a back injury after he realized that he either had to get out of the sport or be dismembered by team members during heavy competitive play. He probably used the injury as an excuse to quit and to avoid admonishment from his father for quitting.

"He was allowed to stay the year out in Ryan Hall—the school president's concession to appease the Bradfords. But Don's unforgivable mistake was his intimidation of Sam—racial slurs and condescending comments. His life at Ryan was made miserable. There were unexplained incidents such as live cockroaches placed between the bed sheets or telephone awakenings at three or four o'clock in the morning.

"From time to time gift-wrapped packages, addressed to Don, contained fresh animal or human excreta. There was no indisputable proof that Sam was to blame, but everyone strongly suspected it to be so when they saw how Sam was being treated by Don.

"Now here is the part of the story that everybody remembers and laughs about when the topic of Sam's behavior comes up. Don received a package with no return address that contained an inviting array of delicacies. Don, suspicious from past experiences, offered Sam one of the cookies as a test to see if they were edible.

"Sam just smiled and told Don he wasn't hungry. Don then insisted that Sam take one and eat it to be sure it was all right. Sam then reached into the box, took a cookie and ate it, and reassured Don that it was OK. Don then tried one...coughed and choked and ran for water.

"Sam apparently had prepared the package and planted the one single cookie that wasn't saturated with cayenne pepper. I love that story and think about it every time I catch Sam in one of his tricks."

"Don finally reached a time when he could no longer take day after day harassment from an unknown source. He had already pledged a fraternity, and as soon as a houseroom became available he moved out of Ryan Hall, amidst the silent cheers of every resident in the dorm. Sam just smiled and kept right on doing his work."

"So that's the story of Don Bradford, Sr., and Sam. But as I said, if Sam likes you, you couldn't have a better friend. What do you think?"

"I think we better stay on Sam's good side," said Josh.

"Easy to do; just show him the respect that he deserves," said Walt. "Sam, in his unassuming way, demands respect. If anyone—jocks or alumni—ever abuses or humiliates Sam in any way, retribution is dealt in strange ways, most of the time at the victim's unawareness of the perpetrator. But Sam never stops smiling," he added with a chuckle. "I am told that this is the way it has been for years."

"What happened to Don?" asked Josh. "Did he finish at Northwestern?"

"Yeah. He was a bright student; graduated with honors, they say. Returns regularly for alumni events. Big write-ups about his success in the financial world...you know, 'Northwestern graduate success story.'"

"There's a twenty-story skyscraper in Westlake named Bradford Tower. That must be the same Bradford," said Josh.

"I'm sure it is," Walt replied. "I think his company is called Bradford Holdings. It's a Wall Street conglomerate of several companies. When Don Bradford is here for some function, I hear the term 'Bradford Holdings' used a lot in the media stories."

* * * *

Back at Ryan Hall, they thanked Walt for the tour and returned to their room to continue unpacking and getting settled. Josh stood by the third-story window, gazing out over the campus, quiet and appearing pensive.

"Which are you most excited about, Luke?" asked Josh after several moments of silence. "Starting classes or starting football practice?"

"Hard to answer," Luke replied. "I am so curious about what goes on in those classroom buildings and laboratories, I can hardly wait. What about you?"

"Feel the same way," said Josh. "We have to keep reminding ourselves that we are here on a football scholarship, I guess. But it was breathtaking, riding over the campus, winding among the massive buildings. We're in an institution of higher learning, partner! Did you ever think we'd make it?"

"Never had a doubt," laughed Luke. "Let's make the most of both—football and higher learning. They're both just games."

Chapter 6

Josh and Luke managed to get most of their pre-med classes together. The shocker came when they attended their first chemistry class, looked around, and saw five to six hundred pre-med students in the auditorium. With a stiff, militaristic gait, an unsmiling Dr. Hinson entered and took his place at the rostrum. He dropped his glasses low enough so he could see over the rim. He stood erect in one spot, scanning the class for what seemed like a lifetime before he finally spoke.

"Students!" he shouted, without the benefit of a PA system. "Students!" he repeated. Every eye was glued to the rostrum and the auditorium was quiet. "All of you look to your right…look to your left…look behind you…and look in front of you." He paused between each "look" to assure attention. "Only one of you will make it to medical school."

Dead silence prevailed. The students sheepishly looked around, assessing their competitors.

In spite of the scary introduction to higher education, the boys found their classes to be exciting and fascinating. Their grades stayed in the top percentiles. Every class and every day offered new challenges in learning.

* * * *

Fortunately football practice started several days before classes began, which gave Josh and Luke time to build a tolerance to the grueling workouts. After they became physically conditioned, the post-practice fatigue wasn't quite so hard to deal with when it came time to focus on studying.

Some days were worse than others. It was one of those "worse" days. Josh and Luke, bruised and sore from head to foot, dragged into Ryan Hall, looking like they had been run over by a truck. They both were facing tests the next day and were behind in their studies. After the evening meal, while most of the athletes gathered in the lounge to watch TV, Josh and Luke headed for their room to hit the books. On the pretense of checking their room, Sam made one of his routine courtesy visits—after dinner on football practice days—to check on Josh and Luke. Somehow he seemed to know when they were under pressure to study.

"How is yo boys, today?" he said as he emptied the trash cans and straightened up the bathroom.

"We're fine, Sam," said Josh. "How was your day?"

"Jest fine!" he replied. "Yo dun et?"

"Yeah. Good dinner tonight," said Luke.

"Now I'se told yo boys dis before. No matter what dey is tellin' yo," he said, "don't yo boys eat heavy. You fall 'sleep and won't wanna study. Duz I need to bring yo boys some coffee?"

"We're fine, Sam," Josh said, "but thank you anyway. I'll bet you pass out coffee to all the players," he added, with a chuckle.

"No needs to," he replied. "Dey is not into studies like yo two."

They both laughed as Sam walked out of the room and quietly closed the door behind him, smiling all the while.

"Hey Luke, what's your favorite class?" asked Josh, feet propped up on his desk, zoology book in hand.

"I sure don't like zoology," he replied. "I look over there and see you digging into that shark, and I say to myself, 'I think I'll just get a job selling shoes.'"

"Luke, the word is 'dissecting,' not 'digging,'" Josh laughed. "And I see how orgasmic you get in that physics lab—like you're trying to split the plutonium atom."

"Well, I sure as hell don't want to be another Ambrose Paré," replied Luke.

"Hey!" laughed Josh. "You learned something in that boring history of medicine class! Thought you were asleep."

"Yeah, every day I learn that I don't wanna be a surgeon."

"Fine, after we graduate from medical school you just find the patients that need surgery, send them to me, and I'll operate on them,"

"What makes you think I'm going to medical school?"

"'Cause you wouldn't wanna miss the game," laughed Josh.

* * * *

During the first year pre-season football scrimmages and practice games, Josh and Luke earned the respect of the coaching staff and their teammates as being offense team players to be reckoned with. At first the coaches were critical of Josh for always throwing the ball to Luke in the practice games. Josh could hit a twenty-four inch circle at thirty yards, but a receiver had to be conditioned to the speed and impact of the ball from any passer.

Although Luke knew exactly what to expect when Josh released the ball, the other receivers often appeared stunned by the force of a ball that Josh threw and either let it bounce off their chest or flip out of their hands. Before the first scheduled game, however, the other receivers adapted fairly well to Josh's style of passing.

* * * *

The freshman year football season for Luke and Josh was well underway. Josh was the back-up substitute player for Jake Connor, the veteran starting quarterback for Northwestern. Jake had recurring bouts of leg cramps and disabling hamstring muscle strains, which meant that Josh frequently was tapped to replace him during the game, usually in the last quarter. Luke often was sent in to play at the same time Josh was in action, catching impossible passes that Josh threw. The sports reporters quickly caught on to the Leman-Sanders Axis concept and played it up big in their stories.

The last quarter of the last game of the season—against the Torrance University Eagles—was highlighted by Josh and Luke's skills as team players. Jake Connor was sidelined, and there was still ten minutes left to play. Josh was sent in without Luke. After two incompletions due to the starter receiver's juggling Josh's well-placed passes—then dropping the ball altogether—Luke was put into action as a wide receiver. Northwestern scored twice from touchdown passes from Josh to Luke.

After the game, Josh and Luke showered and dressed and were met by the media gang as they walked out of the locker room.

"Nice game, Josh," said one reporter. "Do you think you will replace Jake Connor as the lead quarterback?"

"You'll have to ask the coach," he replied, with Luke guiding and pushing him through the crowd.

"You and Luke showed what you can do if given a chance," said another reporter, chasing after them as they tried to exit.

"Look, Jake Connor is a seasoned, capable quarterback. My role is to be ready to play when he cannot," said Josh, with some anger in his voice. "I have no intention of trying to displace him."

When they were well away from the crowds, walking toward Ryan Hall, Luke turned to Josh.

"All right, football hero," he chided. "Did we play a good game or what? You know we did! Admit how it makes you feel."

"Makes me feel ten feet tall," laughed Josh. "Yeah, I like it! And so do you—just like it was when we played high school. You saw what a difference it makes to have you in there. I have a problem with those other receivers—no confidence in them."

"I need to tell those guys my secret," said Luke, with a broad grin on his face.

"OK, smart ass, what is your secret?"

"Simple. When I look up and see that ball coming, I pretend it's one of those sexy cheerleaders. So I reach up and grab her, hold her close, and throw her to the ground. Then I just smother her with kisses and say, 'You are so beautiful. Why in the hell did Josh throw you away?'"

"Luke, you are a fuckin' freak," said Josh. "From now on, you are going to answer those questions from the reporters."

"No way," Luke replied, with a chuckle. "That's when you are your best—slinging bull-shit with your glib-tongued answers."

* * * *

There were clamors from the commentators—newspaper and television—questioning why Josh was not given a starting position. The season closed before there were any statements forthcoming from the coaching staff. With the grueling practice sessions and the scheduled games behind them, Josh and Luke had more time to devote to their studying. Their jobs at the sporting goods store still took up much of their spare time during the remainder of the school year and extended to full time during the summer months before the conditioning work-outs began for the next season.

* * * *

Their sophomore football season brought a repetition of the same scenarios for Josh and Luke. They were benched most of the time during scheduled games, but were sent in to play with more frequency than the year before. The season ended with their tallying impressive statistics—percentage of passes completed for Josh and yards-gained-after-completion for Luke. The sports writers continued to give glowing reports on the Lehman-Sanders Axis, with predictions of a banner year for Northwestern when Josh and Luke were team starters as juniors.

The talk of the sports community at the school was Jake Connor's contract with an NFL professional team. Working in the sporting goods store put Josh and Luke where the rumors were rampant with regards to sports world activity.

"Who is Jeff going with?" asked Luke during a lull in business.

"He's not saying," replied Josh. "They're not supposed to release the information until after everybody has signed."

"I heard he got a five year contract," said Luke. "You know how much?"

"No, but I'll bet it's in the millions."

"Wow! See what you can look forward to?"

"I don't know, Luke," said Josh. "Say you contracted for five years and then either didn't perform or got injured…What would you do?"

"Hell, I'd just sit back and enjoy being rich," said Luke with a chuckle.

"Yeah, I can just see that," laughed Josh. "You wouldn't last six months."

"It sure would beat working in this pit every day," said Luke.

"Be quiet, stupid! We could be fired, you know."

"I'm not worried. You'd smooth-talk 'em out of it."

"Let's just get through these next two years, smart-ass," replied Josh with a laugh.

"I'm still gonna dream about a million dollars worth in the meantime."

Chapter 7

The beginning of football practice for Josh and Luke's junior year was rapidly approaching. During the summer months their jobs kept them busy enough, but they still found time for regular workouts. Fortunately, they were able to stay in their rooms at Ryan Hall during the summer months. They returned to their room after an hour's racquetball game in the gym to find a note on their door that Walt wanted to see them. They went straight to Walt's office.

"Hey Josh, Luke!" greeted Walt. "Haven't seen you guys in a while. You doing OK?"

"Fine," said Josh. "What's up?"

"I know you've both been working hard all summer. I just wanted to touch base with you and let you in on a possibility to earn a few extra bucks tutoring this year."

"Tell us about it," said Luke. "If there's money to be made, we're all ears."

"OK, listen to this!" said Walt. "You remember the story of old Don Bradford and the Bradford Foundation?"

"Yeah," they both said.

"You said you remembered Donnie, Don's son from Westlake?"

"Yeah," said Josh. "He was two years behind us in school, went to private schools, never heard from him since."

"Well, he's here!" said Walt. "Even with a piss-poor SAT score, his Dad got him admitted, and he's going to need tutors. He enrolled for summer semesters prior to his first full year; grades are in—looks like he failed every subject. A real challenge, but ought to be good money."

"We could use it for sure," said Josh, "but will the coach agree?"

"For you two, I think he will. You both have good grade point averages and you have shown you know self-discipline. Besides, Donnie's father still carries a lot of clout."

"Let us talk about it, Walt," said Luke. "Thanks for thinking of us."

"Yeah, we appreciate it," said Josh.

"Just let me know, guys," said Walt. "Oh, one other thing. If you take this on, you can use the library here in the dorm. Might make it a little easier for you."

They thanked Walt again and returned to their room.

"What do you think, Luke?" asked Josh. "Are we ready to take on tutoring?"

"Sounds like teaching some wet-behind-the-ears kid to drive a car," said Luke, after they plopped into chairs. "Do you think we can work it in?"

"Yeah, I think we can this year," replied Josh. "I can sure use the money. I'm trying to help Dad as much as I can."

"Man, we are strapped for time now," said Luke. "Is the pay enough to justify time with this snot-nosed rich kid?"

"Hell, we can ask for anything," replied Josh. "Old Bradford will cream when he tells his country club buddies that the varsity quarterback and wide receiver are tutoring his son."

"You're an egotistical ass, Josh."

"Just leave the negotiations to me," said Josh.

"Go after 'em, tiger," said Luke. "And remember, you can't always win."

"We always think 'win' though, don't we, Luke?"

"All right, yeah, I know what you are thinking—*it's just another game.*"

"Sure," replied Josh.

"Oh, on another subject, Josh. I've been meaning to ask…how are your mom and dad?" asked Luke.

"Not too well," he answered. "Wish I had time to go visit them. My dad needs to spend full time with Mom, but he can't retire from the refinery now. The company that took over the company he works for wiped out all of his retirement benefits. No one seems to know what happened," he added. "He was just told that his retirement fund was gone. Something's not right there."

"What can you do?"

"Not much now," he replied. "I'm just going to see to it that both of them are well taken care of right now, but some day I'm going to find out what happened to his savings. Have you checked on your mom lately?"

"Yeah, I try to call once a week at least. I don't like to visit," said Luke. "I'm not much in favor of my mother's living arrangements, but she seems happy.

Some horny dude moved in with her. I have no idea where my father is. I really don't give a shit."

"I guess we both have had messed up home lives," said Josh, in a pensive mood. "We've got to be sure that doesn't happen to us."

"I agree, Josh," he said. "We can't look back."

"Right now we've got to figure out how we can find time to help that dumb-ass kid," said Josh. "You have any ideas?"

"What courses does he need tutoring in?"

"Probably whatever he's taking," he replied. "We need to find out."

"You want me to call Walt?" asked Luke.

"Yeah, go ahead," Josh replied.

"Let's take Walt up on his offer to let us use the library and have Donnie come over here for his lessons."

"Good idea," said Josh. "Of course he might mess in his pants if he has to come into this jungle every week and have these animals gawk at him."

"That will be his first test," laughed Luke.

"I have a feeling that this whole undertaking is going to be a test of our endurance," said Josh.

"You're probably right, so see to it you make it worthwhile when you talk to the contact person at Bradford Holdings."

"Don't worry; just get the name and number from Walt."

"What makes you think you can out-deal someone like Bradford, Mr. Big Shit?" asked Luke.

"They're all the same—self centered, puffed-up ego, always have to win. Just make him think he came out ahead, put one over on us."

"Hell, maybe we should just send you to Wall Street."

"Yeah, in time for the next great recession," Josh said, laughing. "You know, Luke, I think I'll go down and talk to Walt again, see what he knows about Mr. Bradford and Donnie."

"Good thinking," said Luke. "May give us a better idea of what we're getting into."

✶   ✶   ✶   ✶

Josh tapped on Walt's door. "Come in, door's open!" said Walt, as always a cheerful tone to his voice. Josh marveled at how Walt always seemed in such good humor considering his disability.

"Walt, I think we are going to take the tutoring job offer."

"Great!" replied Walt. "You're just what this kid needs: you and Luke. He needs a role model."

"What do you mean?"

"This boy has had a very unhappy childhood, I'm told."

"How do you know, Walt? One reason I'm here is to ask you how I might find out more about Donnie's background. You know, what he's like. What kind of problems we will have."

"I can tell you this right now," he said. "From what I hear, he's poorly motivated, overindulged, and snobbish. Yeah, I think you should look at the family history."

"You think we can do this tutoring, Walt?" asked Josh. "From what you're telling me, it may be an impossible feat."

"If anybody can, you and Luke can do it. Let me suggest this, Josh," said Walt. "You need to talk to Dr. Hammonds Quigley. He's the head of the School of Finance. A strange little guy—loves to talk, has accumulated volumes of information, much of it financial information, on every benefactor of this university. He's on the Development Council and he has made that his project. Everyone says he's obsessive-compulsive about it."

"Think he'll know about the Bradfords?"

"Absolutely!" he replied. "He'll have a complete file on the Bradford dynasty. Might not be much on Donnie, but you'll get some idea about the Bradford family. But let me warn you: Prepare to give Dr. Quigley some time. Once he gets an audience, he doesn't know when to quit talking. Weird little man, but plenty sharp. Went all the way through medical school, didn't like it, and switched to economics."

"He graduated from medical school?"

"Yeah, but I'm told he could never adjust to a medical career—difficulty communicating. You'll see."

"Thanks, Walt."

"Oh, one other thing about 'Squig'—that's what the students call him—he's an avid football fan. Never misses a game. Last person on the faculty you'd expect to have an interest in football. He probably can recall details of every touchdown pass play you've ever completed, Josh."

Chapter 8

Chancing that he might find Dr. Quigley in his office, Josh entered the Rothmore School of Finance, checked the directory, and took the elevator to the fourth floor. The receptionist looked up at Josh with skepticism.

"May I help you?" she asked with an air of indifference.

"I would like to speak with Dr. Quigley if he could spare a couple of minutes." *She probably thinks I'm another student here to challenge a grade*, thought Josh.

"Do you have an appointment, Mr....uh?"

"Lehman...Josh Lehman," he answered. He thought he could sense a change in attitude as she fumbled for the intercom switch when he gave his name.

"I'll see if he's available to see you," she said, then turned and spoke into the receiver. "There is a Josh Lehman here to see you."

She had no sooner uttered those words than the door to Dr. Quigley's inner office crashed open and Dr. Quigley bounced through. Walt was right when he said he was strange. Small stature, small features, crew-cut blondish hair, reading glasses hanging from his neck by a bright red cord. He wore athletic shoes that needed cleaning, yellow slacks, and a wrinkled pink shirt with an open collar.

"Josh Lehman! Josh Lehman!" he said, as loud as his high-pitched voice allowed. "Come in, come in, come in. I know, you've come to ask me to join the team heh, heh, heh! Sorry, can't do it. Too busy...heh, heh, heh."

"I was hoping you could find time," said Josh with a laugh. *He must weigh no more that a hundred pounds,* thought Josh, as he watched him move around the office.

He motioned for Josh to be seated and went behind his desk and sat in his own chair. He fidgeted with papers on the desktop for a few moments, then abruptly stood, walked around the desk, and took a chair beside Josh. *My God, he's never still,* Josh observed. All at once Dr. Quigley got up and started pacing around the room, continually staring at Josh.

"I am so glad you came by. I've never seen you up close. Always in uniform, you know. Can't wait for the next game…heh, heh, heh. Have to wait, won't I…heh, heh, heh?"

When he spoke, Josh noticed the tics—twitching of his facial muscles, rapid blinking of his eyes, and spasmodic twisting of his neck. His arms and legs were never still more than a few seconds. There was a jerking motion any time he moved his arms or when he crossed his legs, which he did repeatedly. Even while seated, he shifted positions constantly. *No wonder he gave up medicine,* thought Josh.

"Dr. Quigley, Walt Wasson suggested I come see you," said Josh. "I would like to know something about the Bradford family. Luke Sanders and I are going to tutor Donnie Bradford this semester. We just wondered what kind of person we would be working with. We are from Westlake also, but we know nothing about the Bradfords."

"Ah…Westlake! Westlake!…home office of Bradford Holdings! Oh…Luke Sanders! Other half of the Lehman-Sanders Axis…right? Heh, heh, heh."

With the twitching and jerking, his glasses swayed back and forth. *Nothing is ever still with this man,* thought Josh.

"Yes, sir," said Josh. "Luke and I will work together in tutoring Donnie Bradford this semester."

"Lucky boy. Maybe teach him some football plays, eh?…Teach him that play where Luke races down the field, leads the defense chasing after him, then turns, runs back and is open for a pass."

"Don't think so," replied Josh, with a chuckle.

Suddenly, as if a curtain were drawn. Hammonds Quigley stopped twitching, placed his glasses on the bridge of his nose, focused on his computer, clicked the mouse a few times, and the copy machine whirred.

Dr. Quigley remained motionless while the stacks of pages grew in the copier hopper. At the finish, he stapled the pages together and calmly handed them to Josh. *How can he change from being so hyper to being so placid?* Josh wondered.

"I think you will find everything you need here, Mr. Lehman," said Dr. Quigley, without the high-pitched voice, leaning back in his desk chair, relaxed as if he were going to take a nap. "Of course, I have deleted the list of references. I think you will understand why when you read the history."

"Thank you, Dr. Quigley," he replied, "I understand, and please just call me Josh."

Like a light switch turned on, suddenly Dr. Quigley began the twitching, hopped to his feet, and resumed the purposeless movements of his body.

"Hey!...yeah, yeah, Josh! Josh!" he called out, again in a squeaky tone. "Season starts soon. I'll wave to you from the stands and call out: Josh! Josh!...heh, heh, heh, heh"

"Dr. Quigley, why don't you come down on the field this season with the team?" suggested Josh. "You would be able to see the game better."

Dr Quigley was stunned. He jumped to his feet and pranced around the room.

"Oh, Josh! Do you mean it? Of course you do! Oh, Josh! Josh!," he said as he ran around his desk, came to Josh's side, and kneeled to the floor. "How can I ever thank you? Should I put on a uniform...heh, heh, heh?"

"We'll have a team jersey for you to wear," said Josh.

"Oh, thank you, thank you, thank you!" he cried, grabbed Josh's hand and faked a kiss.

"Thank you, Dr. Quigley, for the information," said Josh as he stood to leave.

"See you at the game, Josh," he said. "Heh, heh, heh, heh...Yeh, Josh! Josh!"

Josh left with the packet in his hand. *He is more than a little weird,* thought Josh. *So what?* With that, he made his way back to the dorm.

* * * *

Once in his room Josh thumbed through the pages of the report. It was meticulously arranged with a table of contents and reference numbers, and with all of the information in chronological order. In many respects it seemed to be in a narrative form, as if the author intended to make a public disclosure of his research.

The report contained the history of John Bradford and his beginning as a roughneck in the oil field. It told of his acquiring his own drilling rig and his fabulous success in finding oil fields.

Josh came to the part about the current Bradford Holdings subsidiaries. There it was! Westlake Refinery, acquired by Western Lake, Inc., one of the Bradford companies, in 1986. Western Lake subsequently became insolvent and the assets were transferred to still another "store front" entity, owned by Bradford Holdings.

"That bastard!" said Josh, as he read Dr. Quigley's analysis of Don Bradford manipulations in the stock market. All of the funds in the employee's benefit account were invested in stock in Western Lake, Incorporated. The stock had a value of zero! The transactions were scrutinized by the Security Exchange Commission, but no wrongdoing was uncovered. Hundreds of employees lost their life savings, according to Dr. Quigley's report, with no clear explanation ever forthcoming.

Luke came in to find Josh poring over the document.

"What's grabbed you by the balls? Doesn't look like study material," said Luke.

"You won't believe this," Josh replied. "I spent an interesting hour with Dr. Quigley in his office in the School of Finance. Walt said he could tell us all about the Bradford family. Dr. Quigley pulled all this up from his files."

"You got this from old Squig?" laughed Luke. "How did you get him to sit still long enough."

"You know Dr. Quigley?"

"Nah," he replied, fidgeting mockingly in his chair. "I just hear his students laughing about him and mimicking him."

"That's pretty cruel, Luke."

"OK, Mr. Nice Guy. I'll back off," he said. "Whatta you got?"

"History of the Bradford family. Nothing specific about Donnie," Josh replied, "But Don Bradley was an unscrupulous lout. That kid probably had a horrible family life. And here we are talking about working for Donnie's father."

"Think we should take the job or just forget it?"

"Luke, we need the money," pleaded Josh. "Let's just make the best deal we can. Besides, from what Walt says we may be able to help the boy."

"Let's give it a try—anything for money," taunted Luke.

"Come on, you don't mean that," laughed Josh. "Luke, you know, I just had a feeling that it was one of the Bradford companies that took over the Westlake Refinery and wiped out my dad's retirement benefits. Dr. Quigley described it in detail in his report."

"You said you were going to find out some day," said Luke. "Maybe this is the day."

"Whatever, we're still taking the job. Right?"

"Right!" Luke's answer was followed by a high-five.

✷   ✷   ✷   ✷

The coaches gave Josh and Luke the green light on setting up the tutoring sessions as long as they didn't interfere with practice, workouts, or the coaches mentoring sessions. Josh and Luke both had free time in the early afternoon—early enough that they would be finished with the tutoring well before the time for their own classes and before football practice.

A call to Bradford Holdings put Josh in touch with Don Bradford's office. He was informed that a Mr. Corbett would speak to him and authorize the tutoring arrangement with Donnie. Luke stood by, trying to distract Josh with his mimicking facial contortions, with Josh waving him off and turning his back.

"This is Jeremy Corbett, Mr. Lehman," he said. "Mr. Bradford has asked me to act in his behalf in this. Will you be able to take on this task?"

"Yes, sir. Luke Sanders and I will work together in helping Donnie."

"Fine," he replied. "What is the customary rate for tutoring at Northwestern?"

"Mr. Corbett," said Josh, evading a direct answer to the question. "Luke and I have a busy schedule, you know, with our own studies plus football practice."

"Are you saying you are not sure if you can do the work or not sure if the standard rate is acceptable?"

"The standard rate is not acceptable, sir."

"Find out the usual rate and double the fee," he said. "Bill this office weekly if you wish, to my attention. How often will he need your services?"

"We think he should have three sessions a week."

"Fine," he replied. "You know, Mr. Bradford expects results."

"We'll do our best."

"Anything else?"

"No, sir," answered Josh. The phone clicked, and Josh turned to Luke.

"OK, lay it on me," said Luke.

"Luke, damn it," said Josh. "Get serious!"

"I'll try. How did you do?"

Josh informed him of the agreement.

"Far better than I would have ever dreamed," said Luke, in all seriousness.

"Whatever, we have our work cut out for us."

"How do you want to divide the time, Josh?"

"Let's do this," he said. "Let's alternate the weeks, but be available to cover for each other if either of us can't make it."

"Sounds fine."

* * * *

The first week was assigned to Luke. Donnie appeared fifteen minutes late for the first lesson. Luke found him wandering around the first floor lobby, studying the alumni portraits.

"Why isn't my father's picture here? He lived in this dump when he was in school," Donnie's first words were uttered in a demanding tone.

"Must be a mix-up," Luke replied, trying to be cordial.

"I want it corrected," said Donnie.

"I'll report it," said Luke, glancing at his watch.

"Which one are you? Josh something or Luke something?" Donnie inquired, as if he were speaking to a servant.

Luke began a slow boil and struggled to suppress it.

"I'm Luke Sanders—at your service!"

"Well, let's get on with it," said Donnie. "This is all my father's idea, you know."

"Fine, but let me remind you: the sessions are for one hour only. If you are late, we have less time."

"What's the big deal?" he said and sneered. "OK, I'll try to be on time. Otherwise you'll tell my father, won't you?"

"Look, this whole deal is between you and Josh and me. If you want us to help you, we'll try, but it's up to you," Luke said with sternness as he led Donnie into the library. "This is where you will come for your lessons."

They sat at the massive table in the middle of the room and Donnie tossed out a copy of his posted grades for the summer semesters; Luke saw that he had passed one course out of twelve hours of basic liberal curriculum courses.

"I guess you want this," said Donnie with a snarl.

"Looks like you'll have to take three courses over."

"Yeah, guess so. Can't you get those firkin' profs to change the grades?"

"Afraid not, Donnie," replied Luke.

"OK, what's next?" asked Donnie, slouched in his chair, picking at his fingernails.

"You'll come here Monday, Wednesday, and Friday at 2:00 pm every week. Josh—that's Josh Lehman—and I will alternate weeks. Make sure you bring any reading assignments with you and make sure you have completed any assigned work before you come."

"Shit, you guys are worse than the profs," said Donnie.

"A lot worse. Get this straight. You're gonna study and pass these subjects! Josh and I are going to stuff these courses into your fuckin' brain or up your ass. Which do you want?"

"OK, OK!" he said. "I get the message."

The first session ended as a disaster. *I don't think we can put up with this shit,* thought Luke. *I know Josh negotiated a neat deal with someone in the Bradford Holdings office, but is it worth it to have to face this worthless, spoiled brat three times a week? We need the money,* he sighed. *We'll give it a try for awhile.*

* * * *

It was Josh's week, and he waited in the library conference room for Donnie. Late again, as usual, so Josh used the time to do some reading on his own. Donnie finally appeared. He was unsteady when he moved about, his eyes were glazed with dilated pupils, and his speech was garbled.

Josh recognized the signs of substance abuse, but pretended not to notice. He tried to get Donnie to concentrate on the study material with little success. Nevertheless, he continued trying*Maybe something will penetrate his clouded mind,* he thought. In the middle of the hour there was a soft knock of the door to the conference room. The door opened and Sam was standing there, holding a slip of paper in his hand.

"Dey is a message fo yo, Mr. Josh," he said, with a semblance of a bow as he handed Josh the note and backed towards the door.

Donnie came alive from his somnolence and glanced up at Sam.

"What the hell is this?" he yelled. "I'm not paying for tutoring sessions to be interrupted by some goddamn nigger with a message."

"It's all right, Donnie," said Josh, hoping Sam had not heard the comment. "He is just the messenger. Sam, this is Donnie Bradford. He is here for tutoring sessions."

"Well, howdy, Mr. Donnie," said Sam, smiling all the while. "I is plumb happy to know yo"

"You don't know me," retorted Donnie, "And you can call me Mr. Bradford, if you call me at all."

"Well, yaassuh, Mr. Bradford!" Sam replied, still smiling. "Does yo happen to be old Don Bradford's son?"

"It's none of your goddamn business, but the answer is yes."

Oh, God, thought Josh. He could see it in Sam's eyes and in his smile. *He's going after the kid.*

"Well, be sure and tell Mr. Don that old Sam said howdy," he said, smiling broadly, as if no slurs had ever been uttered. "And good day, Mr. Josh." And he left with that cunning smile on his face that Josh knew meant retribution in some form was forthcoming.

They concluded their instruction session and Donnie seemed to have sobered up a bit. Josh took the opportunity to counsel Donnie on the dangers of substance abuse mixed with alcohol and how it could impair his learning capacity. After the class, Donnie buried his head in a *Playboy* magazine, obviously ignoring Josh.

Josh just shook his head and waved good-bye. He toyed with the idea of just abandoning the project. He thought of his parents and of Luke and their desperate need for extra funds. He decided to weather it through.

Ten minutes after Donnie left, he returned to ask for help to reach road assistance. Someone had let the air out of two of the tires on his Mercedes Sports Coupe.

* * * *

"Sam, I need the money. I need to keep tutoring that piece of horseshit," he pleaded when Donnie was out of earshot. "Please back off, Sam."

"But Mr. Josh," he replied. "I ain't done nothin' to harm that boy. I jest don't knows what yo means."

"I think you do, Sam."

"He sho seem like a nice boy, Mr. Josh," he said with his usual broad smile. "Why, he is a chip off the old block."

"Sam, please?"

"Yassuh, Mr. Josh," he said, as he walked off, a smile on his face.

Chapter 9

▼

The first game of their junior year at Northwestern arrived with the usual fanfare of excitement. Every member of the team glowed with exuberance and self-confidence as they gathered in the dressing room before the game. Josh and Luke were suiting up and getting ready to hear the last-minute instructions and pep talks from the coaches. Josh noticed one of the security guards whispering to the head coach, both with puzzled looks on their faces.

"Josh!" the coach called. "Come here for a minute!"

"Yes, sir," he replied, as he finished tying his shoelaces.

"Josh, did you tell Dr. Quigley that he could join us at the sideline for the game?"

"Yes sir. I forgot to ask you."

"I don't know, Josh. What brought this on?"

"He's obsessed with football, Coach. Never misses a game. He can recall every statistic you can think of—knows every one of our plays by heart. I think he fantasizes about being on the team. He'll do anything you want him to do—water boy, anything."

"He's head of the damn School of Finance, for God's sake!"

"Give him a chance, Coach," pleaded Josh. "Think of him as a mascot."

"Dammit, Josh! What if he gets hurt?"

"Don't worry, Coach," laughed Josh. "He won't be still in one place long enough to get hurt."

"I've coached this goddamn team for twelve years," said the coach, shaking his head. "I've done everything you can think of for you guys except wipe your asses. I've never faced anything like this before."

"Come on, Coach. Do it for me."

"You and Luke are good, Josh," he said. "I don't know if you are that good."

He paused for several moments, glanced around to see Luke, and a handful of other players gathered, watching it all evolve. He turned to the guard.

"OK, bring him in here. Josh, tell him to sit and be quiet while I talk to the team. And tell him, 'Home games only.' I don't want the embarrassment of trying to explain his presence at out-of-town games."

"Sure, Coach," replied Josh. "Oh! I almost forgot. I told him we'd let him wear a Jersey with a number on it. You know, like the water boys wear."

"Holy shit!" said the coach, his face a brilliant red. "What else did you promise him, Josh? If he sets one foot across that playing field line during play, I'm going to bench you—and you too, Luke, and stop that grinning!"

"Don't worry, Coach," said Josh. "It'll work out fine."

Dr. Quigley was ushered in, wide-eyed with wonder, twitching, jerking his arms and hands, but speechless as he stood by and looked around. Josh welcomed him and introduced him to a few of the players and to the coach who, try as he may, could not erase his skeptical facial expression. One of the trainers handed Dr. Quigley a Jersey with the numbers "00" front and back.

"You'll go out with the water boys and the trainers, Dr. Quigley," said the coach. "Stay close to the bench at all times and don't converse with anyone, especially any of the sports reporters."

"Oh…yes, yes, yes, yes," said Dr. Quigley., his eyes blinking rapidly along with the facial twitching. "Close to the bench…yes, yes…close to the bench!"

The coach turned and walked away, silently mouthing, "Damn, damn, damn!"

*   *   *   *

With Josh and Luke sparking the team during their first year to play as starters, by their junior year, Northwestern was building an impressive record of wins and no losses. In game four—played on the home field—the opponent team was trailing by two touchdowns and was taking wild chances during their offense play. Against all odds of success, their quarterback threw a pass to a receiver—closely guarded by the Northwestern defensive linebackers—just behind the line of scrimmage. He caught the ball, picked up blockers, and ran down the field.

Brent Tower, a Northwestern linebacker known for his speed, overtook him, dived, and tackled him from behind. Brent's helmet was knocked free, and he was struck in the throat by the runner's foot. He grabbed his neck and began frantically rolling on the turf, gasping for breath.

As soon as the trainers and medical technicians realized what had happened, they raced to his side. They started oxygen, but the player grabbed at the mask and tried to pull it away from his face as if the mask were interfering with his ability to breathe. He tried to cough, but made only a crowing sound. His face took on a bluish discoloration. The attendants restrained him with one person on each extremity, holding him down against his almost overpowering strength.

"I can't get an open airway!" the technician cried. "Pull back on his chin! Somebody go for the resuscitation bag! Get that ambulance out here! Quick!"

The emergency technician used the resuscitation bag, connected to the mask, in an attempt to force oxygen into his lungs.

"I can't get oxygen through! His airway is obstructed! Get that ambulance here fast!" he yelled. "There's a scope there! We need to get a tube into the trachea—quick! He's going out!"

Brent's eyes closed; he stopped fighting; his face and hands became deeply purpled; his pupils began to dilate. With the scope, the technician tried to insert an endotracheal tube, with no success.

"I'm afraid it's no use," he said. "I can't get the scope past the obstruction. His throat is crushed…loose fragments of cartilage and blood everywhere."

Brent was motionless during the attempt.

"I think he's gone," said the technician.

Josh, Luke, and a few other players stood around, speechless, spellbound. Unbeknownst to anyone, Dr. Quigley had come out on the field and watched, quietly. As soon as the technician uttered the words, "I think he's gone," Dr. Quigley went into action. He kneeled at the player's side and felt for a pulse in his neck.

"His heart is still beating," said Dr. Quigley in a calm tone of voice. Moving quickly, he removed his pen from underneath his Jersey and a knife from his pocket. He handed the pen to Josh.

"Unscrew the tip and take the cartridge out of the pen," he said, while everyone looked on in wonder.

His voice was calm and came across in a normal tone without the usual squeaking sounds. His words were well-articulated and spoken with a commanding authority that said he was in control. There was none of the usual twitching or jerking or tremor of his arms and hands. It reminded Josh of the calm deliberation he had witnessed in Dr. Quigley that day when he retrieved the data on Bradford Holdings from his computer.

With his knife in one hand and holding the player's trachea firmly with the other, he made one stab through the skin and deep tissue into Brent's windpipe. He twisted the knife blade slightly to enlarge the stab wound, removed the knife blade and inserted the pen casing. He blew into the pen a few times to make sure the chest was expanding, and then turned the resuscitation over to the medical technician.

After a few whiffs of oxygen, the player's skin became pink. He opened his eyes and, although still with a frantic facial expression and a terrified look in his eyes, he didn't fight against the restraints. With each cough he sprayed bloody mucous from the tube that fed life-saving oxygen into his lungs. Soon he was breathing on his own through the make-shift tracheotomy tube. He was loaded into the ambulance and was on his way to the hospital—very much alive.

Josh and Luke sat side-by-side on the bench, waiting for the signal to go in for an offense drive when the game again began. Both were silent and reflective. Luke sat bent forward with his bare, red-haired head cradled in his hands.

"Did you see that, Josh?" Luke said finally. "He was dead, Josh! And Squig saved his life!"

"Yeah, I saw it," answered Josh. "When I saw Brent gasping for air, turning blue, I thought about the many times I have seen my mom looking like that, fighting for air…I'm glad we are in pre-med, Luke."

"I wanna be a doctor, Josh," said Luke. "Don't ask me again. My mind's made up."

"Good! Now, let's win this goddamn game, go have a beer, tell Sam what happened tonight, and catch up on our studying tomorrow."

"I'm with you."

✶ ✶ ✶ ✶

Josh looked around for Dr. Quigley. He had melded silently into the crowd and had made his way back to the bench. When the game resumed, he was his old self again—pacing up and down the sideline, twitching and jerking, staying abreast of the first-down and scrimmage line markers, yelling encouragement to the Northwestern players, and waving his arms at the spectators, asking for louder yelling.

The TV commentators and sports reporters called the incident the "Miracle on the 40 Yard Line." Dr. Quigley refused all interviews by the news media and refrained from discussing the feat with anyone. There was never another question raised about his presence on the "bench turf." The coaching staff insisted that he accompany the team on out-of-town trips from that day forward. For the next game, after that occurrence, he was issued a new Jersey with his name front and back and with a "1" placed in front of the two zeros.

Chapter 10

▼

The next school year, their senior year, was the last for Josh and Luke as non-professional players. The scouts from the professional football teams had watched the two of them closely for their entire career. They began to make recruiting overtures at regular intervals, even during their junior year season.

Josh and Luke both had excellent grades and had applied to three of the state's medical schools. They had been told that they would have no trouble gaining admission to medical school. It was decision-making time.

Both in pensive moods, Luke and Josh stopped by the students' favorite after-class hangout for a beer.

"What are you going to do, Josh?" asked Luke.

"I don't know," he answered. "Those offers are very attractive. I never dreamed they'd make offers like that."

"That would be the end of our financial worries, wouldn't it?" asked Luke.

"For sure," said Josh. "I could help my folks. My dad could stay at home with my mom."

"I know that worries you, Josh," said Luke. "Maybe you should take off and go visit them. It might help you decide. Talk to your dad."

"I tried to get him to come up for the next game, but he won't leave her," Josh replied. "I guess you're right. I'd better go see for myself."

"Have you ever thought of playing professional for a few years and then going on to medical school?" asked Luke.

"I don't think it would work, Luke. We are all steamed up over the prospects of going to medical school. I don't think we could shift gears and put that behind us and then pick it up again later."

"Yeah, I guess you're right," said Luke. "I just don't know what to do."

"While we're thinking, let's have another beer," said Josh.

"Good idea. Won't help us decide, though."

"Think we're becoming a couple of ego-maniacs?" asked Josh.

"What do you mean?"

"We enjoy playing football, that's for sure," said Josh. "Not to mention the roar from the stands that comes with every touchdown. You can't deny it, Luke. It keeps us pumped up to an ongoing high."

"Maybe so," Luke replied. "We sure as hell do enjoy the limelight. Is it worth giving up something we're good at for something we don't know anything about?"

"You are a damn egotist, Luke."

"I saw that gleam in your eyes when you cut into that shark in the lab," Luke said, his speech garbled from drinking the beer too fast. "You think you'll be a good surgeon, don't you? You wanta take those poor unsuspecting creatures into the operating room and cut 'em open, then walk out expecting applause, just like football."

"Hell, I don't know, Luke. You've had too much beer," Josh answered, then became serious. "I really think we both can do just about anything if we believe in it strongly enough."

"But can we walk away from these offers and bury ourselves as unknowns in some medical school, still struggling for enough money just to get by?"

"We have to decide, Luke."

"Talk to your dad, Josh."

"Yeah, I need to do that. Let's go to the dorm."

* * * *

The last game of the regular season was against Crescent University, one of the top-rated teams in the conference. Both teams were undefeated. According to the experts, Northwestern was almost a certain winner. It would be a crucial game, however, since the scheduling of the post-season bowl games depended so strongly on the outcome.

Northwestern was ahead well into the fourth quarter and the team was performing like clockwork. It was beginning to look like a runaway for Northwestern until the Crescent team began to close the score spread.

In the last few minutes of play, Crescent scored a touchdown plus the extra point which left Northwestern still ahead, but only by a narrow margin. They would need to score again or keep possession of the ball to be in a comfortable position.

"OK, Luke, this is it," said Josh in the huddle. "You know the play. This is the third-down play that will cinch the game for us. Just catch the goddamn ball!"

"Do I ever miss, ball slinger?" asked Luke. "Just place it, I'll catch it!"

"It'll be there, smart ass. You just need to be there. Hey, you guys, protect me just a little."

The ball snapped, Josh ran back, dodging defensive linemen until Luke was in position. Luke raced down the sideline and turned abruptly across the field, well ahead of the defensive players. Josh released the ball, watched as it spiraled through the air into Luke's hands. The second he caught the ball he was smothered by Crescent players.

Players were peeled off one at a time by the referees, and after the pile was untangled, Luke was at the bottom. He grasped his knee and rolled to one side in agony in a futile attempt to stand. Josh ran to help him, thinking the worst, and found Luke writhing in pain with a severely injured, flail knee—the same knee that he had previously injured.

The game ended with Northwestern ahead, which assured the team a spot in a major Bowl game, probably against Arizona in the Desert Bowl, but Luke's fate was far less certain.

* * * *

Josh waited outside the operating room for Luke's orthopedist to bring news of the surgery. The procedure had taken much longer than the arthroscopic repair of the cartilage had taken four years earlier. The coach and trainer, a few other players, and Walt waited with Josh. Their joy over winning was dampened by Luke's injury.

"He's fine," the surgeon said. "No complications. It was a complex procedure that took much longer than we anticipated. A badly torn cruciate ligament."

"When can we see him?" asked Josh.

"He should be awake enough to visit in about an hour."

Josh could tell from the surgeon's hesitancy that there was more to the story than they had been told. After being assured that Luke was stable, everyone in the room had the same question in their minds.

"What is the prognosis for future play?" asked the coach finally.

"I'm afraid Luke's football days are over," the orthopedist said.

The room was quiet. No one spoke as they absorbed the reality of those words.

"You played a great game today, Josh," said the surgeon. "So did Luke. Sorry about the injury."

"Thanks," Josh responded, without a smile or another word.

Josh sat back in one of the chairs in the waiting area, staring at the floor while thoughts raced through his mind. He really wasn't too surprised at the answer they heard. It just meant that he and Luke needed to do some soul searching about their futures. There was no question that Luke would not be playing in a Bowl Game. He could accept that.

But what about long term? Josh wondered. *Do we need another opinion? Saying Luke's football days were over sounded so brutally final. Many players with cruciate ligament tears were able to play again after surgery and recovery with a good rehabilitation program. Surely Luke still would be able to go to medical school.*

He needed to talk to Luke as soon as he could hold a conversation. Luke was strong and determined. He would fool the doctors who said that he would not be able to play again. He was a fighter.

"How are you feeling, Luke?" asked Josh, after he was allowed into the hospital room.

Josh could tell by looking at him that he didn't need to ask that question.

"I feel like I've been trampled by the entire Crescent team, including those apes that tried to take you out."

"How do you think they feel right now?"

"If I remember right, just before going under they feel pretty bad," he replied.

"We have a Bowl Game coming up," said Josh, trying to be cheerful.

"What does this look like, Josh?" he said, pointing to his knee. Josh paused before answering.

"Not too good right now," he answered. "We'll need some other opinions."

"Josh, you paused too long to answer," he said.

Josh moved closer, sat on the edge of the bed, and grasping Luke's hand in his, looked into his saddened eyes.

"They don't think you'll be able to play again."

Luke became quiet and thoughtful for several moments, a few tears welling up in his eyes.

"They don't know how tough you are, partner," Josh said, still holding his hand. "We'll get you started on physical therapy, and by next year we'll show them that the old Lehman-Sanders Axis is still alive."

"You ought to take up acting," he laughed. "It's over, Josh."

"Whatever…Right now you need to concentrate on getting well. I'll take over teaching the little son-of-a-bitch for a while," said Josh. "Or better still, I'll turn him over to Sam. He could teach him a thing or two."

They both laughed so hard that Luke grabbed his leg and yelled from pain.

"Enough of that," said Josh. "I'll check with you tomorrow. Get some sleep."

"Josh, thanks," he said, again misty eyed. He turned his head to the wall. Josh knew he wanted to be alone with his thoughts and turned to leave.

Just as Josh was stepping into the hallway, he heard Luke call his name. "Are you going to visit your mom and dad?"

He turned and caught Luke's inquisitive look bearing down on him and knew immediately what he was thinking.

"Yes, I am," he replied. "Get some rest."

Chapter 11

Driving a rental car, Josh started long before daybreak so he could make the trip to Westlake and back in the same day. Luke would leave the hospital in a day or two and Josh needed to make the visit to his mom and dad as soon as possible in order to get back in time to help Luke when he came out of the hospital.

Intensive practice, both on the field and in the briefing room, would start the next week in preparation for whatever bowl game they drew. Josh dreaded the pressure of playing in that game without Luke. Luke's substitute players were excellent pass receivers, but it wouldn't be the same without Luke on the other end of a pass. *I've got to learn to deal with it,* Josh thought.

Josh had notified Donnie that he could lay off his lessons for a few days. That was fine with Donnie. Typical of his self-centered personality, he never once asked about Luke. *Maybe he didn't know about Luke's injury,* thought Josh. *I doubt that football holds much interest for Donnie.*

Josh arrived home just as his dad was preparing breakfast for his mother and getting her spruced up for the day. His dad seemed to have aged so much in the short time since he last saw him. Perhaps he appeared that way because he had just finished his night shift at work. His mother seemed so very weak—hardly able to rise out of the bed without help.

His dad had fashioned a very low bed to facilitate her getting in and out. She always slept with three pillows under her head and chest, and still had difficulty breathing, even with the continuous flow of oxygen. Any time she moved the least bit, she developed shortness of breath plus an aggravating dry, hacking cough. She reached out and pulled Josh close to her. He could hear the rattling in her chest as she kissed him on the forehead. Josh noticed a bluish tinge to her lips.

"I'm glad you came, Josh," she whispered between breaths. "We talk about you a lot. Your dad is so proud of you."

"How are you feeling, Mom?"

"About the same," she replied. "Josh, we haven't given you much of a home life," she added, sadly. "I know it has been hard for you."

To Josh, it sounded too much like some kind of a farewell message.

"The way you and Dad have managed here has given me more than you know," he said. "I only hope I can capture some of that strength."

"You're a good boy, Josh," she said.

"I haven't helped you as much as I would have liked to," said Josh.

"You've helped us a lot, and we appreciate it."

"How is Dad holding up?" he asked.

"He gets tired," she said. "I wish he would give up that night shift work."

"He wants to be near you during the day, Mom."

"I know that," she replied. "I feel so guilty. He has no life except work and caring for me."

"We'll change that someday, Mom," said Josh.

"Josh, I'm not going to be around much longer. I can tell," she said with tears in her eyes. "Promise me you'll take care of your dad."

"Don't talk like that, Mom!" he said. "I'll take care of both of you."

"Any girlfriends, Josh?" she asked.

Josh knew this was coming. He thought about the many times she had asked him the same question.

"None serious," he replied. "I know…you're thinking grandchildren."

"A little late for that," she said, with a wistful smile. "I just want you to be happy," she added. "Your father and I had many happy years. I like to think of those years before I became such a burden on him."

"I think he remembers those years too, Mom."

His dad came in with her breakfast tray, placed the tray on a table in front of the chair, leaned down, and gave her a kiss.

"Out of that bed now," he said, as if he were scolding her. "It's in the chair for you this morning," he added. "We have a special guest."

"See how he treats me, Josh?" she laughed.

"Josh, come join me. I have your breakfast ready too," said Mr. Lehman.

"Thanks, Dad," he said. "It's about bedtime for you, isn't it?"

"Pretty soon, but we have time to talk."

How did he know? Josh wondered. *I guess he could see the troubled look in my eyes and on my face.*

"First, tell me about Luke," he said. "I watched the game on television and saw him carried off the field."

"His knee looks pretty bad," he replied. "He probably won't ever play again."

"I'm sorry to hear that," he said. "What ever happened to his mother?"

"She's living with some guy," he answered. "Luke never sees her or his father and really doesn't seem to care."

"That's sad," he said. "I guess you're the closest thing to family that he has."

"You're right there," Josh said. "I worry about him like family."

They sat across the table from each other, silently eating the special breakfast his dad had prepared. His dad knew just how Josh liked his scrambled eggs—with cheddar cheese and jalapeno peppers. Josh finally spoke.

"Dad, I have some fabulous offers from the professional football teams," he said, and then remained quiet, waiting for his dad's response.

"What are you going to do?" his dad asked after a few moments.

"I don't know. I want to go to medical school, but I can't do both. I would have to agree to a five-year contract."

His dad paused before responding.

"Josh, I never had the opportunity to go to college, as you know," he said. "But if I had, I wouldn't trade a chance for an education for any contract."

"It's a long haul, Dad," he said. "I'm looking at four years in medical school and then four or five years in specialty training."

"Are you thinking professional football just for the money?"

"I guess so to some extent," he replied. "I love football, but I can deal with giving that up. But I need to help you and Mom."

"We manage all right," he said. "I'm still in good health and have a few good years ahead to work. Don't worry about us, Josh."

"Dad, what do the doctors say about Mom?"

"She has what they call 'Chronic Heart Failure'," he replied. "Another term they use is 'Cardiomyopathy.' There is nothing they can do except a heart transplant, and she's too sick for that."

"How much time, Dad?"

"The doctors don't think she'll last another year," he answered, squeezing his eyes to suppress tears. "She's on the maximum doses of medication that she can tolerate now."

"Does she know?"

"I think she does. We just don't talk about it."

"Does Rabbi Joseph visit her very often?" he asked.

"He tries to see her once a week," he answered. "He brings tapes for her to listen to. She tires so easily. Just talking and visiting makes her breathless in only a few minutes. We don't even light Sabbath candles anymore."

"That's not like Mom," said Josh. "I remember well our Sabbath home services and the challah bread Mom used to make every Friday night."

"Hang on to those memories, Josh."

Josh could see the sadness in his dad's eyes as he talked about Josh's mom's long term illness and rapid deterioration. *When he is alone he probably deals with it by denial,* thought Josh. *Having to discuss it with someone else must bring forth the stark truth of finality.*

They had strayed from addressing the dilemma Josh faced. Josh needed some guidance. He wanted to get back to the matter at hand and hear his dad's words of wisdom.

"Josh, I can't tell you what to do," his dad continued. "I can advise you—don't go for the dollars and give up your chance for medical school. 'Fast dollars' is short term. A degree in medicine is long term," he added. "Whatever you do, don't let our situation here influence your decision. We'll get along fine."

Before leaving, Josh went back into the bedroom to tell his mom good-bye. She had eaten only a parcel of her breakfast and had already fallen asleep.

"I'm on the way back to school, Mom," said Josh. "Just wanted to tell you good-bye. I'll try to come more often."

"Thanks for coming, Josh," she replied between gasps for breath. "I know you have studies. And of course, football practice."

"Dad says Rabbi Joseph comes by often."

"Oh yes…and Mrs. Minsky drops by almost every day. Her son's a doctor, you know."

"So I've heard," said Josh, trying to suppress laughter.

"Be careful driving back, Josh," she said. "And tell Luke hello for us."

"I'll do that, Mom," he replied as he bent over and gave her a kiss.

* * * *

The long stretch on the Interstate Highway back to Plainville gave Josh time to reflect on the gnawing quandary—go professional or go to medical school? He turned off the radio and the air-conditioning and lowered slightly the windows of the rental car. *Maybe save on gasoline,* he thought. The refreshing cool air and the noise of the wind rushing past seemed to provide a "playing field" for the debate that engaged his every thought.

He could hear his dad's words: "Don't let our situation here influence your decision." *Did I really want to hear that?* he asked himself. He turned over and over in his mind his dad's remark about "fast dollars" being short term. Still, with the lucrative football contract he could raise his mom and dad out of the quagmire that engulfed their very lives today and every day.

What would a football career be like without Luke on the receiving end of my passes? he wondered. *I have pretty well learned to play with other receivers, but it would never be the same after all these years if Luke were not there with me.*

Luke's silent message to him from that hospital bed seemed to say, "If you want to go professional, go on without me...I'm washed out...but listen to your heart and make your decision based on long term gain, not on short term financial rewards."

How did Luke know that my father would say the very same thing? Josh wondered.

He kept bouncing thoughts back and forth in his mind:

Could I play for five years and then go to medical school? But would I do it? I may become too accustomed to the notoriety and the financial reward to give it up. And then there was the intoxicating excitement of winning, the cheering from the spectators, the thrill of being hailed as some sort of hero. After living a life for five years of professional football, I probably would not be able to give that up any more than an alcoholic could turn down a second drink.

I would miss Luke if I went professional, but I could adjust to other receivers in time. With Luke, however, if I get off a pass and place the ball anywhere in range, Luke will snare it and swivel his way down field for another five or ten yards. Makes me look good. What in medicine could ever replace the self-satisfaction of throwing a touchdown pass?

The image of Brent Tower lying on the football playing field struggling for a breath of air—just like the many times he had seen his mother fight for a breath—kept creeping into his mind. *Brent was given up for dead and this little guy came forth and, with a few heroic measures saved his life. Brought him back from death! What could be more rewarding than that?*

On the other hand, what about those staggering contracts that were being offered by the professionals? How can I turn my back on that? Financial security for myself and my family—never a worry about money again. I could even help Luke in whatever he wanted to do. I could see to it that my mom and dad had everything they needed.

But on the other hand, he wondered, *would I miss more the opportunity of going with Luke to medical school—studying together, graduating together, and maybe even practicing together after our training? Luke always said, "It's just another game." Maybe he's right! And then my mom could say, "My son's a doctor, you know."*

One thing for sure, laughed Josh, while turning these thoughts over and over in his mind, *if I give up professional football for a medical career, no one could ever accuse me of going into medicine to become a rich doctor. I would make more money in football in five years than most doctors make in a lifetime.*

He guided the car into the hospital parking lot reserved for doctors, looked at his watch and realized the late hour. Even though visiting hours were over, he went straight into the hospital, hoping he could talk his way past the security guard. After he parked, he sat in the car for a while and closed his eyes. His head ached from indecision.

Why don't I just take the lucrative offer from one of the professional teams and be done with it? Something just keeps getting in my way, he said to himself. *Something keeps me from jumping for the "big bucks." I feel better about my parents after my visit. I've got to face the reality that my mom will not live too much longer. She is so miserable. I hate to think it, but in a way it would be a blessing.*

My dad is a remarkable person. I realize more every year how wise and intelligent he is. His whole life has been working and taking care of Mom...and never a complaint! If he had had the chance for higher education years ago, there's no limit to what he could have achieved. If Mom dies, he'll manage all right.

As he walked down the corridor toward Luke's room, he suddenly felt as if the dense fog that had been hovering over him had been lifted. He now knew what he wanted to do! It was as clear now as a bright starry night!

"Hell, I could never leave Luke behind," he said aloud. "We're a team and always will be. Luke and I together will find equal self-satisfaction in a medical career. In our own way, we'll save lives just like little Dr. Quigley did on the football field. It'll just be another game! We will suit up in scrubs!"

Josh knocked quietly and opened the door to Luke's room. He was lying in bed, with his head slightly elevated. His injured leg was attached to a machine that slowly flexed and extended his knee. His head was turned away from the door—he didn't look up when Josh entered.

"Hey, swivel hips!" Josh called out. "Climb out of that bed. We're going to medical school!"

Luke's face lit up like a lamp. He said not a word, but his eyes and the expression on his face said a thousand words.

Chapter 12

Josh knew the Bowl game against Arizona University, an unbeaten team for the season, would be a hard one to win with Luke being out of the picture, but he was determined to play his best to win. Sports writers all over the country picked Arizona to win over Northwestern as soon as they saw Luke on the injured list.

Even though football was no longer a priority in his life, Josh didn't want to disappoint the coaches or his teammates with a poor performance. He practiced intensively every day with the other receivers to improve their plays.

The closer the time for the Desert Bowl game, the more nostalgic he became. His last game! It was hard for Josh to accept that he was giving up a way of life that afforded him notoriety and fame that few players enjoyed, but he had made his decision and he was not going to look back.

The day arrived and the team gathered in the dressing room for last minute words of encouragement by the coaches. The roar of the spectators and the vibrant sound of the school bands filtered through every time an outside door was opened. Josh checked his shoelaces one more time for security. *Where is Luke?* Josh wondered. *I thought he'd be here.*

It was time to race out on the field; Josh was expected to lead the pack. He was met by a deafening clamor from the crowd when he appeared on the playing field. He felt an empty, sick feeling in his stomach. *My last game!* it was the thought foremost in his mind as he waved to the spectators. *I have never started a game before without Luke.*

While warming up before the kick-off, Josh glanced at the sidelines and saw Luke standing on crutches at the bench. Without warning, Josh suddenly stopped his warm-up, turned and trotted off the field toward Luke. All eyes in the stands were glued to Josh as he bear-hugged Luke, both boys with tears in their eyes. The crowd roared.

The game started at a slow pace, with each team testing the other for weaknesses and trying for opportunities to score. During the first half and through the third quarter neither team could be said to have an edge over the other.

The score was tied going into the fourth quarter. In the last few minutes, the Northwestern team clicked. The wide receivers and Josh, by then more relaxed, found each other—as if for the first time during the entire game. The final outcome was a last minute "cliff-hanger." A field-goal from the twenty yard line, set-up by a pass from Josh to one of the receivers, put Northwestern ahead by two points and the game ended.

Next came the media reporters' interviews that Josh had tried so hard to avoid since he had decided not to go professional.

"Josh, have you made a decision for next year?"

"Yes, I have," he replied, "but I'm not ready to announce it yet."

"There is a rumor that you may give up football for medical school."

"Medical school is a viable option," he answered, which caused a flurry of questions coming from everywhere at the same time. The sports reporters finally backed off that line of questioning as Josh edged toward the dressing room.

"You managed very well today without Luke," someone said.

"I missed Luke, especially in the last quarter, but we all managed to connect—finally. The replacement receivers played very well."

After the interviews, the TV sports announcers analyzed and commented on Josh's response:

"Josh Lehman would not give a direct answer to questions about possible professional career contracts today. If anything, he seemed to be telling the sports world that this was his last game of football of any type. He has an enviable record for his last four years at Northwestern. It will be a tremendous loss to professional football if he decides to pursue a different career."

✱   ✱   ✱   ✱

The excitement of winning the bowl game settled into normal routine. Luke and Josh turned their attention to their pre-med courses. They had applied to three of the state's schools, and had yet to hear from any of them. Their anxiety from waiting escalated each day that they found the mail box empty of a notice from any one of the schools.

"Why is it taking so fuckin' long?" asked Luke.

"You're too impatient," replied Josh. "No one has heard yet."

"Josh, if we do get accepted," asked Luke, "how the hell can we afford it?"

"We'll find a way, Luke."

"Dammit, Josh," said Luke, "do you always have to be so goddamn optimistic?"

"Student loans, bro," answered Josh. "Borrow the money now and pay it back after we graduate."

"What about scholarships?" asked Luke.

"Yeah, we both will be eligible with our grade point average."

"How do we apply?"

"I've already applied for both of us. We should hear soon," Josh replied.

"You applied for both of us?"

"Yeah," Josh answered.

"Dammit, Josh," he said. "I don't need a keeper."

"Cool it, man," said Josh. "You can always change your mind."

Finally, their acceptances came from all three state medical schools. Now came the decision of which one to choose. The most difficult school into which to gain entrance was Metcalfe Health Science Center in Dallas. Metcalfe offered attractive student assistance programs and was recognized nationally as a top grade research and training center.

So Metcalfe it would be. Both Luke and Josh agreed. They were assured that they both would qualify for scholarships and student loans, plus there would be off-hour job opportunities.

* * * *

They still had the problem of Donnie to deal with for the remainder of the year. Their agreement carried them through the second semester of their last year at Northwestern. Even though they would like to throw in the towel, they had made a commitment and they would see it through. With the expense of medical school on the horizon, they needed money now more than ever.

Salvaging Donnie seemed hopeless at times. They were tired of his lackadaisical approach to his studies. His attitude mirrored his very basic philosophy of life. With his dad's money, he could have anything he desired. Josh and Luke were fed up with making excuses for his ineptness. They were weary of propping him up for classes after one of his raucous nights of revelry.

They had managed to get Donnie through the first semester with enough grade points to keep him in school, but it came only after badgering, threatening, and coercion. The drug and alcohol problem was getting worse. Some days Donnie was so stoned the tutoring session had to be canceled altogether.

While Luke was recovering from surgery, Josh took over the tutoring every week. Each time Donnie came in zonked from coke or alcohol or both, Josh tried to counsel him, but never seemed to reach him. *What is wrong with this kid?* he wondered.

"Why do you do this, Donnie?" asked Josh.

"Whatta you care, man?" he answered, his speech so thick as to be barely understandable.

"Don't you see what you're doing to yourself?"

"Hey, dude, don't wanna teach me? Just haul ass."

"Look, Donnie, Luke and I want to help you. You have got to help yourself."

"Yeah, look who's talking," Donnie replied. "Big football star! All the girls chasing after you. What the hell you know 'bout how it feels?"

"What do you mean, Donnie?"

"How it feels!" he said. "Shit, you wouldn't know! You wouldn't know how it feels—when nobody gives a rat's ass about you. Not even your mother and father."

"Donnie, your dad is very concerned that you pass your grades and succeed."

"Come on, man," said Donnie. "He's just trying to avoid the embarrassment that his son is a dumb-ass. You don't know how it feels, Josh, growing up in a house where the houseboy and the chauffer take care of you—and laugh at you and make fun of you."

"I am so sorry, Donnie," said Josh. "It must have been hard to take."

"Yeah, where you never get a hug or a kiss from your mother or father—always busy with parties or society shit. You don't know how it feels, Josh, to be so lonely you want to kill yourself. I used to wish sometimes that my mother or father would spank me. At least they would show some feeling."

"Donnie, turning to drugs is not the answer," Josh pleaded. "You can turn this around. Get some help, man! Get into a treatment program!"

"What are you?" he retorted. "Some kind of fuckin' shrink? Yeah, go to group meetings and tell strangers how some maid or butler taught you to ride a bicycle or took you to your soccer game when every other kid had a dad or mom by their side."

"You've got a problem, Donnie. Something you're not telling me, something you're not telling your dad."

"I can't tell him, Josh! I can't tell him!" he said, as he dropped his head into his cupped hands and began sobbing. "He'd never understand. He'd never listen. All he wants to do is to travel all over the world with some bimbo tagging along. They never wanted me to be born in the first place. I know that. I feel that."

Josh came over to him and placed his arm around his shoulders, trying to comfort him. *How pitiable!* thought Josh, *I can't believe what I'm seeing. He's showing emotions that I never thought he was capable of. Instead of his usual attitude that Luke and I are his servants, it's like he's crying out for help. What is he trying to tell us?*

Donnie suddenly straightened his back and stood. He looked past Josh as if he weren't there and, with a scowl on his face, headed for the door.

"I'm getting out of here," he said, and left the room without turning back.

Will I ever know what that was all about? wondered Josh. *I'm going to tell Luke that we must never say our childhood days were messed up. Nothing could be worse that what Donnie experienced as a child.*

Donnie's abrupt departure left Josh in a quandary over his behavior. *Something is going on in that poor kid's life,* thought Josh. Whatever, Josh was glad to see that Luke could now resume the every other week sessions with Donnie. The last few weeks had stressed his endurance.

* * * *

Josh stripped down to his skivvies, popped open a diet Coke, and settled at his desk to study for an exam the next day when the phone rang. It was Lola.

"Josh, it's me—Lola."

"Yeah, I know, Lola," said Josh. "What's up?"

Even though the switchboard operator's voice was a fixture after years in Ryan Hall, Lola still identified herself.

"There's a gentleman here to see you and Luke. It's about you guys tutoring that Bradford boy."

"Damn, Lola, I'm trying to concentrate on studying for an exam tomorrow and Luke is still in one of his labs. Can't it wait? Is it Donnie's father?"

"No, try again."

"Come on, Lola." said Josh, even more exasperated. "Is it one of Donnie's profs?"

"This dude looks more like a bank president. Nice to see someone with a little class around here for a change—someone who doesn't smell like an athletic dressing room."

"Lola, can't he wait until Luke gets here?"

"Josh, get your sweet ass down here now! He's in the library."

Josh dressed, grumbled to himself, and went down to the first floor lobby and into the library. A distinguished-looking, slender man in his early thirties stood to greet Josh with a smile and a handshake.

Lola was right. He was class—immaculate dress, a charcoal pin-point suit, an expensive-looking tie. His blondish hair had been styled, not a strand out of place. He had a firm handshake and Josh noticed his manicured, smooth-skin hand.

"You're either Josh Lehman or Luke Sanders," he greeted with a broad smile.

"Yes, sir, I'm Josh. Luke is still in classes."

"Josh, I'm Jeremy Corbett. I work for Bradford Holdings as Mr. Don Bradford's executive assistant."

"Nice to meet you. I talked to you last year when Luke and I started the tutoring sessions with Donnie. You're here about Donnie?"

"Yes," he replied. "First, Mr. Bradford asked me to convey his sincere appreciation for the work you've done with Donnie."

Ho, man! thought Josh. *He's setting me up for something. What's next?*

"Thank you, Mr. Corbett," said Josh. "It's been an interesting experience."

"You can be honest with me, Josh," he said, with a twinkle in his eye. "It's been a nightmare for you and Luke and I know it. Now let me tell you why I'm here."

"Please do," said Josh, a bit taken aback. *This guy is crafty.*

"To give you some background," said Jeremy. "Mr. Bradford is very resolute that Donnie should be trained to take over the reins of Bradford Holdings some day. The company has opened a branch office in Dallas and I will be placed in charge. One of my responsibilities will be to see that Donnie is groomed for a leadership position in the company."

"We are aware that this is your last year at Northwestern and we will need a replacement at the end of this semester. For now, I will relieve you of your tutoring duty for the rest of the year. You and your partner will continue to draw the agreed-upon stipend. I am hopeful that you will assist me in setting guidelines for Donnie's studies."

Josh wanted to scream "Thank God!" and yell out the window to the world, "It's over! It's over! We've been blessed!" Instead, he restrained himself and made a weak effort to fake remorse.

"We will be happy to help you in any way, Mr. Corbett. And in all honesty, we will miss the opportunity to help Donnie."

"Thank you, Josh," he replied. "I am confident Donnie has gained from being around you and Luke. I will commute from Dallas and meet with you for each session for a while until I feel capable of filling your role. Oh, please feel free to call me Jeremy."

"I'll do that, Jeremy," said Josh, and they parted.

* * * *

Jeremy welcomed the time with Josh and Luke to familiarize himself with some of the strategies they used to pound even a fragment of knowledge into Donnie's pickled brain. He didn't look forward to the task ahead, but he could perceive the advantage of taking on this chore. *One more step in the right direction,* he thought. *It fits well into my long-range plan.*

Chapter 13

Jeremy Corbett grew up in the squalor of a near-poverty existence. His father worked in the Westlake Refinery until his untimely death from end-stage lung disease when Jeremy was only ten years old. Jeremy, the youngest of four children, watched his mother scrape and slave to keep the family fed and sheltered.

There were no retirement or death benefits when Jeremy's father died. The employee health and benefit plan had mysteriously disappeared when the company was taken over by a different owner. His mother managed, however, to provide for her family by working various night-shift jobs in a convenience store and taking in laundry and ironing during the day.

As soon as he was old enough to work, Jeremy helped his mother with the expenses of daily living by doing odd jobs wherever the opportunity arose—delivering papers, mowing yards, or baby sitting for neighbors' children. By the time Jeremy was sixteen, his older brother and two sisters managed to escape their miserable existence at home and pursued interests elsewhere, leaving Jeremy the sole helping-hand for his mother.

* * * *

Jeremy hurried home from school; one of his counselors had recommended him for a bus-boy job at the country club. He needed to spruce up a bit before going for his interview. His mother was sitting in a chair in their small living room. *Most unusual for her at this time of day*, Jeremy thought.

"Mom, are you all right?" he asked, then noticed her labored breathing.

"I'm fine, Jeremy," she replied between gasps for breath and coughing. A trash basket beside her was filled with tissues soaked in blood.

"You're not fine, Mom," said Jeremy. "You need to go to the doctor."

"Jeremy, you know we can't afford a doctor," she said. Her breathing became even more difficult with wheezing and gurgling. Her lips and fingers were blue and her skin was covered with beads of perspiration.

"I'm calling a taxi."

"Jeremy, wait!" she called out as he ran to the phone.

"I'm not waiting, Mom."

The taxi dispatcher sensed the urgency for help when he asked Jeremy's destination and was told that it was the hospital. An ambulance was sent instead, and with Jeremy at her side, his mom was taken to the nearest hospital emergency room. In spite of a constant flow of oxygen by mask in the ambulance, she was getting worse by the minute. At the E.R., a physician quickly evaluated her, ordered a chest x-ray and blood gasses.

Jeremy was standing by his mom's stretcher when the E.R. doctor motioned for him to follow them to the consultation room.

"Your mother is very sick, young man," he said. "Are you her son?"

"Yes sir."

"How long she has been having trouble?"

"I don't know…she never complains," he answered. "What's wrong?"

"Looks like she has a severe pneumonia, probably has been coming on for several days."

"She's been coughing a lot at night for a long time," said Jeremy. "I tried to get her to go to a doctor but she wouldn't go—said we couldn't afford it. She just got worse today."

"We're going to have to put her on a ventilator; that's a machine to help her breathe."

"Will she be all right?"

"We'll do everything we can, son," he replied as he put his arm around Jeremy's shoulders. "It looks pretty bad."

The memory of his mother being told those same words, just before his father died, flashed through Jeremy's brain. He remembered the panic-stricken look on her face—as vivid in his mind as it was on that fateful day.

"She's gonna die, isn't she?" asked Jeremy, staring at the floor.

"We're going to do our best," said the physician. "We'll have to put a tube into her windpipe and connect it to the machine. The ventilator will breathe for her—try to expand her lungs."

"Will she be in pain?" asked Jeremy.

"I won't let her be in pain," he replied.

"Can I stay with her?"

"I'll see to it that you can," he answered.

The doctor looked down into the saddened face of the frightened boy and held him close for a few moments.

"You're a brave boy. I know it must be hard for you to go through this."

"I'm all she has," said Jeremy.

She was admitted to the Intensive Care Unit. Although there were visiting hour restrictions, the doctor arranged for Jeremy to stay by her bedside. In spite of the ventilator support and the intravenous fluids—saturated with antibiotics and medications to keep her blood pressure stable—she deteriorated rapidly. She aroused once during the night, long enough to smile reassuringly at Jeremy, then lapsed into a coma and died within an hour, with Jeremy holding onto her hand.

Jeremy had no idea where to find his brother and sisters to notify them of their mother's death. The hospital social workers arranged for her to be buried in the pauper's section of the cemetery, with the only attendees being Jeremy and a few of the women for whom she had done laundry or with whom she had worked. After the burial, Jeremy returned home, alone, to their empty house.

There were no casseroles or plates of tuna sandwiches that are usually brought in by the good ladies from some church after a funeral. No teary-eyed relatives or friends, mourning and consoling each other with hugs and kisses. There was only sixteen-year-old Jeremy Corbett, left alone to make his way in the world by his own devices.

Jeremy wandered through the house from room to room. The ironing board was still standing in the kitchen, with stacks of clothing nearby that his mother had never finished. In her bedroom, as always, everything had been left in perfect order. The chest of drawers contained a scattering of her personal possessions—birth and marriage certificates, a faded picture of Jeremy's father, a wedding band that must have been his father's. A few items of well-worn clothing hung in the closet.

Everywhere he looked, memories of his mother's self-sacrifice and deprivation flashed back through his mind. He sat on his mother's bed and pulled her pillow onto his lap. He buried his head into the downy softness and smothered his face with the pillow for a few moments, letting the fragrance that he remembered of her presence penetrate the higher centers of his brain. No tears flowed as he sat there. He stood and replaced the pillow on the bed, careful to straighten the coverings just as his mother had always done every single morning. He stared at the empty bed for several minutes.

"I hate this place!" he finally said aloud, anger building up to a boiling point.

He stormed into the kitchen, grabbed the unironed clothes, ironing board, and iron and threw everything out into the street. He went back into the house, slammed closed the door to his mother's bedroom, and then sat on the porch steps, thoughts whirling through his mind. With his hands cupped around his head, he began sobbing.

"Whatever will happen to me now? I am so scared!" he cried.

From that day forward Jeremy set two goals for himself: first, to pull himself out of the despair of destitution; second, to avenge somehow the cruel impoverishment that had caused the suffering and death of his parents. Grief and self-pity were pushed aside. Bitterness over the misfortunes in his young life took over and became the motivating force that drove Jeremy on the road to achieve his goals.

* * * *

Graduation from high school with honors made Jeremy eligible for tuition and textbook scholarships. He worked the lunch and dinner shifts at the country club as a bus-boy in order to have time for his morning and afternoon accounting classes at the college. In his country club job, Jeremy quickly learned how to use flattery and politeness to his advantage. Within six months he was promoted to assistant waiter.

Waiting tables at the country club gave him a glimpse of the affluent society element in the community and a look at the business world at lunch time, complete with the two and three martinis. Being attentive to the patron's needs and never missing an opportunity to shower compliments at just the right time and place brought him a generous share of tips and made Jeremy one of the most popular waiters at the club.

A frequent customer at lunch time was Don Bradford, Sr. He was accompanied always by business associates or executive assistants who never failed to show that they were impressed when Jeremy promptly placed Don's first martini, with two large stuffed olives speared by a toothpick, on the table as soon as Don was seated. Don had become so accustomed to Jeremy and the other waiters attending to his every need—from pulling out his chair, unfolding and placing his napkin across his double "spare-tire" paunch, to jumping when he beckoned—that he rarely ever looked into their faces. They were servants, without identity, put there for his pleasure.

When handed the menu, Don always placed his reading glasses over his puffy face and vicariously tasted every item offered for the day, oblivious for the most part of everyone around him. Until he had thoroughly scrutinized the menu, he kept his head buried in the folder. He even carried on conversation with his luncheon guests without ever looking up until he decided what to order.

It had been a trying day for Jeremy. He had final examinations the next day, needed every bit of time to study, and wanted to go home as soon as possible. He had no sooner asked Ivan Dominique, the head waiter, if he could leave early than Don Bradford's secretary, Miss Stafford, called the club for Ivan.

"Ivan, Mr. Bradford will be there for lunch. He has two VIPs from Wall Street that he's bringing; they might be a little late," said Miss Stafford. "You know what to do, don't you, Ivan?"

"Oh, yes ma'am," he replied. "Everything will be ready."

"Don't let anything go wrong, Ivan," she warned. "This is a very important meeting."

"No ma'am," he responded. "Don't worry. I know just what Mr. Bradford expects."

"Ivan, please remember that Mr. Bradford likes two large stuffed olives in his martinis," she said. "The last time he was there the waiter brought his martini with only one olive."

"Yes ma'am," said Ivan, as he eyed Jeremy. "I know Mr. Bradford was upset because there was only one olive. There was a different waiter that day. Jeremy will be here today, and we'll see that everything goes well—and that he has two large stuffed olives in his martinis."

"Thank you, Ivan," said Miss Stafford. "It has to be perfect today."

Jeremy was standing by, waiting for an answer to his request to leave early. He heard only one side of the conversation, noticed how pale and sweaty Ivan had become, and turned to go back to his work, for he knew what the answer would be. *I'd like to stuff those two large stuffed olives, with the toothpick, up that old bastard's ass,* he thought.

Don Bradford and his entourage arrived and were met with the usual fanfare performance by all of the club employees, from the valet parking area all the way to the private dining room. Ivan was waiting, a clean white towel draped across his arm. He opened the door and escorted the group into the room just as Jeremy placed Don's drink—a martini with two large stuffed olives—at his place at the table.

Jeremy filled glasses with ice water and took drink orders from the others as he passed out menus. As usual, Don immediately turned his attention to the menu—his moment of fantasizing over the choices of culinary delicacies. While Jeremy recited the specials of the day, Ivan stood by the door in surveillance, waiting for Don to raise his head as a signal that he was ready to order.

"Ivan, what do you recommend?" asked Don.

"Mr. Bradford, I think you would like the Filet of Sole, stuffed with fresh crabmeat and covered with our rich, creamy Béarnaise sauce. Very tasty, sir."

"Fine," said Don.

The others followed suit and Ivan retreated to the kitchen to make sure the plates were prepared to perfection. Jeremy stayed available for any additional requests while the men began their business discussions. Words like "liquidity" and "short and long-term liability" filled the air and reminded Jeremy of his accounting finals.

The food cart arrived promptly and Jeremy began placing the plates on the table. *I'm glad they all ordered the same thing,* he thought. *The only thing I can think about right now is getting out of here and back to my studies."*

Jeremy had just delivered Don's third martini and turned to stand back away from the table when Don motioned that he needed his water glass filled. Jeremy grabbed to pitcher to fill the glasses. Over and over again Ivan had instructed him to always gently shake the pitcher before pouring so the water and ice would flow without splashing. In his haste, when he poured into Don's glass, a glob of ice hit the glass, caused it to overturn into Don's plate, washing food and ice cold water into his lap. Turmoil erupted!

"Ivan!" yelled Don as he pushed his chair back, scraping food and water off his clothes and onto the floor, saturating his shoes and socks on the way. "Ivan! Where are you?"

Jeremy began cleaning the mess off of Don. "I'm so sorry, Mr. Bradford," he said. *God, what have I done?* he asked himself. *This is the end of this job.*

"Just get away from me, you idiot! Where is Ivan? Ivan!" he called just as Ivan arrived.

"How did this happen?" said Ivan to Jeremy.

"I'm sorry, sir," Jeremy replied.

"Get him out of here!" said Don. "I want him fired!"

"Of course, Mr. Bradford," said Ivan, still trying to clean some of the "rich, creamy" Béarnaise sauce off of Don's clothes. The "VIP's from Wall Street" observed the scene with expressionless faces.

Jeremy quietly stole out of the room, cleaned out his locker, left his white coat behind, and walked out of the club. "If I do well on this examination I won't have to put up with this shit anyway," he muttered to himself. "I'll come back later for my check. I don't think I'll get my share of the tips for today."

*   *   *   *

With whatever other daytime jobs he could manage and with weekend work waiting tables at other restaurants, Jeremy was able to finish his college curriculum and achieve a degree in accounting. He handily passed his CPA examination on his first try. Part time employment by an accounting firm in San Antonio enabled him to continue in graduate school and to gain a masters degree in economics and a law degree from Trinity University.

In the course of his studies in accounting and economics, Jeremy became knowledgeable in the mechanics of setting up employee benefit trust funds. Even though he was very young when his father died, he could still remember how proud his father was of the benefit funds he had created at the refinery—his retirement plan and the college fund for his children. His father often commented to his mother, "There will be money enough here for our kids to go to college."

The employee benefit funds disappeared when the refinery was taken over by the new corporation. By searching a few internet web sites, Jeremy found that Westlake Refinery had been acquired by Western Lake Corporation, a subsidiary of Bradford Holdings. The answer to the question of what happened to the employee benefit funds was no longer a mystery to Jeremy. With a few accounting manipulations, Bradford Holdings invested the employee's funds into corporations that they owned and then bankrupted the companies.

Chapter 14

The next step in Jeremy's plan was to find the Wall Street brokerage firm that handled Bradford Holding's transactions. With little effort he found the firm, applied for and secured a position there. He managed to get himself assigned to the Bradford account.

Within a short time, Jeremy was on a first-name basis with the Bradford executives. They relied strongly on Jeremy's research and recommendations when Bradford embarked on a hostile takeover of some unsuspecting corporation. Driven by his determination to learn more about Bradford Holdings, Jeremy led the Bradford executives through one acquisition after another—all successful.

Jeremy spent hours on end every day and most weekends seeking to unravel and understand the complexities of the stock manipulations he observed by Bradford Holdings. On the surface, everything looked perfectly legitimate. He dug and dug until he finally found the key. *How clever!* he marveled. *How very simple! How shrewd! No wonder the Security Exchange Commission attorneys and auditors had missed it.*

Jeremy revealed to no one what he had discovered. He filed it away into the depths of his computer-like brain. Someday, when the time was right, he would open that file again. He knew their secret. Now he would wait until the time came when he could use it to his advantage.

Working alongside the Bradford cadre almost every working day, Jeremy quickly gained their respect for his Wall Street savvy, all the while careful not to disclose all he knew about their methods of operation. He was frequently consulted by Bradford executives for an opinion of prospective targets for acquisition.

When an opening on the Bradford management staff came available, he discretely showed an interest. That's all it took! With his proficiency and experience, he was offered a position as a corporate executive with the core holding company: Bradford Holdings!

Just what I have been waiting for! thought Jeremy, silently shouting his enthusiasm as thoughts whirled through his brain. Once in an executive position, with electronic access to all of the company's confidential dealings, Jeremy dived headlong into the heretofore secretive transactions of Bradford Holdings and all of its subsidiaries.

* * * *

While Jeremy was still with the Wall Street brokerage firm—just before joining Bradford Holdings—Rob Stewart, one of Bradford Holding's top echelon executives, leaned heavily on Jeremy's advice on a possible acquisition. Renvorken, Ltd., Rob's prospect that he had spent months researching for a hostile takeover, appeared to be a "sitting-duck."

"What do you think, Jeremy?" Rob Stewart asked.

"Good prospect," Jeremy replied. "They have some lucrative space program contracts on the board, both here with NASA and with space programs in Europe. Their engineers are the best in the industry."

"Do you see anything in their financial reports that I should be concerned about?" asked Rob.

"Their problem has been debt load and poor cash flow. That can be corrected with minor adjustments in their operating statements and balance sheets," Jeremy answered. "Great opportunity!"

Jeremy watched Rob's response to his remark. *He didn't even hear me; he showed no sign that I know how they make "minor adjustments" and manipulate the numbers on their company's financials,* observed Jeremy. *He's too eager to get on with another corporate slaughter.*

"Thanks, Jeremy," said Rob. "You've never been wrong. When are you coming with us?"

"Soon," he replied. "I've been offered a position and I look forward to joining you guys."

"Great!" said Rob. "Then I won't have to pick your brain on every turn for info like this."

"When do you intend to move on this takeover?" asked Jeremy.

"Within a few weeks. You'll be with us by then. Probably will be an agenda item at your first board meeting."

"What will you do with a company like this?" asked Jeremy. "It looks more like long-term payoff, which is not Bradford's forte."

"Oh, we'll manage it like the others. Spin off parts of the company, keep stock options, work on one subsidiary at a time to jack up the stock price, and then have one of our partnerships sell high. You know, Jeremy. You've seen us do that. Lastly, we'll bleed the company's cash—including the employee benefit funds—into a partnership and the dissolve the whole entity after we distribute the cash. Neat deal, huh?"

"Yeah, neat," said Jeremy as he looked out the twentieth-story window and thought of his father working all of his life to have all of his savings jerked away by "neat deals" like Rob described. *My father and mother paid for their "neat deals" with their lives,* Jeremy reflected with vehemence. *Bleed the company's cash! You bled my mother's life blood, you bastard.* Memories of that bucket filled with blood-soaked tissues flashed through his brain.

"You don't know the half of it," said Rob. "Giant bonus for me, plus I'll take the family on an extended vacation to Hawaii on the corporate plane. I've worked my ass off for this deal, Jeremy. Good to know you're always right and that you'll be joining us at Bradford."

"What's it like working for Mr. Bradford?"

"Oh, old Don's OK," said Rob. "You have to put up with a lot of bullshit. He's an egotistical windbag; but if any of us come up with a good deal—like Renvorken—that makes him money, he rewards us handsomely."

"I guess that's what keeps all of you guys around."

"Absolutely! And we have free rein to seek and search for money-making transactions. Don doesn't micro-manage. He turns us loose to do as we please."

"That gives you a lot of power on the street then, doesn't it?" said Jeremy.

"Oh, man, yeah!" Rob replied, his face lighting up with a fiendish grin. "We're feared everywhere we go, like, 'Barbarians at the Gate.'"

* * * *

Jeremy's first board meeting was scheduled for seven a.m. a week after he joined the top management echelon. On the agenda was the proposed acquisition of Renvorken, Ltd., a manufacturer of critical parts for propulsion rockets used in the space program.

The top executives of Bradford Holdings were sitting around the massive oval shaped table when Jeremy entered the conference room. They were all dressed as if they had just stepped out of a fashion plate from "Gentlemen" magazine. Jeremy knew most of them from previous meetings when he had been with the Wall Street firm.

The bright young men who made up Don Bradford's platoon of "warriors" paused momentarily from their raucous story telling and noshing on Danish to welcome Jeremy. He took a seat in one of the few vacant chairs. When Don came in and took his place at the head of the table, the chattering, even the chewing, stopped.

Rob Stewart, appearing eager to get on with his presentation on Renvorken, Ltd., spoke first, addressing Don.

"Don, this is Jeremy Corbett, whom we have been telling you about. He has been a great asset to us over the months and now has been kind enough to join our group."

Don, without uttering a word, looked at Jeremy—straight in the eye, up and down—with a strange, puzzled look on his face.

"Where have I known you before, Mr. Corbett?"

"You must be mistaken, Mr. Bradford," he answered. "I don't believe we've met, sir."

He treated me like dirt on his feet when I worked as a waiter at the country club, Jeremy reminisced. *Maybe I'll get a chance to remind him of that some day.*

"Let's get on with it," said Don. "Rob, you have a report on the company you've been studying?"

"Yes, I have, Don."

Rob jumped to his feet, his remote control in his hand, and pulled the laser pointer from his pocket. With a click on "slide show," doors covering the giant screen at the far end of the room slid open. The first slide flashed on and Rob began his Power Point presentation. First he gave an overview of the company that he had researched:

"The name of the company is Renvorken, Ltd. It was founded in the 1950s by Hans Renvorken, a German immigrant engineer, during the early days of rocket technology. The company has designed and manufactured various parts for rocket engines for the space programs in this country and in Europe."

With each comment made by Rob, a new slide was projected on the screen. The room was quiet during the show.

"It became a publicly traded company in the early 1960s when funds for development financing were needed. The Renvorken family retained twenty percent of the stock in the company and still has control, along with the fifteen percent owned by long-time employees."

He continued the show, with slides showing the current and the preceding ten-year graphs of sales, expenses, debt ratios, cash flow, inventory, price-earnings ratios, and market price.

Jeremy winced when Rob projected the sizable balance in the employee benefit fund. He glanced around the room and witnessed each guy smiling and licking their lips. *I'm going to sink this ship,* vowed Jeremy. *This is one fund they are not going to rape.*

Rob finished his presentation and asked for questions. The room was quiet.

"Our new associate, Jeremy, has helped me with this prospect," said Rob. "Jeremy, do you have anything to add?"

Jeremy squirmed for a few moments before answering. He could feel every eye in the room focused on him. *I want my answer to hit home,* he thought.

"I apologize, Rob," Jeremy? said. "I assumed you had researched the status of the foreign contracts. Most have been canceled because of defective products. I project that the present forty-eight dollars per share will drop below ten within the next few weeks. I thought I made that clear when we talked last."

Don slammed shut the brochure that Rob had so neatly prepared, stood and started for the door, then turned.

"Rob, I'll see you in my office in ten minutes."

"Yes, sir," said Rob. Once Don was out of the room, Rob faced Jeremy.

"You son-of-a-bitch," he screamed. "Do you know what you've done? I have plane and resort reservations; I'm taking my wife's parents. I've placed an order for a new BMW. You've wiped that out."

"I'm sorry, Rob," said Jeremy, remaining cool as if nothing had ever happened. "I thought I told you that Renvorken was a long-term pay-out."

*   *   *   *

The repetition of similar scenarios whenever any occasion arose that involved the other executives brought Don's attention to Jeremy's astuteness and capability. In short order, Jeremy won Don's confidence to the point that Don depended on him for advice on every turn—both financial and personal. Jeremy became Don's confidant and consigliore. In time, Don became nothing more than a "fixture" in Bradford Holdings, with Jeremy making all of the administrative decisions.

Jeremy had access to all electronic records of each one of the companies that comprised Bradford Holdings, as well as access to Don's personal accounts He was able to transfer funds in and out of any of the Bradford Holdings accounts. Don had implicit faith in Jeremy's integrity, and Jeremy never missed a chance to enhance that trust. He provided Don with regular statements of his personal accounts. Don disliked electronically transmitted information, so Jeremy always delivered hard copies of the reports to him personally. Don never questioned their authenticity.

Any time Jeremy appeared with a briefcase in hand, Miss Stafford knew to usher him straight into Don's private office.

"Time for another report, I see. Mr. Bradford's going to clog the shredder again, I'm sure. He'll be out in a minute," she said, pointing to the adjacent restroom.

Jeremy smiled when he heard those words about the shredder. *Just as I have always suspected,* he thought. *He never looks at the reports.*

The toilet flushed and Don emerged, drying his hands on paper towels, but had failed to zip up his pants. Jeremy decided not to comment.

"Jeremy!" he said. "What a nice surprise. Must be urgent to drag you away from your office," he added with a chuckle.

"Nothing serious, Mr. Bradford," said Jeremy. "Just time to give you another report on your personal accounts. There is one bit of urgency, however, that needs attention."

"Come sit down, Jeremy," he said, motioning toward a chair near his desk. "I can't imagine anything being too complex for you to handle."

"Thank you, sir," Jeremy responded. "If you would like, I can pull up the data on your computer, Mr. Bradford."

"No, no, Jeremy, you know I have an aversion toward computers," he said. "Whatever the problem I'd rather you just handle it."

"That will be fine, sir. Here's what concerns me" said Jeremy, spreading sheets of paper across the desk. "One of your personal Swiss bank account balances shows a sharp increase compared to the previous statement. I know it's secure, but I worry that someone would leak information that there has been an unusual increase in activity and tip off one of the regulatory agencies in this country."

"My God!" said Don, a frantic look on his face. "Then here would come the probing to find out where the money came from."

"Exactly!" Jeremy replied.

"What do you suggest?" asked Don.

"I think we should transfer the balance to an off-shore bank—open a new account. Create a new entity. Label it 'Bradford Research Foundation' or some similar name."

"Good idea, Jeremy!" said Don. "Get with legal and get it done. Do I need to do anything?"

"Not necessarily," said Jeremy. "I'll put in a code number so you can have access. Be sure you place the number in your safe."

"Fine, Jeremy," he replied. "Of course you know I'll never use it. What else is going on in the company?"

"Moving along on schedule, sir."

"Jeremy, I'll be tied up with other business next week," said Don. "Could you preside at the board meeting in my absence?"

"Certainly, sir," said Jeremy. A cunning smile flashed across his face that he hoped Don didn't notice.

"I know I can always depend on you, Jeremy," said Don as he leaned back in his chair, his face distorted by a deep yawn.

Jeremy by-passed legal in the process of setting the new account for "Bradford Research Foundation" with an access code that only Jeremy knew.

*   *   *   *

Jeremy returned from one of his many trips to Wall Street, checked into his office, and started perusing the long list of e-mail messages. He was tired of these trips to New York and longed for a way to accelerate his scheme. There was a message from Miss Stafford, Don's secretary. Don wanted to see him in his office as soon as he returned.

Well, he's back from his QE2/Concorde trip to Europe. I wonder which playgirl he took with him this time? Jeremy pondered.

Jeremy announced his arrival in Don's office to Don's secretary.

"Mr. Bradford is expecting you, Mr. Corbett," said Miss Stafford, with the same stereotypical smile he had seen on every executive secretary he had ever encountered—polite but with total indifference. *How do they do it?* Josh wondered.

"He will be with you in just a moment," she said in a tone that oozed cordiality.

"Thank you," he said and seated himself with a magazine.

Don came through the door within a few minutes, his face stretched in an ear-to-ear smile.

"Jeremy!" he called out. "Thank you for coming. Come on in. Miss Stafford, bring us coffee. Maybe something else for you, Jeremy?"

"Coffee will be fine, Mr. Bradford," he answered. *Something besides coffee is brewing,* he thought. *The old man is too patronizing.*

"Jeremy, you know I don't have a chance to talk to you very often—business pressures and all," he said, "but I'd like to say, I appreciate the respect you show when you address me. Don't think it goes unnoticed."

What's he up to? wondered Jeremy.

"You certainly deserve respect, sir," answered Jeremy. "You have certainly earned it. You're our role model."

"The other team members don't seem to think so," he said.

"I'm sure they do, Mr. Bradford," said Jeremy. "They probably just don't know how to show it."

Miss Stafford entered with a tray of coffee service and a few sand tarts on the side. She poured Don's cup first, adding a generous amount of cream and sugar.

"How will you have your coffee, Mr. Corbett?"

"Black will be fine, Miss Stafford."

They sat across from each other, sipping their coffee and discussing trivial company matters before Don revealed his reason for summoning Jeremy to his office.

"Jeremy, I am restructuring our top level management," said Don at last. "I would like you to open a branch office in Dallas. You probably already know this, but I want Donnie to be groomed to take over leadership of this organization someday. He can't do it without assistance, and you are just the one who can fill that need."

"I would be pleased to take that on, Mr. Bradford," he said. *Great opportunity to win favor with this old fart,* thought Jeremy.

"We will make a big splash when we announce Bradford Holdings is opening an office in Dallas. That will get a lot of attention from investors. We'll take a prestigious office in the financial district with a staff of clerical and secretarial personnel.

"I want you to have enough assistance that you will have time to take Donnie under you wing and guide him through the complexities of the company," said Don. "The most important thing right now is to get him through the next two years in college and get him degreed. As you know, we have arranged for him to have tutoring. If you could assume that responsibility yourself, I'm sure Donnie could be molded into an executive that would be credible to the company.".

"I can handle that, sir" said Jeremy. "For one thing, it would give me the opportunity to bond with Donnie."

"Just what I was thinking!" Don said.

"One thing, Mr. Bradford," Jeremy remarked. "You mentioned new employees. I'm concerned about new, untried employees. I'd like to screen everyone we hire."

"That will be your call, Jeremy," he replied.

"I don't want just anyone having access to our computer system," said Jeremy.

"I agree," he said. "Confidentiality is a top priority."

"We'll program the system so I can communicate directly with management of each company, and of course I'll put you on-line for direct access to information."

"Don't worry about me," he said. "I depend on people like you to keep me informed by direct contact. You know I'm just not a computer person."

Those were the words that Jeremy wanted to hear. His long-range plan was shaping up just as he had hoped and was evolving faster than he had ever dreamed possible. His timetable was ten years, and he was already well ahead of his projected schedule. Getting a shot at molding Donnie to his liking was more than he had ever bargained for. It was as if Don had given him a passkey to the vault.

With the company's sophisticated information system, he would be in touch with every office daily, even while he traveled back and forth to Donnie's tutoring classes. The company's electronically-equipped limousine would serve as an extension of his office.

He would have to travel to New York less frequently now and would have ample time to develop a close relationship with Donnie. His first priority would be to visit with Josh Lehman and Luke Sanders and make plans for a smooth transition. The boys would be winding up their school year and graduating soon, so Jeremy needed to contact them right away.

Chapter 15

The approaching graduation exercises posed somewhat of a problem for both Josh and Luke. Should they join the other graduates, don cap and gown, and march across the stage to receive their diplomas? Josh knew his father likely would not be able to attend and Luke had not even communicated enough with his mother recently for her to know that he was graduating from Northwestern or that he had been accepted to medical school.

"Are you gonna suit up in all that formal garb just to get a piece of paper?" Luke inquired of Josh.

"I guess we should. We've worked hard enough for this day for sure," he replied. "What do you think?"

"I really see no sense to it," said Luke. "I won't have any family here...probably make me depressed to look around and see all the other guys' moms and dads and girlfriends."

"I know how you feel," replied Josh, "but we have a lot of friends here at the school, you know," Josh replied.

"Yeah, you're right," he said. "I guess they're family in a way."

"And all our profs will be there," said Josh.

"I'd like to look old Dr. Hinson in the eye and say, 'Look this way, you old fart, Josh and I have been accepted to medical school. How does that grab ya?'"

"I'm sure he remembers who you are," laughed Josh in a sarcastic tone.

"I know, you want to walk across so you can get one last round of applause from the student body," Luke retorted.

"Not a bad idea," Josh replied, then grinned. "You gonna join me?"

"Let's do it!" answered Luke.

"You're on!" he said.

* * * *

Graduation day arrived, and with it came the throngs of family and well-wishers. When Josh's name was called, he stood to start the walk across the stage. Immediately the announcer called Luke's name, even though it was not his turn. They went across together as the auditorium vibrated from the applause and shouting. When they reached the center of the stage, Dr. Quigley arose from the row of seated faculty members and came forward to hand them their diplomas. There was no tremor, no twitching, but there were tears in his eyes. He was at least ten inches shorter than both boys, but he was able, standing on tip-toes, to reach up and give each a hug.

* * * *

The summer months before medical school enrollment passed rapidly. Fortunately, they were able to continue their jobs at the bookstore at Northwestern during the summer before medical school started. Luke had recovered nicely from his surgery, and with the rehabilitation program, he was seemingly as agile and functional as ever. He and Josh worked out every day with muscle-resistance training plus low-impact jogging. They even passed the ball back and forth some.

Josh used some of his time prior to medical school to visit his parents again. He would be in a real time crunch during the first year or two of medical school, so he wanted to check on his mother's status beforehand. He came away from each visit more despondent than ever about his mom; she seemed to deteriorate so rapidly between his visits. Also his dad seemed more distressed. *Did I make the right decision in giving up football?* Josh asked himself while transient clouds of guilt swept over him. *I have to get that thought out of my mind and move on.*

* * * *

Josh and Luke cleaned out their room and came across the old backpacks they had brought with them from Westlake four years earlier. They had since been issued new luggage by the athletic department that they were allowed to keep.

"Look familiar?" asked Josh, tossing one to Luke.

"How could I forget?" he replied. "We were blown in by a sandstorm. How do you think we'll leave?"

"With heads held high—and a hellavuh lot smarter than when we came," said Josh.

"That's for sure," said Luke. "It's kinda sad. I'm gonna miss this place."

"Me too," said Josh. "We've made a lot of friends and have seen some great athletes come and go."

"How are we gonna get along without Sam?" asked Luke.

"Maybe we ought to take him with us," laughed Josh. "I think you're getting sentimental. You've got tears in your eyes!"

"Nah, it's just sand," he replied. "Let's get out of here."

They left their packed bags in the lobby, while they had their last meal in the dining room before calling a taxi. They made rounds to every table in the room saying their good-byes, and then went in search of Sam, Lola, and Walt. Sam was helping the taxi driver pack their bags into the cab and giving him instructions about proper handling when they went to the front door to exit.

"Sam, be kind to these guys," said Josh. "Especially those new boys coming into Ryan Hall for the first time."

"Yassuh, Mr. Josh...I always is." He laughed, shook hands with Luke and Josh, and gave each a warm hug. For a brief moment, he was not smiling. He turned to walk away, and then stopped and turned around. His usual smile was back in place, but his cheeks were moist from tears.

"Mr. Josh, Mr. Luke," he said. "I knowed you'd do this. Yo is different. Yo is goin' to be fine doctors."

"Thank you, Sam," they both replied.

"That means a lot to us, coming from you," Josh added.

✳   ✳   ✳   ✳

Metcalfe Health Science Center...Dallas, Texas

During orientation the entire environment at the medical school seemed so different from what Josh and Luke had been used to during the pre-med years. They were welcomed now as a part of a culture of individuals with common goals and objectives. Everyone seemed to say, "We want you to succeed and we are here to help you."

Josh and Luke soon faced the decision of which fraternity to join. The fraternities in medical school served an entirely different purpose than those in colleges. Medical students were motivated to focus on study and learning, and the fraternities provided a communal housing arrangement where all of the student-residents were readily available to assist each other with any study problem. With their sports world notoriety, Josh and Luke had offers from all of the fraternities. They liked the guys at the Sigma Chi house, joined the group, and began the process of moving in.

Classes had been underway no more than a few days when both Josh and Luke were convinced that they had made the right decision to go to medical school. They were intrigued with every facet of medicine. Josh and Luke strolled toward the fraternity house during the lunch break after a lecture in embryology.

"What are you thinking, Luke?"

"Never thought I'd be so fascinated with embryology."

"Me either," said Josh. The prof doesn't have much personality, but he sure gets the message across. Sometimes it's hard to follow his drawings on the chalk board."

"Yeah. I sat there thinking, *it's an absolute miracle that babies can develop from cell division,*" said Luke. *An absolute miracle!*

"How about that video?" Josh replied. "Showing the stages of development of all the body organs, skeleton and muscle—even the genitalia."

"I was spellbound," said Luke. "It's something that happens, but we never give it much thought."

"Of course, when I look at you in the shower I see you haven't finished developing," Josh said with a laugh and jumped aside to escape Luke's swing.

"Damn you, Josh!" Luke retorted. "You're just jealous."

"Think where we were a year ago," said Josh.

"Yeah, I miss those guys. A lot of excitement right now—new kids moving into Ryan Hall, scared and trying to act like 'big shits.'"

"And Sam, Walt, and Lola," said Josh. "Miss them a lot."

"Quit looking back, dude," said Luke. "We're moving on to greater things."

*   *   *   *

Josh was in the Anatomy Laboratory when he got the call that he had dreaded for years. It was his dad, and it was an emergency call.

"What is it, Dad?"

"She is much worse, Josh," he said, his voice breaking as he spoke. "I brought her to the Emergency Room…she wouldn't let me call the 911 number. She couldn't get her breath, Josh. Her face was blue. I'm scared."

"I'll be there as soon as I can, Dad," he said. "You did the right thing."

"The doctors are working with her now," he said. "It doesn't look good."

"I'll be there, Dad."

He explained to his professor why he had to leave and asked Luke to notify other professors and to update him when he returned.

Josh fought to stay awake, drinking tons of coffee, as he drove through the night from Dallas to Westlake. He went straight to the hospital and to the ICU and found his father sitting alone in the waiting room, bent over with his head in his hands. He looked so tired and forlorn. Obviously he had not slept since arriving home from work that very same day. He looked up when Josh came to his side.

"She's about gone, Josh," he said as tears welled up in his eyes. "She did not want to be kept alive by machines. Is that best, Josh?"

"Yes, it is, Dad. She's been so miserable."

"She's ready to go, Josh," he said. "She wanted to see you. I think that's the only thing keeping her alive."

Josh went to her bedside. In spite of the oxygen, she struggled to breathe. From time to time she would gasp for a deep breath and then stop breathing for a few seconds before taking another breath. Her skin was drenched with perspiration and had taken on a blue discoloration superimposed on a morbid appearing pallor.

Josh thought she was unconscious. He took her hand in his, bent over, and kissed her on the forehead while he fought back tears. She opened her eyes and looked at him, smiled and tried to speak, but could not. She closed her eyes, gripped his hand tightly for a moment, and then stopped breathing altogether. Within a few seconds the monitor showed a flat line.

After consoling his dad as best he could, Josh called Luke to let him know he would stay around for a few days to help his father with funeral arrangements and to get him settled. Even though his dad knew it was going to happen, Josh knew this loss and abrupt change in his life would be difficult for him.

"Let me know the details of the service, Josh," said Luke.

"Luke, I don't expect you to come here," he said. "You have too much to do. Just stay there so you can fill me in on what's happening."

"I'll be there, Josh."

Josh was quiet, his throat so tight he couldn't find words to say for a moment. He finally answered.

"Thanks, Luke."

Josh's Dad had long ago made funeral plans. He had prepaid all expenses, including the traditional wooden casket. He had made prior arrangements with the rabbi and the synagogue and had selected a burial plot in the cemetery that was large enough for two.

There would be a short service in the chapel and burial in the adjacent Jewish section of the cemetery. Josh called Luke to let him know that the funeral would be the next day and to give him the time and the location. He knew there was no stopping Luke from coming, so he didn't try again.

His mom had been so ill and inactive for so many years, he didn't expect that very many congregants would attend. He and his father waited in the anteroom with the rabbi. Josh wore the yarmulke that his mother had knitted for him years ago.

When the time arrived for them to take their places in the area assigned for family, Josh and his father emerged from the adjacent room, accompanied by the rabbi. Josh looked out across the chapel and was astonished at the number of people that filled the pews. He spotted Luke near the front of the chapel. Then he saw them.

Surrounding Luke was every single member of the Texas Northwestern University Conference Championship Team from the year before—all of the players, coaches, trainers, and even the water boys. They were all dressed in their athletic jackets and wore yarmulkes on their heads. On the front row was Hammond Quigley, M.D., PHD., sitting still and quiet with no tremors or jerking.

Josh tried every trick he could think of to keep from openly sobbing. He managed it fairly well until he saw Sam, sitting behind the team, dressed in a dark suit and tie and freshly starched shirt and proudly wearing a yarmulke. For one of the rare occasions in his life, Sam was not smiling.

*　　*　　*　　*

Josh's dad assured him that he would be all right and that Josh should return to medical school promptly.

"I'm prepared for this, Josh," he said. "As much as anyone could be. I'll gain comfort in knowing you and Luke are on the right path. Don't worry about me."

"I'll stay until you get settled."

"Josh, I really need time alone," he answered. He put his arms around Josh and pulled him close. "You'll never know how pleased I am that you and Luke made the decision to go to medical school. Your mom was so pleased when she heard your decision."

"I wonder if she ever had a chance to tell Mrs. Minsky," laughed Josh.

"You know she did," his dad replied with a chuckle.

* * * *

Josh and Luke left together early the next morning, hoping to get to Dallas in time to make a few of their classes. The day was clear and the traffic light so they could put the miles behind at a rapid rate. The solemnity of the funeral services left both boys in a pensive mood. Unlike his usual self, Luke came up with only a few wisecracks and one-liners.

"Your dad's a strong man, Josh," said Luke.

"I see that more every day," replied Josh. "I know I'm fortunate, Luke, but neither of us had a normal life. You know—a dad that we could cling to, play ball with, wrestle with."

"I never had a dad I could be proud of. You have that, Josh," Luke said. "I feel cheated."

"I know it's been rough, Luke," replied Josh. "I'm proud of the way you've dealt with it. Things could have turned out different, you know."

"I'm grateful to you for keeping me on the right path, Josh," said Luke, "but it's sure as hell hard to keep up with you. Work, work, work…practice, practice, practice…study, study, study. You're about to kill me, Josh Lehman."

They both chuckled and gave a high five while Josh herded their rental vehicle down the highway, a little over the speed limit.

"Do you ever think about settling down, getting married, having kids, and all that sorta stuff?" asked Josh.

"Yeah, I think of it a lot. I want to have kids. I want to be the father to them that I never had. I want to find a naïve, sweet thing, marry her, and worship her for the rest of my life. That's what I want, Josh."

"You'll find that, Luke. You'll find it," said Josh. "Let's stop for coffee and a doughnut. We're going to make it back just in time for Physiology class."

Chapter 16

Ann Wilson lived most of her life in a small West Texas town where her father was a physician and her mother was a nurse. She was born in Dallas while her father was still in medical school and her mother in nursing school. With her medical family background, Ann had never thought of any career other than health care.

She applied for and was accepted to nursing school at Metcalfe. With trepidation, leaving her small home town, she moved to the expansive Metcalfe Health Science Center in Dallas and into the nurse's dormitory. Her roommate was Linda Searcy from Amarillo.

From the day they met, Ann felt ill at ease around Linda. She was made to feel inferior and not as worldly-wise as Linda. They came from different backgrounds and from some the remarks Linda made, Ann did not think they embraced the same values or lifestyle.

"You know any medical students here?" Linda asked while they were unpacking and arranging their room.

"Not really," Ann answered. "My dad has a classmate whose son is here. I have his name written somewhere. I'm supposed to look him up."

"Great!" she said. "Find out who he is. Maybe we can get invited to some of the fraternity parties."

"I imagine we are going to be pretty busy with classes and studying," laughed Ann. "Probably no time to party."

"Always time, dear," Linda responded with a grin. "I've heard the medical students here are cool. And hey—we're in 'Big D'!"

"It's kinda scary," said Ann.

"Guys are all the same, dear," replied Linda. "All have the same thing on their mind. What O.C. do you take?

"What?"

"Birth control pill!"

"I don't take any. No need to," said Ann, feeling her face turning red.

"Hey, aren't you the brave one? Pretty risky, you know."

"I'll take my chances," Ann replied, turning her back and moving on with her unpacking.

Linda looked at her and smiled furtively. "You've never had sex, have you?"

"Look, we've just met," said Ann, her anger showing. "I do not intend to answer your questions like that."

"I'm sorry," said Linda. "You're right, that was presumptuous of me. Look, I'll be a good roommate; give me another chance."

"Sure," said Ann, and both girls laughed.

"Going outside for a cigarette. Wanta join me?" asked Linda.

"No thanks," Ann replied.

In spite of their different personalities and background, the girls were compatible as roommates from that time on and shared some fun times. Although Ann spent most of her after-class time studying and reading, she accompanied Linda to some of the fraternity parties.

* * * *

Ann met Luke at one of the Sigma Chi affairs. Linda strayed off somewhere with one of the medical students, leaving Ann to mingle on her own. She was talking with another nursing student she knew when that person was dragged onto the dance floor by one of the med students, leaving Ann alone. When Ann turned around, she found herself face-to-face with Luke Sanders.

"Saw you standing here and didn't think you oughta be by yourself," he said, with a broad grin on his face.

"So this is your life's endeavor?" she laughed. "Rescuing lonely maidens?"

"This could be the start of a lasting relationship," he retorted.

"Never can tell," she replied with a coquettish wink.

Oh my God! What did I do? Am I flirting? I must have learned that from Linda, she thought.

"Where are you from?" asked Luke.

"You wouldn't know where it was if I told you," she answered. "Ever hear of Prairie Gulch?"

"Don't think so, but sounds exciting."

"Maybe on Saturday night," she replied with a laugh. When she smiled or laughed, the dimples on her cheeks popped up like two beckoning signals that to Luke said, "I like talking to you."

"Can I get you a beer?" asked Luke.

"Thanks. That would be nice of you."

"Anything for a lady in distress."

Luke returned with two long-necks. The loud music and chattering in the room made conversation almost impossible. They moved toward the door to an outside patio area.

"Let's sit out here for awhile," said Luke. "Unless you'd rather stay in here and dance."

"We can always come back in," she replied.

But they didn't go back in. Instead, they stayed on the patio and spent the rest of the evening talking and telling each other about themselves. Too soon the hour was late and almost everyone else began drifting away.

"I hate to tear myself away," said Ann with a laugh. "I guess I'd better find my roommate and go to the dorm, but really, I've enjoyed talking with you. Seems like I've known you for ages,"

"Same here," he said. "We didn't do much dancing, though."

"We'll save that for later," she replied. *I'm flirting again!* she thought. *So what? I like this big lout.*

"I'll wait here while you find your roommate," said Luke. "I may just have another beer while you're looking."

Ann went indoors but couldn't find Linda. The music had stopped and no one seemed to remember seeing her lately.

"If you see her, tell her I've gone on home," she told one group, and then went back outside to tell Luke good-bye.

He was sitting on the low brick wall that encircled the patio, sipping his beer. A gentle breeze had blown spiral locks of his long red hair across his forehead and down over his eyes. "God, what a lovable hunk!" she said to herself.

"I couldn't find her. I guess I'll go on with out her."

"I'll walk with you," said Luke.

"You don't need to. It's not too far."

"Look, you don't walk the streets of Dallas at night by yourself for even a half-block."

"I guess it's a little different from Prairie Gulch," laughed Ann. "I'm too much country."

"You know, I think that's what I like about you."

"You mean a plain and simple country girl?"

"I didn't mean that. To me you seem honest and straightforward," replied Luke. "I can't say that about many girls raised in the city. They always seem to try to be something they're not."

"Hey, have you had too many beers?" laughed Ann.

"Maybe so," he said. "Whatever, let's go."

They walked hand-in-hand to the dormitory, parted with a peck on the cheek, and made promises to see each other again.

Ann entered the dorm foyer, spoke to the security guard on her way to the staircase to the second floor, and wondered if her exhilaration was showing. She floated up the stairs while humming a tune she remembered from somewhere and then twirled like a ballet dancer down the empty corridor on the way to her room.

"I can't get him out of my mind," she said aloud, and then added, "Cool it, gal. You've only known him a few hours."

She reached her room just in time to catch the ringing phone. "Maybe it's Luke." She said, her hand trembling as she reached for the receiver.

"Hi, sweetie, it's me," said Linda. "Heard you were looking for me. Been trying to call. Bet some big stud carried you away."

Linda's speech was as garbled as if she had a mouthful of mush. Ann could hear rap music in the background.

"I just wanted to tell you I was leaving," said Ann. "It was getting late. Where are you? I can hear music."

"At the Downbeat Club, baby," she replied. "This place is rocking. Wanta join us?"

"It's late, late, Linda," said Ann. "We have classes in the morning."

"Yeah, I know," she said. "But this is a swinging crowd. Don't wait up for me, sweetie. The way the night is shaping up I probably won't get home tonight. Cute guys, sweetie."

"What about classes, Linda?" asked Ann.

"I'll drag myself in for the class, dear," she replied. "Don't worry about me. Sure you don't wanta party?"

"No, thanks," said Ann. "I'm just gonna go to bed and dream about a guy I met tonight."

"Is he there with you?"

"Linda! Of course not!"

"See you tomorrow, sweetie, and you can tell me all about him."

* * * *

From that day forward, neither Ann nor Luke dated anyone else. They spent every spare moment together. Before the first school year was over, Luke pinned Ann with his fraternity pin.

"Why do you want to get tied down to one dude when there are so many other cute ones all around us?" Linda chided Ann.

"I'm happy with this guy, Linda. I feel good when I'm around him."

"We've known each other long enough now that I can advise you again. Birth control pills, sweetie!"

"I'll tell you when," she laughed. "You know why I like being with him? He makes me feel safe. He reminds me of my father. Not in looks, just the way he talks and acts. His mannerism—so much like my dad."

"You're hooked, sweetheart. I sorta envy you."

"You need to meet his roommate. They were both football players at Northwestern."

"Yeah, good idea. Introduce me."

* * * *

Luke and Ann took a couple of days off to visit Ann's parents in Prairie Gulch, a small West Texas community that depended on farming and ranching for its economy and survival. Ann's father, Dr. Burton Wilson, took great pride in having served the area as its only physician for thirty-odd years. Luke and Dr. Wilson hit it off fine. Luke was going to the same medical school that Dr. Wilson had attended, and both were members of the same fraternity. Visiting with Luke gave Dr. Wilson the opportunity to reminisce about some of his medical school experiences.

"Is old Dr. Scoggins still teaching anatomy?"

"Oh, yeah!" Luke replied. "Not well-liked by the students—still as obnoxious as ever."

"I can just see him now," said Dr. Wilson with a chuckle. "Short, fat, bald-headed, little guy. Used to climb up on top of the dissection tables in the anatomy lab so he could be seen when he shouted to the class."

"He still does," laughed Luke. "I don't know how he does it. He must be close to eighty years old. Everybody makes jokes about what should we do if he falls off the table. Should we try to catch him or just let him bounce off the floor?"

"Medical students never change!" said Dr. Wilson, laughing. "But whatever else is said about old Dr. Scoggins, he taught human anatomy in a way that you never forget."

"That's for sure," said Luke. "I learned a lot from the old guy."

Several minutes passed with the two of them discussing other members of the medical school faculty, changes in curriculum over the years, changes in medicine, and exchanging stories of life in the Sigma Chi house.

"Have any idea yet what field you want to go into, Luke?" asked Dr. Wilson.

"No sir," Luke replied. "I know I don't want to do surgery."

"Ever thought of rural primary care?"

"Yeah, it has an appeal," said Luke. "I'm sure it is a rewarding practice."

"Absolutely!" said Dr. Wilson. "You get to know everything about your patients, like being a member of their families. You can't beat it."

"Ann tells me Mrs. Wilson is a nurse."

"One of the best!" he replied. "She's been right by my side in building my practice—worked in my office until a few years ago."

"I'll bet you miss her."

"Every day!" he said. "We've been fortunate. Able to raise three healthy children…all gone from home now. Ann is the youngest. I was floored when she announced she wanted to go to nursing school. I never suspected she was interested in any health career."

"You have been fortunate," said Luke, "to have a close family."

"What about your family, Luke?" asked Dr. Wilson.

"I was hoping you wouldn't ask, sir," Luke replied, dropping his head as if pondering how to answer. "Let me tell you this, Dr. Wilson; ever since I met Ann—we met by chance at a party, I tell myself every day, 'everything happens for a reason.' If I am ever lucky enough to have a family like yours, it will start with me. Do you understand what I'm saying?"

"I think I do, Luke," he replied, with a gentle pat on Luke's shoulder. "And I like what I hear."

Ann and her mother left the kitchen long enough to check on Luke and Ann's father.

"How are you two doing?" asked Ann's mother.

"We're doing fine," said Dr. Wilson, his eyes fixed on Luke. "We've gotten to know each other pretty well."

"We have a lot of mutual interests," laughed Luke.

"OK, Burt, you've had enough time with Luke," she said. "It's my turn. Ann, take your father out of here. Go do something!"

"Mother!" said Ann. "I know what you're up to! Luke, she's an avid football fan…has probably watched every Northwestern football game you've ever played in. She's going to talk football until you're sick of it."

"I can handle it, Ann," said Luke with a chuckle.

I see where Ann gets her beauty, thought Luke. Mrs. Wilson had question after question about his and Josh's football experiences and about the game itself. She could even recall details of some of their games and she remembered the meaning of the "Lehman-Sanders Axis." Ann and her father returned and Ann dragged her mother back into the kitchen to complete dinner before time for their return trip to school.

* * * *

Traveling along the highway back to Dallas, both were quiet for several moments. Luke broke the silence.

"Thanks for taking me to your home, Ann," said Luke. "You have had a beautiful home life."

"Luke, my father told me about your conversation and what you said about family," she said. "He thinks you're a keeper. If I haven't told you lately, I love you."

"If I'm a keeper," said Luke, "will you marry me?"

"I thought you'd never ask," she said as she laughed.

* * * *

Luke and Ann announced their engagement and approaching marriage. No one was surprised. They married in Ann's home town—a small, quiet wedding at Ann's request, in spite of her mother's clamoring for an elaborate affair. Linda was the bridesmaid and Josh was Luke's best man.

Within a year after they were married, Luke and Ann had their first child: a beautiful, healthy boy. The baby changed their lives drastically. They were totally absorbed in being parents. Ann and the baby were Luke's life. Other than his fascination with medicine and medical school, he had no interests other than his home life. When Luke was not in class or studying, his every waking moment was consumed with doing something with the baby—from changing diapers to talking baby talk.

Any time Josh could break away from studies or from classes, he went straight to Luke's home. He, too, was enthralled with the marvels of the growth and development of this newborn child. The baby was named Joshua, after Josh, and was called Jay to avoid confusion when they were all together. When Jay was only a tiny child, Josh would hold him in his arms and talk to him, and sometimes rock him to sleep.

"Luke, he looked me right in the eye, smiled and cooed at me!" said Josh. "Every time I pick him up and talk to him, he does that. He recognizes me, Luke!"

"Sure he does. And me too," replied Luke. "You know, even at an early age babies learn to recognize familiar voices and smells."

"Yeah, we learned that in that class, remember? Never thought I'd see it first hand," said Josh.

"Ever been around a baby before?" asked Luke.

"Never," Josh answered. "Knew they were around somewhere, but I've never been this close. Jay always smells so fresh and clean."

"Wait until you have to change his diapers," said Luke, holding his nose. "That's when I call his mother."

"Think his 'soft spot' is normal?" asked Josh as he palpated the top of Jay's head.

"Yeah, it is," said Luke. "I measured it. It's just the size the textbook said it was supposed to be. And it is not bulging."

"I never knew it pulsated before. When does it close?"

"Dammit, Josh!" said Luke. "I don't remember. I'll look it up. I know it's not supposed to close too early."

"What do you want him to be when he grows up, Luke?" asked Josh, cradling Jay in his arms and swaying back and forth.

"I think he'll want to be like his daddy and his Uncle Josh. He'll want to be a doctor."

"I think you're right," said Josh. "Think he'll want to play football?"

"Yeah, he might," Luke replied. "Think we oughta push him?"

"Don't think so," said Josh. "But I'll bet he'd be good at it."

Ann came to their side. "All right, you two. I need to get him ready for bed, and I hope he sleeps the night without awakening."

"Do you wake up when he cries out, Luke?" asked Josh.

"Yes, he does, Josh. We both do," said Ann, "We both do, and don't ask me why."

"I think I know without asking," replied Josh with an all-knowing smile on his face.

* * * *

In his Early Childhood Development classes, Luke became well-versed on what to expect during a child's growth stages. He learned at what age babies were expected to hold up their head, roll over, sit without support, crawl, stand alone, take their first step, or say their first understandable word. Luke, as well as every other medical student, learned in class what an average newborn would likely achieve during its early development. Still, with Jay, whenever a developmental stage was reached, Luke would announce the new accomplishment—generously colored with superlatives—to everyone within audible range.

Luke had twenty minutes before his ten o'clock laboratory, so he dropped by the cafeteria for a mid-morning snack and a Coke. A group of other students who had the same idea had captured a large table and beckoned Luke to join them.

"Hey, Luke!" one of his classmates said, an impish look on his face. "Come tell us about your little girl. How is she doing?"

"All right, you scabs!" he said. "You know damn well my baby is a boy."

"How could we remember? You haven't told us anything about the baby since yesterday," another classmate exclaimed. Laughter around the table followed his remark.

"And it just so happens that I have photographs today to show you," said Luke. "I told you he was pulling himself up to a standing position. Look at this! Standing alone without holding on to his crib! Is this proof, man, or what?"

"I thought he'd be walking by now," said still another medical student, a broad grin covering his face.

"Come on, smart ass," said Luke. "He's only eleven months old. And he has four teeth. Bet you won't find that in the well-baby clinic. Check this out! Those are my hands holding his mouth open while Ann took this picture of his teeth."

"Show us some more pictures, Luke."

"God, don't tell him that! We only have ten more minutes," said another classmate, with a chuckle.

A couple of the students looked at their watches and stole away, their faces blossoming with smiles.

"Saying any words yet, Luke?" one of the guys asked.

"Ha! I'm glad you asked," said Luke. "He can say 'da-da', 'ma-ma,' and listen to this: when Josh comes over, he looks at Josh, smiles, and squeals 'ja-ja.' What do you think of that?"

"Maybe he'll be a football player some day."

"You better believe it!" said Luke.

A few of the guys remained around the table. Luke didn't realize that Josh had come up behind him just in time to hear his response.

"He's gonna be a doctor, Luke," said Josh. "Anybody here have any doubts?"

"No doubt about it, Ja-Ja!" one of the students called out as the group chuckled in unison and stood in readiness for a hurried exit. "So long, Ja-Ja," said another.

* * * *

Months passed and Jay passed normally through all of the developmental stages under the watchful eyes of Luke and Josh. They hovered over the little guy like two FBI surveillance agents, watching his every move. They coaxed him, taught him, and cheered him on at every chance. Ann could be heard to say, almost daily, "Leave him alone, Luke, and you too, Josh. He's coming along fine."

As he grew older and began walking, running and saying more words, Jay developed a strong attachment to both Luke and his Uncle Josh. Josh would melt every time Jay would look up at him with those deep blue eyes and with that angelic expression and hold out his little arms to be picked up. The bonding was beautiful and grew stronger as Jay grew older.

Seeing Luke and Ann so happy in their home environment struck a chord in Josh's mind. He longed to experience the same enjoyment of having a family and children of his own that he could watch grow and could have a part in molding them into mature individuals. He wondered if Linda could fit into the picture.

* * * *

Josh's first encounter with Linda was during Luke and Ann's wedding activities. There was an attraction there that Josh couldn't ignore, but there always seemed to be something missing. He couldn't explain it. He and Linda were thrown together on many occasions after the wedding, usually those arranged by Ann and Luke. They each dated others, but even so, they seemed to be drawn back to each other. Sometimes weeks passed before either Josh or Linda would call the other.

Josh saw Linda at one of the fraternity parties. The wave of guilt that swept over him—guilt that he had not called her earlier—was mixed with a bit of resentment that she was at the party with someone else. He promised himself that he would call Linda within the next day or so.

* * * *

The anatomy lab lasted longer than Josh had ever remembered. Walking home to the fraternity house alone at that late hour accentuated the fact that he was alone. He thought of Luke and Ann and the comfortable home life they enjoyed. "I need to call Linda when I get home," he said aloud. He settled in his favorite study chair, and instead of opening a book to study he reached for the telephone. Before he as much as touched it, a loud ring came forth.

"Hi! It's Linda," she said, in her sexy, purring voice. "Haven't heard from you for a while."

"I was just thinking about you," replied Josh. "What have you been up to—other than having a gay time partying."

"Really nothing exciting," she answered. "Why don't you ever ask me out so we can do something exciting?"

"I could say I've been busy with school and studying."

"Won't work, handsome" she said. "Saw you out with that streaked blonde last week. Bet you could have had more fun with me."

"Just a friend," said Josh.

"Come on, Josh. That won't fly," she said. "Why don't you say it was your cousin?"

"From what I hear, you haven't stayed home knitting," Josh retorted. "Also I heard about the Phi Chi party when you danced on the table."

"Ok, ok…just a little fun when my favorite healer is too busy to call."

"Give me another chance. OK?"

"Sure, call me sometime when you can't find anyone else to play with."

"I may do that," said Josh as he hung up the phone.

Josh told himself to ignore her enticing remarks, but he couldn't erase from his mind the intimate moments they had enjoyed together just a few weeks earlier. Within the hour he called.

"I'll pick you up tomorrow at six," he said without asking if she agreed.

"I'll be ready," she answered. "What shall I wear?"

"Something exciting!" he said. "We'll go somewhere—after I see what you're wearing."

* * * *

Josh needed to talk to Luke, but there never seemed to be a good time. Finally, an opportune time came one day while they were both waiting in the student lounge for the pathology class to start.

"Luke, you are the most fortunate person I know," said Josh.

"What brought this on, Josh?" Luke asked, thinking, *Josh is leading up to something. He's getting sentimental.*

"You have everything any man would want: a devoted wife, a neat kid, a warm home environment," said Josh.

"Maybe you should try it."

"I guess that's what I have wanted to talk to you about," he said. "What do you think about Linda?"

Luke was silent for an inappropriate length of time, apparently contemplating his answer.

"You took too long to answer," said Josh.

"What are thinking of, Josh?" asked Luke, finally.

"Well, you know——what would you think if I proposed marriage to Linda?"

"I can't answer that, Josh," he replied. "You have to look into your heart. Is this the right person for you?"

"We have known each other too long, Luke," he said. "There's something you are not telling me."

"Look, if you are thinking that Linda can fulfill the same role as Ann as a mother and a homemaker, forget it," he said.

"What do you mean, Luke?"

"Josh, promise me you won't breathe a word of this to Ann," said Luke.

"Promise," he replied.

"Linda has one objective in mind: marry a rich doctor and have fun. I'm going on what Ann has told me about her. She has known Linda for a long time. Linda is not interested in being burdened with children or supporting a fledgling physician trying to get started. The only time she shows any interest in children is when we are all going out together and she sees you watching her. She's a party animal, Josh."

"I think you're wrong there, Luke," he said. "She admires your family and is absolutely carried away with Jay."

"I wish you hadn't asked me," said Luke. "If you feel strongly, go for it."
"I don't know, Luke," he replied. "I just don't know."
"If you're not sure, wait!" he said.
"Yeah, I guess you're right." With that they made their way to the classroom.

Chapter 17

During the first two years of medical school, Luke and Josh worked closely together—in classes and during study time. It was much like their pre-med and football days, with the difference being that they had to be more self-disciplined now. But just like their football days, their objective was to succeed and to win—win with passing grades, not passing and receiving, as in football—but still, it was just another game.

Very soon their individual interests became apparent. Josh was fascinated with surgery. Luke couldn't care less. He drifted more and more toward an internal medicine field, especially pulmonary diseases. Luke had always liked physics, and he was intrigued by the changes that occurred in blood gasses in patients with lung disorders.

By the time they neared the end of their fourth year in medical school, each had decided definitely on the specialty field he wished to pursue. Josh had already lined up a residency in General Surgery at Metcalfe and Luke a residency in Anesthesiology at the same center. Their first year as interns would include rotating services prior to starting their residency training.

With graduation day came the excitement of family and friends arriving for the ceremony. The graduation exercises were held inside the large auditorium in the administration building. A reception for students, families, and faculty was held in a nearby meeting hall.

To Josh's delight, his dad was able to attend. Josh introduced him to everyone as the person responsible for his reaching this point in his life. He would frequently say: "I want you to meet the person that I have more respect for than anyone on the face of the earth…my father!"

"Thanks for coming, Dad," said Josh.

"Wouldn't miss it for anything!"

"I wish Mom could have known that I made it," he said.

Josh could feel his eyes getting moist, and looked away for a second. He then turned back to face his dad and laughed.

"I remember so well, even before I went to high school, whenever she referred to Mrs. Minsky across the street she would say, 'Mrs. Minsky, her son's a doctor, you know,' and look straight at me."

"She knows you made it, Josh," he said, his face glowing with paternal happiness and pride.

"I think you're right, Dad."

"What's next, Josh?" he asked.

"I was accepted to the General Surgery residency program, so I'll be staying here. Luke got accepted to an Anesthesia residency here also."

"How is Luke?"

"He's fine, Dad," he replied. "He's a little despondent that he has no mother or father to share this special day with, but wait 'til you meet little Jay and Luke's wife, Ann. Jay looks just like his father—red hair and all. Luke and I already have him in training for football," he added with a chuckle, "but we think he should go to medical school too."

Luke and Ann approached, with Jay in hand. Ann had him dressed in a suit, complete with tie and a white captain's hat, which Jay kept rearranging on his head. When he saw Josh, he broke away from his parents and ran to him, ready to be picked up.

"I believe he knows you," Josh's father said and laughed.

"Jay, this is my daddy," said Josh, facing his dad, with Jay in his arms. Jay frowned, with a puzzled look on his face as he carefully studied Mr. Lehman for a few moments. He turned back to Josh and gave him a sloppy kiss on his cheek— as if his way of saying he wasn't sharing Josh with anyone.

Without Josh even being aware that she was around, Linda had edged through the crowd, and after tossing her cigarette into the grass, appeared at Josh's side.

"Congratulations, Josh!" she said. She turned to Luke, "You too, Luke. You both deserve a lot of credit."

She reached for Jay, who immediately recoiled into Ann's arms.

"Linda, this is my father, Joseph Lehman. Dad, this is a friend of mine, Linda Searcy."

"I've heard Josh speak of you so often," she said, moving close to Josh's dad and grasping his arm.

"Thank you, Miss," Mr. Lehman replied. "I am pleased to meet you." *Who is this girl?* he wondered. *I don't remember ever hearing Josh mention her name.*

"Josh, I haven't seen you lately." She purred as she spoke. "Maybe you will have more time for me now."

"Maybe so," he said, blushing uncontrollably.

"I heard you were going to stay at Metcalfe."

"Luke and I both were fortunate to be able to get residencies here," he answered. "Are you still at the center hospital?"

"I guess you didn't get my message," she said. "I have finished my training for certification in ICU nursing. I'm sure we'll see a lot of each other now."

"Well, congratulations to you also," Josh said. *I didn't get the message because it was probably never sent,* he thought.

"Nice seeing all of you," she said as she turned to leave. "Ann, you and Luke and your boy are a picture of happiness."

"Thank you, Linda," she said, "You must come by sometime."

"By all means," she said, with a devilish smile. "I need to see first hand what family life is like."

Luke winced in silence.

*   *   *   *

The first-year internship, before entering their respective residency programs, gave Josh and Luke the opportunity to experience and gain an appreciation for all of the many specialty fields. For any elective rotation service, Josh chose surgery at every chance. Luke spent every free day shadowing one of the anesthesiologists in the operating rooms.

As interns, they were under the supervision of the residents. The surgery residents picked up on Josh's interest in surgery and quickly became aware of his surgical skill potentials. They all encouraged him and helped him by allowing him to actively assist in certain cases.

When the year of intern service rotation ended, Josh moved into the position of a first year surgery resident. He was allowed to do select surgical cases under the watchful eye of a senior resident or one of the department staff physicians. In his evaluations Josh was given excellent scores, both for his technical ability and for his diagnostic acumen. He scored very high in his ability to work with others, in his interaction with patients, and in his sensitivity to patients' problems.

Luke started his anesthesiology residency at the same time Josh started his surgery residency. Once he was well into the first year of the training program, he began to focus more on complex cases such as open heart and lung resection cases.

Josh and Luke used every opportunity to manipulate the surgery schedule so the two of them were present for the same cases. Whenever they had a case together they each looked at the other with a special gleam in their eyes as if to say, "The Lehman-Sanders Axis has been reactivated!"

* * * *

Josh saw more of Linda than ever. As a surgery resident, he participated in the care of patients that required post-operative admission to the Surgical Intensive Care Unit.—often major, complex surgery cases. Part of his training was the follow-up management of those cases of which he had been an assistant surgeon in the operating room. Linda was assigned duty in the Surgical ICU, so she and Josh worked side-by-side almost every day.

Josh assisted one of the general surgeons in an emergency colon resection of a seventy-year-old man with high risk medical problems of coronary artery disease and diabetes. After the surgery and after a period of time in the recovery room, the patient was moved to the Surgical ICU and place under Linda's nursing care. Josh was at the dictation desk finishing his paper work for the day when the call from Linda came.

"I need your help here, Josh," pleaded Linda, with a tone of urgency in her voice that told Josh he needed to head for the ICU.

A quick glance at the monitors showed Josh that the man, pale with a frantic expression on his face and slipping in and out of consciousness, was in acute distress—fast heart rate, fast respiratory rate, and a barely discernable blood pressure. He had sustained his surgery with no problems and had left the operating room in a stable condition.

"What happened, Linda?" asked Josh.

"Weird," answered Linda. "He was doing great...vital signs stable, alert with minimal pain. Then his pressure started to drop, he complained of chest pain, shortness of breath, and became extremely anxious."

"Must have had a heart attack," said Josh.

"Just doesn't look like a heart attack," she replied. "Look at the heart rhythm monitor strip."

"Yeah, I see what you mean," replied Josh. "Let's get an EKG."

"Already have; this is what concerns me," she said. "Look at the changes from previous EKG's. Something's going on. It doesn't look like a heart attack. Looks like the heart has changed positions. Shifted to the left! X-ray is on the way for a portable film."

"Incredible!" said Josh. "No sign of blood loss?"

"None," she said. "I've increased the flow rate of fluid through the subclavian line…but every time I increase the fluid he seems to get worse."

"I can't hear any breath sounds on the right, Linda," said Josh, checking both sides of his chest with his stethoscope. "Get me a thoracentesis tray, stat! We can't wait on an X-ray."

"I already have it ready," she said. "You're thinking the same thing I am—we have a tension pneumothorax for some reason."

Josh inserted the large core needle into the patient's chest, and to everyones surprise, clear fluid under pressure sprayed out through the needle.

"Oh my God!" yelled Josh. "The subclavian line is in the chest cavity. Turn off the I.V. fluid!"

He had no sooner uttered those words than one of the radiologists rushed to the bedside.

"I just now looked at the X-ray that was taken in the operating room after the I.V. line was placed. The line is in the chest cavity!" he called out. "The IV fluid is going into the chest cavity!"

With a few adjustments, replacing the I.V. line, inserting a chest tube connected to suction, and draining the fluid from the chest, the patient awakened with normal vital signs. Josh and Linda looked at each other with simultaneous sighs. Linda asked for one of the other nurses to take over for a few minutes. She and Josh, both physically and emotional exhausted, retreated to the lounge, sat side-by-side on the couch without either saying a word. Josh finally spoke.

"You saved his life, you know," he said. "Another minute and he would have been dead."

"Let's don't talk about it," she replied.

"When do you get off duty?"

"About an hour."

"Wanna go for a beer?"

"Yeah, wait for me."

They stopped at their favorite after-work bar for a beer, but they didn't stop with one beer. Linda's apartment was within walking distance. Holding on to each other, they managed to navigate the trip, giggles and stumbles along the way, climbed the stairs, and made enough noise to pique the verbal wrath of Linda's neighbor. They turned out the lights, fell into the bed fully clothed, and then undressed each other, throwing their clothes on the floor.

* * * *

At the surprise of no one, Josh and Linda soon moved into an apartment together. Fairly often, whenever their time off work allowed it, they arranged to visit Luke and Ann and little Jay. Luke softened a little in his attitude toward Linda after seeing her professional performance. He even mentioned to Josh that he felt very secure when one of his post-operative cases was moved to Linda's unit. This served as a signal to Josh that maybe he would have Luke's approval for a more serious consideration of marriage.

Any time they were all together for an outing of any kind—a trip to the zoo, a picnic, a movie, or even a fast food restaurant—Jay always stayed glued to Josh, either in his arms or holding onto his hand. Josh glanced at Linda, hoping to see some sign that she approved of his fondness of Jay. He was met with a weak smile of sorts, leaving Josh skeptical of its sincerity.

Chapter 18

▼

Josh was in the lounge, ready to start his next operation, when Luke entered. Josh could see in Luke's eyes that he was distressed about something. He had a worried look on his face that Josh had rarely seen before.

"Something's wrong with Jay, Josh," he said.

"What is it, Luke?" he asked as he jumped to his feet.

"I just talked to Ann," he replied. "He woke up this morning with pain in his abdomen. We didn't think much of it at first, but when it lasted all morning and kept him from playing, Ann took him in to the clinic."

"Who checked him?"

"One of the HMO doctors," he replied. "He reassured Ann that Jay was all right...told her that he was just constipated and gave her some suppositories. He's getting worse, Josh. The pain is worse and Ann says he just lies quietly in bed between the spasms of cramping."

"What about the suppositories?"

"He passed a small stool that Ann said looked like dark grape jelly. I'm worried, Josh," he said, almost tearful. "They did no X-rays, no lab work. The doctor didn't even do a rectal exam."

"That's the HMO policy: do the least you can get away with and move 'em out in a hurry," he replied, with bitterness. "You should be worried, Luke. I'm worried too. You remember your Pediatrics. You're probably thinking the same thing I am. I'm canceling this case. Let's go see what's going on. If it's a surgical abdomen, every minute counts."

Jay lay in bed, his face wet from tears that he couldn't suppress when the intermittent cramping hit. His skin was feverous and dry. He didn't jump into Josh's arms as usual, but did manage a heart-warming smile when he looked up at Josh as if pleading with him for help. Josh bent over and gave him a kiss.

"My 'tummic hurt, Uncle Josh."

"You're gonna to be all right, big man," he said. "Let me look at that sore tummy."

With even the lightest pressure Jay cringed and tears welled up in his eyes when Josh touched his abdomen. He listened with his stethoscope for a few moments until he heard the characteristic high-pitched tinkling sound when the pain spasms came. Ann stood by quietly, but looked as though she were about ready to burst into tears when she read the expression on Josh's face.

In the next room, Luke and Josh conferred.

"We've got to move fast, Luke," he said. "He's obstructed and he's getting toxic. This is probably intussusception. Try to keep Ann calmed down and get Jay to the hospital emergency room. I have some phone calls to make."

"We're ready to go, Josh," said Luke. "Make your calls here. Just pull the door closed when you leave."

"I'll be right behind you."

* * * *

Milton Mintner, M.D. was probably the most qualified, dexterous pediatric surgeon in the country, but was sadly lacking in personality. He never learned how to communicate with patients or family—even depended on his residents to fill in that void in his patient care. As an intern, Josh had fulfilled that role a few times, providing families explanations of procedures that Dr. Mintner would be performing on their child.

Josh was convinced that Jay needed emergency surgery, and with trepidation he placed a call to Dr. Mintner.

"Dr. Mintner," he said when he finally reached him. "This is Josh Lehman. I'm one of the third year surgery residents. I have an emergency and I need your help." There was a long pause that told Josh Mintner probably was checking the surgery duty roster.

"What is your problem, Dr. Lehman?" he asked, with a rather cool tone to his voice.

"This is a four-year-old son of one of our anesthesiology residents," Josh replied. "I think he has intestinal obstruction, probably an intussusception. I believe he needs surgery right away."

"How did you get involved in this, Dr. Lehman?"

"His father, Luke Sanders, is a close friend of mine."

"Have Dr. Sanders take the child to the clinic," he said. His response was too indifferent for Josh's liking.

"Dr. Mintner, they took the boy to the clinic earlier," he said. "The E.R. doctor told them it was constipation and gave him suppositories. There were no X-rays, no lab work. They sent him out without even doing a rectal examination."

"Tell them to take him back to the clinic!"

"Dr. Mintner, let me make myself clear. This child is sick and getting sicker!" said Josh, with fervor in his voice. "He likely will need emergency surgery. He is my godson. I want the best for him. That's why I'm calling you."

"I appreciate the compliment, Dr Lehman, but we must follow protocol. He will need to be referred to the surgeon on call by a primary care physician."

"We are going to the emergency room, sir," said Josh, his voice echoing firmness. "I am in hopes that you will call and notify the E.R. that you will assume care. Otherwise we have no choice but to carry him to Parkdale E.R."

There was a long silence on the other line. Josh could hear Dr. Mintner's heavy breathing. Parkdale Medical Center had the one competitive Pediatric Surgery Department that, for years, was known to be the greatest threat to the reputation of Mintner's program at Metcalfe.

If Josh was right in his diagnosis, and if a Metcalfe resident's son was transferred to Parkdale with a missed diagnosis, Metcalfe would be the laughing stock of the medical community. Then Mintner would have to face the Metcalfe president and likely the president of the board of trustees. Now, Mintner had no choice.

"I probably will report you to the Medical Ethics Committee, Dr Lehman," he said. "And I will certainly write you up for insubordination."

"I understand, sir," he replied. "Will you assume care of this child?"

"Yes!" he exclaimed, as he slammed down the receiver.

By the time Josh reached the hospital, Dr. Mintner had already arrived. The E.R. physician had ordered stat X-rays and lab work and had started I.V. fluids with antibiotics. Jay was on telemetry monitoring. To Josh he looked so pitifully small and frightened on the E.R. stretcher. The boy looked up at Josh and faintly smiled, then closed his eyes again. Dr. Mintner had finished his examination and had ordered light sedation for him.

"We're taking him to the operating room," he said, with a stern, blunt tone to his voice. "Will you be scrubbing in, Dr. Lehman?"

"No sir," he replied. "I will stay with Dr. Sanders and his wife." Josh assumed that was the reply that Dr. Mintner hoped he would hear.

Josh, Luke, and Ann stayed in the surgery waiting room without speaking, each with the same somber, worried expression on their faces. The television, with a sit-com of canned laughter, was on, but held no attraction for any of them.

"He passed out just before we got here, Josh," said Luke. Ann was still trembling from the thought of it.

"He was in septic shock for sure," Josh replied.

It seemed like hours, but was only a little over one hour when Steve Boller, the surgical resident who was assisting, came to the waiting room. He was all smiles, which signaled that Jay was all right.

"He's fine," he said. "It was an intussusception, just as you had thought, Josh. There was a small segment of gangrenous bowel that had to be resected. No colostomy, thank God. Dr. Mintner did a masterful job, as always," he added. "I imagine the boy will be bouncing back quickly."

"Thank you very much, Steve," said Luke, as he stood with his arm around Ann, who was sobbing softly.

"Josh, you did a brave thing here," said Steve.

Dr. Mintner never appeared. "I guess he took his 'protocol' out the back door and home," Josh said to himself.

Ann and Luke stayed at Jay's bedside without a break, in spite of Josh's plea that only one should stay at a time so both wouldn't become totally exhausted. Josh spent the night in the doctor's lounge, waking up every hour or two to check on Jay.

On his last check, before starting his morning case, Jay, Luke, and Ann were all dozing. Josh placed his hand on Jay's forehead while studying the telemetry monitor readings which showed normal temperature, heart rate, and blood pressure. Jay opened his eyes, looked at Josh, and flashed a broad smile. *It's going to be a beautiful day*, thought Josh. Luke roused briefly, but before he could speak Josh shushed him and quietly left the room.

Chapter 19

Josh had just finished his first case when the call that he expected came on his cell phone. It was President Roever's office calling to arrange for an appointment as early as possible in the president's office.

Josh had visited with the president only briefly on rare occasions. He had no idea what kind of person he would face. He was pretty sure of the reason he had been summoned and couldn't help but be a little apprehensive about any possible forthcoming disciplinary action.

The secretary busied herself with the routine tasks of the day while Josh sat in the waiting area, waiting to be called in. She politely offered him coffee or juice, which he declined. He heard the faint sound of a bell and the secretary stood and motioned for him to follow her.

The president's office was impressively spacious with darkly stained wooden tile flooring in a mosaic pattern and a colorful Oriental oval area rug that almost reached each of the mahogany paneled walls. Near the center of the room was a huge dark oak desk, behind which was a matching credenza and a leather upholstered desk chair. At one side of the desk, a computer table held a flat panel monitor. The keyboard and server were hidden somewhere out of sight.

The opposite wall was devoted to library shelves and compartments for a gigantic television screen and a sound system. Uniformly framed pictures, citations, and diplomas adorned the walls. Several comfortable-appearing leather chairs were placed near the desk.

President Roever immediately stood to his feet when Josh entered and came from behind the desk to greet him. Josh hadn't remembered his being so tall and having such an athletic build. *He is well into his fifties and obviously stays physically fit,* thought Josh.

"Dr. Lehman!" he said, all smiles as he extended his hand. "Thank you for coming in on such short notice." *He couldn't be more gracious and amicable,* Josh thought. *What's coming next?*

"I regret that I haven't been able to spend more time with our staff physicians," he continued. "I believe I have had the pleasure of meeting you before."

"Yes, sir," said Josh. "Usually with a group of residents. There are so many of us, I'm sure no one could keep everyone's identity straight," he added with a laugh.

"Not all come to us with such colorful athletic background," he said as he directed Josh to a chair and resumed his position behind his desk. "I've watched many of your college games, which brings me to my next question. Was it difficult for you to pass up professional football?"

Josh pondered the question for a few moments before answering. The president seemed to be sincerely interested. Josh hadn't expected this.

"As a matter of fact, it was very difficult," he replied. "I loved football. It was a very difficult decision."

"I played college football for Nebraska," he said. "I had to make the same decision years ago. I know how hard it was for you, but I have never regretted it. Neither will you, Dr. Lehman."

"I already feel that, sir."

"This is your third year, I believe," he said, as he thumbed through what appeared to be a freshly prepared dossier.

"Yes, sir," Josh replied. He wanted to tell Dr. Roever to get on with it. He could feel his anxiety building up and hoped it wasn't noticeable.

"You certainly have an impressive record so far," he said. "Your evaluations have been excellent."

"Thank you, sir," he replied. He wished he hadn't emphasized the "so far."

"I'm sure you know why I have asked you to come," he said.

"I'm reasonably sure," he answered. "I was expecting your call."

The president was silent for a few seconds, still looking through Josh's record, as if contemplating his next remark.

"Dr. Lehman, how well do you know Dr. Mintner?"

"Only casually—from assisting him in the operating room."

"What do you think of his ability?"

"He is a superb pediatric surgeon, the best I've ever seen," he replied. "Most everyone else feels the same way."

"What do you think of him personally?"

Josh hesitated in his answer. He smiled and chuckled softly. He looked down at the floor and then looked up at President Roever, who had a devilish twinkle in his eyes and was smiling at Josh.

"That's a hard question to answer," said Josh. "The interns and residents all pretty much feel the same way about Dr. Mintner."

"What do they say?" asked the president, grinning broadly—like he already knew what they said about Mintner. Josh felt crowded into a corner. He continued to grope for the right words.

"Never mind, Dr. Lehman," he said. "I know what you guys say, that he's either chronically constipated or he's in need of a hot piece."

The tension was broken. They both broke into hearty laughter. *The president is crafty,* thought Josh. *I'll bet he was a hell of a football player.*

In short order, after they both had calmed down, the president resumed an air of seriousness.

"Dr. Lehman," he said. "I think I know what happened. I'm going on what Mintner told me and what I know about him. Let me ask you one more question, maybe two more. First, do you think the outcome of your encounter with Dr. Mintner would have been different if you knew him better?"

"I'm really not sure," he replied. "I think it would be pretty hard to get to know him very well."

"My next question is this: under the same circumstances, would your behavior toward Dr. Mintner be any different? In other words, would you do it again?"

"Yes sir," he replied. "I'm sorry, sir."

"I'm in a difficult situation, Josh," he said, calling him by his given name for the first time. "You probably saved that child's life by your prompt action. We try to teach our residents the importance of being astute in their diagnoses and in their judgment of a patient's needs. You certainly proved yourself in that regard. On the other hand, I'm faced with a faculty member being threatened, or feeling threatened, by a staff physician and filing a complaint that I have to resolve."

"I understand, sir," said Josh.

"Let me tell you a few things about Mintner," he said. "We all know about his personality quirk. We all know about his competence. Josh, he perceived your presence at Metcalfe as a threat long before you ever threatened him, if it can be called a threat. This dates back to your application for a position here."

"He was on the selection committee. When he reviewed your application, he said words to the effect of, 'He's used to walking out on that football field and winning every time; now he thinks he can come into the surgical field and do the same.' Dr. Mintner is dedicated to his profession and he expects perfection from everyone he works with, but I think he's resentful of your success as an athlete—maybe envious. He can't deal with it. Subconsciously, he hopes you stub your toe as a surgeon."

"What can I do, Dr. Roever?" he asked, "Is there any way I can reach him?"

"I don't know," he replied, in a pensive tone. "I know very little about his social life. I don't think he has any outside interests other than golf," he added. "I've heard that he is fairly good. Very meticulous, I'm sure, much like his surgery technique," he added, with a laugh.

Dr. Roever gazed out the window which overlooked the Metcalfe campus for several moments before speaking.

"Josh, you know I cannot ignore this occurrence," he continued, frowning. "Here's what I'm going to do: I want you to make an appointment with Dr. Mintner in his office and apologize. I'm not asking you to back down on your decision to take the action that you did. I'd probably do the same in that situation. I don't have any idea how he will react when you go to him."

"Next, I want you to think of something during the remainder of this year that you can do that will enhance your relationship with Dr. Mintner. I am not making any suggestions. I'll let you call the play on that, but I will be on the sidelines, watching and waiting. If you do that, Josh, nothing will go into your record."

"I can handle that, Dr Roever," he said, relieved to be given the chance to avoid a black mark on his record.

"Josh, it's been a pleasure to have the opportunity to visit with you," he said. "You have a great future ahead of you. Please feel free to drop by any time."

"Thank you, sir," he said, as he rose to shake hands with the president.

"Oh, Josh," he called out, as Josh approached the door. "I've been told that the little boy was Luke Sanders' son."

"Yes sir, it was," said Josh.

"The old Lehman-Sanders Axis still working," he said. He laughed, as he waved good-bye.

Chapter 20

Apologizing to Dr. Mintner was not going to be easy. In his mind, Josh groped for the words he would need and the approach he should take. Dr. Roever said that he didn't have to back off his position on the sequence of events that transpired on the day in question. How would Dr. Mintner take it if he offered anything less than a "bended-knee, hat-in-hand" apology?

Josh would start his pediatric surgery rotation service soon and would be forced to stand across the operating table from Dr. Mintner while assisting him. Dr. Roever must have known he was starting his rotation on Dr. Mintner's service when he assigned Josh the disciplinary measures. The air had to be cleared if his time on Dr. Mintner's service would be beneficial to his training. Josh decided that the best approach would be one of honesty. *Maybe when I talk to him, the right words will flow,* he thought.

Josh was alone in the surgery lounge, between cases, when Dr. Mintner walked in with his cell phone in his hand. He pretended not to notice Josh—actually turned his back to him while he talked. Josh remained quiet until Dr. Mintner finished his conversation. Josh took a couple of deep breaths and then approached him. With any luck they would have a few minutes to talk before anyone else entered the lounge.

"Dr. Mintner, would you have a few minutes to talk to me?" asked Josh. Dr. Mintner's face was mask-like. He glanced at his watch before replying.

"Yes, I think so," he answered hesitantly.

"I just want to let you know how very much I appreciate your managing Jay Sander's case last week," he said. "I am so sorry we got off to such a bad start."

"How is the boy doing?" he asked. For all the emotion he showed, he could as easily be asking about the bus schedule.

"He's doing fine; he bounced back quickly," he replied.

"I'm glad to hear that."

"Dr. Mintner, I will be starting my pediatric surgery rotation soon. I was hoping we could perhaps clear the air a bit beforehand. I am looking forward to working with you, both in the clinic and the operating room. I feel very fortunate to have that privilege."

"Thank you, Dr. Lehman, for being straightforward about this," he said. "I probably overreacted to your phone call last week. I agree. We do need to 'clear the air.' It will make both of us more comfortable."

"I hope you understand that my behavior that day was an emotional response," said Josh. "I care a great deal for that little guy, and I just panicked."

"Thank God you did, Dr. Lehman," he said. "He was near total organ failure from profound septic shock."

Other physicians entered the room and their conversation had to shift to other subjects. They changed their discussion to general medical and hospital-related issues. Dr. Mintner definitely seemed to have softened by the time they shook hands and parted. Josh had completed "phase one" of Dr. Roever's assignment.

* * * *

Josh's on-call hours, which consisted of eighty hours per week, occasionally gave him an afternoon off beginning at two o'clock. He rarely took off, using that time to catch up on records or to read professional journals. He frequently took calls for any one of the residents who had some unforeseen reason for being off.

It was a little after two and he was pretty well caught up with routine chores. He needed to visit Jay and Luke and Ann, but first he had to run some errands. This would be a good time to get together with Luke's family for dinner and maybe a movie. He dropped by the Surgical ICU to see if Linda would be available, but found that she wouldn't finish her shift until late. He called Luke on his cell phone while he was doing a case.

"I'm sorry, Josh," he said. "Ann has already announced she's planning dinner at home tonight. Let me call and tell her you'll join us."

"That will be great, Luke," he replied. "I haven't seen Jay for a while. I don't want him to forget what I look like."

"Not a chance," he laughed. "He asks about you every day. Will Linda be with you?"

"She's working late, but I'll ask her to come when she's finished."

* * * *

As soon as Josh entered the front door, Jay came running to him and jumped into his arms. Josh lifted him up to his shoulders and carried him around the house while he greeted Ann and Luke. As usual, Jay stayed as close as possible to Josh's side.

"My 'tummic dun't hurt anymore, Unca' Josh," he said, holding his abdomen with his hands.

"He tells everyone that his Uncle Josh fixed his stomach," laughed Luke. "You've got an admirer here."

"Great!" Josh replied. "I need all the help I can get." Then he turned to Jay, still perched on his lap.

"Jay, I'm glad your 'tummic is well. OK, now show me your hand." Jay's eagerness showed that he loved this trick. He held his right hand up to Josh's, palm to palm with the webs of their hands matching.

"Now, tell me what you will be when your fingers grow to here?" he asked, pointing to his fingertips.

"A doctor!" Jay called out loud and clear.

"Right!" said Josh and gave him a tight hug.

Ann pried Jay loose, in spite of loud resistance, and sent him to another room so Josh and Luke could have some time together.

"How did it go with Mintner?" asked Luke.

"It really went very well," he replied. "I managed to apologize without saying I was wrong."

"He knew you were right."

"And he admitted that. Now I have to come up with one more element of this disciplinary action plan."

"I have thought about that, Josh," he said. "Let me tell you my idea. You know old Mintner is a golf enthusiast. You will find out when you are on his service. He stays glued to the television every spare moment whenever there is a golf tournament."

"I'm not going to play golf with him!"

"Wait, Josh. Listen to this," said Luke. "Do you remember the little guy who moved into Ryan Hall at midterm our first year at Northwestern?"

"Yeah, I remember. We had to come to his rescue when the jocks were ridiculing and harassing him. What was his name? Haynes something, wasn't it? Where are you going with this?"

"OK, smart ass, look at this Sports page. If you kept up with golf you'd know. Brantley was his last name, Haynes Brantley. You can bet your left nut that old Mintner knows who he is."

The headlines, in large print on the front of the Sports section of the "Dallas Morning News" read: *"Haynes Brantley Expected to Win the Dallas Country Club Open."*

"Now here's the clincher, football hero," said Luke. "He will be visiting here soon to check out the golf course ahead of time for the tournament. They say he always sneaks in unannounced before every tournament he plays in."

Josh began to see the light. Luke had a plan and lights were beginning to flash in his own head.

"Luke, didn't we turn over the 'protective duty' to Sam before we left?"

"Right!" he said. "And you know he was well protected. He won every match for Northwestern and turned professional as soon as he graduated," he added. "Without asking, we can be sure he is grateful for all we did for him and gives us credit for putting him under Sam's wing."

"OK, what's the plan?"

"We get in touch with Sam. He probably can tell us how to find Haynes," he said. "If I know Sam, he keeps up with athletes like Haynes."

"Then what?"

"We contact Haynes, explain to him what we want him to do, and see what his response will be."

"Come on, Luke," he said. "What do we want him to do?"

"Let us know when he is coming and arrange for him to play a round with Mintner, just the two of them. We'll make it an early morning game before the media even knows he's in town. What do you think?"

"I think you are out of your mind," Josh replied. "What makes you think someone that famous would go out of his way for some hair-brained scheme?"

"Simple," said Luke. "People who are winners don't forget how they got there. Trust me. I'll take care of the details."

"You're a genius, Luke, and a firkin psychologist yet. Let's go for it."

Chapter 21

In her position as telephone operator at Ryan Hall, Lola Watson prided herself in knowing where just about everyone in the building was at any given time.

"Lola, this is Luke Sanders."

"Hi, Luke!" she said. "How have you been? How's Josh?"

"He's fine, Lola. We are still in our residency training at Metcalfe," he answered.

"Sounds exciting! You are both doctors now. I can say I knew you two boys when you were two scared freshmen." She laughed.

"Lola, I need to talk to Sam. Can you find him for me?"

"Sure can, Doctor," she replied, emphasizing *Doctor*.

"Thanks a lot, Lola."

"Just stay on the line, sweetheart."

Some things never change, he thought, as he waited to hear Sam's voice.

"Mr. Luke!" he said. "This here's old Sam."

"Good to hear your voice, Sam. How are you doing?"

"I is jest fine, Mr. Luke. Jest a few of my old miseries. How you? And how is Mr. Josh?" he asked. "I sho misses yo boys."

"We're doing fine, thank you," said Luke. "Sam, I need to find Haynes Brantley. Do you have any idea how I can get in touch with him?"

"Yassuh, Mr. Luke," he replied. "He done give me a number to call if I needs him. I ain't supposed to give it to nobody. But I knows he'd wants yo to have it. Yo and Mr. Josh wuz there when he needs yo. Wait right there 'til I gets back."

Sam came back to the phone in a short while with the number.

"Sam, thanks for your help," said Luke, "And don't worry, it's safe with me."

"I knows dat, Mr. Luke."

"Oh, Sam, one other thing. I have a little five-year-old boy."

"Dat is jest fine! Mr. Luke, jest fine!" he replied. "Fore yo knows it he be here at Ryan Hall. Yassuh, dat is jest fine, Mr. Luke."

* * * *

Luke dialed the number, thinking he was probably going to reach some dumb flunky or a secretary that he would have to go through to ever talk to Haynes. To his surprise, Haynes answered.

"This is Haynes Brantley," said the soft-spoken voice on the other end.

"Haynes, this is Luke Sanders. I wanted to…"

"Luke! What a nice surprise!" he called out before Luke could even finish his first sentence. "How is everything? How is Josh?"

"Fine, Haynes," he replied. "Josh and I are both in our residency training at Metcalfe Center in Dallas. I see you are going to be here soon."

"Right! Do you think we can get together?"

"That's why I'm calling, Haynes," he said. "Do you have a minute to talk?"

"Absolutely."

Luke launched right into the whole story about Josh's problem with Dr. Mintner that began with Jay's surgery, and about their scheme to get him to play a round of golf with the doctor as a way of creating a more pleasant atmosphere while he and Josh worked together. Luke waited for a response from Haynes, not knowing what it would be.

"Luke, I think that is a wonderful idea," he said. "You know there's nothing I wouldn't do for you two guys. I would never have made it without you two and Sam. And I know you're responsible for Sam's helping me."

"Thanks a million, Haynes," he said. "I can't wait to tell Josh."

"Look, my manager Bob Salyer will set everything up," he said. "No one else is to know when I'll be there. He'll arrange for the match to be at an early hour before the media finds out. He'll let you know all the details."

"Thanks again. We are in your debt."

"Not at all," Haynes responded. "It's been great talking to you, Luke, and congratulations on medical school. Looking forward to seeing you."

* * * *

The pediatric surgery rotation was well under way. Josh's schedule was packed—surgical procedures each morning and follow-up clinics each afternoon. As always, emergency surgeries punctuated the day and night.

Each day on the service, Josh developed more and more respect for Dr. Mintner's surgical skills. Josh made a sincere effort to assist Dr. Mintner in the operating room every chance he had. Their relationship developed into a smooth-working team, both in the operating room and in the clinic.

For Josh, time spent in the clinic was a delightful experience, except for those children with illnesses for which there was no hope of recovery. The steady stream of children of all ages through the treatment rooms so often brought to mind his disappointment that he had no children of his own—children like Jay. That he had no home life to compare with Luke and Ann's.

Josh finished examining his last patient for the day, a five-year-boy, and was busy making the boy an airplane out of tongue blades and band-aids—a trick he devised that always made kids laugh—when Dr. Mintner called.

"Before you leave, Josh, check the patient in Room 5 for me and let me know what you think."

Josh entered the room to find an anxious mother with a two-month-old baby who appeared malnourished and far smaller than would be expected for its age. Josh noticed a cloth diaper draped across the mother's shoulder.

"He just won't gain weight, doctor," she said, her voice trembling.

"And he spits up all of the time, doesn't he?" said Josh.

"Yes, he does. How did you know?"

"Just guessed," he said, pointing to the diaper. "How long has he been vomiting?"

"For about two weeks. I keep telling the doctors he's getting worse," she replied, and then broke down in tears. "They just give me medicine to give him, but it doesn't help."

"Has he had any X-rays?"

"None," she answered, blotting tears with a tissue. "My mother and I both asked and they said it wasn't necessary."

Josh tried to comfort her while he examined the baby.

Dr. Mintner came into the room and watched while Josh palpated the baby's abdomen. Even though the baby was crying, when it would inhale Josh could feel deep in the pit of his stomach. "We will need some X-rays," said Josh to the mother. "Don't feed him anything for now. Try not to worry. Dr. Mintner and I will talk to you later."

"I'm reasonably sure I feel a tumor," Josh said, after they stepped into the corridor.

"I thought I could also," said Dr. Mintner. "You have sensitive fingers, Josh. I'm proud of you. We hardly need an X-ray for that diagnosis."

"It's nice to find a case that a simple operation, just making an incision across the thick muscle, will relieve the blockage at the lower end of the stomach."

"Right!" said Dr. Mintner, "The baby should do fine. I want you to do this one, Josh."

"Sure," said Josh. "As long as you are standing across the table from me."

"I'll be there," he said. "Oh, Josh, let me give you a tip. If you suspect pyloric stenosis in crying babies, sometimes turning the baby face down makes it easier to find the tumor."

"Thanks, I'll remember that…hadn't thought of it," replied Josh. One more pearl of wisdom to be filed away!

* * * *

After each case they did together, Dr. Mintner accompanied Josh to the consultation room in the waiting area to observe the way Josh communicated with families. At first it was rather awkward. Dr. Mintner simply stood aside and never uttered a word. In time he loosened up a bit and began interacting with the families of the children, using much of the same scripting and body language that Josh used.

Dr Mintner still had a problem when unpleasant news had to be delivered and allowed Josh to do the talking in those cases. When Josh took the lead role in talking, he always emphasized how well Dr. Mintner had handled the case.

"I'm supposed to be teaching you, Josh," he said with a laugh one day after a very busy morning. He had just recently begun to call him by his first name. "I've learned more on how to communicate with people from you than I ever knew before. How do you do it?"

"You're embarrassing me," laughed Josh.

"No, I'm serious. How do you do it?"

"I'm sorry, sir," said Josh. "I don't know how to tell you. When I'm faced with reporting to a family, I put myself in their shoes. I say words that I would expect to hear if that were my child. The right words always seem to come from somewhere."

"That's it!" said Dr Mintner. "It's sensitivity! You're a very sensitive person, Josh. I just want you to know that I'm learning. I'm working at it."

"Thank you, sir," said Josh. "On another subject, Dr. Mintner, I have heard that you are a golf enthusiast. I read in the paper that Haynes Brantley will be playing in a tournament here."

"He's a fabulous player!" he said, hardly able to constrain his enthusiasm as he talked. "I certainly will not miss that. I watch him play on television every chance I get. I'm really looking forward to seeing him live when he's here. Do you like golf, Josh?"

"I've never played," he replied. "The article about Haynes caught my eye. We were at Northwestern together. Luke and I lost track of him after we left. I didn't dream he would become so successful as a professional."

"He's unbelievable," Dr. Mintner said, still beaming with excitement. "Then you know him? Maybe you would like to go watch him play while he's here?"

"Yeah," he said, "I'd like to see him again, for old times sake. I imagine Luke would like that also, if we can get some time off."

"Fine," he said. "I'll work on the scheduling and plan on both of you coming as my guest. Maybe you can introduce me to him."

"We'll sure try," said Josh. "Of course, he may not even remember us now that he's famous."

* * * *

Dr. Mintner and Josh entered the lounge and sat down to unwind for a minute after an unusually difficult case. Both were totally exhausted—physically and emotionally. They would have to take a disheartening report to the family. There was not much hope for the beautiful little five-year-old girl with congenital heart disease whom they had just left on the operating table.

On the communication board in the lounge were the many messages for them that had accumulated over the four hours while they had been operating.

"Who do you think Bob Salyer is, Josh?" he asked, fumbling through his message cards. "The card says that it's not medical, but about the golf tournament."

"I don't recognize the name." *Could it pertain to Luke's arrangement with Haynes?* Josh wondered.

"I guess I'd better call," he said. "Probably something to do with my request for tickets for you and Luke, but I don't remember anyone by that name at the club," he added. "If you don't mind, go on out and talk to the parents. I'll join you later. I know that's going to be a tough one."

When Josh returned, after delivering the heart-breaking news, Dr Mintner was sitting by the phone—quiet, speechless, and pale.

"Josh, you won't believe this!" he exclaimed. "Bob Salyer is Haynes Brantley's manager. They want me to play a practice round with Haynes at the Country Club. It is being set up for three days before the tournament."

"That's great, Dr. Mintner!" said Josh, trying to pretend surprise. "You'll like Haynes. He is one of the most unpretentious people you'll ever know."

"This is top secret, Josh," he said, in all seriousness. "He will try to slip in here for the practice round without the media being aware. The game is scheduled for six o'clock in the morning."

"I guess you won't be coming to the clinic that day, will you?" Josh laughed.

"God, how did this happen?" he said. "I'm not that good a golfer."

"There must be some reason you were chosen," said Josh.

"Josh, did you and Luke have anything to do with this?" he asked.

"I'll ask Luke," he replied with a twinkle in his eye as he turned to leave. "Oh, the family of that little girl wanted you to know how much they appreciate all you did for her."

"Thanks, Josh," he replied. "That was a sad situation. It tempers my good news about the tournament."

* * * *

Dr. Mintner practiced on the golf course every spare minute, and even set up a putting mat in his office. He could talk openly only to Josh about the approaching golf match and still maintain the secrecy of the event, but eyebrows were raised in the department when he was heard making statements in the clinic like: "I've got to stay calm," or "I've got to remember to toe-in a little more," or "I hope I don't drop into that pond on number seven."

Josh finished a preoperative evaluation of a child scheduled for surgery the following day and found Dr. Mintner waiting just outside the treatment room.

"I was going to find you," said Josh. "I just checked the boy we're doing in the morning. He's fine."

"Oh, yes," he replied. "I almost forgot about the case. Josh, could you come in my office for a minute?"

"Sure," said Josh. *I'm sure he has another question about the golf game,* thought Josh. *Probably one I've answered a dozen times.*

As expected, the putting mat was down and his bag of golf clubs was leaning against his desk. *Now I see why I have been so busy in the clinic—I'm doing all of the work,* thought Josh, trying to suppress laughter.

"Josh, watch my swing with this club," he said, motioning for Josh to stand clear. "I'll use this one first and then this second one. Watch my follow-through and see which you think appears more natural."

Josh watched, trying to keep a straight face, as Dr. Mintner pretended to hit a golf ball, swinging smoothly.—first with one club and then with the other. Josh cringed when he missed the ceiling by only inches.

"What do you think?" he asked.

Josh could tell no difference whatsoever, but he knew Dr. Mintner wanted some sort of an answer.

"I believe I like the first one best," he answered.

"Now let me try it again. I want to be sure," he said. "This time watch my feet to see if they stay in place."

He repeated the process with both clubs and then looked to Josh for his comments.

"Very good!" said Josh. *I've got to get out of here and back to work before I break down laughing.*

"Thank you, Josh," he said. "You know, I need to have a full length mirror put on that wall so I can see for myself."

"A good idea," Josh replied and hurried out the door.

* * * *

Bob Salyer called Luke to announce that Haynes would like for him and Josh and Dr. Mintner to have lunch at the club after the practice round. He had already arranged it with the club. That meant that Luke and Josh would have to rearrange their schedules, but it would give them a chance to visit with Haynes.

They arrived at the club before Haynes and Dr. Mintner returned from their round of golf and were met by Bob Salyer.

"I'm afraid we were unsuccessful in keeping this quiet," he said. "The sports reporters are everywhere. But this usually happens," he added. "We're used to it, but we were afraid Dr. Mintner would be embarrassed."

"I think we'll have to get him a bigger hat," laughed Luke. "He can handle it all right."

They looked out the large plate glass window across the lush, green grass fairways and watched Haynes and Dr. Mintner approaching. Side by side, they talked and laughed and gestured with their arms and hands like two long-time close golfing buddies.

The hovering news reporters descended upon them like vultures going after a recent road kill. If there was ever any concern about Dr. Mintner being embarrassed over a press interview, that concern could be put aside. He absolutely glowed with self-confidence as he responded to the many questions thrown at him.

Bob Salyer quickly rescued Haynes and Dr. Mintner and whisked them through the crowd of wild reporters into a private dining room inside, with Luke and Josh following close behind. After greetings between Haynes and Luke and Josh, including questions about family and friends, conversation at lunch centered around current activities of each and reminiscing about days at Northwestern.

Dr. Mintner joined in with praise for Josh and Luke in their residency training. Evidently, from remarks that were made at the table, he had already narrated to Haynes the story of Jay's close encounter. The role Luke and Josh played in bringing them all together was not mentioned. They broke up the gathering with promises to visit again.

* * * *

The sportscaster on Dr. Roever's favorite television station's evening news sport's edition excitedly reported this feature item:

"*Haynes Brantley, well-known championship golfer, made a surprise visit to the Dallas Country Club early this morning for a practice round of golf in preparation for the upcoming open. His partner for the round was Dr. Milton Mintner, chief of the Pediatric Surgery Department at Metcalfe Medical Center. Haynes also used the time to visit and reminisce with Josh Lehman and Luke Sanders, his friends from his days at Northwestern. Dr. Lehman and Dr. Sanders are both residents in training at Metcalfe.*"

Dr. Roever immediately sent Josh a message on his cell phone: "Nice work. Case closed!"

* * * *

Josh and Luke neared completion of their third year in the program at Metcalfe. When Josh was offered a fellowship in cardiovascular surgery at the Metcalfe Heart Institute, he accepted. It was just what he had worked for. As much as he enjoyed working with Dr. Mintner, his greatest ambition was to move into adult cardiac surgery and train under Dr. Michael Dubonet.

Dr. Dubonet was the aging "dean" of cardiac surgery. He had pioneered many of the current surgical techniques commonly utilized in open heart surgery. He was internationally acclaimed as the leading heart surgeon in the Southwest. Patients from every corner of the planet flocked to Metcalfe for heart surgery, based on his reputation.

He had a charismatic personality that won the hearts of every patient he touched. His patients and their families believed that he was a miracle worker. They hung onto every word he uttered with resounding faith in his recommendations for their care.

He had undaunted faith in himself. Not all of his contemporaries shared the same belief in the merit of some of his innovative ideas, but this never deterred him from trying new approaches whenever he was given the opportunity. His artificial heart implantation was a failure and he took a lot ridicule for the attempt. On the other hand, however, he refined the protocol for the heart transplant program at Metcalfe that became a model for the whole country. And he never stopped challenging the old established procedures, ever looking for ways to improve them.

With his advancing years, Dr. Dubonet knew he needed someone to carry on in his place. Every year, and with each new group of residents and fellows, he searched for that special individual whom he could take under his wing and pass on as much of his skill as possible. It would take a unique person who was sensitive and receptive to all he had to offer. Every time he thought he had found the right person, something would disappoint him about his choice and he would be back to searching again.

Josh impressed him early on with his eagerness, his surgical skill and judgment, and his compassion for the patient. Dr Dubonet was principally responsible for Josh's being offered the fellowship. He had had so many disappointments that he was skeptical of choosing anyone, but he believed he was right in his opinion of Josh's potential as his successor.

At the same time that Josh accepted the position with Dr. Dubonet, Luke was recruited by and joined the anesthesiologist group at Metcalfe. Being in a group gave him the benefit of free time to spend with Ann and Jay, as well as the opportunity to expand his training in managing heart and lung cases. With Josh moving into heart surgery, if they were to work together Luke needed to increase his proficiency in handling those cases.

* * * *

Josh took time between mid-morning cases to find Luke. He checked the schedule board in the operating suite ante-room to find which case Luke was assigned. *He should be finishing soon,* thought Josh. *I'll wait for him in the dressing room.*

"I was just going to find you," said Luke. "Heard the good news! You're staying on!"

"That's why I'm here," replied Josh. "The word's out that you're joining the anesthesia group. Great news! I came to congratulate you. We'll still be working together!"

"I think the world's quit trying to separate us," Luke said with a laugh.

"Different playing field, but just another game," said Josh.

"OK, agreed. Now before you launch into another work marathon, listen to your old wide receiver," said Luke. "It's time for you to go to the bench for a few plays while we're ahead. Take some time off."

"Come on, man," said Josh. "What would I do?"

"Go somewhere. Go play. Have some fun," said Luke. "Do it now. Dr. Dubonet's gonna work your ass off."

"I'll give it some thought. How are Ann and Jay?"

"Fine," Luke answered. "Ann's happy to stay here. Jay likes his school. He asks about you every day. We're fine, Josh. Come visit."

"You know I will," Josh replied.

Chapter 22

On rare occasions, Josh and Linda took time to discuss their relationship. Living under the same roof had brought them closer together, but only from their sexual attraction to each other. Their talks just could not bridge the gap that was still there regarding their individual long-range goals. Those differences remained unchanged and consequently were discussed less and less frequently.

Neither Linda nor Josh had taken very many days off work. When Josh had any spare time at all, he stayed busy with some research project or worked on a paper to be published. Their recreation was pretty much limited to an occasional party or movie or visiting Luke and Ann and Jay.

Each time they visited, Josh could sense that Linda became uncomfortable when he spent any time playing with Jay or when he made comments to Luke and Ann favoring their way of life. *Will Linda ever change?* Josh wondered. *Do we stay together just to sleep together? We need something different in our lives.*

* * * *

Mel Jacobson, as director of Human Resources for all of Metcalfe, was inundated with major personnel problems: turnover rates, production percentages, recruitment, and whatever else might be loaded on his plate by administration.

Mel had no time to be concerned about employee's accumulated "Paid Time Off" hours. Nevertheless, one of his assistants regularly placed before him a list of employees who had reached the maximum allowed hours.

He glanced at the list, not wanting his assistant to think he had no interest—which he didn't—to find Josh Lehman's name flashing at him like a strobe light. He yelled to his secretary.

"Find Josh Lehman for me. Get him on the line!"

Mel had become acquainted with Josh a few months earlier when Mel's father came into the Emergency Department with severe abdominal and back pain and in a near state of collapse. Josh was on call; he promptly identified a leaking aortic aneurysm and got him to the operating room for a timely repair with a very satisfactory outcome. Mel thanked Josh so many times it became embarrassing.

"Hey, Josh, this is Mel Jacobson."

"Hi, Mel," said Josh. "What's up?"

"Listen, dude," he said. "Ya got too fuckin' many PTO hours. You need to haul ass out of here. Go somewhere!"

"Mel, I can't afford to go anywhere," said Josh. "How's your dad?"

"Fine, Josh, thanks to you," he said. "Josh, you're changing the subject. Take some time off!"

"Can't afford it, Mel," he replied.

"Yeah, you can," said Mel. "Cash in some of your hours; sell 'em back to the company."

"I'll think about it."

"Another thing, Josh," he said. "The Residency Surveillance Committee will be on our ass if they find out you've been working that long without a break."

"Damn it, Mel!" said Josh. "I don't have time to take off."

"Take off, Josh!" The phone clicked before Josh could answer.

Without being requested, brochures of exotic trips began appearing in the mail from travel agencies. *Mel has to be responsible,* thought Josh. He decided that he and Linda needed to do some serious talking about taking time off to travel. He was thumbing through the colorful pamphlets when Linda came in from her shift.

"Come look at these," said Josh. "Mel Jacobson says I have to take some time off. I'm looking for a place we can go."

"Am I included?"

"Yeah, both of us have accumulated maximum time-off hours. We need to go somewhere or lose those hours."

"Jeez," said Linda. "I never realized how many places I've never seen."

"I thought the same," replied Josh. "I hope you don't want to go to Las Vegas."

"No way," she laughed. "I don't want to compete with all those chorus girls."

"What about Hawaii?"

"What are those girls called? Wahinis?" asked Linda, mimicking a hula dancer. "Do they turn you on with all that gyrating?"

"Come on, Linda, we have to make a decision."

"Hawaii is fine with me. Anywhere we can be together," said Linda as she climbed onto his chair and straddled his lap. "Ever got into lap dancing?"

"No!" said Josh. "Unless I hear otherwise, I'm making plans for Hawaii."

So, Hawaii was the choice. With Mel's help they scraped enough cash together to sign up for a package deal that included air travel. In short order they were on their way to Maui, exuberance at an unprecedented high.

* * * *

Their room in the hotel was ground floor, beachfront. It was luxury supreme. Their first task was to find appropriate bathing suits and to secure snorkeling gear.

Josh was perched on a stool in the swimsuit shop, waiting for Linda to try several styles. When she emerged from the dressing room in her bikini, Josh had to grab hold of the nearest counter to keep from falling to the floor. In the furor of their daily activity at the hospital, he never saw her in anything except scrubs, and in the dark bedroom it never mattered what she had on—or didn't have on.

It was as if he saw her for the first time. She looked stunning, standing there with wisps of blondish strands of silky hair waving across her face and with her newly-acquired bikini accenting her beautifully well-proportioned figure. *I can just see all of those lustful old bastards staring at her when we go to the beach,* thought Josh.

Their every minute was spent sunning on the clean, sandy beach, drinking exotic Hawaiian drinks, or swimming in the clear blue Pacific water. They learned to snorkel after a few lessons and diving each day became a routine. The beauty of the coral formations and the colorful array of fish of all sizes and shapes was captivating. They laughed a lot. They laughed at things they would have considered "school-kid" silly only a few days earlier.

Josh lay on a lounge chair, totally detached, reading a book—something he never seemed to have time to do—when he heard Linda call to him. Unbeknownst to him, she had scampered off into the surf and was splashing around in the waves by herself.

"Josh!" she cried frantically. "Josh!! Come here—now!"

He looked up from his book. *What could be wrong?* he wondered. *She probably saw something in the water.* He ejected himself out of the chair and raced toward her, thinking the worst. She was standing in waist deep water with her arms crossed over her chest.

"What the hell's going on?" he yelled. "Come on out of the water!"

She wouldn't budge. Then he saw the problem. She had lost the top to her bathing suit!

"Wait!" he yelled, grinning and pretending to turn back to the hotel room. "I need to get the camera!"

"Josh! don't you dare!" she pleaded. "You come here this minute and dive for my bathing suit top. I'm in no mood for jokes"

Josh waded into the water, went to her side, and tried to pull her arms away from her chest, with her fighting franticly to stay submerged.

"Josh Lehman!" she screamed. "Find my bathing suit top!"

"Hey, girls don't even wear tops on some beaches," he laughed as he dived under to recover her lost garment.

"Yeah, you'd like that, wouldn't you?" she said. "Help me tie this."

They fell back into the water, both laughing, with Josh faking an attempt to remove the suit top again. Josh thought about how many times they would be telling this story after they returned home. *Mel was right,* thought Josh, *we needed this time away from work.*

Sometimes, when they lay on the beach side by side, Josh would turn toward her without her knowing and study her every feature. He admonished himself that he had never noticed her this closely before. She was a beautiful woman!

They slept late the next morning. They left the sliding glass door open all night and the pleasant, gentle breeze bathed their room with cool, dry air. The sound of the waves washing ashore had a mesmerizing effect.

"I like this place," Josh said aloud as he roused from the bed and started to dress for the day's activity. Then, for whatever reason that it hit him right then, he went to the bed where Linda was still in deep, restful sleep and shook her.

"Will you marry me?"

"Sure, when?" she asked, shaking her head trying to clear the fuzzy feeling from her brain.

"Today!"

"Fine," she replied. "Let me get dressed first."

They took an air shuttle to Honolulu and were married the same day, in a judge's office with some clerk as a witness.

"We need to let Luke and Ann know," said Josh.

"You make the call," she said. "I have a feeling they won't be particularly thrilled."

"Of course they will," he said. "Luke has been after me for months to settle down to a family lifestyle."

"But not with me, Josh," she said. "Ann has told him something about me and I don't know what it is. I never feel relaxed around Luke."

"Just wait and see," said Josh. "They both will be ecstatic. Probably mad that we didn't invite them," he said with a laugh.

* * * *

"Luke," he said, with Linda standing by his side. "It's me. How's it going?"

"Fine, Josh," he answered. "Are you having as much fun there as we are here? You just couldn't stand it without checking in, could you?"

"Get serious, gas passer," he said. "Linda and I have something to tell you and Ann."

"She saw you in a bathing suit and decided to split?" he chided.

"Turn it around. I saw her in a bikini and decided to marry her," he laughed. "We just got married! Wanted you and Ann to be the first to know." There was an uncomfortable long pause.

"That's good, Josh," he finally said, in a rather subdued tone of voice. "Congratulations to you both. Here, tell Ann the news."

"Hi, Ann," he said. "Linda wants to tell you some news."

He handed the phone to Linda and stood aside. *Luke sounded about as excited as a depressed shrink on a cloudy day,* he mumbled to himself. *What's the deal?*

Linda and Ann were talking "girl talk"—complete with squeals and laughter. *What a contrast,* he thought. After they finished talking—with Linda filling in all of the details of when, where, and how—Josh asked to speak to Luke again.

"Luke, how's Jay?"

"You need to come home, Josh. I'm having trouble explaining Hawaii." He laughed. "I tried to explain about snorkeling in the Pacific Ocean and he keeps asking why you don't just come over here and go swimming in our pool. He's fine, Josh. We're all looking forward to your return."

Luke sounded more like himself. Josh decided that he needed to have a long talk with Luke as soon as he had a chance.

* * * *

The drone of the jet engines carrying them back to the real world lulled Josh into a contemplative state—thinking of life ahead with Linda, now as a married couple. *What would be different? They had shared the same apartment for so long that they knew each other's peculiarities and mood swings. There was really nothing to discover about each other in bed. There was no question that they had different long-range goals.*

It was obvious to Josh that Linda did not want to talk about having children. Without her saying a word, Josh could tell that she did not want to be burdened. She was already talking about planning an announcement party and about planning a dream home with all of the entertainment amenities—swimming pool included.

Luke had implied in his talks with Josh a long time ago that self-indulgence was a way of life for Linda. *She'll change,* Josh predicted. *I'll change her mind about children. We'll need to get closer to Luke and Ann and Jay. She'll see.*

"You're anxious to get back to work, aren't you?" asked Linda.

"Yeah, I really am. I'm anxious to start working alongside Dr. Dubonet," said Josh. "He is fabulous, Linda."

"Josh, you've got to find time to help me plan our announcement party. I want a big party!" she said, her eyes and face aglow with excitement.

"We'll work it in," answered Josh.

Chapter 23

Working with Dr. Dubonet was every thing Josh had hoped for. It reinforced his decision to move into cardiothoracic surgery. A day never passed that he didn't gain something rewarding from being around the older surgeon—a refined technique, a new skill, a lesson on gentle handling of fragile tissue.

And more than just operating room tutoring, he observed with wonderment the way Dr. Dubonet bonded with every patient he treated. He took the time to listen and explain complex procedures in simple terms that patients and families could understand.

He never seemed rushed, either in the operating room or in the clinic, but even on the most difficult cases he spent far less time operating than any other surgeon. He was known to be extremely respectful of all personnel and assistants. No one had ever reported any disruptive behavior on his part.

"A sure sign of insecurity in a surgeon is abusive behavior in the operating room," Dr. Dubonet said on several occasions. Knowing his feelings about that kept many surgeons in his department in line.

Josh's curiosity and his challenges of certain case management policies ignited the elder surgeon to expound and to teach. Dr. Dubonet loved being questioned, never showing any indication that he felt that his integrity or skill was being criticized.

Josh picked up so many of Dr. Dubonet's traits, both in and out of the operating room. One trait was the untiring devotion to his work. Regardless of how many cases they did together in a day's time or at what hour they operated, neither the younger nor the older surgeon ever showed any sign of fatigue.

One of Josh's greatest rewards was seeing the smiles on the faces of patients in the clinic who had undergone a revascularization procedure that was successful. These were people who heretofore had been ravaged with chest pain with the least exertion; or who couldn't walk a block without having to stop because of the torture of severe leg pain. This was the same exhilaration he had felt during his football years when he would throw a winning, touchdown pass to Luke in the final minutes of a game.

*   *   *   *

Linda continued to work in the ICU. She was often heard to say that she saw Josh more in the ICU than she did at home. On her time off she looked at houses and condos, visited furniture stores, and shopped. She enjoyed giving parties for small select groups, even if Josh had to miss most of them or had to leave before they were over. She enjoyed the notoriety of being Josh's wife, in spite of the innuendos that floated around the hospital that she had accomplished just what she set out to do—marry a doctor.

When she received the invitation to join the Metcalfe Doctors' Wives Club, she jumped at the chance to get involved in the social whirl that went along with the membership. The club was composed of members whose husbands were either residents or medical staff physicians at Metcalfe. The Doctors' Wives Club was both a social and a service organization. They sponsored regularly scheduled fund-raising events for worthy causes. They were usually festive occasions that included dinner, dancing and entertainment.

Linda proved to be a great asset to the group in planning the events and working untiringly to see that they were a success. The time she spent with the club's activities encroached on her work at the hospital, however, which meant she had to reduce the number of shifts that she worked in the ICU.

She was expected to host club planning committee meetings from time to time in her home, even as small as it was. She convinced Josh that they needed a larger and more elaborately-furnished house instead of the small apartment that they lived in. Josh let her make the decisions in that regard.

He was too wrapped up in his work at the hospital, and really didn't have time to be bothered with those details. This gave Linda free rein to explore moving into a different residence and to decorate it any way she wished. A problem soon arose when she did so without concern for the cost.

They moved into one of the more exclusive condominium villages in a prestigious part of North Dallas. Theirs was a luxurious unit that fronted on the swimming pool and patio. They had access to an adjacent party room that was ideal for entertaining. The new furnishings began to arrive, followed by the invoices showing the charges had gone on their credit card. For the first time, Josh was hit with the reality that their budget was stretched to the limit.

"Linda, we can't afford this!" he exclaimed. "We will just barely skim by with these payments."

"Josh, if I am going to be active in the Wives Club, I have to have a presentable home for meetings and entertaining," she replied.

"You should have checked with me first," he retorted.

"You told me to go ahead. I was just doing what you told me to do."

"But you're getting us deeper and deeper in debt," said Josh, looking at their Master Card statement and studying the invoices.

Her eyes flashed daggers. She pranced around the room, shoving furniture out of her way, grabbed the Master Card bill out of Josh's hands and started tearing it into small pieces.

"I'll send it all back, damn it!" she said, slamming kitchen cabinet doors and drawers shut. "We'll just move to some dumpy apartment and let everybody laugh at us. 'Oh, that's Dr. Lehman's wife,' they'll say. I can hear it now, 'She has to work extra shifts to pay the bills.'"

"Now you're trying to put a guilt trip on me," he said, then threw the invoices on the floor and started toward the door.

"Where are you going!" she yelled. "I suppose you're going over to Luke and Ann's house to tell them how horrible I am."

"Not a bad idea!" he yelled back and slammed the door as he left.

He didn't go to Luke's house. Instead he walked to the campus gym and worked out as vigorously as he possibly could. While running the track, he muttered to himself, almost aloud, "I shouldn't have scolded her; she was just doing what she thought was right in creating the expected image of a doctor's wife. I'll call Mel and see if I can borrow money to pay for the new place."

He jogged back to the apartment, arriving there just in time to get drenched by a sudden cloudburst. When Linda answered the doorbell, she faced Josh, soaking wet, hair hanging down over his forehead, streams of rainwater channeling across his face. "I'm sorry," he said, his head hanging.

"Come here!" she said, a soft, misty, seductive look in her eyes. "I've never seen you look so sexy."

She grabbed him and pulled him close to her, wet clothing and all, and began stripping his clothes off, one item at a time, while dragging him toward the bedroom. They never made it that far. She pulled him down to the carpeted floor, and that ended their first argument.

Chapter 24

The Emergency Department at Metcalfe was covered twenty-four hours a day by the junior surgery residents, with the senior residents rotating back-up call. As a designated class trauma center, there were two residents in the hospital at all times. The senior resident was available whenever there was a need. Although he was assigned to the cardiovascular service, Josh took his turn as senior surgery resident on call for all emergency room cases.

He was on his way to the lounge for a brief breakfast break after a busy night of gunshot wounds, stab wounds, and auto accident injuries. He felt the vibration of his cell phone just as he sat down, hoping for a few moments of rest and quiet. The place already bustled with interns, residents, and staff members drifting through for coffee, juice, and whatever else was available for a quick bite.

"This is Dr. Lehman," said Josh.

"Dr. Lehman, this is Brent Kelley, general surgery resident. I was called to the E.R. to see this lady with abdominal pain. I'm having difficulty examining her; she is totally uncooperative. She keeps saying that she wants to go home."

"Who is she?"

"She's Mrs. Salzman," he replied. "You know, Salzman Electronics—makes all of our X-ray equipment. She just wants to go home."

"Is she stable enough to release?"

"I don't think so," he replied. "She is mentally alert and well oriented. She just insists on leaving. She let the E.R. doc examine her when she first came in. He said she has an almost rigid abdomen, more localized in the left lower quadrant. She won't even let me touch her. Her temperature is 102 and she looks sick. She is refusing X-rays or ultrasound or any basic blood work. I need help."

"Let me take a look," said Josh. "If she is competent, we may not be able to do anything if she doesn't agree."

"Thanks, Dr. Lehman."

Josh skipped breakfast and hurried down to the E.R. *What can you do when some cantankerous old lady won't even submit to being examined?* he grumbled to himself. *I need to guard against showing irritability in front of the resident and the patient.* He pushed through the E.R. door and found Dr. Kelley waiting for him, chart in hand.

"What do you have?" asked Josh.

"Mrs. Ruth Salzman is an 81-year-old female with a history of abdominal pain of two or three day's duration," said the resident as he began his presentation. "She appears acutely ill with a temperature of 102, a rigid abdomen, and absent bowel sounds. She is refusing any tests."

"She lives alone, but has attendants close by to care for her. She summoned her housekeeper early this morning for help when she had attempted to rise out of bed and was too weak to do so."

"The housekeeper and the chauffeur managed to convince her to go to the hospital by threatening to notify her son. After loading her into the limousine, they called her son anyway to tell him what they were doing."

"Is her son here?"

"No, only the chauffer and the housekeeper. They are trying to stay out of sight."

"Does she say why she wants to leave?"

"Only that she's cold and she needs to get home—and she has a few choice words to say about doctors."

She lay on a stretcher, parked in one of the many E.R. cubicles, a frantic look on her face as she glanced about at the scurry of activity—nurses, technicians, doctors, all dressed alike, pacing back and forth. She called out to anyone in a scrub suit who happened to venture close by.

"I'm ready to go home. Tell Jackson I'm ready."

"Yes, ma'am," came the reply from anyone near.

She clutched the soft wool blanket that she had brought from home, gripping it tightly around her neck, as if she challenged anyone to try to examine her. Josh walked up to her bedside.

"Mrs. Salzman?" he said. "I am Dr. Lehman. How are you feeling?"

"Another doctor yet!" she replied. "'How are you feeling?' he says. How do you think I feel? I need to go home. Jackson, come get me!"

Josh glanced out toward the waiting area. Her chauffeur stood discretely out of sight of her direct vision and, along with the housemaid who accompanied him, pretended not to hear her beckoning call. *They very likely are anxiously awaiting her son's arrival,* thought Josh.

Josh pulled up a chair and sat beside the stretcher. He took her hand is his and looked compassionately into the eyes of this frightened, aging matriarch of the largest electronic manufacturing company in the world.

He looked at her blanket from home that protected her from the ever-present cold blast from the air conditioning. Scattered across the blanket were the long, white hairs that were the telltale sign of a pet. *Probably a poodle,* thought Josh. He decided to chance it.

"Mrs. Salzman, I know you don't feel well," he said in a clear, distinct voice. He had noticed hearing aids in both of her ears. "I can see in your eyes that you are ill. You have fever and the emergency room doctor is concerned about the tenderness in your lower abdomen."

"That doctor!" she exclaimed. "Can you believe? 'Ruth', he called me. What happened to respect? I want to go home."

"Of course you do. You want to get home to your poodle," he said, with a smile. "And that doctor was disrespectful. But he is young and naïve. He'll learn."

Her head jerked around toward Josh when he mentioned "your poodle." *How did he know,* she wondered? Her demeanor changed abruptly; she studied Josh carefully, as if she had seen him for the first time.

"You know about Robie? How did you know?"

"I saw Robie's hair on your blanket. My mother had a poodle. She loved that little fellow," he said wistfully. He decided that in situations like this a little lying was sometimes helpful therapy.

"She has no pet now?" she asked.

"My mother died a few years ago. Her little poodle never recovered from the loss and he died only a few days afterward," he answered as he dropped his head in sadness.

"You poor boy. I am so sad," she said. "Were you a good son?"

"I tried to be. But I didn't visit often enough."

"Like my babies—busy, busy, busy. I only see them at board meetings and on Passover and High Holy Days."

"You know, we can have Jackson bring Robie here to the hospital to see you," he said. She immediately brightened up with those words. "We even have kennels for our patient's pets so they can be close to them while they are in the hospital."

"Will I have to stay in the hospital?"

"I'm afraid so, Mrs. Salzman."

"Will I need an operation?"

"You may. We will be able to tell after we do the X-rays and the other tests," he replied. He motioned for the resident, who stood by in wonderment at the dialogue between these two, to get the necessary lab work and X-rays.

"Will you be with me in the operating room?" she asked, a soft, pleading tone to her voice.

"Yes, I promise," he answered as he stood.

"You're Jewish, aren't you, Dr. Lehman?"

"Yes, ma'am," he replied.

"You were a good son."

"Thank you, Mrs. Salzman," he said. He bent over the stretcher and kissed her on the forehead.

Josh left her side and went to the waiting room to report to Jackson and the housekeeper. He was met by a well-dressed, distinguished-looking gentleman in his late fifties with very distinct facial features, dark eyes, and gray streaked hair. He rose from his chair as Josh approached.

"Dr. Lehman, I'm Charles Salzman. Jackson has told me how well you dealt with my mother's behavior, and I want to apologize for her."

"No problem, Mr. Salzman," he said. He turned to Jackson and the lady whom he supposed was Mrs. Salzman's housemaid and introduced himself.

"You both deserve a great deal of credit for bringing her in when you did. She is a very sick lady," Josh continued, addressing all three of them. "We'll know more when we finish with the tests. From what I've seen so far, she very likely will need surgery. I'll get back with you as soon as I know."

"Dr. Lehman, I appreciate your help," said Charles Salzman. "I would like to tell you a couple of things about my mother. Ordinarily she is extremely alert. She is in no way mentally incompetent, in spite of her age, although she may try to lead you to think so."

"She certainly seems mentally clear now," replied Josh.

"Nevertheless," said Charles, "I suggest that you be truthful with her and explain thoroughly what you find, what you recommend, your rationale, and the outcome that she may expect. My suggestion is based on what I've seen in our corporate board meetings. Sometimes she appears to have no idea what is transpiring, then sends some of our executive staff members scampering for answers to questions on critical issues that we all overlooked."

"Thanks for the warning" said Josh. "I think I've already seen some of that," he added with a laugh.

"Also, she has a remarkable ability to judge character," he said. "You must have passed the test."

"I hope so," he replied, as he turned to follow the stretcher carrying Mrs. Salzman to the radiology department.

Josh returned a few minutes later to give Charles Salzman a report.

"The X-ray and the ultrasound of the abdomen confirm the suspicion that she has acute diverticulitis that has ruptured. This means she has acute peritonitis. She needs immediate surgery. We will remove the infected portion of the bowel; but, I must tell you, she will need a colostomy."

"She'll accept whatever needs to be done, Dr. Lehman," said Charles. "Just explain it to her."

With Charles present, Josh described to Mrs. Salzman what he had found. He explained to her that she would need an operation to remove the infected segment of her bowel, but with the acute infection he would not be able to re-attach the two ends of bowel for several weeks.

"A colostomy I'll need, then," she said calmly. "Is there a chance that I may have cancer?"

"That's a possibility," he replied. "The ultrasound pictures do not indicate that, but we can't always be sure."

"How long will I be in the hospital?"

"From the operating room you will go to the ICU for a few hours. As soon as it is safe to do so, you will be moved to your room. If all goes well, you'll be home in eight to ten days."

"Make it eight already," she said with a laugh. "The colostomy—will someone train me in care of the colostomy?"

"Yes, we will have a colostomy care nurse give you detailed instructions," said Josh. He marveled at the appropriateness of her questions. Charles had been right in his advice. *I just hope she doesn't ever find out that my mother couldn't stand to be in the same room with a cat or a dog.*

"Will you do the surgery, Dr. Lehman?" she asked.

"Yes, ma'am," he answered.

"Let's get it done," she said. "Your mother…Josh, she called you?"

"Yes, ma'am."

"Then Josh it is," she said. "But don't call me 'Ruth,'"

"Never, Mrs. Salzman," he replied, and again bent over and kissed her. "You'll do fine, Mrs. Salzman."

* * * *

Josh found Luke to be available. He did not want to be under this kind of pressure without Luke at the head of the operating table. He recruited the general surgery resident and an intern for assistance and notified his staff surgeon to be on standby.

He checked on her one more time while she was in the holding area. She was still clinging to her blanket, trying to stay warm. She now was having hard chills from the overwhelming infection. He convinced her to trade her blanket for one that had been heated in the operating room suite.

Intravenous antibiotics and fluid were flowing into her veins. Luke had started oxygen by nasal canula and had given her a mild sedative though the tubing. She was relaxed and drowsy when she looked up and saw Josh.

"One more kiss, Josh," she whispered as she dropped into deep sedation.

The surgery went very well. Josh was able to resect the bowel with no difficulty and then fashion the colostomy through the abdominal wall away from the surgical incision. There was no evidence of malignancy anywhere. He would not have a final report until after the pathologist had examined the specimen, but he was reasonably certain there was no cancer.

Josh went out to tell Charles and the others who were waiting the good news. In addition to Charles, Jackson, and other loyal household employees, there were other family members present. Charles introduced them to Josh one at a time, attempting to identify their relationship to Mrs. Salzman.

"My two brothers are out of town, Dr. Lehman, and can't be present," he said. "But my oldest brother, David, is ably represented here by my niece, Leah Salzman."

"I'm very pleased to meet you, Dr. Lehman," she said. "I have heard that you have already experienced some of my grandmother's abrasiveness," she added, laughing.

Josh was struck by her beauty. The way she tossed her head to one side when she laughed was tantalizing. He held eye contact an awkwardly bit longer than he should have before he answered her.

"We got along fine, Miss Salzman," he replied. "She's a remarkable person. She's already started giving me advice."

"She's good at that," said Leah. "I'm sure she's asked you if you were married and if you were Jewish."

"Both," laughed Josh.

He excused himself and walked away, but the image of Leah Salzman in his mind didn't go away. *Get your head out of the rut, you bum!* he told himself. *You're not going there!*

✶   ✶   ✶   ✶

Mrs. Salzman's post-operative progress couldn't have been smoother. She was very cooperative with her colostomy training and with her physical therapy. Josh visited her daily, sometimes twice daily. After she improved to the point that she could be conversant, they had some lively sessions.

"I met your granddaughter," said Josh. "She's a lovely girl."

"Information you want, now," she said and laughed. "You're fishing, Josh. An old fool, you can't fool."

"I'm married, Mrs. Salzman."

"That I know," she said. "I'll tell you anyway. Leah's not married…thirty years old already! Whatever will happen to her? Thinks of nothing but her career. A good lawyer, she is. I tell her—find a nice Jewish boy to marry. At thirty, three babies I had."

"Does she work for the company?" asked Josh.

"Lawyers! Too many we have, already!" she said. "Too smart for her own good. Defense lawyer, she is. In the law firm named Hall, Cranston, and somebody, I don't know. Work, work, work, that's all she does. Her home, the courtroom yet."

"Mrs. Salzman," he said. "It's nearing time…" Before he could finish, she interrupted him.

"Changing the subject, you are," she said. "No more about Leah. But I guess I'm through telling you about Leah. I wish you had known her earlier."

"When you go home, Mrs. Salzman," Josh continued, "you will need nurses to care for you for a while. The case manager here at the hospital will make arrangements for nurses to visit you in your home. For the next few weeks I will need to see you in the clinic each week. Of course, if you need anything before then you should call me any time."

"Maybe Leah will bring me to the clinic," she said with a twinkle in her eyes.

"Just make sure you come in," said Josh, and then chuckled. "Or I'll come after you."

"Oy, vey! Scolding me now, you are."

Chapter 25

Leah did, in fact, bring her to the clinic on two occasions. While the nurse was getting Mrs. Salzman ready to be examined, Josh had the chance to visit with Leah for a few minutes. He was still intrigued by her attractiveness and by some of her mannerisms when they conversed.

"Dr. Lehman, I'm sure you've noticed this about my grandmother," she said. "She is a manipulator of the first degree. She deliberately gives Jackson a day off when she knows she has to come here. Then she calls me or my Uncle Charles to bring her. It's her way to force us to visit."

"She's probably very lonely," he said. "I imagine she's reluctant to go around other people with her colostomy."

"That may be true," she said. "I hate to admit it, but I dread being around her sometimes. She makes me feel like I'm a disappointment to her because I don't have a husband and a house full of children."

"You should remember this," said Josh. "She raised three sons; she had no daughters. She looks upon you as the daughter she never had."

"I know you're right," she replied. "I love her with all my heart. She is a remarkable person—could be a professional 'shadchen', you know. She is constantly lining me up with some eligible guy who usually turns out to be a nerd," she laughed.

"Don't give up," Josh chided. "Maybe the next one will be Mr. Perfect."

"I've already given up," she replied, then smiled and tossed her head again.

* * * *

Mrs. Salzman progressed rapidly toward full recovery. It was nearing time to take her back to the operating room for a "take-down" procedure on the colostomy. Josh hated to think he would need to release her from his care soon, bringing an end to their lively visits—visits that always lasted longer than the allotted time.

At every chance during their conversations, Mrs. Salzman used the opportunity to interrogate Josh. She was as inquisitive as a nosy neighbor about every aspect of his life, including his married life. Josh tried to avoid giving direct answers, but that didn't work with Mrs. Salzman. He could imagine what she would be like at a corporate board meeting.

It was her last time to come to the clinic; her take-down procedure was scheduled for two weeks. With her on the examining table, Josh did a quick physical to verify she was ready for another operation. He had noticed the tell-tale tattoo on her forearm many times before, but avoided talking to her about the horrors of the Holocaust, although his curiosity was at a high level.

"Tell me about your husband," Josh said, thinking perhaps he could lead her into relating some of her earlier life experiences during those dreadful years.

"A good marriage. Sixteen, I was," she replied. "Arranged by my aunt, Aunt Sarah, a matchmaker yet."

"You have no regrets, do you?"

"None," she said. "A fine man, Julius. A nuclear physicist, he was. For the Nazis, he would do no work. So, for us, the labor camp."

"Concentration camp?"

"Oy, all Jewish people we knew, taken. Gone, pulled off streets, pulled out of their homes."

"Your family?"

"Questions, questions, you ask," she said. She turned her head to the wall, trying to hide her face. "We learned not to cry, Josh. Cry and they shoot you, Josh."

"What do you mean?"

"My sister…they grabbed our friend…my sister cried, they shot her. My eyes, I closed. 'I'm next,' I say, but they walked away, laughing. Our girlfriend, they dragged with them. My sister, in the ghetto, lying in the street, bleeding. In my arms, she died. Animals, Josh! Animals!"

"Did you lose all of your family?"

"More questions, already! No one I tell, Josh, no one, ever" she said. "Not even my children. Mama, Tateh, my other sister, my brother. Gone, Josh."

"Did you try to find out about them?"

"The AID society searched and searched for records…none. In Treblinka, last they were seen. I would have been with them, but to America with Julius, I went."

"So sad, Mrs. Salzman, so sad. Can you ever forget? Can you ever get over the pain?"

"Memories, Josh," she said. "Deep in your brain. You try to bury them. Like demons, they are. Then to the surface, they rise, they haunt you. You can't stop them. You never forget."

"How did you escape the camp?" asked Josh.

"Jewish Underground," she replied. "The Nazis, oy! Julius they wanted. The resistance fighters knew. From the labor camp they rescued us, escorted us out of Germany, smuggled us on a ship to America. Two little boys we left behind, and pregnant I was with another."

"What happened to your boys?" asked Josh.

"In Warsaw they stay. David, six, Charles, four, with a brave Polish family. To America they come after the war to meet their little brother, Phillip. My three boys I hugged close, Josh! I could not turn them loose! I could not turn them loose! I cried then, Josh," she said, tears streaming down her face.

Josh tried everything from clamping his jaws to biting his cheeks to suppress tears while she told the story. When she reached the part about the family reunited after being torn apart for years, he could feel the moisture spreading from his eyes.

He sat down beside the treatment table, held her small, wrinkled hand in his, placed it on his face, glanced again at the tattoo on her arm, and they both sobbed. Without a word said aloud, when they looked into each other's eyes the story was told in a way that Josh knew it must be retold over and over again.

* * * *

Bit by bit, Josh learned the fascinating history of the beginning of Salzman Electronics, and the more he heard, the more respect he developed for the founder and the woman behind the man.

The Salzmans entered America through New York and Ellis Island. With courage and perseverance and the help of other Jewish families, they overcame the countless hardships of adapting to life in a new country. Julius took a teaching position at Columbia University for a short period before venturing into his own business.

Julius envisioned the impact technology was having on modern society and started a small company to build computer parts for larger manufacturers. Salzman Electronics grew into a major corporation over the years. It gradually expanded into developing radiology equipment—more specifically, computerized tomography scanning and magnetic imaging.

Each of the sons trained to take positions with the company. Charles graduated from M.I.T. and took over the position of head of research and development. David graduated from the Wharton School of Finance and joined the company as the Chief Financial Officer. Julius remained the CEO of the corporation until his death. David then stepped into that position. Phillip, the youngest, became head of the marketing department.

* * * *

Mrs. Salzman's second procedure went smoothly, with no adverse events. Following the procedure, Josh went to the waiting area to give his report to the family, not sure whether or not he hoped Leah would be there. He had promised himself that he was going to block her out of his mind; but there she was, alluring as ever. He tried to avoid staring at her.

"Mrs. Salzman's fine," Josh reported. "I expect her to be ready to leave the hospital in a few days, barring any complications."

"Will she need nursing care at home?" asked Charles.

"We will want a nurse to visit her each day for a couple of weeks. Mrs. Salzman is a tough lady," said Josh with a laugh, "and if the nurse stays too long, she'll probably be chased out of the house."

"I see you know her pretty well," said Leah.

"I'm going to miss her visits," said Josh. "We had some enlightening conversations."

"I expect that she'll find some way to see you again," said Leah.

"I hope so," replied Josh. As he turned to leave, Charles beckoned him aside.

"Dr. Lehman, I'll be leaving town for several days and may not have a chance to speak to you again," said Charles. "I would like to invite you to come visit my office and laboratory some time so I can show you what we do at Salzman Electronics."

"I would like that very much," Josh said. "I am especially interested in learning more about using the Salzman Thoracoscope."

"When I return, my secretary will contact you for a definite time," he said. "I want to take this opportunity, on behalf of all of the family, to thank you for the care you've given our mother. I know it hasn't always been easy," he added with a laugh.

"It's been a pleasure," said Josh. "And I am looking forward to seeing all of you again some day."

He glanced over at Leah; she was looking straight into his eyes. There was that captivating way she tossed her head, as if she were sending him some kind of message. Josh reprimanded himself. *Come off it, nebbish, you've got to stay focused on your work.*

Chapter 26

Josh was well into his last year at Metcalfe and had to make some decision on where he would go after finishing his fellowship with Dr. Dubonet. He had several good offers to join groups, but none seemed to satisfy all of his expectations. None could equal the satisfaction of staying with Dr. Dubonet. Josh was reasonably sure Dr. Dubonet would make him an offer.

Josh had already decided that he preferred to work where Luke would be available to manage the anesthesia on his cases. It was the same feeling he always had when they played football. Having Luke at the head of the operating table gave Josh the same confidence he felt when Luke was on the other end of a pass. Luke liked working with the group at Metcalfe Heart Institute and probably would want to stay if Josh accepted an offer from Dr. Dubonet.

The thought of staying in Dallas, however, just didn't appeal to Josh. There was certainly enough work there to be done, but something was holding him back. Linda was well entrenched in the Dallas social circles. She was working less and less all the time. She had been invited into the Junior League, which meant more social activities for both of them.

Josh thought that might be the reason he was reluctant to stay in Dallas. The social whirl was just not for him. He had resigned himself to go along with Linda's lifestyle, and although they were going deeper in debt every month, he told himself he would find a way to catch up eventually. Josh had a call from Dr. Dubonet's office to set up an appointment. He surmised that it was about his future plans. He was down to the wire—a decision had to be forthcoming.

When he was ushered into Dr. Dubonet's office, to his surprise Dr. Roever was present. A brief wave of panic enveloped him. *Why would they both want to see me?* he wondered.

"Josh!" Dr. Roever exclaimed. "Nice seeing you again. How have you been?"

"I'm fine, sir," said Josh, waiting expectantly to hear what was next to come.

"Mike tells me you've been kinder to him than you were to old Mintner," he laughed. "When I saw Mintner on television, I knew exactly what you boys had done. A perfect touchdown play, Josh," he added with a chuckle.

"Josh, I'm sure you're wondering why we asked you to come here today," said Dr. Dubonet. He paused for a few seconds, prolonging the agony for Josh.

"It just doesn't seem possible that you are this near finishing your work here. I think you know I would like for you to stay on with me," he added. "But I can't ask you to do that without your hearing some other options. I'm going to let Dr. Roever take it from here."

"Here's the pitch, Josh," said Dr. Roever. "You know you have a position here with Dr. Dubonet. But here's what's coming up. This is strictly confidential, so I can show you nothing in writing. Metcalfe Heart Institute has been planning to expand for quite some time to cover the south Texas area for cardiovascular procedures."

"We have looked at several cities and have decided that the most strategic location will be Westlake. It is a growing community with a well-balanced medical community and well-run hospitals. "We will finalize negotiations with Westlake Regional within the next few days. A public announcement will be made then. This will be a joint venture between Metcalfe and Westlake Regional. We will build the physical plant, manage and operate the new facility, and Regional will provide ancillary services."

"We will grant privileges to the Westlake Regional medical staff for general medical services and will recruit cardiothoracic surgeons for the surgical services. We need a medical director, Josh. That's why we are here with you."

"Dr. Roever and I want you to consider assuming the position of medical director," said Dr. Dubonet.

Both Dr. Roever and Dr. Dubonet remained quiet while Josh absorbed the full impact of the offer.

"A Medical Directorship?" said Josh, finally. "That's not exactly what I had in mind as a career."

"You won't be giving up surgery, Josh, if that's worrying you," said Dr. Roever. "You'll be starting a practice and at the same time playing a major role in planning and building the heart hospital."

"You'd do well at it, Josh," said Dr. Dubonet. "You like challenges. I have watched you long enough to know. I've seen the way you've tackled some difficult situations in the operating room."

"And on the football field," Dr. Roever added with a laugh.

"What exactly will I be doing?" asked Josh. *Does this mean a lot of administrative work?* he wondered.

"The project will take about three years to build, start to finish," Dr. Roever replied. "During that time you will be developing a referral base for your surgical practice. You'll be operating there, just as you have been doing here. Same type of cases. As your work load increases, we will recruit additional surgeons to help you.

"You will be available to assist in architectural decisions and planning during the building phase. You will be on salary from the Heart Institute, plus the reimbursement you receive from your patients. Of course you will stay in close contact with Dr. Dubonet. There will be times that you will return to Dallas to work with him on certain special cases."

"It does sound appealing," said Josh. "I want you both to know that I feel quite honored to be considered."

"Before you ask," said Dr. Roever, "we will do everything possible to get Luke to agree to join you."

"I'll need Luke," said Josh. "I can't imagine working without him."

"In case you're concerned about administrative duties, Josh, we'll provide you with administrative assistants to manage the day to day issues," said Dr. Roever. "Your role will be more in communicating with the medical staff and in reviewing certain quality and outcome studies. It should take very little of your time."

"I'll need to talk to Luke and my wife," said Josh.

"I imagine your wife will be reluctant to leave Dallas," said Dr. Dubonet. "My wife tells me she has been very active in the wives' club and the Junior League."

"Then you know what I'm facing," said Josh. "I'm sure she'll be reasonable."

"Josh, a nice salary goes along with this position," said Dr. Roever.

"That will go a long way with Linda," Josh said with a laugh.

"Josh, again, this is very confidential, and we need an answer as soon as possible."

"Thank you both for considering me. I'll call you with an answer by tomorrow at the latest."

Josh left the office, wondering *What am I getting into? When I tell Luke he'll say, "it's just another game." I can hear him now.*

* * * *

His first stop was finding Luke. He knew he wouldn't see Linda until the end of the day—until her last committee meeting was finished. Luke had just finished a case when Josh walked into the O.R. dressing room.

"Of course I'll go!" said Luke after Josh told him of the opportunity. He was ecstatic. "I've always thought I'd like to see my children grow up in my home town. Ann wants to have another baby, you know. And I might even take Jay to see his grandmother."

"I want to get out of Dallas," said Josh. "This will be a good chance for both of us."

"Josh, come over tonight when I tell Ann," said Luke. "And Jay hasn't seen you in a while."

"Great idea! I'm off call tonight; I'll find Linda and we'll be over."

He called her cell phone number and got no answer. He left a message that he was going to Luke's and for her to join them, and in the message told her that he would surprise her with some exciting news. He was on the freeway to Luke's house when she called.

"I'm so sorry, Josh," she said. "Georgia Van Zant has called an urgent meeting of the League tonight and I can't miss it. What is the news?" she asked.

"I'll tell you later," he said, his voice reflecting disappointment.

"Josh, you're angry with me," she said.

"Just disappointed," he said. "It seems we never have any time together anymore."

"We'll catch up some day," she said. "If you are asleep when I get home, I'm going to wake you. I love you."

"Be careful driving at night. I love you, too."

* * * *

Once again, Linda had something else to do that kept her away from home in the evening and kept her from going with him to visit Luke. Then when she did get home, there was strong suspicion that she had drunk more than "one glass of wine," which was always her answer when questioned. Driving to Luke's house gave Josh time to contemplate over the many times Linda avoided going to Luke's. *She's uncomfortable being there, even for a short period of time,* thought Josh. *Will she ever change?*

As soon as Josh hit the front door of Luke's house, Jay was all over him. He dragged him over to the television and begged him to watch cartoons. How could he refuse? Jay climbed up in his lap and snuggled as close as he possibly could. Josh couldn't remember when he had last taken time to watch anything on television. The usual animated cartoons were of little interest to Josh, but he enjoyed the closeness of Jay beside him. Luke was busy in the kitchen helping Ann with dinner when it hit Josh. He called to Luke.

"Luke, come here! Quick!" he yelled.

Luke came running, not knowing what to expect.

"Luke, watch the cartoons!" he exclaimed. "Look how they make the characters move their lips and change facial expressions."

What's happening to him? He's talking out of his head, thought Luke. He had to drag Jay away from Josh and into the kitchen for his dinner so the three of them could dine in peace.

"Josh, what are you talking about? You've seen that before."

"It just came to me, Luke," he said, excitedly. "Those are still, inanimate images that they are making move. Think, Luke! If they can make still images move, why couldn't moving images be made to appear still?"

"What are you driving at, Josh?" he asked.

"Think how easy it would be to do a "beating heart" procedure through a scope if the operating field was motionless. Luke, I think it can be done," he said. "Do you remember the movie, 'Forrest Gump'? There was a character who had lost both legs and he was made to appear as a bilateral amputee."

"Ok, Spielberg, how do you propose to research this goofy idea?"

"Laugh if you will," he replied. "Everything starts with an idea. I'm going to see Charles Salzman."

"Let me know when you go," he said, "so I can rescue you when he laughs you out of his office. I can see the word spreading now. Who is that surgeon over at Metcalfe who is going to produce a science-fiction movie?"

"You should go with me, Luke," said Josh. "Charles Salzman is a brilliant man. And believe me, he won't laugh."

"Maybe his good-looking niece will be there," said Luke. "Mrs. Salzman told everyone in the hospital that you should have married her granddaughter."

"Come off it, man!" Josh retorted. "You're trying to aggravate me. How did Ann take the news?"

"Excited as she can possibly be," he answered. "She's really never felt at ease in Dallas."

"I wish I could say the same about Linda. I don't know what to expect when I tell her."

"Leave her here!" Luke said, without the laugh Josh expected.

"Luke, you did it again!" Ann stepped into the room just in time to hear Luke.

"I want you to stop that, Luke," she said. "Josh, I'm sorry. Don't worry; it will all work out fine. I do wish Linda would come visit us more often. Or just come over and visit me."

After dinner, Josh drove home through a sudden downpour, thinking the same as always when he left Luke's home—glad to see the family so happy—but feeling the void in his own marriage. The rhythmic slapping of the windshield wipers lulled him into a pensive state. How would he approach Linda with the offer from Dr. Roever? She would probably be as plastered as she often was after one of her committee meetings. "I just had a second glass of wine," she would say.

No matter how he described opportunities and benefits to her, Josh expected that there would be another shouting quarrel. Josh had to let Dr. Roever know his decision the next morning. He had already made up his mind, but he wanted Linda to hear the proposal before giving Dr. Roever and Dr. Dubonet a final answer.

When Josh reached home, Linda still had not arrived. He worried about her driving at night on streets wet from a recent shower and debated about calling her on her cell phone to see if she needed him to help her drive home. As tired as he was, he needed sleep in the worst way before his early morning case, but he had to stay awake so he could talk to Linda about the move.

He heard tires screech and a car door slammed. She let herself in, unsteady on her feet and acting surprised to see Josh. Josh couldn't help but notice her disheveled appearance and her glassy eyes.

"I thought you would be asleep," she said. Her speech was definitely slurred.

"I stayed up to tell you the news."

"Must be important not to wait until morning," she said, moving toward their bedroom, drifting into the walls of the hallway as she walked.

She's avoiding eye contact with me, thought Josh.

"It is important," he said. "We're moving to Westlake when I finish here."

"We're what?" she screamed and almost fell when she whirled around. "I'm not going to that hick town. You want me to give up life in Dallas—and move to Westlake?"

Josh tried to explain what would be involved with Metcalfe expanding its heart program and the opportunity that lay ahead for him. She paced around the room while she undressed. She had to grab onto furniture to keep from falling.

"We'll talk about it in the morning," he said. "You're in no condition now. You really shouldn't drink so much if you are going to drive, especially with the rain and the wet slippery streets."

"Don't lecture me, Josh!" she exclaimed. "And the first thing you do in the morning is tell that son-of-a-bitch Roever you're staying in Dallas."

She fell into bed, naked for the most part, and passed out. Josh hoped he would be able to talk to her when she was more capable of reasoning. Whatever, he definitely was going to call Dr. Roever's office and confirm the offer. The confrontation with Linda reinforced his determination to get out of Dallas.

* * * *

She was sleeping soundly when he dragged himself out of bed. He could have used a few more hours of sleep. He should be through with his first case in a couple of hours and he would then call Dr. Roever.

He finished the case and immediately called the president's office to leave his message. He was walking down the corridor when he ran into Dr. Van Zant.

"The wives must have had a lively time last night," he said with a chuckle. "I think Linda had a little too much wine."

"What do you mean, Josh?" he replied, an inquisitive look on his face.

"I thought I heard Linda say she had a League meeting at your house."

"No...some mistake, Josh," he said. "Georgia and I dined out and took in a movie."

"She must have said someone else had called a meeting," said Josh, grinning. "I can't keep up with all of her chasing around."

There was not a doubt in his mind that he had heard her correctly. As inebriated as she was, he hoped she hadn't been holed up in some bar somewhere. She would be in such a foul mood after his announcement about the move that he dared not approach her on her drinking. However, her aberrant behavior of late could not be ignored. He had to do something.

With the prospects of leaving Dallas soon, he wanted to follow up on Charles Salzman's invitation to visit his office and laboratory. *What kind of reception will I get from Charles when I approach him on the idea of a motionless operative field?* Josh wondered. *Will he think me meshuga?*

Chapter 27

Josh studied the directory in the well-guarded lobby of the Financial Plaza Building. Salzman Electronics was labeled simply as the eighteenth floor, which meant the executive offices occupied the entire floor. His appointment with Charles was for one-thirty; he was a few minutes early.

After signing in with security with a thumbprint, and after his identity was verified, he was allowed to proceed to the elevators. Once in the elevator, he had to place an imprint of his thumb next to the floor number in order to activate the elevator.

On the eighteenth floor he stepped out of the elevator into an empty lobby and faced a solid black mirrored wall on which was another thumbprint pad. He had an eerie feeling that somewhere, someone was watching his every move.

When he placed his thumbprint on the pad, the black glass wall parted, leaving a doorway to a large anteroom. Two armed security guards sat behind a tall counter. Everywhere Josh looked, from the time he reached the lobby, he saw discretely placed surveillance cameras that constantly scanned the rooms.

Monitors for the cameras must be behind the counter, he thought. He had to go through the identity check again before being allowed in the inner reception area. This time, however, he had to speak his full name into a recording device.

"If you come again, Dr. Lehman," said one of the Salzman guards, his hand extended for a handshake, "you'll only have to speak your name to gain entrance. Sorry for the inconvenience, but we have to be extra cautious here."

"No problem," Josh said, still astounded at the thoroughness of the security checks.

A smiling receptionist motioned for him to follow her. She led him into a massive, well-appointed office with a panoramic view of downtown Dallas. Charles rose from his desk immediately and greeted him.

"Josh, nice of you to visit. I'm told you initiated this appointment," he said.

"Yes, I did," he replied. "First, how is your mother?"

"How kind of you to ask. She's fine, thanks to you, Josh," he said. "At least once a week she asks me to take her by to see you. I tell her that you are busy. That doesn't stop her."

"Please do bring her in," said Josh. "It's always a pleasure to visit her. She is a unique lady."

"She asks me also why you don't come to Friday evening services at Temple Shalom sometime," he said.

"I know that I should. I keep telling myself that. Some day, maybe."

After they visited for awhile, discussing generalities in the medical world, Charles turned to Josh.

"Josh, I want to show you my personal laboratory," he said.

He reached over and pressed a code number into a dial on his desk. With a whirring noise, surveillance cameras dropped down from the ceiling and a door that at first appeared to be a wall panel slowly slid open. Josh followed Charles into a large brightly-lit room, filled with electronic equipment with complex control panels and monitors of various sizes.

"This is where I do most of my work. Much of what you see here are simulators. I can bring into focus every piece of equipment that we produce and put it into a simulation mode. What you see on the screen then is an exact replica of the imaging that it is designed for. Let me show you an example. I'll walk you through a heart catheterization procedure and you'll see what I mean."

"Awesome!" said Josh, glancing in wonderment at the expansive array of technical instruments, not knowing which to look at first.

"This is what I'm working on right now," said Charles. "We are developing a catheter with a tiny scope on the tip that will allow the operator to actually visualize the vessel opening and the lining of the vessel that the catheter enters."

"Unbelievable!" said Josh. "We can actually determine if there is ulceration of any plaque on the wall of an artery that we enter."

"Correct," said Charles. "Also, Josh, we are constantly working to improve our stents—not only those for the coronary arteries but also for the many other vessels that could be stented."

He let Josh try some procedure simulations which led to a discussion of the thoracoscope. Josh went through a simulated scoping of a lung lesion. He felt as though he was performing a biopsy of a lung tumor with a scope. He encountered the same problems of working on a moving target that he wanted to discuss with Charles.

They went back into his office. As they did so, the door gradually slid shut and the cameras receded into the ceiling. Josh couldn't distinguish which panel was the door.

"Why all the cameras, Charles?" asked Josh.

"We record and date everything that happens in this office. Every visitor's identity is recorded and kept on file. Much of that is for patent protection purposes. This is a very competitive business, Josh. Other companies are constantly trying to duplicate our products. They will go to extremes to steal our designs and ideas."

"There are no other manufacturers locally that are competitors, are there?" asked Josh.

"There are a few smaller companies, but they mostly make replacement parts and renovate older equipment. The only real competitor is Scoetec," said Charles. "It is a fairly large company that moved here a couple of years ago. They are trying desperately to capture some of our market and some of the confidential information on our products. The company started in Taiwan and somehow was acquired by Bradford Holdings and was moved here.

"Bradford is unscrupulous in their dealings. We are always on the alert for patent infringements. Also, they have made some token efforts to raid and take over our company. Fortunately, family and loyal employees own a sizable block of our stock, and we are always able to block any attempt of a raid. It's always a threat."

Charles had a tray of bottled water and soft drinks with snacks brought in for the two of them while they talked. Josh decided he wouldn't tell Charles about his relationship with Donnie from years past. It would serve no purpose to admit that he even knew Donnie. While they conversed, Josh had the opportunity to talk to Charles about the main reason he was there.

"Luke says you are going to roll on the floor laughing about the idea I have," said Josh.

"I never laugh at ideas," replied Charles. "We take all suggestions seriously, Josh. That is what has made this company."

"Your mother has given me much of the background of Salzman Electronics—a fascinating story."

"Then you can appreciate that my brothers and I have a lot to live up to," said Charles. "Oh, forgive me, Josh. Back to your idea. Of course I want to hear it."

Josh described to Charles that one of the difficulties using the scope for heart and lung procedures was the pulsation of a beating heart and the movement of the lungs breathing that caused the operative field to move.

"My idea is this: if the field, with the use of the scope, could be made to appear motionless during the operation, there would be a tremendous benefit, both from the ease in performing the procedure and from the reduced time in the operating room."

"If the images of inanimate objects or animals can be changed to show facial movements, for example, could not that process be reversed in the operative field—projecting an image of a motionless field, while in reality there is movement? Is that too wild to even consider?"

Charles was quiet for several seconds. He swiveled his chair around to face the window, with his back to Josh, as he gazed out across the city, to all appearances lost in. deep thought. *Anyway, he didn't laugh,* Josh thought to himself. After a while Charles turned back to face Josh.

"I think you may have a very valid idea," he said. "We may be able to do it. In these few seconds, I can think of innumerable obstacles that would have to be overcome. Synchronizing the camera light rays with the rhythm of the heart or lung movement—a different rhythm for every patient, developing instruments that you could use that would not be affected by the magnetic rays of the camera—just to name a few."

Charles turned away from Josh again and gazed out the window as if in deep thought. After a period of time that seemed endless, he swiveled his chair and faced Josh.

"Josh, I am going to get our engineers on this," said Charles. "I can't answer your question right now. I hope you have not mentioned this to anyone else."

"Only to Luke, and he accused me of getting too close to his anesthesia gas," said Josh with a laugh.

"I promise you, we'll work on it. It is not a wild idea," Charles said. "While we are in a research mode, I'd like for you to drop by here as often as you can to check our progress. Whatever the engineers develop, I'll have access to it right here in my laboratory."

"I can hardly wait to tell Luke that you didn't call the goon squad on me," said Josh. "I will tell him that you don't want this mentioned to anyone. You have no worry there."

"Thanks for coming in, Josh," he said, "I am looking forward to your return visits. And I'll tell my mother you were here. She'll be mad that I didn't drag you home for dinner—which, incidentally, would be a good idea some day."

"Give her my regards, Charles," he said. "I think of her often."

They shook hands and Josh left, reversing the process of going through the same security checks that he had passed through when he entered. Once in the high security parking garage level, exclusive for Salzman Electronics, he found his car and backed out of the parking space to exit. Everywhere he looked he saw surveillance cameras tracking his every move. *Is all this necessary?* he asked himself. *What else is going on in this company?*

He guided his car into the late afternoon traffic and headed back into the real world. Why pursue this crazy idea with Salzman? He had enough challenges ahead. Of highest priority was his personal conflict. He turned over and over in his mind the dilemma he faced with Linda's attitude about moving to Westlake and with her drinking. How could he deal with anything else? Something was driving him on.

Chapter 28

Linda's pouting about the move to Westlake didn't keep her from her social whirl. She continued to come home late at night, long after Josh had gone to sleep. Josh decided not to question her about the night she had lied about being at the Van Zants' for a meeting. Probably she would only reply with another lie. He was now concerned about her alcohol problem—more so than about her pouting.

As usual, when she went into a pouting phase she compensated by going out and buying something—always something that they couldn't afford. Josh rarely paid attention to the bank account statement, but after the last expensive purchase, he checked the account to see how much more he was going to have to borrow to cover overdrafts.

He was appalled at how deeply they were in debt. What really disturbed him were the unexplained cash withdrawals from the bank. He didn't want to question her about it with her being in such a foul mood. He just didn't want to foment another tirade. Their relationship continued to deteriorate as they neared the time to make the move. Josh needed her to go with him to Westlake to arrange for housing, but she refused. She acted as if she had no intention of leaving Dallas.

Josh was totally distraught over what to do. He was afraid his mental turmoil would affect his work. He certainly couldn't afford to let that happen. What could he do? He felt like everything was closing in on him.

He needed to go to Westlake, make contact with the medical staff there, and confer with the planning group on the new hospital. Winding up his work at the hospital and the clinic consumed time. He had records to complete, referral letters to write, and multiple last minute details to attend to. Farewell events had already been planned. This was a time when he desperately needed help from his wife.

Luke and Ann were busily making arrangements to move, finding housing in Westlake, and locating a school for Jay. Josh hesitated to take his personal problem to them. He missed not being able to see Jay as much as he would like, but pressure on his time kept him away. Linda now absolutely refused to visit Luke and Ann under any circumstances, continually saying Ann had been telling untruths about her.

Charles Salzman expected him to make regular visits to his laboratory during the development stage of the new scope. He had to find time to keep that relationship kindled. If the motionless field imaging could be accomplished, ultimately it would mean better quality of patient care with fewer deaths and lower cost of care.

Linda was asleep when he arose early to get ready for another seven o'clock case in the operating room. It was a complex case, and Dr. Dubonet was going to assist him. Dr. Dubonet was always prompt in starting his cases on time and Josh did not want to be even one minute late.

Linda had come home late, as usual, from another of her purported meetings, and from the looks of clothing scattered about the room she was inebriated when she arrived. Her purse had hit the floor and snapped open, scattering the contents over the floor.

Josh bent down to pick up the purse and gather the spilled articles to replace them in her purse. Two things immediately caught his attention: one, an unlabeled bottle of pills that he could not identify, and the other, a small plastic bag containing a fine white crystalline powder.

Next he found a receipt from a pawn shop. He checked her dresser where she kept her jewelry, and found that several pieces that he remembered her having were missing. Overcome with rage, he crumpled the pawn ticket and placed it in his pocket.

He had to leave shortly in order to reach the hospital in time for his surgical case, but before leaving he took a small sample of the powder and one of the pills and placed each in an empty medicine bottle. He carefully replaced all of the scattered objects back in the purse and left it lying on the floor.

He knew what the report from his friend Jeff Wahlberg, the director of the laboratory, would be before he heard the words. Josh told Jeff the samples were found in a patient's room, and he needed an unofficial analysis in order to determine how to deal with the problem. Cocaine and methamphetamine! Josh felt his throat tighten. Thoughts raced wildly through his head.

"This can't be happening!" he whispered to himself. "How did this happen?"

Then he recalled Linda's unusual behavior after they moved into the condo, soon after they married. He had been amazed at how she maintained such a busy schedule—club activities, country club tennis matches, shopping for their new home, and still working shifts in the ICU. And then the unexplained weight loss and the mood swings—euphoria alternating with despondency! *How dumb can I be?* he thought. She was being fueled by "speed" and "coke"! How could he have missed it?

What can I do? Josh wondered. *I can't think of a worse situation—moving into a new town, starting a practice, and bringing a wife who was a "coke" addict.*

He had to talk to Luke. He wanted to salvage this marriage if it was at all possible. He had to put Linda's welfare first. The move could be delayed if necessary. In spite of what he had gone though, he still felt a deep attachment to her. He felt a strong sense of guilt about the whole thing. If he hadn't been so intensely involved with his training and had devoted more time to their marriage, this might not have happened. He felt guilty also that he hadn't detected it before. *I should have known,* thought Josh.

* * * *

"Luke, can you meet with me this afternoon?" Josh asked when Luke answered his cell phone.

"What's wrong?"

"Who said anything was wrong?"

"Something has happened, Josh. I know you too well," Luke replied. "I'll be through here in thirty minutes."

"I need your help, Luke," he pleaded.

"You've got it. I'm in O.R. 18. I'll get someone to take over for me."

The dressing room between 16 and 18 was empty. Josh looked through the glass panel into 18 and saw Luke make last minute adjustments to the anesthetic gas manifold and talk to someone in scrubs, apparently one of the junior residents. The surgeons had already left the room. Luke turned and entered the dressing room.

"Josh, you look like shit. What the hell is wrong?" asked Luke.

Josh told him the whole story and ended it with the finding of the "coke" and speed, the missing jewelry, and the pawnshop receipts.

Luke said nothing for several seconds. His head slumped forward, he covered his forehead with the palm of his hand and stared at the floor. When he finally broke the silence he said, "Josh, how have you lived with this alone?"

"I guess I just couldn't believe it was true. What can I do, Luke?"

"You don't have too many options," he replied. He stood and paced around the room, kicking discarded scrubs on the floor out of his way.

"If you don't act quickly, you could be wiped out. Think what would happen if she bought from an undercover agent and they raided your home and found illegal drugs. Your career would be wiped out. You've been lucky so far. Any DWI arrests?"

"None that I know of."

"Is she screwing anybody?"

"I don't know," he replied. "Our sex life has been zilch for months."

"You could just walk away, you know; but I know you are not going to do that," said Luke. "The next option will be to try to get her to voluntarily agree to treatment. If she refuses, you can forcibly commit her. If you do that, you lose your chance of keeping this quiet, and you could lose her."

"I don't think she would ever agree to go into a treatment center," said Josh. "I don't know how I would pay for it. I am already so heavy in debt."

"We need a psychiatrist who specializes in substance abuse. If it becomes necessary for her to be admitted to a center, we'll find the money. I'll help you, Josh."

"I can't ask you to do that, Luke. You have a family to provide for and you're making a move that is going to be costly. I couldn't do it."

"You're not asking, Josh. I'm telling you," said Luke. "You know how I feel about Linda, but I know you care for her, and we care for you. So let's take one step at a time," he added. "First, you have to confront her, even if it does make her angry. Next, I'll check out the shrinks and find out what's available. Whatever you do, don't say anything to anyone."

Chapter 29

Josh signed out to one of the senior residents at the Heart Institute. Without going into detail, he explained to Dr. Dubonet that he had a family emergency and would need to be gone for two or three days. He called Mel Jacobson at Human Resources about his "paid time off" status.

"You have almost reached the max again, Josh," he said. "I've already heard about your move. You'll still be on our payroll, so you may want to sell some of your hours back to the company. I suggest you wait until you take on the new position. Your accumulated hours will be worth more then. We will miss you around here, Josh."

"Thanks, Mel. I'll still be in and out of here, I'm told," he replied. "Thanks a lot for your help."

"Oh, Josh," he said. "Linda was in here a few days ago and formally resigned and cashed in all of her hours. I guess you knew that."

"Yeah...thanks again, Mel."

Another blow! *She is going to extremes to get cash,* thought Josh. He had hoped he could convince Linda to help him plan the Heart ICU in Westlake. Maybe if they worked together like they used to, they could recapture some of the devotion and mutual respect they once shared. Now she was acting as if she wouldn't even make the move.

He was on his way home when he received Luke's call.

"Josh, I just thought of Jim Mayfield. He's the assistant director of the Psyche Unit at Metcalfe and is in charge of detox. He also manages private patients. He's a nice guy. He has a kid in Jay's kindergarten class. I think he may be the one to turn to for this. Let me ask him."

"Fine, Luke," he said. "I'm almost home now. Who knows what I'll find, but go ahead and ask him. I'm taking a few days off, so I'll be available. Psyches don't like third parties in the picture, so tread cautiously. Try to get him to agree to see me without telling him too much."

"I agree," he replied. "Good luck with Linda."

"I'll need it."

* * * *

He surprised Linda when he let himself in through the back door. She must have just awakened—puffiness of her face, eyes glassy, disheveled hair, wearing nothing more than one of Josh's old T-shirts. She was seated on a bar stool, and as Josh entered, was reaching for a half empty vodka bottle that Josh remembered as being almost full the night before. A lit cigarette smoldered in an ash tray on the counter top.

"What are you doing home?" she demanded, frowning, the bottle still in hand and ready to be poured. She appeared neither embarrassed nor disturbed that he had found her in that situation.

"We need to talk, Linda," he said.

"Is this going to be a lecture, Josh?" she snapped. "Like, we agreed I wouldn't smoke in the house?"

"A little more serious," he said. "You need help, Linda, and I want to help you. I love you and care for you. I want you to be the same person you were when we poured our hearts out to each other."

"What about you? All you do is work! That's all you care about!"

"Linda, I work for both of us. I want you to be my partner in work. We are starting a new life, a new venture. I need you! I need for you to get off alcohol and get off drugs. Let's start a new life together."

When he mentioned drugs, she stiffened and jerked her head around, glaring at Josh.

"What do you mean 'drugs?'" she retorted.

"Last night when you came in, you dropped your purse and the contents were scattered over the floor."

"You son-of-a-bitch!" she screamed. "You were snooping around in my purse! How low can you get?"

"Linda, I hoped you'd be reasonable about this."

"Reasonable?" she yelled. "You be reasonable! Get your ass out of here and leave me alone! I don't need your help!"

"Linda, look at me! You're hooked! You're a professional. You know the signs as well as I do. You can't stop the craving without help. You'll do any and every thing to seek drugs. We can whip this together, but you have to admit that you are in trouble."

She was quiet and pensive for several seconds. *Had he reached her?* he wondered. But then she deliberately poured an almost-full glass of vodka and started sipping on it without any mixer.

"Come on, Josh!" she said. "You're not worried about me. You're worried about yourself, afraid I'll embarrass you."

"That's not true, Linda," said Josh.

"I can hear Ann now, telling everyone in Westlake: 'Oh, yes, Josh has a wife. She's a drug addict.'"

"Linda, let us help you," Josh pleaded.

"Take your goddamn precious Luke, Ann, and Jay and go! I want to be rid of all of you!" she said. "Let 'us' help you. Ha!"

She stood, staggering as she tried to walk, and then swept her arm across the counter top, sending the glass, bottle, and ash tray crashing to the floor.

"Linda, please," said Josh.

She made no attempt to clean up the mess. She sat in a chair and looked at Josh with a pitiable expression on her face and began crying. Josh came to her side, kneeled on the floor and placed his arms around her.

"What do you want me to do, Josh?" she asked.

"Get under the care of a qualified alcohol and drug abuse specialist and follow his recommendations."

"What if he recommends a treatment center?"

"Then that's what it should be."

"I'm not going to any group therapy sessions, Josh."

"Just get well, Linda, please!"

She fell into his arms and sobbed. Josh held her closely and kissed her tenderly.

"I've missed you, Josh. I haven't been a good wife, have I?"

"Don't look back. We have such a great future ahead."

"Make love to me, Josh," she said, between sobs.

He picked her up and carried her to their bedroom. She pulled off her T-shirt and began undressing him. They melted into each others arms, their bodies welded together as one.

* * * *

Josh was jolted from a sound slumber by the faint sound of his cell phone vibrating. Linda was asleep at his side. He looked at the clock. They had been lying there, detached from the rest of the world, for over an hour. He punched the "talk" button.

"Dr. Lehman," said Josh.

"Are you all right?" asked Luke.

"Yes," replied Josh, without elaborating.

"Jim Mayfield will see you when you're ready."

"Thanks," he answered.

Linda roused briefly, dropped back asleep for a few moments, then opened her eyes and faced Josh. He smiled at her. She sat up in bed and pulled him close to her.

"Please don't leave me, Josh," she pleaded. "What's next?"

"We'll get an appointment with Dr. Mayfield. We'll go together. I won't leave you," he assured her.

"Who is Dr. Mayfield?" she asked.

"He's a psychiatrist. He can help us, Linda," said Josh. "That call confirmed that he would see us. I need to call him."

"Fine," she replied, covering her head with the pillow. Josh dialed the number given him by Luke.

"Dr. Mayfield, this is Josh Lehman. I'm a senior resident at Metcalfe Heart. Thank you for taking my call."

"I have been expecting your call. How can I help you?"

Josh described briefly what his concerns were about Linda. Dr. Mayfield politely interrupted him before he could continue in detail.

"Dr. Lehman, before you go any further, let me tell you this. I will be glad to see your wife. There is one restriction that you need to be aware of: she must voluntarily contact me for an appointment. After I have evaluated her, we can all get together and discuss treatment options, if in fact treatment is needed."

"I understand, sir," said Josh.

"Will she be calling soon?" said Dr. Mayfield. "It sounds rather urgent from what you and Dr. Sanders have told me so far."

"She's sitting by my side right now, sir," said Josh.

"I'll transfer you to my appointment secretary. Put her on the line."

* * * *

Linda hurriedly went through the process of dressing and making herself presentable for the early afternoon appointment. She was already shaking a little. She reached into the cabinet above the bar counter and picked up another vodka bottle, started to uncap it, and then put it back. She glanced at Josh, standing by patiently, watching her.

"You don't trust me, do you, Josh?" she asked.

"Why do you say that?"

"It's like you're standing here guarding the bar," she said.

"I'm here for you, Linda. I have to trust you."

"I can't do it, Josh," she said and moved forward and reached out for the vodka bottle, then she looked into Josh's sad eyes and at his deeply furrowed brow. "Yes I can!" she exclaimed, and continued to dress.

* * * *

The two-hour wait in Dr. Mayfield's waiting room was the longest two hours he had ever spent. He could do a mitral valve replacement procedure in less time. The waiting room was empty and quiet, far different from the waiting room in his post-operative surgery clinic.

Dr. Mayfield emerged from his inner office and invited him to come in. A tearful Linda, sitting across from his desk, looked pitiful with her head hanging down, dobbing at her mask-like face with a tissue. Josh sat in the chair next to her and took her hand in his. He felt uncomfortable, as if the psychiatrist scrutinized his every movement and reaction.

"Dr. Lehman—I'm going to call you 'Josh' unless you tell me otherwise," he said. "I would like for you to call me Jim."

"That's fine, sir," said Josh.

"And please, leave off the 'sir,'" he laughed. "This is not the surgery department."

"Josh," he continued. "Linda and I have had a very productive session. Let me tell you this; I will only speak to you about Linda in her presence so you can hear what she says and she can hear what you say. This may have been one element that has been missing in your marriage. Possibly neither of you has communicated optimally with the other, for whatever reason."

"Let me begin with telling you my opinion. There's no question that Linda has a problem. From my one brief encounter, I believe it stems back to a very disruptive, dysfunctional family environment as a child. Her father abused her mother and abandoned both of them when Linda was quite young."

"She has never recovered from that emotional trauma. Without her knowing it, she is guilt-ridden from the ideation that she was responsible for her father leaving, that she was a disappointment to him. The result at this age for her is this: she is lashing out at the world for her loss, she is punishing you by her behavior, and she is punishing you and society by not having children."

"That's a synopsis of how this has happened to her. I won't go into depth with either of you until I have had several more sessions with her. Do either of you have any questions so far before we go into the urgent need?"

"Why is she punishing me? What have I done?" asked Josh.

"You've committed nothing, Josh," he replied. "You possibly omitted a few things in your marriage that can be corrected. Linda equates her relationship with you to that with her father. Remember, she is not consciously aware of this. When she punishes you, she is punishing her father."

Dr. Mayfield paused for a few seconds to let his words find the receptor centers in Josh's brain. He avoided eye contact with either Josh or Linda as he pretended to straighten objects that covered his desk top. After a while he continued.

"In her subconscious mind, she sees you as a male image who will abandon her, just as her father did. As a necessary part of your training, you have been forced to neglect your marital responsibilities to some extent. Linda sees this as abandonment."

Josh became pensive and gazed out the window. He could appreciate what Dr. Mayfield said. With counseling, that hang-up of Linda's could be treated and resolved. He just needed to make an effort to be more understanding of the demon that Linda is fighting and to be more attentive. He told himself that he could do that.

"What about her immediate need?" asked Josh.

"Linda will need a few days of detoxification and close observation for any serious withdrawal effects. This will be followed by about three to four weeks of treatment as a patient in the center. Linda has very good insight. I am impressed with her response to what I have said so far. Her outlook is very good, Josh."

Josh turned to Linda, tears still streaming down her face, and put his arm around her. She looked up at him with that lovable expression that had always enthralled him.

"I'm so sorry, Josh," she said. "I understand what Dr. Mayfield is saying. I want to get well. I love you, Josh."

"I love you too," he replied. "We'll beat this. I'm with you all the way."

"Josh, in order for her to show true commitment to her wish to get well, she has agreed to being admitted right now," said Dr. Mayfield.

"I'll go get her clothes," said Josh.

"For the first few days during the detox phase we ask that you not visit. We'll let you know when. During the treatment phase, families may visit weekly—on Sunday afternoons."

"Thank you for helping us, Jim."

"She'll do fine, Josh," he said.

Josh had to tear himself away. Linda avoided eye contact with him as he was leaving. Her head drooped, and he could detect a tremor in her hands when she moved. He exited Dr. Mayfield's office and as he walked away toward the parking lot he said to himself in an almost inaudible voice, "We have done the right thing, but it will be easier to accept if I stay busy while she is in the center."

Chapter 30

Over a month had passed since Josh had presented his idea to Charles Salzman. He visited Charles' laboratory any time he was asked—usually to give an opinion on an improvement being made on one of the other Salzman operative instruments. If Charles was not present, Josh dictated his report into the tape recorder.

Josh now had free access to the highest security areas in the building by simply speaking his name or pressing the fingerprint pad. The simulators fascinated him every time he visited the laboratory. On more than one occasion, using them so absorbed him that he was late for appointments in the clinic.

Charles had sent him a message that he wanted him to stop by at his convenience for an update on the MIS—the name they had dubbed his idea for the motionless imaging scope. He made his way through the security checks once again, was met in the office by the secretary, and was led immediately into Charles' office.

"We think we have a breakthrough, Josh!" said Charles, the broad smile on his face signaling good news. "The engineers are excited about the project. They are reasonably certain it can be achieved."

"Great news, Charles!" said Josh. "What is the time line? I'm ready for it to be in place now."

"Josh, remember that anything new like this takes months to develop and perfect before it can be marketed," said Charles. "We will test the first model of the product on animals. This will require months of documenting results, defects, and finally the outcome. The testing will be highly confidential, Josh. Trained technicians will do the preliminary testing and the filming of their procedures will be downloaded on the simulators here at the same time that they are being performed.

"Here is where you come in, Josh. As often as possible, when we go live on animals, I would like for you to be here in the laboratory. I know your time is limited, and I propose we unveil this whole concept to Dr. Dubonet and solicit his blessings on the time you spend here."

"You will gain by the notoriety of conceiving this innovation, Josh; we will gain by your expertise with the equipment in my laboratory. Also, we gain by enhancing our relationship with one of our large customers, and Metcalfe gains by an exclusive usage contract in the entire state."

"I'm excited, of course!" said Josh. "But Charles, you know that I'm moving to Westlake. I'll still be with Metcalfe, but I won't be living in Dallas."

"I know that, Josh," he said. "We've thought of that, but with our private jet you are only minutes away. We know Metcalfe's plans for Westlake. When it is fully developed, we believe the volume at Metcalfe Heart Institute, Westlake, will be tremendous," he added. "Whatever else can be said about my brother, Phillip, he has never been wrong in his market analyses."

"When will you meet with Dr. Dubonet?" asked Josh.

"As soon as possible," he replied. "I want to describe the project to him personally."

"I think he'll be as enthusiastic as I am," replied Josh. "Look, Charles, I'm not looking for recognition for this idea. You guys develop it, and if you can make it work, that's all the reward I want. Your people deserve the credit."

"You're too modest, Josh."

"I can live with that," he laughed. "Anything new with your mom?"

"She's fine," he replied. "Still drives us wild at the board meetings."

"Deal with it, Charles," Josh said with a laugh.

"She asks about you a lot. Oh, my niece sends her regards."

Josh felt his face turning red and hoped Charles didn't notice.

"Thanks, Charles. Keep in touch."

*   *   *   *

Josh saw Linda every visitors' day. The change that had come over her amazed him. She was bright and alert and relaxed. She seemed happy to see him and happy just to stroll together through the garden, discussing the move to Westlake and plans for their married life anew after she was discharged.

"I want to start over, Josh," she said. "I've wasted so many days that I can never recover."

"We'll make up for lost time," said Josh.

"I'm so embarrassed for putting you through so much turmoil."

"Don't give it a thought. It is such a delight to see you looking so well. You should go without make-up more often," he laughed. "Makes you look bedroomish."

"I need to look ICUish, Josh," she said. "I want to go back to work. I think about it every day."

"Are you ready for that?"

"Yeah. I've been taking refresher courses on the Metcalfe Education Web site. I'll be ready to dive back in soon."

"Good, as long as you don't overdo it. Have you asked Dr. Mayfield?"

"He just says, 'Re-enter slowly.'"

"I'll bring you some pictures of the condo. I think you'll like it. It's much like our place here…the same amenities."

"Don't bother, Josh," she said. "Surprise me."

"I'll ask Ann to help me pack, if that's OK with you."

"Sure," she replied. "I feel so helpless, depending on other people for so many things."

"That's short term. You're getting out soon."

"I'm ready, Josh," she said.

They found a bench on the bank of the small lake. Ducks and geese swam around the fountain in the center. They sat as close together as they possibly could. Linda leaned her head against Josh's shoulder.

"I want to go home, Josh. Take me home. I just want to be near you."

"In due time, loved one."

She hung on to Josh tightly, silently asking him to stay. He had to tear himself away when it came time to leave, but took solace in knowing that soon Linda would be ready to come home with him.

✶   ✶   ✶   ✶

Josh's last few days at Metcalfe, Dallas, were filled with winding up his affairs at the hospital. He had records to sign and complete and farewell visits with the many friends he had made. He got a little nostalgic about leaving a place that had been his home and his life for so many years.

During his final days at Metcalfe, he often walked purposelessly through the hospital corridors and operating suites, greeting everyone he met. Sometimes he just sat in the doctors' lounges for no reason and reminisced about the many experiences he had faced—some humorous, some tragic, all educational.

He was grateful that he had been given the opportunity to train at Metcalfe, especially under Dr. Dubonet's mentoring; he was ready to go out into the world and put into practice the skills he had acquired.

The day arrived that he had looked forward to for so long—the end of years of training. Still, it saddened him seeing his name on the surgery schedule and knowing that these were the last cases he would do at Metcalfe. It looked like another busy day, packed with two high-intensity procedures. The first was assisting Dr. Dubonet on a thoracic aortic aneurysm resection. Dr. Dubonet was listed as the lead surgeon, but Josh knew from past experience that his mentor expected him to do the procedure.

Just before going into the operating room, Josh noticed that their second case had been canceled for some reason. *This will give me a chance to talk to Dr. Dubonet about what's expected of me in Westlake,* he thought.

While sitting together in the lounge, sipping coffee after finishing the first case—a three hour ordeal—Josh glanced at the aging "dean of cardiovascular surgery" with admiration. He wondered if he could ever achieve such stature.

"Nice job, Josh," said Dr. Dubonet. "Ready to face the world?"

"It's scary!" Josh responded.

"Watching you in there just now, you're ready for anything," he said. "I'm gonna miss you around here, Josh."

"Do you think this Westlake move is the best thing for me?"

"Great opportunity!" he replied "As much as I'd like for you to stay here, I can see what you will be able to accomplish there. It will be a challenge. But we all do better when we have challenges, don't we, Josh?"

"I think you've proven that," Josh answered. "You have a reputation for exploring the unknown, going where others have feared to tread."

"It hasn't been easy, Josh. Lots of criticism, a few failures. But it's been fun. You'll see."

"I'm a little apprehensive about what is expected of me from an administrative standpoint."

"You'll handle it OK," he said. "You'll have a well-staffed, well-equipped office. You should start contacting doctors on the Westlake Regional medical staff right away. Let them know who you are, what you're doing. Let them know about plans for the heart hospital."

"You think they'll accept that?"

"Sure," Dr. Dubonet replied. "Patients are leaving there and going to larger centers for their surgery. They'll welcome the chance to keep their patients in Westlake. You're going to build a major center, Josh!"

"Has Charles Salzman talked with you about the new scope that is being developed?"

"Yes, he did," he said. "Exciting! Absolutely incredible! You know how I like innovative ideas, Josh. You must keep up your relationship with Salzman. They need your advice on new projects like this...and there will be more to come."

"I agree it's intriguing, but I'm worried if I will have time for all this—building a practice, helping with the hospital plans, consulting with Salzman Electronics..."

"Don't worry," Dr. Dubonet reassured. "You'll find time. Metcalfe wants you to continue with your consultation role, both with Salzman and with the planning and developing the hospital."

"Thanks for you help, Dr. Dubonet," said Josh. "I guess I'm a little despondent about leaving here, maybe a little scared, leaving the comfort and security that I have enjoyed so much...leaving you."

"Hey, Josh, you're not leaving me!" the elder surgeon said, with an ear to ear smile, as he slapped Josh across the shoulders. "For one thing, I'll be right by your side in spirit every time you walk into the operating room. You're taking part of me with you, man. And another thing, you will be called back here with some frequency to help me with complex cases. I have faith in you, Josh."

Josh could feel his throat tighten and his eyes moisten as he faced his role model and educator.

"Thank you, sir," he said. "I won't let you down."

"I know you won't," said Dr. Dubonet. "How are the moving plans coming along?"

I'm sure he's heard about Linda's problem, for he has made no mention or inquiry of her welfare, thought Josh. *He is just being considerate of my feelings, but maybe he needs to know the whole story.*

"Fine," he replied, with some hesitation. "We're packed and ready to leave. We've already found a condo in Westlake, so we'll be making the move in a few days. I still have a lot of last minute details to attend to before we go."

"Good luck, Josh," said the elder surgeon, and surprised Josh with a hug.

"Sir," asked Josh, "are you aware that my wife, Linda, has been in a treatment center?"

"Josh," he replied, showing no astonishment, "I hear rumors all of the time. I get concerned only if what I hear seems to adversely affect an individual's performance. I have not seen that with you. Remember, Josh, I am here to help you in any way if you need me."

"Thank you, sir," he said. *Just the response I would have expected,* thought Josh. *He is telling me that he is not interested in sordid details, but is confident that I can deal with whatever happens. He has confidence in me—just like Coach Staggs did years ago after I had been sacked twice with the fourth down coming up. It's just another game.*

Josh's exuberance about starting a new life in Westlake with Linda was tempered with his sadness of breaking up the strong relationships he had cultivated at Metcalfe, Dallas, but with this kind of support from Dr Dubonet, he was now ready to move on and would carry with him pleasant memories of his days at Metcalfe.

Josh changed out of his scrubs and into his street clothes. He took one last look around the locker room, thinking how many times he had dressed and undressed there—going into or returning from the operating room. He thought about the many times when he had met with apprehensive family members to report on the outcome of a difficult heart surgery case—often bringing good news, but sometimes bad.

With memories of the ten years of training at Metcalfe flashing through his mind, he opened the dressing room door to meet a throng of the cardiac surgery unit personnel. A table with cake, coffee, and drinks had been placed in front of a large banner which read: "We'll Miss You, Dr. Lehman." Dr Dubonet stood by with that charismatic smile on his face and handed Josh a knife.

"Will you please carve the cake, Dr. Lehman?"

"Will you assist?" replied Josh with a chuckle.

"I will be honored."

"Was that second case really canceled?" asked Josh.

"You'll never know," said Dr. Dubonet, with a twinkle in his eyes.

* * * *

As Josh left the building, he felt his cell phone vibrate. It was Charles's secretary.

"Dr. Lehman, Mr. Salzman asked me to call you and see if you could come by the laboratory. You'll be leaving town soon?" she asked.

"Yes, in a few days," he replied. "Is Mr. Salzman there today?"

"He'll be out of town for several days, but he left taped messages for you," she said. "He hoped that you could come by before you left Dallas."

"I'll come by this afternoon, if that's all right."

"That'll be fine," she replied. "Engineering brought over a disc. I think that may be what Mr. Salzman wanted to talk to you about."

"I'll be there within the hour."

Josh entered the building lobby as he had done so many times before and was met by the same building security guards. Every time he went through the access procedure in the building entrance lobby, there was one security guard who seemed to be especially curious about his visits.

"Back to see Mr. Salzman?" the guard asked.

"Yes, sir," Josh replied, as he submitted to the identity process.

"A lot of people go up there every day."

"It's a busy place," said Josh.

"You must be one of those engineers from the Salzman plant?"

"No, sir," Josh replied and chuckled. "Guess I just look like an engineer."

"Just wondering," he said. "See you in here pretty often. Work for Mr. Salzman?"

"No, just a friend," said Josh.

Josh saw the green light flash, showing he was cleared to proceed, so he turned toward the elevator before the guard could ask another question. Ordinarily the building lobby attendants were friendly and courteous when he would come and go. Was this guy probing for information? Josh decided he was being overly suspicious and put the thought out of mind.

Charles had left the familiar access-controlled message tape. After clearing the code, Josh listened to the message in a sound-proof booth designed especially for transmitting confidential messages. In addition to wishing him well on his move to Westlake, Charles wanted Josh's opinion on an upgraded piece of equipment that his engineers had just finished.

After he reviewed the disc from the engineering department on the simulator, Josh dictated his report, returned the cassette to the secretary, and began to reverse the access procedure in order to exit the office suite. Even though Josh had become familiar with the Salzman armed guards at the office entrance, he still was required to go through the same identity verification. He thought it a little extreme, but couldn't find fault in anything Charles Salzman did—including his strict security measures.

Once he was in the main building lobby, he went to the elevator that took him down to the parking level designated exclusively for Salzman employees.

After pressing his thumbprint to exit, he stepped off the brightly-lit elevator into the darkened garage and walked toward his parked car. He beeped the car door lock and reached for the door handle when he caught a glimpse of movement in the shadows near the fire exit door. He hesitated a moment, then opened the car door and prepared to start the engine.

In his rearview mirror he saw the fire exit door open and close, but he could not identify the person leaving. The fire exit doors were clearly marked with warnings that opening the door would trigger an alarm, but there was no alarm, so it must have been deactivated. He reached for his cell phone to notify the secretary in Charles's office of the incident, and then decided that it was not worthy of any serious concern. Anyway, there were too many more pressing issues hanging over him right then.

* * * *

The moving van arrived, and with Ann's help and supervision, they emptied the condo and packed the van for transfer to Westlake. Josh packed a handful of necessities to keep behind for his use while he waited a few days until Linda could leave the center.

The day arrived finally for her discharge. Josh waited in Dr. Mayfield's office for their exit conference. When Linda came in, she looked beautiful—no extreme make-up, simple dress, a relaxed, self-assured expression on her face.

It reminded Josh of the way she looked in the early morning, lying in bed after awakening, opening her eyes and smiling at him with that entrancing look before they made love. To Josh she was more alluring at those moments than at any other time.

The exit conference was brief. Dr. Mayfield advised them to continue their regular visits for counseling, even though they would be living in Westlake. He wanted to see them as a couple each week for a while. Later he could transfer their follow-up visits to someone in Westlake.

The shocker came when he told them that they should wait at least a year before even considering pregnancy. They both had discussed children and both showed disappointment at the recommendation. Without asking, Josh presumed Dr. Mayfield wanted a full year to verify that she was under control and remained in remission.

* * * *

They arrived at their condominium in Westlake about midday. Josh studied Linda's face for her reaction, He prayed that she would not be disappointed. She was all smiles as they reached the front door. Josh unlocked the door, then picked her up and carried her across the threshold like a new bride. They both laughed and giggled like newlyweds.

"It's perfect, Josh," she said. "You know just what I like. And everything is in place. How did you do it?"

"I know a few things about you," he said with a laugh. "Of course Ann helped me a little."

Linda walked through the unit, gazing at the ten-foot ceilings, awestruck with the marble bathrooms and kitchen, inspecting every closet, and trying every appliance. Their few pieces of furniture were arranged in the rooms much like it had been in their condo in Dallas. Josh had left picture hanging and placement of trivial decorative items to Linda.

"I like it, Josh!" she said.

"Let me show you around the place," he said.

He showed her the workout gym, the swimming pool, and the common party room for the use of all of the occupants. The expansive outside grounds were exceptionally well kept, with a wide, hard surface running track that meandered around the periphery and through the many landscaped garden areas. There was a strategically placed gazebo close to a grove of trees. Josh could envision Linda sitting there, reading or painting or just relaxing.

"Can we afford this, Josh?" she asked.

Josh reflected that this was the first time in their married life she had ever asked about finances.

"We can't afford anything less," he replied. "I love you, little one. I want you to be happy and to stay your same sweet self."

He kissed her tenderly and they led each other to the bedroom to recapture those moments of closeness that they had been deprived of for so many days.

Chapter 31

▼

It was a little after ten o'clock when Jeremy Corbett received Don Bradford's usual Monday summons to see him in his office as soon as possible. *Another session about what's going on at Salzman Electronics,* thought Jeremy. He'd tried every strategy he could think of to unravel the mystery—every legal means, that is. The old bastard was going to be irritable today. He had to think of something.

"Jeremy!" Bradford's face beamed, but Jeremy knew the smile was insincere. "How was your weekend?"

"Just fine, Mr. Bradford," he replied. *It always starts this way,* thought Jeremy. *He couldn't care less about my weekend.* Jeremy remembered the time he said he was bit by a water moccasin in his swimming pool. The old man never blinked an eye. The next question will be about Donnie.

"How is Donnie coming along, Jeremy?"

"Donnie has really proven himself to be a great asset to the company, sir," said Jeremy, tongue-in-cheek. "I depend on him for much of our overseas surveillance." What I'm really saying is, 'I keep him skiing in Switzerland or sailing the company yacht off the coast of Monaco.'"

"Well, I know he must be staying busy since his graduation. He's never around here. I never see him" he said. "I appreciate all you have done for Donnie, Jeremy. You've made that boy into an executive to be proud of."

"Thank you, sir," he replied. "It's been a pleasure to work with him."

"Jeremy," he said, with a furrowed brow, "what the hell is going on at Salzman?"

"I wish I could tell you, Mr. Bradford," he replied. "We know something is happening, but we just can't unravel it yet. However, I think we may be getting close to a breakthrough."

"Update me on what you have so far," he said, leaning forward in his chair and tapping his pen on the desk top.

"I know this is very important to you," said Jeremy, "and we're working very hard on trying to get information."

"Good, good!" he exclaimed. "I know I can depend on you, Jeremy. Do whatever you have to do to find out. You know you have my permission."

Without saying it, thought Jeremy, *he has made it clear: do whatever you have to, even if it is illegal, as long as you keep me from being blamed if you're caught.*

"Yes, sir," said Jeremy as he continued. "Here's what we've got: We've been tracking everyone who comes and goes through the Salzman private garage. We have been able to buy off one of the building security guards in the lobby."

"He identifies everyone who visits the eighteenth floor from their car license. He reports to us daily, and then we do a complete check on the individual, in hopes of linking him or her to the new project. This has given us only limited information so far, but it has proven to be useful."

"But you haven't identified the project?" asked Don.

"Not yet," Jeremy answered, "but we may be getting close."

Bradford leaned back in his oversize leather chair, folded his hands across his protuberant belly, and gazed out the window while Jeremy gave his report.

"From time to time two or three engineers from various divisions of the plant visit Charles Salzman's office, carrying briefcases, and usually stay longer than most visitors. I suspect they run this assortment of engineers through there as decoys. There is one young, low-level engineer whom we have been able to buy; but he has a very minor role in the new project. This kid managed to get himself heavily indebted to Lennie from gambling."

"When I told Lennie you needed some information from the boy, he said for me to tell you that he's at your service. Just tell him when. The only information we could extract was that he is working on a special instrument that will be manufactured from a rare substance called Xentallium. The young engineer doesn't know what the instrument will be used for; but he thinks it is part of the job everyone is so excited about. According to this guy, Xentallium has the characteristic that it is totally resistant to magnetism and is stronger than steel."

"He has no idea why the instrument has to be made from Xentallium, but he knows the entire project is highly secretive and complex. He has had to take his work back to the plant over ten times to refine its performance."

When Jeremy mentioned Lennie's name, Don immediately stiffened and his face took on that fiendish, malicious look that Jeremy had seen before when the old man was about to order a strike of some sort. Jeremy could see the wheels turning in Don's sordid, ignoble mind. *He is thinking of bringing Lennie into the picture*, thought Jeremy. *Damn it, I wish I'd never mentioned that contemptible, small time hoodlum.*

Don sat upright, leaned forward, and turned to Jeremy.

"You know, Lennie has a way of getting information; and he has a lot of connections," he said.

"Yes, sir," replied Jeremy. "If I may say so, sir, I think it would be unwise to use strong-arm tactics in this situation. I suggest we move along as we have been doing for a while."

"Very well, Jeremy," he said. "I'll trust your judgment, but I want some results on this endeavor before too long," he added sternly. "If you can't get information, call Lennie."

"I understand, sir," said Jeremy. "Back to our scared engineer, he says the company knows about his compulsive gambling. He expects to be fired any day, but they need him during this development stage because he's the only one who knows how to work with Xentallium."

"I don't know whether to believe him or not," Jeremy continued. "He may just be another one of their decoys to try to steer us in a different direction. Whatever, this kid does enjoy the money we're dropping on him."

"If Lennie worked him over, you wouldn't have to worry about whether to believe him or not," growled Don.

Jeremy wondered how he could ever get Don off this mind-set.

"We have been unsuccessful in reaching anyone in Charles Salzman's laboratory or in his inner office," Jeremy continued. "Every time we try, it only brings on tighter security."

"There has been one new visitor lately that we are having trouble linking to Salzman," he added. "Our pay-off security guard picked this up. After we ran a check on him, we found it to be a Dr. Joshua Lehman. He goes to Charles Salzman's office with some regularity. Not always the same day of the week but he's there at least every two weeks. He never brings anything with him; he stays sometimes as long as two hours, and he takes nothing out with him when he leaves."

"What else have you found out about him?" Don asked, suddenly gaining interest.

"He's a cardiac surgeon. Just finished his training at Metcalfe in Dallas. He has just moved here to Westlake to start his practice. Probably that's his tie to

Salzman—something to do with their high-tech X-ray stuff. But I can't find out why he keeps returning to Charles's office so often."

"That name sounds familiar. A cardiac surgeon?" asked Don, suddenly becoming more alert, his eyebrows raised, his hands clasped, and his elbows on his desk, straining to hear every word Jeremy uttered.

"I have thought the same thing," Jeremy replied.

"Jeremy, do you remember the two football players that tutored Donnie a few years ago before you took over?" asked Don. "Wasn't one of them named Josh?"

"You're right! Josh Lehman!" replied Jeremy. "He gave up a professional football career for medical school…a lot of sports media hype about it. Yeah. I remember. We paid them the rest of the semester."

"It has to be the same one," said Don. "There was another one. Both played football at Westlake High School. Donnie knew them and we hired them to do the tutoring. Luke was the name of the other boy. That's it—Josh Lehman and Luke Sanders! They went to Northwestern on a football scholarship."

"We don't have anything on Luke Sanders, but I remember now. That is his name."

"So Josh is returning to Westlake as a doctor. He'll be applying for the medical staff at Westlake Regional, you know," Don said, staring out the window in deep thought.

Jeremy could almost hear the wheels turning again in Don's corrupt brain, and could predict with near certainty what the old fart was thinking before he said another word. Don finally broke the silence.

"What else do you have on Lehman? Is he clean?"

"Yeah, nothing comes up. Clean record," replied Jeremy. "He's heavily in debt with the Metcalfe Credit Union. Apparently lived pretty high while he was in training. His income potential is pretty good, so the debt will not be a problem."

"He and his wife moved into one of the exclusive Lakeview luxury condos. Of interest, his wife was in a treatment center for drug abuse. Checked out and moved directly to the condo here in Westlake. She must be cured. We checked with a few dealers and didn't turn up anything."

"Did you alert Lennie?"

"No, I haven't," he said. "Probably should."

"Yeah, they never get cured," said Don. "You need to talk to Josh Lehman. He's your best lead."

"I agree," said Jeremy. "I would like to suggest, sir, that you talk to him. With your position on the hospital board, you have some leverage that I don't have."

"Can you bring him in?"

"I'll try," he replied.

Chapter 32

Josh made good use of his slack time before formally starting his practice in Westlake. His contract with Metcalfe provided him with an ongoing salary until his surgery volume grew to a predetermined level, giving him an income during that interval. He needed that income, since he still had substantial debt from Linda's extravagance during their last several months in Dallas. Also, the cost of Linda's treatment in The Willows hung over them, in addition to their present living expenses in Westlake.

There was a myriad of trivial items to address before he would ever do his first surgical case: register his license in Westlake County, apply for privileges at the hospital, apply for membership in the county medical society. As advised by Dr. Dubonet, he scheduled professional courtesy calls on every cardiologist, general surgeon, and primary care physician in the area.

The other cardiothoracic surgeons welcomed his arrival. Previously, many of their complex cases had to be transferred to larger medical centers in Houston or San Antonio. With Josh's support, those cases now could be done locally and remain under the care of their regular physicians during the post-operative period. To Josh's benefit, he could arrange an on-call schedule with the other surgeons that would give him time off after his practice grew.

* * * *

Josh and Linda now had time to do things together. They set a routine for themselves of getting up early in the morning, jogging on the track for five miles, working out in the gym for thirty minutes, and then soaking in the hot tub together before breakfast. It helped Josh get started every day with renewed spirit and optimism.

They had time to visit Luke, Ann, and Jay and to plan activities together. Josh marveled at the change in Linda when she was around Jay. At first Jay was a little distant, but in time he warmed to Linda. Josh watched with fascination as Jay, his eyes fixed on Linda's face, sitting in her lap, while she looked down at him with a tender, motherly look that said more than a thousand words. To Josh, Linda was saying, "I think it's time we had a baby."

Linda busied herself with decorating their new home to her liking, but with a common-sense approach. Josh marveled at her conservative buying and spending, so different from the past. Everything was different now. Their relationship was so different than before. It was based on a devotion and respect for each other that they had never before experienced. There was an element of sensitivity—of tenderness and concern for each other that was new. It was as if they were sharing the same bed for the very first time.

Linda had been able to transfer her Junior League membership to Westlake. That gave her the opportunity to interact with others on the same social level. She had been a valuable asset to the Junior League and the Metcalfe Wives' Club in Dallas—before the drug and alcohol nightmare started—and she had a lot to offer the group in Westlake in organizing activities.

Josh was afraid she might have carried some of her treatment history with her, but thanks to the confidentiality at the treatment center, either her history was not known or it was downplayed by organizations in Westlake. She was automatically offered membership in the Medical Society Alliance when he applied for his membership in the medical society.

Another benefit from his association with Metcalfe was the privilege of a membership in the Westlake Country Club. That gave Josh and Linda another opportunity to enjoy their time together. They played singles tennis at least twice each week. Josh was amazed at Linda's tennis skills and at how close she often came to beating him. Playing mixed doubles with other couples at the club helped them expand their circle of acquaintances.

They continued their visits to Dr. Mayfield in Dallas. With Linda's progress, she was given permission to increase her work activity whenever she wished and to reduce the frequency of their visits to every two weeks. Josh was able then to coordinate their counseling sessions with his visits to Charles Salzman's office.

* * * *

When Josh entered Charles' office, he was met with unprecedented smiles and exuberance.

"We're getting there, Josh!" Charles said. "We should be able to finish the project within the year. Then we go live."

"It's overwhelming!" said Josh.

"Josh, I need to warn you about something," he said. "Scoetec has done everything short of armed robbery to find out what we're doing. They know something is coming down the tube. Their efforts have been rather amateurish, for the most part, but have been aggravating. We know what they are doing and have been able to block their attempts on every turn."

"One thing that is disturbing them is your visits. We know that they have identified you and have done an in-depth background check on every aspect of your life. Don't be surprised if they contact you in some way."

"Sounds scary!" said Josh.

"I don't think they would be so foolish as to cause you any physical harm," said Charles, "but they might try to use some other leverage to reach you."

"What should I do?"

"Nothing right now," Charles replied. "Let me know if you notice anything suspicious. This whole scenario is like a spy-versus-spy novel. They want to know what we're doing, and we know everything they are doing to find out. In a way it's like a Peter Sellers comedy." He laughed.

Josh didn't share his amusement.

"It may be funny to you, but it's still scary," said Josh, "but I'll be on guard."

"If you come with us on this, Josh, you are going to continue to be at risk," warned Charles. "I know this is all intriguing to you, but I also want you to know you can cut out any time you become uncomfortable with the risk."

"No way!" he said. "I don't scare easily, Charles. Count me in!"

"How are things going in Westlake?" Charles asked.

"Great!" replied Josh. "I'm picking up more and more cases now from referring doctors and from the emergency room."

"Jim Ewalt is the executive director of Metcalfe Heart Institute there, isn't he?"

"Yeah, we're working together on developing some patient care standards and on upgrading policies and procedures for caring for cardiac patients," Josh answered. "He's easy to work with."

"A very bright young man," said Charles. "You don't regret making the move, do you?"

"Not at all," he replied. "I can see that I'm going to get busier and busier. That worries me. Linda is doing fine right now. I'm just afraid that if I get too busy, we'll slip right back into that same lifestyle pattern that drove us apart."

"Well, you know it can happen, Josh," said Charles, "so you need to take some preventive steps, don't you?

"I agree, and I'm trying," he replied.

"Josh, again, if the consulting position with Salzman becomes too time consuming, you can drop it any time," said Charles. "You know that, don't you?"

Josh was quiet for a few moments, as if contemplating his answer. Charles watched him expectantly.

"Yeah, I know. But I think I'm hooked, Charles," said Josh. "I just couldn't ever walk away from the MIS project."

"I understand, Josh," said Charles, "and it will take less of your time once it's finished. How is Luke?"

"Luke's fine," replied Josh. "Busier than ever. He's helping me with the planning, but he still reserves time for his family."

"Thanks for coming by, Josh," he said. "Oh, I almost forgot. My mother sends her love."

"Give her my regards," said Josh, as he prepared to leave.

✳   ✳   ✳   ✳

With Josh's surgical volume increasing steadily and with Linda now working more shifts in the ICU and becoming more involved with her social obligations they were returning again to their old lifestyle habits that entrapped them in Dallas. Getting home late at the end of the day and the more frequent night-time meetings, kept them from following the quality-time-together routine they had set for themselves.

In conjunction with her Junior League and Medical Alliance activities, Linda was expected to entertain, just as she had done before in Dallas. Josh made a concentrated effort to be present as often as possible for the many parties and gatherings that were held at the country club, or sometimes in their party room, but still he was often absent or detained because of emergencies or a heavy work load at the hospital.

As the social pressure increased, Linda was forced to abandon her plans to continue working in the ICU. She played tennis at the Country Club more often—usually with the same elite group that she mixed with in her social world. Whenever Josh and Linda were scheduled to play in a mixed doubles tournament, Linda never knew whether or not he would show up. With increased frequency, Linda found herself looking for a substitute doubles partner.

*   *   *   *

Josh's cell phone vibrated in the pocket of his scrub suit just as he finished his early morning case—a fifty-five year old patient with five-vessel coronary artery disease, crippling angina, and a weak heart muscle. Coming off the heart-lung machine was harrowing and required a third round of electro-shock to restart the heart.

Josh was exhausted, both from the difficult case he had just finished as well as from the sequelae of horrendous chest trauma cases the night before. He was in no mood for even one more phone call, regardless of who was calling. It was his office secretary, Melba.

"Dr. Lehman, a call came through this morning from a Mr. Jeremy Corbett who said he needed to speak with you. He sounded as if it were urgent, but said there was no emergency. I thought you should know about it. He said he was not a patient and it was not medical."

"Thanks, Melba," he said. "I don't recognize the name, but I'll return his call when I finish here."

Unless she felt like it was important, it was unusual for Melba to interrupt him when she knew he was doing a case. *There was something about the call that alerted her sensitive antennae,* thought Josh.

He went out to talk to the anxiously awaiting family and to explain the procedure, the difficulties encountered, and to answer the many questions that he knew would be forthcoming. He checked on the patient one more time and then retreated to the lounge to make the call Melba had given him.

A lilting voice on the other end of the line said, "Bradford Holdings. How may I direct your call?" with enthusiasm that reflected someone who had been carefully instructed in the importance of scripting and telephone etiquette.

"Mr. Jeremy Corbett. I am returning his call," said Josh. "This is Dr. Lehman."

"Oh, yes, Dr. Lehman," she replied, her voice bubbling with politeness. "He's expecting your call." A short wait and a click followed.

"Dr. Lehman, this is Jeremy Corbett," he said. "You may not remember me; we met while you were in Northwestern. I picked up the tutoring assignment for Donnie Bradford when you graduated."

"Yes, sir. I remember now," he said. "I didn't connect the name at first."

"Well, it's been a few years," said Jeremy. "You and your partner did a great job with Donnie, made my job easier. Your partner—Luke Sanders, I believe?"

"Yes, sir," said Josh, waiting to hear the reason for the call.

"Dr. Lehman, Mr. Bradford wants me to convey his appreciation for your work with Donnie. Also, he wants to welcome you to Westlake. He would like to meet you personally and has asked me to set up an appointment with you at your convenience. He will come to your office, you can go to his office, or he can meet you at the club."

This had to be the call that Charles Salzman had warned him about. Josh had to make a quick decision. He would agree to meet, but where? Although Josh wanted to get this over with as soon as possible, he had to stall for time until he could call Charles.

"Mr. Corbett, I will be tied up at the hospital all day today," said Josh. "I will have free time tomorrow and probably the best meeting place would be at Mr. Bradford's club."

"That will be fine with Mr. Bradford, I'm sure," he replied. "I will reserve a conference room at the Country Club for noon. Will that be all right with you?"

"Yes, sir."

"Thank you, Dr. Lehman," he said. "I will confirm the time and place with your secretary." Another click and he was gone, leaving Josh in a quandary. What was he getting into? He needed to talk to Charles.

He called the number he was told to memorize and soon found out why only a select few people had access to the number. There was a slight delay between the dialing and the beginning of the signal, after which Charles answered.

"Charles, I need to talk to you about a phone call I received," said Josh.

"Hi, Josh, You can talk to me now," said Charles, a calm tone to his voice. "We don't worry about security on this line. I'm in Switzerland right now, so it would be pretty hard for us to get together for the next two to three days. I already know about your phone call. You handled it very well."

"Charles. I'm talking about the call from Jeremy Corbett, ten minutes ago!"

"I know, Josh," he said. "We monitor every call that goes out from that office. If it goes to a flagged recipient, the information comes to me immediately. You're on that flagged recipient list, Josh."

"What do I do now?" asked Josh, trying not to sound a little annoyed with it all.

"Here's what we would like for you to do, Josh," he said. "Keep your appointment with Bradford at the Country Club. We want to record your conversation with him, if you are willing."

"How can I do that, Charles?"

"Josh, listen closely," he answered. "By the time we finish this conversation, there will be a technician knocking on your door with the equipment. We sent him on the way when we first learned of the contact because we were afraid you might have decided to meet with Bradford today. His name is Tom Weston. He will explain everything to you. Josh, you don't have to do this, you know. I told you that before, if you remember."

"I know, Charles, and I made some grandiose statements about my bravery," said Josh with a laugh. "Bring 'em on, Charles!"

"I felt sure you'd say that," he said. "Thanks, Josh. I'll get back with you after your visit with Bradford. It should prove quite interesting."

Almost immediately, a hospital employee knocked on the lounge door with a message.

"Dr. Lehman, there is someone here to see you; he says you are expecting him."

"Yes, I am. Please ask him to come on in. Thanks."

A well-groomed young man in a coat and tie, carrying a briefcase, tapped on the door and entered. He introduced himself as Tom Weston, and in a very business-like manner, explained the use of the recording device to Josh.

He must have performed this task before, thought Josh. His appearance and self-assured demeanor was another reflection of Charles Salzman's efficiency. Josh didn't question him, except to ask how to return the equipment.

"When you leave the Country Club, drive to your office. I will be close by to see if you are being followed. If not, I'll meet you at your parking place. If I don't show there, call Mr. Salzman—you have his number—and he will give you instructions."

"We appreciate your help, Dr. Lehman," he added. "On the side of the recorder is a button. Press it once after your meeting. That seals the tape and it can only be played on our tape player. I don't think you'll need it, but the button is also a panic button. Press it twice and we will be by your side in seconds."

With that good news, he excused himself and left Josh to ponder over whether there was real danger out there. He hadn't quite adjusted to this cloak-and-dagger business. What was the reason behind it all? All of these precautions seemed to him to be escalated out of proportion, but he trusted Charles and would go along with it as instructed.

Chapter 33

▼

Josh went to the front of the club instead of the usual back entrance that he and Linda used for tennis. At the front of the club you were expected to use valet parking—five dollars for some kid to park your car so you wouldn't have to walk a hundred feet.

Josh parked his own car, checked to make sure that the recording device was well concealed, walked the hundred feet, paid the kid two dollars anyway, and entered the club. At first, he felt that same bit of apprehension that he remembered from football days when facing an opponent and not knowing what to expect. Then he laughed at himself and said, "Relax, dude, it's just another game!"

When he announced that he was meeting Mr. Bradford, a receptionist smiled politely and beckoned him to follow. She escorted him down a wide corridor that led into the depths of the club. They passed several rooms—women playing cards in one; loud, garrulous chatter from another room where balding, overweight men in gym clothes, played gin. He wondered if any one of these creeps ever worked a day in their lives?

Near the end of the hall were a series of private meeting rooms—quiet, well appointed, furnished in "library" vogue, with a medium-size round table and cushioned chairs in each room. Josh was ushered into one of the rooms, where he faced a wall which held a huge television screen plus a music center with a DVD player and CD changer.

"Mr. Bradford and Mr. Corbett will join you in a moment," she said and handed him a menu. "In the meantime, you may wish to look at the menu. I can take your drink order now."

"Thank you," said Josh, "I'll just have water."

Within minutes Don Bradford and Jeremy Corbett entered, an explosive entrance such as one would expect from busy executives rushing from one meeting to another. Josh expected them to start looking at their watches before they introduced themselves.

"Dr. Lehman!" the big man bellowed. "I'm Don Bradford! Nice of you to take time from your busy day to visit with us. I have followed your career with interest and it is a privilege to meet you."

"Thank you, sir," replied Josh. *I have never seen such a broad, fake smile,* Josh thought. It completely covered his fat face and deepened every wrinkle. Don's skin was deeply tanned; his hair was uniformly gray. His suit was impeccably tailored; everything he wore reflected custom tailoring.

"I want you to meet Jeremy Corbett," Don Bradford said. "Jeremy is my executive assistant. In fact, he is my confidant. He knows more about me than I know myself." He laughed.

"Nice meeting you, Dr. Lehman," said Jeremy.

"I am pleased to know you, Mr. Corbett," said Josh, without revealing to Don Bradford that they had met before when the tutoring chore had passed to Jeremy.

After placing their drink order, a waiter appeared from somewhere, already carrying a martini with two large stuffed olives. Don began the expected interrogation.

"I understand you grew up in Westlake, Dr. Lehman."

"Yes, sir," he replied. "I was born here."

"Always good to see hometown boys do well and return to their roots," said Don, without taking his eyes off the menu.

"I'm happy to be back," said Josh.

"How about family? I believe you are married, are you not?"

"Yes, sir," Josh replied. "And my father lives here."

"And what does your father do?" asked Don, still studying the menu.

"He works in the Westlake Refinery," said Josh. "He should have retired some time ago, but he lost all of his retirement benefits and has to keep working."

Josh watched closely for Don's reaction to his comment. He showed no interest. In fact, Don never looked up. Josh glanced at Jeremy and was certain he detected a change in facial expression—tightness of his jaw muscles and a fleeting, hostile look in his eyes.

"How were things at Metcalfe?" asked Don. Jeremy was silent during the dialogue. Josh wondered why.

"I was fortunate to be there," Josh answered. "I trained under some great teachers."

"You remember my son, Don Bradford, Jr.—Donnie?" asked Don, finally looking up.

He must have made his choice from the specials of the day, thought Josh.

"He's with the company now. Doing great! Jeremy's Donnie's teacher," he proudly added. "Right, Jeremy?"

"Yes, sir," replied Jeremy, as a faint wincing smile crossed his face.

"Donnie works directly under Jeremy. He has just returned from foreign assignments under Jeremy's direction," said Don proudly. "He's come a long way from the time you tutored him at Northwestern."

"I'm glad to hear that," said Josh.

"I want to thank you again for helping Donnie become a success."

"It was a pleasure, sir," Josh replied, struggling to suppress laughter. "I'm sure you're very proud of Donnie."

While they ate lunch, their conversation centered around generalities for the most part, intermingled with Don's attempt to tell jokes that Josh didn't find funny. Jeremy and Josh were content with a very light lunch—soup and salad. Don's meal, preceded by two martinis, each with two stuffed olives, seemed to Josh more like a festive holiday dinner than a lunch. Following their meal, Don again began his discourse, this time more with an air of seriousness.

"Dr. Lehman, it's been a real delight having you here today," said Don. "I wish we had the opportunity to visit with our new doctors more often. As president of the board of trustees of the hospital, I have a keen interest in everything that is going on at the hospital, especially with Metcalfe Heart Institute joining us."

"I'm sure you're very busy, Mr. Bradford, and I appreciate the chance to visit with you and Mr. Corbett. It's been nice to hear about Donnie again. Please give him my regards."

"Yes, I'll do just that," he said. "Perhaps we could all get together some time." Josh noticed again an unmistakable wincing smirk on Jeremy's face. "Dr. Lehman—do you mind if I call you Josh?"

"Not at all," he replied. *I really wish you wouldn't call me at all,* thought Josh; *I just want to get out of here.*

"I want to take a couple of minutes and tell you something about our company. Jeremy is here to answer questions if I can't." He laughed. "Jeremy runs the company—heh, heh, right, Jeremy?"

Jeremy was silent, but smiled faintly as Don continued.

"Josh, Bradford Holdings is a diversified, organization. We own and control many companies all over the world; that's why we need the large office building we have here in Westlake. This is our home base, but our companies are traded on Wall Street. This means we have to be constantly aware of the economic trends in the country. It's a complex business with trading, buying, and selling going on every minute.

"One of our very successful companies is Scoetec," he said, as he continued. "This company produces high-tech instruments: endoscopes, X-ray and nuclear imaging equipment—just about anything used in a hospital radiology and special procedures department. You have probably seen our name on some of the equipment you use every day in the heart program," he added, a prying, inquisitive look.

"I don't recall, sir," said Josh, "but I probably didn't notice." *Get to the point, you old fart*, thought Josh. *He is one big windbag!*

"We're in a very competitive business, Josh. Our biggest competitor is Salzman Electronics. Much of the equipment carrying the Salzman name is Scoetec equipment that Salzman has copied, after we've spent millions in research and development! Then, one way or another, they undercut us and market our equipment to hospitals as if it were there own."

Josh could barely constrain outright laughter at what he heard. He could feel Jeremy's eyes in a fixed stare toward him. Josh hoped he had been able to mask his disbelief of Don's absurd remarks.

"Oh, yes, I do remember seeing the Salzman name on the equipment we use," Josh said. "Then that is really made by your company?"

"Copied from our model! Patent infringement!" he yelled and slammed his fist so hard on the table that dishes and glasses shook.

A good actor, thought Josh. *Could anything he said be true? He is certainly convincing.*

"Now, that's not your problem, Josh. I just wanted you to know the truth, and I wanted you to know why we are so interested in the new Heart Institute—and interested in you, Josh. You have a very important role assigned to you for this project. You want it to succeed, and of course we want you to succeed."

"Yes, sir," said Josh. "We do have that in common."

Don burped loudly, looked at his watch, then at Jeremy, signaling by his action that they needed to end this meeting and move on. Josh was certainly ready.

"Josh, please feel free to contact me or Jeremy if there's anything you need," said Don, shifting his weighty carcass forward in his chair in preparation to stand, clearly saying that the meeting was over. Jeremy moved accordingly and Josh stood.

"Jim Ewalt tells me you have been granted temporary privileges while waiting for your credentials to clear," said Don, looking Josh straight in the eye as if he were trying to get a message across, "and I've heard good reports of your work already. I'm sure there'll be no problem. Good luck to you, and let's keep in touch."

"Yes, sir; thank you for lunch."

They shook hands and Josh walked out first, leaving the two behind. He wondered why the credentials thing was brought up at all. He had the highest recommendations possible from Metcalfe.

* * * *

He went straight to the parking lot, pushed the button on the recorder as instructed, backed his car out and headed down the street toward his office, watching his rearview mirror constantly for any sign of being followed.

When he parked in his space at the hospital, his forehead was sweaty and he could feel perspiration dripping inside his shirt from his armpits. "I don't need this," he said aloud. "I've faced life-threatening open-heart cases with less anxiety."

He looked through the windshield and saw the same young man who earlier had instructed him on the use of the recorder walking toward his car. He opened the passenger door and entered. Josh passed the recorder over to him without a word.

"Mr. Salzman will be in touch, Dr. Lehman," he said as he hurried away from Josh's parked car. He was gone in a flash.

When Josh entered the side door to his office, Melba hurriedly approached him with the news that Charles Salzman was on the line.

"Josh!" said Charles. "You performed beautifully."

"Charles," said Josh. "What is this all about?" How did Charles know what went on? He was in Switzerland!

"Come to Dallas to my office after I return, any time after tomorrow," he replied. "We need to talk."

"Any time?"

"Whenever you can make it."

"I'll find the time."

"Josh, they were setting you up. Today they were just sizing you up to see what you could take. Expect another call in a few days. Be careful, Josh. Don't do anything or say anything without checking with me."

"OK, Charles, but you need to fill in some blanks for me."

"I know what you mean. Don't worry."

"Yeah, easy for you to say," said Josh with a laugh. "You're halfway around the world."

"But I know what's going on," he said. "It's my bedtime, Josh."

"Sleep well, Charles," said Josh. "I'll see you in two days."

"Oh, Josh, I forgot to tell you. Mother wants you and your wife to join us for Passover Seder."

"I think I'd like that. We'll be there."

"Goodnight, Josh," he said, and with a click the line was dead.

Chapter 34

Two days passed and Josh had not heard from Charles or from Don Bradford. He decided to wait one more day before contacting Charles. He needed some answers before he talked to Bradford again. Charles said he could expect another call. "How did I get into all of this?" Josh asked himself.

Josh just wanted to do what he knew best—cardiothoracic surgery—but he knew he couldn't back out now, even though Charles said he could any time. He had already committed himself. "Quit kidding yourself," he said, laughing aloud. "You're intrigued by it all; deal with it! It's just another game."

He finished his first morning case, talked to the family, and was preparing to start the second case when the call came. Melba said Mr. Salzman wanted him to call…that Josh knew the number. Charles had just arrived in Dallas and wanted to talk to him. Instead of Josh making a trip to Dallas, Charles wanted to meet at the Westlake airport in two hours. Josh had time to finish his second case before Charles' arrival.

He checked out to one of the other surgeons and raced to the airport to be there by the time Charles arrived in his private jet. The private hangar facility provided a conference room that they could use that was secure from any outside surveillance. Josh watched as Charles stepped off the plane, unshaven and clothes ruffled. *Far different from his usual appearance,* thought Josh. *Probably jet lag.*

They sat across from each other; both remained quiet for a while before speaking. Charles struggled to keep his head from nodding.

"You look tired, Charles," said Josh.

"I'll be all right as soon as my biological clock realizes I'm back in Texas," he laughed. "I've needed some time with you, Josh, to try to help you understand the complexities of the corporate world."

"I'll admit it is quite confusing, yet fascinating in many ways."

"Yes, it is in many ways," said Charles, "and terrifying in some ways when you see the extremes people like Bradford will go to for personal gain. He uses unscrupulous tactics to achieve his objectives. But enough of that! How are you doing?"

"Fine, thanks; staying very busy and enjoying every minute of it," he replied. "The heart program is shaping up nicely, and the building plans are well under way. Construction should start soon."

"Good to hear," said Charles. "Let me update you on the Motionless Imaging Scope project. We are on target! Much of the work is being done now in the laboratory in our Switzerland branch. Before long I likely will ask you to spend a few days there. I want your opinion of the final product before we start the fine-tuning phase. It gets more exciting every day, Josh. It's your baby, Josh!"

"Wow!" said Josh. "Hard to believe you're that close."

"Can you work it into your schedule?"

"I'm sure I can," replied Josh. "I need as much notice as possible."

"I'll see that you get it!" said Charles. "Josh, I have cleared this with Dr. Dubonet and President Roever," he said. "They are highly supportive of what we are doing and have no problem with the time you spend with us."

"Good to know. Just tell me when."

"Josh, let's talk about Bradford and Scoetec," said Charles. "You may already know much of what I'm going to tell you. I'm going to hit the highlights of the medical technology field. Salzman Electronics is a leader in the industry, along with companies like Gentron, Dynatron, and a handful of others. These are all ethical companies and you already know something of our background."

"We compete, of course, but we often share ideas and work collaboratively with each other. The competitive edge for any one of the companies is related to management and marketing—and service, of course. We all pour millions into research and development every year, and are all publicly traded stock companies, responsible to our shareholders. We are under constant scrutiny by the Securities and Exchange Commission. Independent accounting firms carefully audit our financial reports, and their findings are a part of our quarterly reports that we deliver to our shareholders and to Wall Street investors."

"Scoetec has to play by the same rules, insofar as Wall Street is concerned. However, from a day-to-day business standpoint, they stand by, much like a generic drug company, waiting until a product is developed and approved for use, and then produce duplications, some times with minute changes to avoid patent infringement. They are able to market their equipment at a reduced price, far below our price."

"They fall short on integrity and on service. We stress the importance on upgrading our products, many times at no expense to the customer, and we always respond promptly to any question or problem with equipment failure. That's why we have so many repeat customers like Metcalfe."

"Scoetec cannot compete on that level. Their customers are, for the most part, small hospitals or clinics who fall into the trap of trying to economize on equipment or fall prey to Scoetec's deceptive advertising."

"Now, here's the story of Bradford Holdings; Much of what I am going to say is based on the opinions of our finance and accounting department. Bradford Holdings is a multi-billion dollar entity. They own controlling interest in several companies that they have been able to acquire one way or another, often with shady deals of questionable legality. No one has been able to prove it, but our accountants are reasonably sure of the methods they use."

"By creating partnerships into which they transfer debt of any one of their companies, they are able to manipulate the financial reports of the subsidiary to show glowing earnings. On the surface, the company appears to be healthy, growing, and showing an attractive net profit."

"After the reports come out, legitimate Wall Street brokers start buying and the stock price goes up. Bradford, then—using other dummy holding companies—either sells stock that they have acquired for practically pennies, or they exercise options they hold for stock at a very cheap price and then sell for fabulous profits."

"With further manipulation, Don Bradford and a few of his cronies drain the cash off the partnerships into their personal accounts in foreign banks. Another trick they use is robbing the employee retirement accounts of their companies. They cause one of their weak corporations to borrow funds from the employee benefit funds, transfer the money to their personal partnerships, and then bankrupt the company. Lifetime employees, working for years toward the day they could comfortably cease work and retire, suddenly find that their accounts have been stripped and they are left with nothing."

"That is what happened to the company my father works for, exactly what you have described," said Josh. "Bradford acquired the company that owned the refinery, and the next thing my father knew he had no retirement benefits."

"Exactly!" Charles replied. "That has happened over and over again, all over the country, and they are clever enough to get away with it."

"If our analysis is correct," Charles continued, "they will eventually be discovered as the crooks that they are. It's hard to believe that they could deceive the SEC and the Wall Street brokerage firms for so long, while the rest of us in the industry have to comply with such stringent accounting practices. I'm sure there is pay-off some where in the picture.

"Now, back to Scoetec," said Charles. "Using illegal accounting practices, Bradford Holdings has bled Scoetec on at least three occasions. None have yet to be detected by auditors. Meanwhile, the executives of the company, including old Don, have made off with fortunes at the expense of the public.

"The only thing that will save them now is to announce some innovative product that will make their stock go up and will salvage the company. If you compare it to drug companies again, it would be like announcing a Viagra-like drug.

"They can't take a chance on manipulating the financial report again, and they have to do something to keep government auditors at bay and to keep the company alive. This is why they are so desperate to find out what we're doing. If they could identify our new prospect, they could leak information to Wall Street that they are coming out with the product before we are, and then start the duplication process as soon as we hit the market, claiming that we copied their model.

"They have never been quite this desperate before, which explains the extreme strategy they're using. They have already reached one of our lesser engineers—a nice little guy named Herb Bowman—who has a compulsive gambling habit. He knows more than he's telling them, according to what he's telling us, but they will keep on working on him.

"Josh, they know about your visits to the laboratory. That's why they are pursuing you so vigorously. They are looking for some weakness in your character or some unusual need that you might have. I have to tell you this; we have done a complete character and financial check on you, and find neither."

Charles paused to give Josh a chance to respond. Josh was quiet for several seconds before speaking. He stood and walked around the table and gazed out the window at the Salzman plane, ready to take Charles back to Dallas. Could he believe Charles? His integrity and morals are beyond reach for old Bradford. Charles has given me opportunity. Bradford has left me with suspicion and bitterness.

"I guess what I object to in this whole scenario, Charles," said Josh, "is the wiretapping! Being followed! Background checks! You know, in medicine, we like everything to be above-board."

"I know you do," he replied. "That's why I've gone to this extreme to explain the picture to you. In this case, a certain amount of undercover activity on our part is necessary. The other reasons I have explained all this to you are: one, you can get out any time, as I have said before; two, you must be very careful. I cannot stress enough to you how ruthless these people can be."

"I can handle it, Charles," said Josh. "Your narrative does answer the questions that clouded my brain. Go home, Charles! Get some sleep! You're making me feel bad, just seeing how exhausted you are."

"I think I'll do just that," he replied with a laugh.

They shook hands and Charles signaled his pilot that he was ready to leave. Josh turned and went to his car. As he was driving along the frontage road leading to the freeway, he looked into the sky and saw the beautiful blue and silver 747 airship soar into the sky, the name "Salzman" clearly showing on the fuselage.

Chapter 35

Melba had that same subdued but frantic tone to her voice that always meant to Josh that there was some urgent matter that needed his attention.

"Dr. Lehman, there is a Mr. Jeremy Corbett here to see you," she said. "He does not have an appointment, but he says he thinks you will want to see him. What shall I do? You have a busy schedule today."

"Tell him I will be a little late getting to the office. If he insists on staying, try to make him comfortable."

He called Charles immediately.

"Stall him as long as you can," said Charles. "The same technician that you met before will be there in minutes. Meet him in the same lounge as before. Your office phone line is probably wired now. Talk to you later."

He called Melba to reassure her that he would be in shortly.

Just as Charles said, Tom Weston arrived within minutes and was ushered into the lounge. He attached the recording device and gave Josh the same security instructions before leaving.

"You remember how to activate and deactivate the recorder, don't you, Dr. Lehman?" asked Tom.

"Yeah, I think so," said Josh.

"Just to be sure, let's go through a test run," said Tom. "Show me how to work it."

I feel like a dumb-ass student, thought Josh as he went through the maneuvers.

"Perfect!" Dr. Lehman. "Now, I'll be watching for Jeremy to leave. After he's gone, I'll pick up the recorder from your secretary."

"Then what?"

"You are to call Mr. Salzman from a hospital phone on his private line."

"Thanks, Tom." Josh paused for a few moments, then turned to Tom. "Did you ever play football?"

"No, I didn't," replied Tom with a laugh. "Why do you ask?"

"I don't know," said Josh. "When you were giving me those instructions, it reminded me of being in a huddle during a football game, giving each other instructions."

"It's just part of another game, Josh," Tom said with a chuckle.

Josh left the hospital and hurried to his office.

* * * *

Josh really didn't have time to visit casually with Jeremy with an office full of patients, but he would give him time to say why he was there. He called Melba to bring him into his office.

"Dr. Lehman!" he exclaimed. "Thank you for seeing me on such short notice."

"How can I help you, Mr. Corbett?" he said. "I am sure you are not here to discuss open-heart surgery."

"If I were in the need, this would be the first place I'd go," he replied, with a chuckle. "This visit is a follow-up on our last visit, Dr. Lehman."

"I guess I don't understand, Mr. Corbett," he said, "Do we have more to discuss?"

"Well, yes," he said, looking straight into Josh's eyes with a look that might have frightened some individuals. Josh held the stare until Jeremy dropped his eyes.

"I will get straight to the point, Dr. Lehman. Mr. Bradford has asked that I bring you this message," he continued. "We know that you know more than you have told us about what is going on at Salzman Electronics."

"You have made frequent visits to Charles Salzman's office and we want to give you a chance to tell us what you know. We are prepared to make you an offer for the information that would be quite lucrative for you. If you refuse, your action could lead to unpleasantness for you."

"I think our meeting has come to close, Mr. Corbett," Josh said with a firm tone to his voice. He pressed his intercom button for Melba. "Melba, Mr. Corbett is leaving. There are no charges for today."

"Think about it, Josh," he retorted.

"Give my regards to Mr. Bradford, Mr. Corbett," he said. "And kindly address me as Dr. Lehman in the future. On second thought, I don't think there will be a future insofar as our visits are concerned."

Jeremy appeared agitated as he stood to leave. Josh was slightly tremulous as he opened the door for him; but, at the same time he felt invigorated with his ability to stand up to this threat. In his office alone, Josh said aloud, "This guy threatened me! Do they take me to be some kind of pushover?"

He pressed the security button on the recorder and placed it in the carrying case. He called for Melba to come in.

"Anything you need, Dr. Lehman?" she asked, a concerned look on her face.

"No, I'm fine, Melba. Thanks," he replied. *This lady is remarkable*, thought Josh. *She can sense that something is not right.*

"Melba, someone from Mr. Salzman's office will come by soon to pick this up. I won't need to see him."

"Yes, sir," she said and left without another word.

*   *   *   *

At the first lull he had after checking his post-operative cases in the hospital, Josh went to the lounge in the hospital to call Charles.

"Josh, they've drawn the battle lines. Listen carefully," said Charles. "Is anyone else in the room with you?"

"No, not right now."

"The technician that you met is Tom Weston. Tom is one of our highest trained service technicians. He also is in charge of security. He has at least two armed guards working close to him at all times. You won't recognize them, but they will be close by.

"We want you to wear an electronic locator strapped to your ankle. It transmits a signal so we know where you are at all times. You will carry an instrument that appears to be a pager, but it is actually a panic device. Tom will show you how it works. Josh, I hate to put this on you, but we have reason to believe it is necessary."

"Do I need to carry a gun, Charles?" he asked, trying to remain calm.

"You won't need to. If you are approached, just activate the 'pager' and you'll have plenty of firearm protection immediately. Josh, this will be over soon. Trust me."

"I have no choice."

"We've had one casualty in the company. We don't want another."

That ended their conversation. He didn't elaborate on the "one casualty."

Tom was prompt, as usual, and attached the devices and described the use of the pager. He was matter-of-fact in his instructions and he made no other comment except to say with a laugh, "Another huddle, Dr. Lehman." *Why couldn't he just say, "Don't worry,"* Josh thought, still apprehensive about Charles' remark about a casualty.

I feel like some sort of sex offender or parolee, thought Josh. *I hope no one sees the transmitter on my leg when I change clothes in the dressing room. Of course surgeons never pay much attention to anyone when they change clothes after an operation anyway. They always seem to be in such a hurry when they rip off their scrubs and shoe covers and scatter them about the dressing room floor.*

* * * *

After the last hospital patient was visited, charting completed, and families counseled, Josh made his way to his office. Melba met him at the door, that same quizzical look on her face that signaled that something was not quite right.

"This envelope was delivered a few minutes ago by some courier service," she said. "There is no return address. I decided not to open it," she added.

"Did you have to sign for it?"

"No, sir," she said. "Also, I thought it was unusual that the messenger had no uniform. I have no idea where it came from."

"Thank you, Melba," he said. "I'll open it in the office later."

"Good," she replied. "You have a packed scheduled for the rest of the day."

Josh tried to put all of the happenings of the day out of his mind while he saw patients—one after another all afternoon. No sooner had the last patient walked out the door than Josh sat at his desk and opened the mysterious envelope. By a stroke of luck, Melba was not in the room to witness his startled reaction. Inside the envelope was a newspaper clipping from the Dallas Morning News that read:

"Police identified the badly beaten man who was found in the ditch alongside Turtle Creek Road yesterday as Herbert Bowman, an engineer and long-time employee of Salzman Electronics. He is still in the intensive care unit at Metcalfe Medical Center. Spokespersons there state that he is still unconscious but stable at the present time, with multiple head and body injuries. There are still no details of the cause of the beating and no suspects have been identified.

Administrative officers at Salzman Electronics were unable to shed light on the event, expressing their shock and commenting that Mr. Bowman was a valuable employee with an excellent employment record.

No members of Mr. Bowman's family were available for comment."

Josh's hands trembled as he quickly returned the clipping to the envelope before Melba could see it. He wondered what he should do. *This is obviously a message from Jeremy and Bradford. These bastards are threatening me again!* he thought.

He decided not to call Charles. Nothing to be gained right now, he told himself. *I'm not going to run to the phone to call for help for something this trivial. But is it trivial?* he wondered. *These people are desperate! Whatever, I have gotten himself into this mess and I have to deal with it.*

There was a faint knock on the door and Melba entered.

"Are you all right, Dr. Lehman?"

"I'm OK, Melba; thanks."

"You look a little pale," she said.

"Your mothering instinct is showing, Melba," he laughed. "I think it's about time to shut down and go home, don't you?"

"Yes, sir. Dr. Lehman, a strange phone call came in just now," she said. "When I answered, some man said, 'Tell Dr. Lehman to call this number if he wants to talk,' and then hung up without identifying himself." She handed him the slip of paper with the number.

"Thank you, Melba," said Josh, trying to act nonchalant. "I'll check it out."

Chapter 36

Josh wondered why Charles had not informed him about Herb Bowman. *Probably didn't want to frighten me,* he thought. Josh told himself that it could be that Herb's injury was not linked to Scoetec at all. Charles said that Herb had a gambling habit. But what about the clipping and the phone call? Charles needed to know about the threat—if he didn't already know. Josh decided to wait until he heard from Charles.

Josh's agenda was packed with his surgery schedule, with his consultant role with the new hospital development, and with building his referral sources. He went about his routine, attempting to put the threat out of his mind and stay focused on his work. Still, he maintained his vigil everywhere he went and always had his panic button close at hand. Sometimes he thought that he would just push the button and test the response from his "bodyguards," but decided otherwise.

Every couple of weeks Josh traveled to Dallas, at Charles' request, for an update on the scope initiative. On those visits he reported his progress also to Dr. Dubonet and President Roever. Even though he felt engulfed by a cloud of mystery, Josh had to admit that he was intrigued by this fast pace of activity.

What was missing in his life were the plans that he and Linda had made to spend more time together. He could feel the same erosion in their relationship that had occurred during residency training when Linda drifted into the horror of drug and alcohol abuse. He had to be ever alert to the possibility of a recurrence of that nightmare.

Linda compensated for their drifting apart by staying busy with her social life, just as she had done when they lived in Dallas. When she was not involved in

Junior League, Medical Auxiliary, or community organization committee meetings, she was on the tennis court or in the recreation room at the country club.

The night meetings worried Josh. Frequently he would come home at the end of the day, exhausted, to an empty house and a note saying that she would be getting home late from some meeting, and that there was a frozen dinner to be thawed. This usually led to a fast peanut butter sandwich and a collapse in bed, hoping there would be no calls during the night.

When Linda finally did arrive, he awakened just long enough to verify that she appeared normal, with no telltale signs of drug or alcohol use, and then dropped back into an almost comatose sleep. Their sex life had diminished to zero. Linda even stopped trying to arouse him when she finally crawled into bed after one of her late night sessions.

Linda's calendar called for some party or social gathering for couples every week, and sometimes two times a week. Josh tried to make as many as possible, frequently having to beg off the event, or if he did attend, having to leave before the ending.

* * * *

Donnie Bradford was on the invitation list for every party. He brought a different companion to each event. It was always the same pattern; he would bring some pretty, innocent-appearing young girl for all to see and then abandon her and begin his rounds among the other women. Donnie reminded Josh of an old dog sniffing around trying to find a bitch in heat. Most of the time, whatever girl he brought would leave alone in disgust. It was no wonder that he never brought the same girl twice.

Josh had a hard time being even the least bit cordial to Donnie at the parties. When he looked at Donnie, he was reminded of the contemptuous Don Bradford, and remembered how Donnie had to be tutored through college. He thought about the many times he had to get him sober enough to beat just some bit of knowledge into his pickled brain.

On no occasion—social events or otherwise—where Josh and Donnie were together casually did Donnie ever make any comment that would indicate that he was aware of the unpleasant encounters Josh had had with Jeremy and Donnie's father *Jeremy must have reason enough to keep Donnie out of the loop in sensitive situations like this,* thought Josh.

Even though at every gathering it was obvious that Donnie was on some kind of chemical high, no one seemed to care. Donnie was the eligible, wealthy playboy in the community, and the social world practically idolized him. He could do no wrong in their eyes. Some parents even remarked to others that Donnie would make a good match for their daughters.

On the occasions when there was dancing, Donnie never missed a dance. He grabbed any female who was nearby and dragged her to the dance floor. Linda was one of his favorite targets, and what's more, it seemed to Josh that she enjoyed every minute of it when Donnie wheeled her around the floor and led her perfectly through every step.

Whatever else that could be said about Donnie, he knew his dance steps. When a slow piece was played, where couples danced close, Donnie always pulled Linda to the dance floor. Josh watched as they wound themselves around each other and swayed with the rhythm like two copulating snakes. Josh tried to ignore the scene as much as he could, but it was too obvious and too embarrassing. This was not Josh's world, attending such functions. He went along with it for Linda, hoping that in some way his being there might help to preserve their marriage.

They no longer had the same relationship with Luke and Ann and Jay. For a while it appeared that Linda had developed an enviable admiration for Luke and Ann's lifestyle. Now, however, Luke and Ann were about as far removed from Linda and Josh's social whirl as they possibly could be. The two couples no longer had any common interests, and when they were together for whatever reasons, the awkwardness was unbearable for everyone.

✼ ✼ ✼ ✼

At least two weeks passed before Josh heard from Charles. Josh had just finished a simple femoral artery by-pass case when he received the message to call Charles. He changed into street clothes before placing the call to Charles. Josh hoped Charles had some news that would let me take off the monitor from his ankle.

"Josh!" said Charles. "It's good to hear from you. How are you doing?"

"Fine," replied Josh. "I've meant to call you sooner, but didn't want to bother you with every trivial happening."

"And I've needed to bring you up to date," said Charles. "Don't hesitate to call any time, Josh. I know about the call and the phone number. It was traced back to a Bradford Holdings entity. Have you heard anything else?"

"No, I haven't," he said. "But just before I received the call, an envelope was delivered containing a newspaper clipping about Herb Bowman. That shook me a bit."

"I'm not surprised. That story is gradually unraveling."

"How is Herb?" asked Josh.

"He's better," he answered. "We have been able to communicate with him for the first time. He gave the police a pretty good description of the assailant, but not enough to make a positive identification."

"What was the motive—the gambling thing or the new product?"

"It was a Bradford thing," replied Charles. "They tried to make him talk, and according to Herb, he told them nothing. The little guy is tough. He deserves a lot of credit for holding out."

"What's next, Charles?"

"We stay on the same course," he said "I know you must be apprehensive about all this, but you are well protected. Believe me. You are under our surveillance every minute."

"That in itself is scary," said Josh.

"I know, but necessary," he said. "Josh, one reason I called is to tell you that I would like for you to spend a few days at our Switzerland plant. We are making great progress with the scope. It is in the final stages of development and will be ready to market in Europe soon—long before we will be able to get approval for use in this country. We need you to do some live test runs on animals with the scope within the next few weeks."

"I'll need some time to rearrange my schedule," said Josh. "Let me get back to you. What is your timetable?"

"We need you there as soon as possible."

"I'll let you know," said Josh.

"Josh," said Charles, "don't let down your guard for a minute, and don't tell anyone where you're going—why or when."

"Thanks for the warning, friend," he laughed. "Don't worry, I can handle my end of this."

He wished he were as confident as he sounded.

* * * *

With the assistance of a fellow cardiothoracic surgeon and Luke at the head of the table, Josh struggled through a difficult ventricular septal defect repair in a thirty-four-year-old man who had waited too long to have the surgery. An ineffective attempt had been made to close the defect when the patient was a boy, and for one reason or another—probably financial—the man failed to have another procedure.

The poor guy gradually reached the end stage of heart failure, which placed him in a high surgical risk category. However, without surgery his life expectancy was only a matter of months. As always, Luke did a commendable job of keeping the patient stable during the procedure. When they placed the last suture in the patch over the defect in the wall of the heart, Luke weaned him off the heart-lung machine, and with the first electroshock, the heart started a normal rhythm. Applause erupted from everyone in the operating room. It was a victory!

As they wound down, Luke made a casual remark to Josh.

"Josh, will you be staying around for a while?" he asked.

"Sure," said Josh. "We haven't talked in a while. You need to update me on what's going on in your life."

"Not much to report," said Luke, but the way he said it told Josh otherwise. "I'll need to stay with this man for a few minutes in the ICU. Meet me in the conference room in the ICU."

"I'll see you there," said Josh.

Josh went immediately to the conference room to unwind a bit after the exhausting case. It was an eerie feeling always for Josh when he went into the consultation room alone. The walls seemed to echo the unpleasant announcements that he had been forced to deliver to some families in the past.

Waiting for Luke gave him time to confirm his travel plans with Charles for the next day. The company plane would arrive at an early hour and departure time was set for daylight. Josh had made arrangements to be gone for up to ten days.

Josh had a bit of a problem explaining to Linda that morning where he was going and for what reason without betraying Charles' warning regarding the need for confidentiality. She had not felt well the last two or three days, probably an intestinal virus, and he hated to leave her. This meeting with Luke would give him a chance to ask him to check on her.

In less than twenty minutes, Luke appeared.

"How is the patient?" asked Josh.

"He's doing remarkably well," Luke replied. "We'll have him off the vent in a couple of days. You did a great job on this guy, Josh."

"Thanks, Luke," said Josh. "I couldn't have done it without your expertise. How are Ann and Jay? I miss seeing them."

"They're doing fine, Josh," he answered, "and we all miss seeing you. What has happened, Josh? I know you're super busy, but we're losing touch."

"I know, Luke," he said. "It bothers me. We're in a trap, Luke. A man-made trap. This is not supposed to happen."

"I thought for a while that with all of us working together we could keep the flame kindled. Ann never visits with Linda any more."

"Different lifestyles, Luke," said Josh. "I don't like it. I miss seeing Jay. He's going to forget who I am."

"I don't think so," said Luke. "He worships you and brings up something every day about what Uncle Josh said or what Uncle Josh is doing. You should hear him trying to explain a coronary artery by-pass graft to his friends," said Luke, laughing.

"I'm sure that would be a rich discussion to hear."

They both laughed, and then were quiet for an awkward moment, each waiting for the other to speak. Luke finally broke the silence.

"Josh, this is hard for me to say, but I have to tell you," he said. "There are lots of rumors out there about Linda and Donnie Bradford."

He waited for Josh to respond, not knowing what to expect. Josh stared off into space for a few moments.

"Tell me what you hear, Luke."

"You know, about the only thing we go to the club for is for use of the swimming pool for Jay and for an occasional dinner and for the kid's summer activities," said Luke. "Every time Ann takes Jay, she sees Linda playing tennis with Donnie. After they play, they retreat to the club room, then come out in bathing suits and cavort like a couple of teenagers in the adult pool in front of everyone."

"Is that all?" asked Josh.

"A lot of people are talking, Josh," he replied. "There are stories of Linda and Donnie leaving the club together in Donnie's car and returning two or three hours later to let Linda off at her car. Stories about the way they dance together. I don't like it. I've tried to ignore it as long as I can, thinking it was all tongue wagging, but it goes on and on and I'm worried for your sake."

"I know it's taken a lot of fortitude on your part to bring this up, Luke, and I appreciate your honesty," said Josh. "I am to blame for whatever has happened. It's because of my workload. Losing a wife is a hell of a price to pay for success in a profession. I don't know what to do, Luke."

"What's going on at home, Josh?" asked Luke.

"About the only time we're together is when we go to some dinner party or dance," Josh replied. "Ninety percent of the time either I have to leave early or

Linda is involved in some way as a sponsor and has to stay and come home with someone else. We have no 'intimate time' anymore. Luke, we haven't had sex in over two months."

"What about the substance abuse problem?"

"I watch closely for that. No signs at all," said Josh. "We are not seeing Dr. Mayfield any longer. He warned me to watch for relapses. I think I would recognize the signs."

"Josh, can you restructure your time in anyway?" asked Luke. "That seems to be the key. You are going to have to intervene here, if there's any truth to these rumors. And when you do, you are going to have to spend more time with Linda."

"I can't give this up now, Luke," he replied. "We've come too far in building the heart program at the hospital. I can't back off now."

"What about your deal with Salzman?"

"It ties in with the heart program," he answered. "At daylight in the morning I am flying to Switzerland in the company jet for a week or ten days for some last minute refinement of the new scope. I tried to get Linda to go with me, but she was too committed to some project here. I don't know what to do, Luke."

"And I don't know what to do to help you," he said, "but we always find a way. Sounds like it's time to call for a sweeping end run," he laughed.

"I wish I could throw the ball to a wide receiver down field," grinned Josh. "As you say, we always find a way. Thanks for everything, Luke. When I get back from this trip, I know I have to do something."

"You know we're ready to help in any way we can."

"Oh, Luke, I almost forgot," he said. "Linda has had some sort of stomach problem. I told her she may have to get a prescription from you for nausea."

"No problem, Josh," he replied. "Have a good trip."

"One of the first things I'm going to do when I return is come over to see Jay and Ann. I miss them both," he said. "Luke, I think I've told you before, but this Salzman thing is still highly confidential."

"Yeah, you told me," said Luke. "See you soon."

As they parted, a handshake was followed by an unprecedented hug, which seemed indicated after Luke had dropped his bombshell.

Chapter 37

Daylight would come sometime between six and six-thirty. Josh wanted to allow himself plenty of time to get to the airport—about a thirty-minute trip. He packed before retiring, but slept fitfully, thinking of his talk with Luke.

He awakened at five, shaved, showered, and dressed without waking Linda. Before leaving, he leaned over her side of the bed and gave her a kiss. She opened her eyes, smiled, and then went back to sleep.

He made his way quietly down the stairs, through the kitchen, and to the back door to the garage. No time for breakfast, but he had been told that he would be served meals aboard the plane. He clicked the garage door opener and started the engine. It was pitch black outside. There would be little traffic this early, so he should have plenty of time to get to the airport.

As he backed out of the garage, he became aware of the lights of an approaching car in the street. The car stopped directly in front of his driveway, effectively blocking his exit.

"What the hell?" he uttered and started to get out of his car when he saw, in his rear view mirror the driver of the car and another man emerge from the parked vehicle. Both carried crowbars as they came toward him at a fast walk. Josh slammed his door shut and searched frantically for his cell phone. It was in his briefcase, locked in the trunk of his car!

The two men came to either side of his car and motioned for him to open the door. They held the crowbars, as if ready to smash the windows. Josh thought of his panic button that he always carried around his neck, as he had been instructed. He pushed the button. All he could do was wait. He would give these two goons a good fight before he gave up, hoping beyond hope that Tom Weston would respond before he was subdued.

If he ever had any concern about a prompt response from Tom, he could put that out of his mind. The two assailants shouted a countdown through the window to give him a last chance to open the door. Josh had already decided to open the door and give these guys a fight when a car, traveling at high speed, screeched to a halt, after jumping the curb alongside his driveway. Tom Weston and two Salzman guards, each swinging semi-automatic handguns, rushed to Josh's car.

"Drop the crowbars, scum bags!" shouted Tom. "Place your hands on top of the vehicle—unless you want your legs shortened!"

They obeyed as ordered. Both guys dropped their crowbars and with terror-stricken faces looked about for a possible way to escape. Even in the darkness, Josh could see that one of the men had lost control of his bladder as urine ran over the tops of his shoes. There was no question who was in charge now. Tom opened the door to help Josh out as the other two guards frisked the men for weapons. Each of the thugs had a hand piece in a shoulder holster. Tom removed both and placed them in his car.

Tom told the assailant with the wet pants to walk away. He told the other to get in his car, after the first man was well away down the street.

"Keep your inside lights on and your hands on the steering wheel," warned Tom. "If you remove your hands from the wheel for any reason you'll get a nice refreshing shower of bullets from all three of these guns. Pick up your partner and keep going. Oh...wait! Take a message to Lennie for me. Tell him that in the future, he shouldn't send boys to do a man's job. This is no business for amateurs."

"Wet-pants" did not walk, but ran as fast as he could down the street, without looking back. The other started his car, turned around in the street and raced away, stopping briefly to pick up his partner.

Josh still trembled a bit when Tom came to his side.

"Nice work, Dr. Lehman," said Tom. "You handled that very well. You need to start moving, if you feel like it. Do you want us to take you?"

"I'm all right," said Josh. "I want my car at the airport."

"Fine," said Tom. "We'll follow you to the airport. We suspected something like this would happen. The Salzman plane came in late last night and we detected some unusual activity around the hangar early this morning. I don't think you'll hear from those two again. Their boss, Lennie, is a small-time mobster who wants to be big. He'll never make it."

"Tom, thanks for being there for me," said Josh.

"No problem, Dr. Lehman. Have a nice trip," he said. "I need to report in to Mr. Salzman."

"Tell him I'm still in the game," Josh said, followed by a chuckle.

"I'll do that," said Tom, grinning as he turned his face into his cell phone.

Josh parked his car and walked across the tarmac to the waiting Salzman private 747 jet plane. Over his shoulder he spotted Tom and his two assistants covering him as he walked from the parking lot to board the plane. *That's reassuring to see,* he thought. *What would have happened if Tom and his men had not gotten there in time?* He decided not to think about it.

Josh boarded the plane, met the pilot and co-pilot and the steward. He was introduced to the other two crew members: the communications engineer, Kevin Brant, who stayed in the compartment that housed the complex electronic components of the company's sophisticated information system, and Dak Wang, who was responsible for preparing food and drink as needed by the passengers.

The steward, Jason Morris, showed Josh to a sleeping compartment where he could dress, shower, or take a nap. He left his baggage there, except for his briefcase and cell phone, which he kept close by his side.

Next, Jason escorted him to the lounge area. This was the focal point of the plane's interior design. It was elaborately finished with mahogany paneling and thick carpeting. In the center was a small oval table with padded edges, firmly secured to the deck. Surrounding the table were five leather-upholstered, comfortable, swivel chairs that, with a push of a button, would do everything short of dance. They too were anchored to the deck. One button brought up a tray for meals or drink. Another push of a switch and a notebook computer and keyboard appeared, and still another provided earphones and a dial for a choice of music. On one bulkhead was a large screen that served as a computer monitor, as well as an oversized video movie and television screen.

Josh sat in one of the comfortable chairs, picked out a magazine from the rack, and relaxed while the plane became airborne. Soon after they were under way, Jason appeared to take his order for breakfast. Josh checked the menu—a far cry from the fare at the hospital cafeteria or doctor's lounges.

He was studying the choices when he noticed for the first time that someone other than the steward stood at his side. He looked around. It was Leah Salzman! What a surprise! Josh sprang from his chair and turned toward Leah just as the plane lurched. The motion threw him back into the chair, awkwardly grasping for something to steady himself and leaving him sprawled halfway on the chair and halfway on the floor. They both laughed as Leah moved forward to help him stand.

"I rarely have that effect on men," said Leah, with that same smile and that same toss of her head that Josh remembered.

"I have these visual hallucinations occasionally," Josh said with a nervous laugh, "where images of people appear before me when I know they are not real."

"I'm real, Dr. Lehman," she said. "Sleepy, but real. Obviously you weren't told that I would be here. Are you all right?"

"Fine," said Josh. "No injuries—just a bit stunned."

"I hope you don't mind," she said, taking a seat across the table from Josh. "I'm representing a Swiss drug manufacturer in a product liability suit, and I'm taking depositions in Geneva tomorrow. When Uncle Charles found out, he suggested I go on the company plane."

"I don't mind at all," said Josh. "Did Charles tell you why I'm here?"

"He just said that you were helping him on some research project," she answered. "He thinks a great deal of you, Dr. Lehman."

"He's a remarkable person," said Josh. "Who would ever have thought that my encounter with your grandmother would bring me this close to the company? It's been an incredible experience. I feel fortunate to have this opportunity to work with your uncle."

"My grandmother asks about you constantly," she said. "Charles tells me you may come to Passover Seder."

"I hope to," said Josh. "It's been years since I've attended a Seder. Tell me about your lawsuit."

"It's a case of a plaintiff attorney convincing a family that they have a good case against the drug manufacturer," said Leah. "The drug is a blood pressure medicine. The patient had a dizzy spell and fell after taking one dose of the medicine…developed a clot on his brain, and subsequently died. They contend that the patient was not given adequate warning."

"Do you have a good defense?"

"I think so," she replied. "Thousands of people have taken the same medicine for years with no adverse effect and there are multiple reasons why this elderly gentleman could have had a fainting spell."

"Were they warned?"

"The doctor says yes," she replied. "The family admits that the gentleman was warned, but says the patient was not capable of understanding the instructions. Everybody reads the PDR these days."

"Is the doctor named also?" asked Josh.

"Oh, yes!" she said. "Everybody is named. Even the pharmacy that dispensed the medicine. It's always the same. Frivolous suits with no grounds."

"Do you think this malpractice thing will ever end?" asked Josh. "What's the answer?"

"I'm not sure you want me to get wound-up on this issue, Dr. Lehman." She laughed. "We'll only be in the air twelve hours."

"I'd like to hear your views," said Josh.

"You may not like to hear my opinion," she said. "Why don't we eat breakfast first so I don't ruin your appetite?"

"I *am* curious now," Josh said.

Jason served their delectably prepared trays. The topics of their conversation shifted to generalities—family, college days, careers, and ambitions. Josh felt relaxed talking to Leah and she seemed comfortable in discussing issues with Josh.

"You know, it's a nice change, talking to someone other than a health care professional," said Josh.

"I was just thinking the same thing," Leah replied. "We lawyers get so involved speaking legalese to each other that we lose sight that there are other people in the world—people with other interests, other problems."

"You're describing the medical profession, you know," said Josh. "I think we're probably worse. So often we fail to communicate adequately with patients and families."

"There is your answer, Dr. Lehman. Communication!" said Leah.

Jason removed their trays and added fresh coffee to their cups.

"Are you ready to launch into the so-called malpractice crisis debate?" asked Josh.

"Dr. Lehman, you are relatively new to the medical world," she replied. "You will have to pass judgment on the quality of health care as you see it. I am not going to try to persuade you one way or another."

"Could you just call me Josh?"

"I'd love to," she said, and then laughed. "Sounds less abrasive, doesn't it."

There again was that tantalizing smile and toss of her head that fascinated Josh. He was gawking at her and hoping she didn't notice! He felt as unnerved as a teenage kid on his first date. While turning his head to one side to break his fixed gaze on Leah, Josh lectured himself, *Stay focused, dumb-ass, don't go there.*

"I am waiting to hear your opinion," said Josh, after regaining some composure.

"Here is what I see, Josh," said Leah. "Only the doctors who are responsible for malpractice litigation in the first place can cure this problem. They have to clean their ranks. They have to rebuild their patient's trust."

"You don't do that by asking patients to pay in advance or by having some beady-eyed clerk stopping your patient as he or she leaves and demanding payment. Or having your appointment secretary ask about your insurance before she inquires about your reason for needing to see the doctor. Every office I go to has a prominently displayed sign that says, 'Payment Is Due When Service Provided.' It should say, 'Satisfaction Guaranteed.'"

"There are some bad actors in your profession, Josh," she continued. "I have to defend them. That's my job, but it's getting harder to do. You guys have not set any standards of care for yourselves as a group. Every doctor marches to a different drummer. I am lost when I try to show that acceptable standard of care has been followed in a case. You all apply different standards."

"So what do you do?" she said. "You scream 'Foul!' You say the problem is the greedy lawyers and biased judges. Then you try to get tort reform that is specific to your needs: caps on judgment, caps on attorneys' fees. You call for legislative help when you should be helping yourself."

"You try to buy elected officials during election campaigns, which is the very thing you're exclaiming is wrong with the system. You whine about your insurance premiums going up. As a percent of your income, they are no different today than they have ever been. You never mention the percentage increase in your fees."

Leah paused to take a breath. She had risen from her chair with fire in her eyes and was pacing about the compartment while she spoke, as if she were speaking to a jury. Josh was awe-stricken. He could imagine what she was like in the courtroom. Should he ever have the misfortune of needing an attorney, he would turn to Leah.

"I'm sorry, Josh," she said. "I got carried away. I asked you not to get me wound up. OK, it's your turn."

"This may come as a surprise to you, but we have no issue to debate," said Josh. "I agree with you."

"Josh, when I referred to 'you' and 'yours,' I was not referring to you personally," she said.

"I know that," said Josh. "I hate to admit it, but I've seen everything you've described. Regarding standards of care, you might be interested to know this—at Metcalfe Heart we are creating practice guidelines and clinical pathways for the most common procedures that we perform."

"If our surgeons follow these guidelines—from using appropriate criteria in selecting cases for surgery, to preoperative evaluation, to post-operative care—I think we can make a difference. Also, we have established a monitoring system to track and trend patient care. We can determine which doctors have the best and worst outcomes. We've had great acceptance by the medical staff.

"I agree with you," he added. "The system needs cleaning. If we don't do it, some regulatory agency is going to do it for us."

They were quiet for a few moments, sipping fresh cups of coffee while Jason removed food trays. Leah broke the silence.

"I'm encouraged to hear that someone is waking up," she said. "If I could go into that courtroom and show that recognized protocols of care were followed, I could get favorable verdicts and rulings. We'll always have human error—those cases should be settled by mediation—but we shouldn't have the gross negligence that I see every day. What you are doing at Metcalfe is the answer. More medical centers need to do that."

"It'll happen," he said, "but it will be slow coming. Changes in practice patterns and in better patient-physician relationships need to start during training. I had a mentor during my residency who avoided going out to talk to patient's families after an operation. Can you believe that? He would do some complex surgery procedure with skill and then panic when it came time to talk to the family."

Thinking of Dr. Mintner, Josh turned to gaze out the window while he allowed himself a few seconds to reminisce about those days when he had been assigned to Dr. Mintner's service. It seemed like ages ago.

He turned back to face Leah's dark, soft eyes staring at him with an affectionate look, as if she were seeing him for the first time ever. She dropped her glance and seemed a bit embarrassed that he had "caught" her.

"I think we've about whipped this subject to death," said Josh.

"You're right," she replied. "I've enjoyed hearing your views, Josh. I think there's some hope after all. I have some work to do, getting ready for my depositions, so I guess I'd better get busy," she added, standing and taking her briefcase to another chair.

"See you at lunch," Josh called out.

"By all means," she answered. "We'll find something else to talk about. Maybe we'll find something to fight about," she teased and flashed that smile and the head-toss.

Josh found a medical journal in his briefcase and busied himself catching up on the latest published studies. He knew he would be expected to contribute to these professional publications someday, once the Heart Hospital was fully operational.

The compartment was quiet except for the drone of the jet engines. Jason came by to see if he needed anything, but Josh declined. He put the chair in a reclining position while he read. The comfort and the quietness, other than the jet noise, soon lulled him to sleep and the journal dropped from his lap onto the deck.

Chapter 38

Josh awoke with a start from the light touch on his arm and opened his eyes to see Leah smiling down at him.

"I hate to disturb you," she said. "You have been sleeping so peacefully. I just stood here and watched you for a while. I sort of feel guilty," She laughed.

"Did I snore?" he asked.

"Not at all," she replied. "You looked like a small child. Oh, the reason I woke you! Uncle Charles needs to talk to you. I told him you were sleeping...he thought that was a good idea," she grinned. "He must have a lot planned for you at the plant."

"How do I call him?" he asked as he struggled to stand.

"In the communications compartment there is a soundproof booth," she said. "You will sit facing the cameras and a large video screen. You and Charles will talk to each other just as if you were in the same room face-to-face. It's all computerized," she added. "Your images will actually be three-dimensional. It's sort of weird at first, as if the other person is really right there, but you get used to it."

"Did Charles say what he wanted?" asked Josh.

"No, he said it wasn't urgent," she replied. "I think you are the only person he would ever tell that to. Everything is urgent for Uncle Charles." She laughed. "I'll show you where to go."

She took him to the communications room and left him with Kevin. The compartment, packed with electronic equipment, looked much like a small version of Charles' laboratory in the office building in Dallas. Kevin greeted Josh with a handshake.

"Nice having you aboard, Dr. Lehman," he said. "I'm sure I don't have to tell you, but this is all quite simple," he added as he placed Josh in the booth. "After I close the door, the booth is completely soundproof."

'There's nothing for you to do but wait for Mr. Salzman to appear on the screen. I will be right outside making adjustments. After you make contact with Mr. Salzman, you will be in total darkness except for the image on the screen."

In an instant Charles appeared on the screen, life-size and in three dimensions. Leah was right! It was a weird feeling, talking to Charles just as if he were there. At first there was a slight pause between the lip movement and the sound of his voice, but Kevin made some adjustments to correct the delay.

"Hi, Josh," said Charles. "How is the trip going so far?"

"Very smooth ride," he replied. "And the crew members have been super attentive."

"Good," he said. "Josh, I'm sorry about your unpleasant experience this morning. I got the report that it was dealt with promptly."

"You are absolutely right," said Josh, "Tom is a real champion."

"Josh, I want to brief you on your visit to the plant," said Charles. "You will arrive in Geneva at about two or three in the morning, local time. I suggest you take a short-acting sleeper on arrival. Jason will have it available. You will need some sleep to offset jet lag. The plane will stay on the tarmac until daylight, allowing you time to sleep and dress for the day."

"The customs officials will visit you on the plane and clear you to debark. A car will be waiting to take you directly to the plant. At the end of the day you will be taken to your hotel. Your agenda will be faxed to you before you arrive so you can study it."

"Sounds intriguing, Charles," said Josh, marveling at how organized Charles was in everything he did. "I'm looking forward to seeing the final product."

"I think you'll be pleased, Josh," he said. "It will be much like you have experienced on the simulators. As soon as you are familiar with the actual feel of the instrument, we've arranged for you to train several surgeons in its use before you return home."

"How long do you think I'll be needed?" asked Josh.

"I predict you will master using the scope in one day and be ready to instruct the others for the next day or two," he replied. "I have arranged for you to stay longer if you like."

"Thanks, Charles," he said. "I'll probably be anxious to get back."

"I thought so," laughed Charles. "That's why I'm leaving the plane there."

"I've enjoyed visiting with your niece, Charles," said Josh. "Quite a surprise to find her here. She's a delightful person."

"A last minute surprise for me, too, to find out she was going to Switzerland," he said. "My mother will be ecstatic that the two of you traveled together." He laughed. "I may not tell her."

"How is your mother?" asked Josh.

"She's fine," he replied. "We presented an update yesterday on the new scope initiative at the board meeting. She listened to every word, and then promptly ripped us apart. As always, she amazes everyone."

"Give her my regards," said Josh.

"I'll do that," said Charles. "Josh, I'm looking forward to tomorrow evening to hear how your day went. After you finish your work, I'd like for you to return to the plane so we can discuss your opinion. Kevin will be available to bring us together. Enjoy your trip, Josh."

"Thanks, Charles," he replied.

In a flash he was gone and the booth was pitch black. The door opened and Kevin was by his side.

"Take a few moments to accommodate to the real world, Dr. Lehman," said Kevin, grinning at Josh's astonished appearance.

"I'm not going to ask how you did that, Kevin," laughed Josh. "I'm afraid you might try to explain it to me."

"Quite simple, compared to some of the things you do."

Josh made his way back to the lounge area. Leah was waiting until he returned to have lunch.

"What do you think, heart healer?" she asked.

"Unbelievable," said Josh. "I even reached out to shake hands with Charles when we parted."

Josh plopped into one of the lounge chairs. Jason came to his side immediately with a menu. Josh and Leah both asked for a light salad, which Dak had ready in seconds.

"Are you ready for tomorrow?" asked Josh.

"I think so," she replied. "In cases like this, you take one step at a time. Usually wait for the other side to make a mistake."

"I'm going to ask you a personal question," said Josh. "You don't have to answer. Why have you never married?"

"You *are* getting personal!" She laughed. "Well, first of all, I'm not gay, if you are wondering. I've had a couple of serious relationships, maybe close to being serious, that never got past the bedroom stage. You know, 'have to leave early this morning…important appointment…I'll call you.' Which left me thinking, *Is this all there is to sleeping with someone?* Right now, my work is my life."

"You sound like me," said Josh. "And I am married."

"Are you happy with your marriage, Josh?" she asked.

"Let's just say for now that I'm confused," he said. "I question whether striving for success in a career and marriage are compatible."

"Using your expression, 'you sound like me,'" she said.

"Again, I think we need to change the subject," said Josh.

"I agree," she replied.

They thumbed through their briefcases without conversing, concentrated on the first document they found, even if it was something meaningless. They avoided eye contact and avoided any semblance of a comment on the topic of conversation that they had just visited. After a few minutes, Josh broke the silence.

"Care to watch a movie?" asked Josh, searching through the stack of videos.

"Sure," she answered. "I'm sure you want something with action or about sports."

"What do you like?"

"Find a good tear-jerker where the hero wins. One that has action plus drama," she replied. "No death scenes."

"What a request!" he said with a laugh. "I'm gonna just close my eyes and pick, unless you want to choose."

"No way! Might give you some insight into my personality," she said, then smiled and tossed her head. "Just close your eyes and grab! See what fate will hand us."

Josh laughed, scattered the videos on the table, closed his eyes, picked one, and handed it to Leah.

"Well, look at this!" she said. "We both win: 'Field of Dreams!'"

"How do I win?" asked Josh, chuckling. "I played football."

"You'll love this one if you haven't seen it," she said. "A moral to the story. Applies to both of us."

They settled into chairs as the movie began on the giant screen. Jason discretely took a portable seat behind them.

This is a welcome respite for me, and probably for Leah as well, thought Josh. *For me, a break from thinking about my failing marriage; for Leah a break from thinking about what I suspect is emptiness in her life.*

After the movie, Jason appeared with glasses of wine, without asking their preference. He had a glass of white and a glass of red wine for each.

"You won't have a choice from the menu this evening," said Jason. "Dak has prepared a gourmet meal for you. I have no idea what it is, but I appeal to you both to pretend you enjoy it, even if you don't," he laughed. "Dak is sensitive about his cooking."

"Don't worry, Jason," said Leah. "We are both masters at faking, aren't we, Josh?"

"Oh, absolutely," he said, giving Leah a quizzical look.

Jason left them to sip on their wine of choice.

"What did you mean by that remark?" asked Josh.

"Come on, Josh," she replied with an undertone of vexation. "You're not happy in your marriage. I make my living detecting when people are not being honest with me. There's something going on that you're not telling me. You don't have to tell me a damn thing, but don't think you can deceive me."

She was getting that fiery-eyed courtroom look again. For a moment, Josh thought she was going to stand and pace the deck. He was quiet for a few seconds. He could feel a mixture of anger and irritation building up and wanted to choose the right words to respond to her outburst.

"We're having our first argument!" he finally said with a laugh.

"And our last," she replied, and did not laugh.

"All right, damn it!" he said. "My marriage sucks. My wife—on the brink of a relapse from treatment for drug abuse—is running around with a freaked-out playboy, we haven't had sex for over two months, and I don't know what to do about it. Does that satisfy your curiosity?"

He turned away from Leah and gazed out the window. Neither of them spoke for a long interval. Leah stood, came to Josh's side, and sat on the table facing him.

"I'm so sorry, Josh," she said. She reached out and grasped his hand with a touch of tenderness that Josh had not felt in ages. "It's not curiosity. I care for you, Josh. It hurts me to see you in pain."

He turned to look at Leah. Their gazes locked. They held the look, while they silently said words to each other that they did not dare to speak aloud at this time.

Jason broke the spell when he came to refill their wine glasses. Soon thereafter he served the meal courses, each delectably prepared. Josh and Leah spoke little during the dinner. There were a few awkward moments. They seemed to avoid looking at each other. They both made glowing comments about Dak's creation. Jason asked Dak to come out from the galley and Josh and Leah showered him with compliments, as he bashfully took his bows.

The plane touched down at two-thirty a.m., Geneva time, and came to rest close to the assigned gate without actually connecting. Kevin delivered the fax to Josh that described in detail his agenda for the day, and again instructed him to stay on board until the customs officials cleared him, Leah, and the crew for debarking.

As usual, Charles had thought of everything—except what to do about the turmoil that churned in Josh's head and clouded his every thought. Luke was right. He had to do something. He needed to get back home as soon as possible.

Should I have told Leah about Linda? Josh wondered. *Am I getting too close to Leah?* Every time he closed his eyes, he saw Leah's face, her eyes like bottomless, dark pools, beckoning him to come closer. He had to sweep the cobwebs from his brain. How could he perform the task ahead of him in this state?

Jason passed out the sleepers, with a warning that they had a rapid onset and would wear off in about four hours. Josh, Leah, Jason, and Dak retired to their respective compartments after a few casual goodnight remarks. Jason announced that he would awaken them in time for breakfast and dressing before they had to leave the plane.

★   ★   ★   ★

A continuous soft tone from the speaker, followed by Jason's voice, awakened Josh. His watch told him it was seven o'clock. He climbed out of his bunk and hurriedly shaved, showered, and dressed in preparation for the day. He packed his carry-on and made his way to the lounge area. Soon afterward Leah arrived, fresh and lovely as ever, with a demeanor that said she was ready for whatever she faced.

"Good morning, Dr. Lehman," she said. "Did you sleep well?"

"Like a rock," he replied. "And no hangover feeling. What's with all of the formality?"

"Professionalism." She laughed. "Time to go to work. Just rehearsing for the day."

"You look like you're ready," he said, grinning. "How long will the depositions take?"

"It'll take all day," she answered. "I hope I can wrap it up today. I need to catch a commercial flight back home tomorrow."

"Where are you staying tonight?" he asked.

"The agenda from Uncle Charles says we both have reservations at the Swissotel Geneve Metropole. It's convenient to the airport," said Leah.

"Good," said Josh. "Let's get together after work."

"Sounds great!" she said.

Jason brought their breakfast on a cart that offered them multiple choices.

"How about your day?" Leah asked. "Are you nervous at all?"

"Much like going into a football game against a team favored by two touchdowns," he laughed.

"Your football experience really conditions you for situations like this, doesn't it?"

"Yes it does," answered Josh. "I learned a lot from football that has helped me in medicine. What I do now is just another game—suit out in scrubs instead of a football uniform," he added with a laugh.

"Do you ever regret leaving football?" asked Leah.

"What is this?" he grinned. "Some sort of psychoanalysis?"

"I withdraw the question," she said with a laugh.

"I'll answer it anyway," he said with a smile. He couldn't help but meet her laughter with a smile. "The answer is no. Just think, if I had gone on to professional football, we wouldn't be here now."

"Good point," she said. "We'll file your answer 'of record.'"

Soon after breakfast they were all cleared for entry. Leah and Josh left in the same limousine that Charles provided. Leah was let off at the office building where she would spend the day in legal entanglements and Josh was taken to the Salzman Electronics plant.

Chapter 39

At the Salzman Geneva plant, two operating suites had been constructed and completely equipped, no different than the operating rooms that he was accustomed to at Metcalfe. Josh performed four cases, all coronary by-pass procedures, using the Motionless Imaging Scope—now referred to as the MIS.

The difference here was that the "patients" during this training stage were all chimpanzees, chosen because their coronary artery system is almost identical to humans. In no cases did the chest have to be opened.

The ease with which the procedures were done far exceeded Josh's expectations. He made only two suggestions—one for a finer adjustment of the eyepiece on the MIS and the other for slightly subdued light to reduce reflection. After he completed his last case he visited the cages housing the chimps. His post-operative patients were climbing around, jumping from one platform to another, as if they had never been in the operating room.

After winding up his work, dictating his reports, and congratulating and thanking his assistants, Josh left the plant for the waiting vehicle to take him back to the plane for his conference call to Charles. Kevin escorted him to the communications booth again, closed the door, and soon Charles's image appeared.

"How did it go, Josh?" asked Charles, his three dimensional face beaming with curiosity and eagerness.

"Fine, Charles," he replied. "It was fantastic! I feel like I'm still floating in space. Absolutely unbelievable!"

"Good!" said Charles. "Wish I could have been there. Tomorrow is the big day. Are you ready?"

"I think so," he answered. "I've rehearsed my part so many times I say it in my sleep."

"Any suggestions for the engineers?"

"I made a couple of observations and passed them on to the technician. Nothing of any great magnitude," said Josh.

"Good luck tomorrow, Josh," said Charles. "Phillip will meet you at the conference center and guide you through the day. Josh, once again, I appreciate all you have done and are doing for us."

"My pleasure, Charles."

At Josh's signal, Kevin stopped the show and Josh stepped out of the booth.

* * * *

The Metropole was a five star hotel on Lake Geneva. Charles had arranged for a room for Josh with a beautiful view of the lake. The room's spaciousness and elegant furnishings were wasted on Josh. All he wanted right then was a place to plop and relax after an exhaustive day.

He found a Heineken in the room refrigerator, took a chair on the balcony overlooking the lake, and watched as sailboats maneuvered their way into the marina. He hadn't drunk a beer in ages because of the lingering smell on one's breath; he had forgotten how good it tasted.

As Josh became enveloped in a warm glow of contentment, he thought of Leah and the dinner they had planned for the evening. He had truly enjoyed being with her on this trip. He knew he had to put her out of his mind and leave this fantasy world for the real problems ahead.

The thought of Leah leaving tomorrow brought on an empty feeling that he couldn't explain. He would miss their lively conversations, but he had to admit to himself that there was more there, and maybe more to come. "Maybe the beer is making me think this way" he said aloud. These thoughts were torturing him when the phone rang.

"Hi, what are you doing?" asked Leah.

"I'm sitting on the balcony having a beer," he said. "Come join me."

"I'd love to. Where are you?"

He gave her his room number.

"I'm right next door!" she said. "I'll be right over."

"The door will be open," he replied.

"Oh, my God!" he said to himself. "Right next door! Can I deal with this?"

He looked at the wall. Yes, there was a connecting door. He panicked. Should he open that door or the door to the hallway? He opted for the latter and gave a sigh of relief to find Leah standing there. Maybe she hadn't noticed the door between their rooms.

"I just got here," she said. "Nice to find you so close."

"Come look at this view while I get you a Heineken," he said.

"Thanks, I need that," she replied. "A beautiful place. Wish I didn't have to leave tomorrow."

"How was your day?" Josh called out from across the room.

"Great!" she said. "I got exactly the information I needed in the testimony, plus the enemy predators now have a greater respect for Dallas lawyers."

"Are you bragging?" he laughed.

"Of course," she said and smiled, sipping her beer. "No one else will give me credit. Tell me about your venture at Salzman Electronics."

"It went very well," he said. "Leah...has Charles ever mentioned the new company initiative...why I'm here?"

"You know better than that," she said. "Uncle Charles is the most secretive person in the world. The only thing you could find out about his business is what you'd find in public records. Leave it that way, Josh. Just tell me, were you pleased with what you found?"

"Absolutely," he replied. "It was a fabulous experience. When the facts are made public, you'll see what I mean."

"What a fantastic view, Josh," said Leah, leaning back in the balcony lounge chair with her feet propped up. "That beer was just what I needed."

"I think we both must have needed these few moments to break from a busy day," said Josh.

"Here we are, Josh. Just the two of us," Leah chuckled as she spoke, her eyes were closed. "Half-way around the world, drinking beer together, in a paradise setting, as if we had no worries. I wish it could last forever."

Josh was a bit surprised at her remarks. Was this beer talk?

"It would be nice if we could just pull the curtain on our problems," said Josh. "There's no Shangri-la, Leah, but we can dream, can't we?"

"Right," she said. "Let's not even talk about waking up."

"Agreed," he replied. They laughed and "high-fived" each other to seal the deal.

They decided to have dinner in the formal dining room in the hotel. Josh read the hotel services brochure. *Reservations required. Dress code: Formal Wear.*

"What do you think?" he asked.

"Let's throw protocol to the wind," Leah answered.

"Good, I'll call for reservations," said Josh.

"We'll probably be refused," said Leah.

"So what! If they don't want us, that's their loss."

"Go for it, tiger!" she said. "I'll add some make-up and be ready in minutes."

She went through the connecting door to her room. *She had unlocked it from the other side,* Josh noticed.

"Do you want another Heineken?" he called out.

"Wait for the wine," she replied, partially closing the door.

Josh barely finished ironing the wrinkles out of his sport coat, shaving, and brushing his teeth when Leah reappeared, looking as pretty as ever.

"Think they'll seat us?" she asked.

"Sure, you look great."

The maitre-de greeted and welcomed them cordially.

"Good evening, Dr. Lehman and Miss Salzman," he said, bowing and kissing the back of Leah's hand. "I have reserved a special place for you on the terrace overlooking the lake."

"Thank you," Josh said, and then turned to Leah and grinned. "I think your Uncle Charles has had something to do with this."

"Probably," she laughed.

A small band played soft dancing music and a few couples ventured out onto the floor from time to time. Josh was given the wine list and had to show his ignorance about wine. He looked at Leah.

"Don't ask me, Josh," she said with a laugh. "No one knows less about wine than I do."

They finally asked the wine waiter to make a choice of white wine for them.

"Maybe we should stick to beer," he chuckled. "After all we're from Texas."

They stuck to their agreement and talked about everything except personal problems. After dinner they danced a few times, to find that they did exceptionally well together on the dance floor.

The euphoria from the wine lingered past their dinner. As they made their way back to their rooms, they found themselves giggling inappropriately—especially on the elevator—to the delight of the fellow passengers.

Josh accompanied Leah to her door to say goodnight and to give farewell greetings, since she would be leaving early the next morning.

"Josh, come in for an after-dinner drink," said Leah. "I saw some cognac in the bar cabinet. Let's sit out on the balcony for a while."

"Good idea," he said. "Let me get out of this coat and tie."

"Here," she said, pointing to the door connecting their rooms. "This door is unlocked. You can go through here."

They sat on the balcony in the cool breeze, watching the reflection on the water of the lights from the distant shore. Neither of them said a word, each consumed with their own thoughts; probably thinking about what they faced when they returned to the states. The cognac, on top of beer and wine, was taking its effect on each of them. Leah finally spoke.

"Josh, do you plan on climbing into my bed tonight?" she asked. "I want you to, but our lives are so complex right now, I don't think you should."

"I understand," he said. "May I kiss you goodnight?"

"Please do," she answered.

They kissed and neither wanted to let go. *Can I sleep in that room, knowing there is only an open doorway between us?* thought Josh.

"You are a wise person, Leah," said Josh, as he broke away to enter his own room, staggering a bit as he went through the connecting doorway. Neither locked it.

Josh finally dropped off into a deep sleep after turning the events of the last two days over and over again in his mind. He was awakened by Leah's kiss; he had forgotten to set his alarm clock and was not even aware that she had entered. She was dressed, packed, and ready to depart for her early morning flight.

"Call me sometime, Josh," she said as she slipped through the door.

*　　*　　*　　*

The agenda called for him to be at the plant at eight-thirty. Josh needed to be ready to step into the limousine at eight if he were to avoid being late. He dressed and rushed out of the room at seven-forty-five on his way to the lobby. All he could think of was Leah's kiss.

She came through that connecting door on her way out! Wow! He could still taste and feel the softness of her lips. *What did she think? My breath at that time of day must have been horrible.* He lectured himself again and pushed forward, trying to focus only on the crowded schedule of the day.

He dashed into the dining room and grabbed a cup of coffee and a bagel with cream cheese to eat along the way to the meeting. He didn't want to be late. There would be thirty surgeons, as well as executives from major medical centers all over Europe gathered in the auditorium, eager for information about the MIS.

Phillip Salzman met him at the entrance.

"Good morning, Dr. Lehman," he said. "I'm Phillip Salzman. Thank you for coming. I've heard many favorable reports from Charles on your work back home."

"Thank you, Phillip," said Josh. "It's a pleasure to meet another member of your fabulous family."

"Thanks for including me among the fabulous," he replied with a laugh. "I'm just the work horse in the family."

"I am told a different story, Phillip."

"Everything is in order, sir," he said. "The Power Point equipment is in place with the same floppy that was prepared for you by Charles' office."

"Good. I have run it enough that I almost know it by memory," said Josh.

Phillip was impeccably dressed and portrayed the typical extrovert personality traits of a marketing person: the perpetual smile, the charismatic charm, the positive attitude. Josh remembered the stories of Phillip's earlier college days—his metamorphosis from the wild erratic behavior of a non-conforming student into the position of vice-president of marketing for the company, with incredible success in sales.

"I will introduce you," said Phillip. "The doctors all have headphones and there are interpreters for each language. You should deliver your presentations in English, and the surgeons may choose which language they wish. If they have questions, after a short pause the interpreter will make the inquiry and transmit your answer to the doctor."

After his introduction by Phillip, filled with glowing accolades, Josh took the group through a one-hour session of orientation, using the Power Point slide show. He gave an overview on the development of the MIS: the initial concept, the research, the technology of creating a still image of a moving object while still allowing the introduction of a moving scope into the field.

Josh could tell by their facial expressions that they were spellbound during the presentation. Afterward, he fielded questions from the group through the interpreters. From the nature of the inquiries, Josh knew that Phillip had chosen high-intellect participants. If Josh stumbled on any question, Phillip rescued him with some sort of answer, many times with humor.

Following a short recess, during which Josh visited with several of the doctors, he and Phillip divided the group into smaller cells of five surgeons each. Josh then took each subgroup through a live coronary artery by-pass procedure on a chimpanzee, using the MIS, which allowed each surgeon the experience of handling the scope. There were no interpreters in the operating room, but from the tone of the remarks, Josh could tell they were impressed.

While Josh was busy with the subgroups, Phillip used that time to give his spiel to the remaining doctors, along with administrative persons from their respective medical centers. It was a long grueling day before they finally finished.

Josh and Phillip retreated to the hotel for some quiet time, a couple of drinks, dinner, and much needed rest before repeating the process the next day. After dinner they sat in the piano bar for a few minutes, sipping cognac, before retiring. Josh got the chance to know Phillip better. He was so different from Charles, but Josh could tell he was as dedicated to the company.

"You gave a great presentation today, Josh," said Phillip. "Are you up to another?"

"The next should be easier. I won't be as nervous," he answered.

"I can't imagine you being nervous. If I had to go into that operating room like you do, I'd have to wear triple-fold diapers," he laughed.

"I am fascinated by the way you have all of this organized, Phillip," said Josh. "I think it all went well today."

"Absolutely," he said. "You know, every waking moment I feel like my brother, Charles, is looking over my shoulder. Everything has to be right, where he's concerned."

"I get the same feeling," replied Josh. "He's a remarkable person."

"I agree completely," said Phillip. "Don't get me wrong. I worship Charles. I couldn't get along without his guidance. I owe so much to him. He lifted me out of a horrible quagmire of hopelessness when I was in college."

"How long will you stay in Geneva?" Josh asked.

"I'll be here two or three days longer," he said. "There's a lot of cleaning up to be done, then I have to finish my reports. I'll make last minute visits to the vets on the conditions of our 'patients.'"

"By all means," said Josh. "Let me know what you find."

"You definitely will be in the loop on that, Josh," he said. "I'll send you copies of the reports, even before Charles tells me too." He grinned.

They parted to go to their rooms. Being with Phillip gave Josh a welcome respite from thinking about Leah. Opening the door and entering his room brought back the memory of her kiss, this very morning, before she had left to return home.

* * * *

The second day of activities at the plant went every bit as smoothly as the first day. Josh felt more confident in what he was doing, both during the power point presentations and in working alongside the surgeons in the operating room. There was favorable feedback from the doctors on both days.

They finished the day early, compared to the day before. He looked for Phillip among the crowd of participants to confirm that they had accomplished the task at hand. Josh wanted to make plans to leave as soon as possible. He was wandering about when he looked up and saw Phillip racing toward him, an unusual expression on his face.

"Josh, I've been looking everywhere for you," he exclaimed. "Charles wants to talk to you immediately."

"What can it be?" asked Josh.

He trembled in anticipation as all sorts of thoughts raced through his head. Was his father ill? Had something happened to Luke, Ann, or Jay? Or to Linda? Josh waited while Phillip moved to a quiet corner and placed the call to Charles.

Chapter 40

"I have him on the line, Josh," said Phillip, handing him the cell phone.

"Josh," said Charles in a sober tone. "Something's happened here. I had a call from Luke Sanders, Josh. Some time ago, Luke promised me he'd call me if anything happened to you that I needed to know about. I'm going to transfer this call to him. After you've talked to him, I'll be back with you."

"I had to let you know, Josh," said Luke. "Linda is in the hospital."

"What happened, Luke?" asked Josh.

"She had a miscarriage," he replied. "She's all right…I'm so sorry, Josh."

"I'll be there as soon as I can, Luke," said Josh.

He paused for a few moments to regain some bit of composure.

"Thanks, Luke. Thanks for everything."

Charles was back on the line.

"Josh, I know just enough to know that you need to get back home," said Charles. "The crew will be ready to leave as soon as you get to the airport. Don't try to talk to me, Josh. Just go!"

Within an hour they were airborne. Josh collapsed into one of the lounge chairs, the impact of the disturbing news hitting him with full force. He and Phillip had been near euphoria over the success of their two-day seminar. Then the bombshell! He needed time to think through his next move when he reached home.

Luke had warned him when he passed along the rumors that floated around. Josh had intended to intervene in some way when he returned, but he never imagined this predicament. What should he do? Donnie had to be responsible for the pregnancy. *Maybe I should just shoot the bastard.* He laughed at himself for even having the thought.

Jason had no way of knowing what was going on in Josh's life, but he was clairvoyant that something was not quite right. He brought Josh a glass of Chardonnay, without Josh requesting it. A warm glow engulfed Josh as the wine took effect.

"How could I have been so blind?" he said to himself. At every gathering, Josh now recalled how often he had seen Donnie and Linda together, in a corner talking or wandering about, sometimes to the outside or into another room. He really thought nothing of it at the time.

Josh never dreamed that their flirtation was leading to an affair. He had no respect for Donnie, and was uncomfortable being around him for even short periods of time. He assumed that Linda had the same opinion of Donnie.

As he thought back about some of the scenarios of the last few months, thoughts whirled through his mind like a tornado, touching down first on one center of his brain, then moving on to another, each time leaving chaos behind. Chaos turned into anger and guilt—anger at himself for getting so involved in his work that he had not realized what was happening and guilt that he had neglected his marriage. Could he ever forgive Linda? He just didn't want to go there right now.

Jason refilled his wine glass. Josh began to feel drowsy, but welcomed the relaxation. He needed time to think and formulate a methodical approach to the problems he faced upon arriving home. Doing away with Donnie was not an option. He laughed at himself again for letting the thought cross his mind. His deep concentration was broken by Jason's return.

"Dak will have dinner ready shortly, Dr. Lehman," Jason announced with his characteristic lack of emotion.

"Thanks, Jason," Josh replied. "Oh, Jason, may I go into the communication room and speak to Kevin? I need to let my friend, Dr. Sanders, know that I am on the way home."

"Certainly, Dr. Lehman," he answered. "If you wish, Kevin can bring a phone for you to use where you are."

"That would be better, Jason. Thank you."

Fortunately, Josh reached Luke between cases.

"How's it going, Luke?" he asked.

"She's all right, Josh," said Luke. "She's distraught and teary-eyed, as you would imagine. Ann went by to see her. Linda knows you are on the way."

"I'll go straight to the hospital when I get there," said Josh.

"Then I'll meet you there."

"No need to, Luke," he said. "My visit with her will be brief."

"Josh, you know Ann and I both are ready to help you," said Luke.

"Thanks," said Josh. "Luke, thanks for not saying, 'I told you so.'"

* * * *

After dinner, Josh tried to watch a movie, but couldn't concentrate enough to follow the plot. The wine, the dinner, and the exhaustion from all of the events of the day put him into a somnolent state. Instead of going into one of the sleeping compartments, he dozed off in one of the reclining lounge chairs. Jason placed a lightweight blanket over Josh and even removed his shoes without waking him.

* * * *

Jason touched Josh's shoulder lightly and awakened him enough to inform him that they would be arriving in the States in a little over an hour. Josh stirred from the chair, looked at his watch, and staggered to his feet.

He felt groggy and unsteady. Jason must have slipped him some sort of sedative in his food. If that was the case, Josh was grateful. He certainly had enjoyed a full night's sleep, which he needed in order to face the day ahead.

He went into one of the compartments, shaved, showered, and made himself ready to face whatever the day might bring. Within the hour, the plane was on the runway and nearing the airport debarking gate.

Josh returned to the lounge. In an unprecedented move, Jason sat in one of the lounge chairs facing Josh, with a look of genuine concern on his face.

"Dr. Lehman," he said, "I have no idea what has caused you to be so disturbed. I have worked in this position for several years and I have learned to recognize when someone is upset. Whatever it is that's bothering you, I hope it will get better."

"I appreciate that, Jason," Josh said. "It is purely personal, and it will get better in time. Also, I am grateful for your kind attention during the flights. Hope to see you again."

"Thank you, sir," said Jason and then stood and resumed his duties.

* * * *

As Josh exited the airport parking lot, the sky was just taking on the golden hue of dawn. He had an hour or so to carry out his plan before going into Linda's room. He went straight to the condo, deciding not to let anyone know he was back.

It was no surprise that the interior of the condo was exactly as he had left it. Nothing had been moved. The refrigerator contained the same food. Everything was in its place. There was a huge stack of unopened mail, dating back to the last day he had been there. Linda had not spent a single night in their condo since he had left.

His first call was to Nathan Greller. Nathan was a long-standing friend whom Josh had helped several times on previous occasions, the most recent was arranging for a liver transplant for his indigent sister. Nathan was Medical Director of Laboratory and Pathology Services for the Westlake Regional System.

"Nathan, this is Josh Lehman. Forgive me for calling you so early," he said. "Were you asleep?"

"I must be dreaming, Josh," he answered. "Pathologists don't get called at this hour."

"Nathan, I need your help," said Josh.

"I gave up surgery in my residency," he laughed. "You must be in jail."

"This is serious," said Josh. "I know I can confide in you. Can I come over to your house?"

"Sure," said Nathan, no longer making jokes of this impromptu call.

Josh was there in minutes, and the two of them sat at the breakfast table. Nathan had made fresh coffee.

"Barbara is a sound sleeper, Josh. Feel free to talk."

Josh told Nathan the complete story, along with his suspicions that the aborted fetus was not his.

"It will take a DNA test to confirm that, Josh," said Nathan. "Are you ready for this? Sometimes not knowing is better than knowing."

"I have to know, Nathan," said Josh, "but I don't want the whole hospital to know."

"I have to make a record of the test, Josh."

"I know that, Nathan,"

"But I can block anyone else from access to the test results," he said. "We need to go to the lab now, before too many people are up. I'll get a tissue swab from your mouth and tissue sample from the fetus. I'll do the test myself, enter the results in the computer, and then block access."

"Will you need to get approval from the gynecologist?"

"That will be no problem. Most of the time they want some type of genetic screening to predict the outcome of future pregnancies."

"Let's go," said Josh. "Nathan, I appreciate this."

"I'm so sorry for you, Josh," he said. "I wish I could do more."

"Thanks, Nathan," said Josh. "I'll meet you at the hospital lab."

After the "sample harvest" by Nathan, Josh went straight to the Women's Services floor, checked the first computer he found and entered his code name to locate Linda's room number from the census.

"Maybe I am imagining this," he said to himself as he walked down the long corridor toward Linda's room. "Everyone I meet seems to avoid eye contact." There were none of the usual cheerful "good morning" greetings that he was accustomed to in the hospital. He dismissed the thought, wondering what he would say when he entered the room, and what Linda would say when confronted with results of the DNA test.

Since she was a physician's wife, Linda was placed in one of the elaborately furnished suites in a special section of the floor. Josh rounded the corner of the hallway leading to the suite and found himself face to face with Donnie. Josh hadn't expected this surprise. He hesitated for a moment, trying to maintain composure. He could feel rage building.

Donnie was just leaving Linda's room. His disheveled appearance said he had slept in his clothes and had not shaved in the last twenty-four hours. He showed no surprise or panic at confronting Josh. To the contrary, his face brightened into a broad smile.

"Josh!" he said. "Glad to see you're back."

"Wipe that shit-eating grin off your face, you worthless son-of-a-bitch, and stay out of my sight or I'll kill you."

Two or three nurse attendants working nearby quickly left the scene. Donnie cringed. His face took on a ghostly pallor as he stepped aside, well away from Josh, in preparation for a hurried exit. He turned to face Josh.

"I'm sorry, Josh," he said when he was a safe distance down the hall.

"Stay away, dope head, or I'll kill you!" yelled Josh, well within earshot of several others in the corridor.

Josh took a deep breath and entered Linda's room. She was dressed in a loose-fitting hospital gown and seated in a chair beside the bed. Breakfast trays and coffee service for two were on the bedside table.

"Josh!" she said. "I wasn't expecting you this early."

She reached out for him, tears in her eyes, with outstretched arms.

"I lost our baby, Josh," she cried. "I'm so sorry."

"Cut the dramatics, Linda. It wasn't our baby, and you know it."

Linda dropped her arms; her facial expression changed abruptly. She lowered her head and gazed at the floor. Josh remained standing, waiting for any further response. Linda finally broke the silence as she faced Josh with a cold, emotionless look. There were no tears.

"I'm leaving you, Josh," she said.

"You've already left, Linda," he replied. "Sorry it didn't work out."

He turned and walked to the door without looking back or uttering another word.

Chapter 41

Twenty-four hours after his return from Geneva, Josh had a call from Charles' secretary. Charles wanted to set up a conference with Josh, but preferred to fly in for an "across the table" discussion rather than a telephone conference. They planned a lunch meeting the following week aboard the plane—Josh presumed for security reasons.

"Glad to see you, Josh," were Charles' first words as Josh entered the plane's lounge. Jason was as attentive as ever and seemed genuinely glad to see Josh again.

"Glad to be back," said Josh.

"Sorry about your wife's unfortunate experience," said Charles.

"Yes, it was unfortunate," he replied. Josh wondered how much Charles knew about his personal affairs. He soon found out.

"You were certainly justified in being angered," said Charles. "What do you intend to do?"

How did he know? wondered Josh. *His information network is at work again. Unbelievable!*

"Probably divorce," answered Josh. "If I can afford it." His laugh had a bitter edge.

"I'm sure old Don's son can afford it," said Charles. "I feel sure you will make wise decisions. We support you in whatever you decide."

"I appreciate that very much," said Josh.

"Josh, the seminars in Geneva were a huge success. Phillip tells me that you did a magnificent job with your part," said Charles. "Let me bring you up-to-date. We no longer have the threat of Bradford's and Scoetec's harassment."

"I welcome that one bit of good news," said Josh. "How did it happen?"

"They discovered what we were doing with the MIS from their contacts in Europe shortly before you left for Switzerland," said Charles. "They initiated the attack on you that morning as a last-ditch attempt to slow our marketing plans and to cause us embarrassment in the European medical sales community."

"So now the MIS is no longer under wraps?"

"Right! We've made full disclosure of our research and development of the product to the industry. We're not worried about anyone gaining on us now—too much technology involved."

"Will Scoetec now try to duplicate the MIS?"

"They've already started, we're told. They are already making claims that we pilfered the concept from Scoetec laboratories and are threatening an injunction suit against us to prevent marketing the MIS in the States. Our attorneys assure us that we have no real worries. They are having trouble processing Xentallium, just as we expected."

"What about Herb Bowman?" asked Josh. "Won't they still go after him?"

"We don't think so," replied Charles. "Herb alone can't help them with Xentallium, but we have transferred him to a remote laboratory in Switzerland anyway."

"Has Herb fully recovered?"

"Yeah, he's fine—and under treatment for his addiction," said Charles. "Josh, the purpose of my visit is, one, to let you know we are sensitive to your emotional trauma; and two, to let you know that we don't believe that you are in danger any more. However, Tom wants you to keep the panic device in place, and he will continue to monitor your activities."

"After my experience with the 'goon squad,' I won't disagree."

"Also, Josh, we want you to stay on as a consultant. We should eventually get approval for the MIS in this country, and we will need you for the marketing. And, of course, we are working always on new ideas. We'll need your help in both areas."

"I would like that, Charles," he said. "I am fascinated by all you do at Salzman Electronics. I can handle my personal problems. They won't interfere with my performance."

"Good," he replied. "I was hoping you'd stay with us."

"Of course, if Scoetec makes me a better offer…" He chuckled.

"As long as you can make jokes, we are in good shape." Charles laughed. "Call me if you need anything, Josh."

"Thanks, Charles," said Josh. "How is your family?"

"Fine," he replied, then flashed an impish expression on his face. "They ask about you often. Josh, you used to ask only about my mother. Does this mean that you've expanded your interest?"

"Good-bye, Charles." Josh grinned and kept grinning as he left the plane.

*   *   *   *

The divorce was quick and without complexities. Linda took only her clothing, car, and personal items and left Josh with all of their community property, uncontested. She even paid for her own legal expenses in connection with the divorce. *Likely with Donnie's assistance,* thought Josh.

Josh avoided going into the condo except to sleep, make coffee, and microwave breakfast rolls each morning. He couldn't tolerate the loneliness and feeling of emptiness that overwhelmed him if he stayed in the condo very long.

Each time he entered the place, memories of happy times with Linda were mixed and tossed about in his mind, along with anger, bitterness, and guilt over what had occurred during the last months of their marriage.

Josh spent much of his leisure time with Luke, Ann, and Jay. Having that outlet was a blessing. He even arranged his busy schedule, as much as he possibly could, to allow time to attend Jay's soccer games. Even at the age of eight, Jay still raced into his arms any time Josh appeared on the scene.

Being with Luke's family not only became Josh's compensation for his failed marriage, it gave him a taste of family life that he had never known. With his mother's chronic illness and his father's night shifts at work, as a child he was deprived of the many pleasantries of being a part of a close-knit family like Luke's.

During the working day, Josh focused on his objective of promoting the heart program and the Metcalfe Heart Institute satellite in Westlake. Other than time with Luke's family, he had little room in his life for any other activity. Two or three times a week he managed to exercise—either running the track or joining the spinning sessions at the gym.

In time, thoughts of Linda came to Josh's mind less and less frequently. Ann occasionally and casually reported to Josh the rumors that circulated. Linda moved into Donnie's living quarters that were attached to the Bradford mansion. She and Donnie traveled abroad extensively.

According to Ann, Linda continued to attend some of the community social affairs, with Donnie at her side, but she soon dropped out of the scene altogether. The worldwide travels to remote resorts with Donnie kept her away from Westlake for long periods of time and threw the two of them into a "fast-lane" international social crowd.

Ann reported, with some sadness, that she had heard from several sources that Linda had relapsed into habitual substance abuse, and to a much more intense degree than before. Apparently there had been no attempts to institutionalize her for treatment.

* * * *

It was early afternoon when Josh placed the final row of sutures in the chest incision of a coronary artery by-pass graft case. Luke was at the head of the table, and turned to Josh, cell phone in hand.

"Hey, Josh! Our next case has been canceled by the internist. He said the risk is too great right now," said Luke. "Let's go home. Jay has been wanting to show you something for days, anyway."

"Sounds great!" Josh answered. "What's he got?"

"You'll have to wait and see."

Josh and Luke arrived at the same time and were met by Ann and Jay at the door. Jay ran to Josh, as usual.

"Uncle Josh!" Jay cried. "Can you come to my game tonight?"

"Sure can," Josh answered as he grabbed Jay and twirled him around the room. "Are we going to win?"

"Of course," he answered. "Just like you and Daddy."

"Now wait a minute," said Josh. "Give me your hand."

"I know what you're going to ask," said Jay.

Josh placed Jay's hand in his palm. "Hey, look how those fingers are growing. OK, when they get to here," Josh said, pointing to the end of his own fingers. "What will you be?"

"A doctor!" Jay screamed, then said, "or a football player."

"Jay!" said Josh. "Come on, what will you be?"

"OK," he replied, "A doctor!"

"That's better."

"Uncle Josh, I wanta show you my picture."

"Good," said Josh. "Did you have your picture taken?"

"No. You'll see," he answered and scampered away to his bedroom.

He returned with picture in hand—a 6 X 9 framed picture of Josh and Luke in Northwestern football uniforms, holding their helmets under their arms, arms around each other, and grinning from ear to ear. At the top of the picture was inscribed: *The Lehman-Sanders Axis.*

"Where did he get this?" asked Josh, turning to Luke and chuckling.

"He found it in an old trunk in the storeroom, along with my old football uniform and helmet," Luke replied. "You remember it?"

"Yeah, it was taken after we won some game at Northwestern," said Josh. "Isn't this the picture *Sports World* magazine used?"

"That's it!" said Luke. "Jay wants to take it to school."

"Sure!" said Josh, then turned to Jay. "But what are you going to be when you grow up?"

"A doctor!" he said.

"And some day, your dad and I will have a picture made in scrubs for you to take to school. We'll label it 'Lehman-Sanders Axis-2004,'" said Josh. Luke and Ann joined him in laughter.

"OK, Jay," said Ann. "Into your room so Daddy and Uncle Josh can talk."

A frowning Jay, holding on to his prized picture, reluctantly retreated after giving his "Uncle Josh" a kiss and a high-five.

"Josh, are you working too hard?" asked Ann. "How much weight have you lost?"

"I don't know," replied Josh. "Yeah, I'm working hard, but it keeps me from thinking. I messed up this marriage big time."

"Josh, it was going to happen anyway," Ann said. "I roomed with Linda, you remember. Quit blaming yourself."

"And Josh," said Luke. "You've got to lighten your surgery load. You've got some great guys with you now. Refer some of those cases or I'm going to talk to Melba," he laughed.

"God, don't do that," he pleaded, with a chuckle. "She watches my every move. I have to sneak around her sometimes. She fusses about my schedule, about missing meals. She fusses if my shirt is wrinkled or if I go too long without shaving."

"Are you still making those trips to Charles Salzman's office?" asked Luke.

"Yeah, that's too intriguing to give up," said Josh, "and it also helps to keep my mind focused."

"Do you still want Ann to keep you updated on what she hears about Linda?"

"You know, I really don't care any more," he replied. "For a while I felt like it was therapeutic. You know, helped me adjust and evaluate my feelings. I just don't care now. I even feel sorry for Donnie, in a way. Ann, I guess I just don't care if I hear anything or not."

"That's sounds like a good sign," Ann replied. "And I agree with Luke. Cut down on your workload. Luke tells me your schedule is so packed that you sometimes don't start cases until 5:00 or 6:00 in the afternoon."

"Hey! You know what would be neat?" said Luke. "Let's go on a trip somewhere, maybe a cruise. All of us. What do you think?"

"Fine!" said Josh, with enthusiasm that Luke and Ann had not witnessed for weeks. "You plan it and I'll be ready. A great idea, Luke!"

* * * *

The team of cardiovascular surgeons that Josh recruited for the heart program was a group of young, well-trained recent graduates from some of the most prestigious medical centers in the country. Most were married and with children. With some frequency, family activities conflicted with their on-call schedule. Josh was nearly always available to fill in when needed.

Josh had just finished a horrendous, exhausting week of nighttime call for gunshot wounds, stabbings, and severe injuries from automobile accidents. Many of the cases kept him in the operating room five and six hours at a time.

Josh looked forward to a couple of days off—sleeping late, visiting with Luke and family, going to Jay's soccer games. He was in the dressing room when Hector Ortiz called.

"Josh, I need your help," he pleaded. "I'm on call tonight, and all of the other thoracic surgeons are out of town and checked out to me. I've got to take my wife and kids to San Antonio for a family reunion. Could you cover for me?"

"Man, I've had a tough week—on call every night this week, which has meant working every night. There's no other way?"

"None, Josh. I've tried every possible solution. You know Joe Herrington is on the premises for general surgery."

"He can't handle thoracic cases, Hector."

"OK, Josh," he said, a despondent tone to his voice. "If you can't do it, I'll just have to tell my family we can't make it."

"All right, Hector," he said, "I'll do it. One more missed night's sleep won't matter."

"Thanks, Josh. I'll make it up to you."

* * * *

It was another night of chest injuries, just like the others. At midnight the E.R. volume slowed somewhat and Josh checked out to Joe Herrington, hoping no more heart or lung cases had to be done. He fought to keep his eyes open as he drove toward the condo, hardly aware of the street signs flying by as he crossed each intersection. He had an early morning surgery already scheduled and would have to set the alarm in order to make his seven o'clock case.

It was a clear, crisp night as he drove along, so he rolled down the windows, thinking the cool air might keep him from falling asleep. He turned off the radio. The humming of the tires on the street seemed to provide a musical-like background for the thoughts that raced through his mind.

Do I really never want to hear anything about Linda again? Will I always carry animosity toward Donnie? How would I handle it if I saw the two of them together? Would that rekindle the hurt and bitterness? Would it rekindle some of the old affection toward Linda? I really can't answer those questions right now.

He pulled into his garage, made his way up to the bedroom, undressed, scattered his clothes on the floor along the way, and crawled into his empty bed—too tired to even brush his teeth. He set the alarm clock for six, thinking he'd get at least three hours sleep. For a moment, thoughts of Linda again flashed through his mind, thoughts of sharing with her that very bed. Was Donnie totally to blame? Maybe not.

He reached to disconnect the phone altogether, hesitated, thought better of it, and then crashed into a deep sleep.

Chapter 42

Josh reached for the alarm clock, "It can't be time...it can't be," he groaned. The annoying sound was not coming from the clock at all. He tried to ignore the clamor, but to no avail. He finally reached the phone and removed the receiver. The sleep-shattering noise that rudely awakened him abruptly ceased, but the shouting voice from the dangling hand-piece kept him from drifting back into his peaceful slumber.

"Josh...damn it, wake up!"

Again, he tried to ignore what he heard and replaced the receiver. Immediately the ringing started again. He couldn't ignore it any longer and made up his mind ahead of time that he was going to be plenty pissed off at this intrusion. Josh was sure it was Luke's voice that he had heard before he hung up the phone. He picked up the phone again and screamed.

"Luke, what in the hell do you want? It's three o'clock."

"Josh, get your ass out of bed. I need you here...now!" said Luke. "I'm sending an ambulance for you...should be there any minute."

"What the hell for?" asked Josh.

"We've got major chest trauma here...probably a ruptured pulmonary artery. I'm fighting every minute to keep him alive."

"Herrington has taken over surgery call, Josh. I just finished my last case less than two hours ago. Call Herrington!"

"He's here now, jerk!" Luke yelled. "Wake up! You know he can't handle it."

"Look, man, I'm wiped out. I couldn't even shave myself safely."

"I don't give a crap about how tired you are," said Luke. "This guy is dying and you are the only one who can turn this around. The old man is on my ass to get something done."

"What old man?"

"Bradford, dammit!" he answered. "It's his son…it's Donnie. He crashed his new BMW convertible into a brick wall." *Why did he have to ask?* thought Luke.

"Let the son-of-a-bitch die," said Josh. "I'm going back to sleep."

"Josh, damn it!" pleaded Luke. "Do this for me. I know how you feel, but this is me begging. There was a long pause…"Josh!" he yelled.

"I'm moving, Luke," he said, "but my heart is not in it."

✳ ✳ ✳ ✳

With Donnie's chest open, with Dr. Herrington assisting, and with Luke at the head of the table, Josh quickly identified the pulmonary artery and clamped the torn segment to stop the blood loss. Before starting the repair, he used a few minutes of time to exam the heart, lungs, and diaphragm for any other injuries and found none.

"I don't see anything else, Luke," he said. "I'm gonna start the repair. Is he holding stable?"

"Doing great, Josh!" said Luke. "He's having a few runs of irregular heart rhythm…an unsustained ventricular tachycardia…controlled so far with small doses of anti-arrhythmic drugs."

"I'll keep the defib paddles handy. I'm going to need quite a bit more time."

"Just keep working, Super-doc," he replied. "I'll have his brain washed so clean he'll wake up a new man."

"Any change will be an improvement," laughed Josh. "Luke, I presume old Don is waiting outside?"

"Yeah, he's got a non-stop broadcast going about being on the Board of Trustees of the hospital, about how he helps doctors like you get started in practice, and how you have never thanked him. Then he starts talking about Donnie…how he will take over the company some day."

"He doesn't mention how he neglected the kid when he was growing up…probably the reason Donnie is the way he is today?"

"I think you're right there," said Luke. "We saw right off the imprint the old fart made on his son."

"So did old Sam," laughed Josh. "He picked up on it the first time he saw Donnie."

"Yeah, I remember that," he said. "Sam said, 'Why, he's a chip off the old block, Mr. Josh.'"

They both laughed heartily as Josh stayed busy with the repair.

"I'm going to muster up all the strength I can to be civil to Don Bradford, Sr.," said Josh. "Is Jeremy out there too?"

"Of course," Luke answered. "And before you ask…so is Linda."

"How am I going to face those people, Luke?"

"I'll go with you," said Luke. "Just pretend we're losing the game and we have to go in the locker room at half-time and face the coach."

Suddenly, the alarm lights and a high-pitched buzzing noise went off, signaling the onset of a lethal heart rhythm.

"He's arrested, Josh!" yelled Luke. "Ventricular fibrillation! I can't stop it with drugs, Josh!"

Josh grabbed the sterile electrodes wired to the defibrillator and placed them on the surface to the heart.

"Stand back!" he ordered and fired the first shock.

"No change, Josh!" said Luke. "Increase the voltage!"

"Stand back!" ordered Josh to others at the operating table, and fired again.

"Nothing!" cried Luke. "It may be hopeless, Josh. Try again!"

Josh repeated the shock with still greater voltage…no response!

"I'll do manual massage of the heart for a few minutes…then we'll try again."

Why do this? thought Josh. *Why not stop now and rid the world of the worthless being?* He kept up the rhythmic compression of the heart muscle, effectively keeping blood flowing throughout Donnie's body and brain, pausing occasionally for a few seconds to see if the heart would resume a rhythm of its own.

"Let's try defibrillation again!" yelled Luke. "You can't keep that up much longer."

"Is there any chance?" asked Josh, a tone of futility to his voice.

"Try once more before we give up," said Luke.

Josh called for fresh, sterile paddles. After placement on the surface of Donnie's heart, and giving warnings to all around, he used the highest voltage available to shock the heart. He glanced at the monitor.

"You did it!" said Luke. "Normal rhythm…as if nothing had ever happened."

"Hey, that was scary," said Josh. "What do you think caused it?"

"Sudden onset, Josh," Luke replied. "Couldn't have been prevented; probably long-term cocaine use has damaged his heart muscle."

"I guess we have to expect irregular heart rhythm from now on."

"Yeah…be sure and watch his potassium during his convalescence. How are you coming along?"

"Almost finished," Josh answered. "Now comes the hard part…going out there and talking to Don Bradford."

"Don't sweat it, man," said Luke.

"All I can think about is what Bradford Holdings did to my dad's retirement, after years of working at Westlake refinery," said Josh. "And then what they tried to do to me with their hired thugs. I can't help it, Luke, I'm angry—about what has happened in the past and about what has happened tonight. Bradford uses his power to manipulate people, with utter disregard for the consequences."

"Come off it, dude," said Luke. "You saved this piece of horse shit from dying. Just go out there and take your bows."

"Luke, believe me," replied Josh, "Bradford will say something abrasive and totally inappropriate. And you can bet Jay's college fund that the old bastard will show no sign of appreciation for what we've done."

"Forget it!" said Luke, as he and the operating room techs prepared to move Donnie to the Surgical ICU. "Wait until I get back. I want to watch his heart rhythm for a couple of minutes, then we'll go out together."

Chapter 43

Both Don Bradford and Jeremy Corbett leaped to their feet when Josh and Luke came through the double swinging doors to the waiting area. It was no surprise to Josh to see Linda seated in the corner, almost as if she were hiding.

On closer look, Josh could see why. She looked like someone with a terminal illness. She had lost weight, her face was gaunt, her eyes glazed, and she was far from appearing like her usual well-groomed self. This was the first time Josh had seen her since they split. *What has happened here?* he wondered. *Ann's reports must have been accurate.* Josh turned to Don and Jeremy.

"He made it through all right," Josh said. "Luke kept him alive by some miracle. With no complications he should recover."

Josh was curt and matter-of-fact in describing the injury, the procedure, and the possible complications. There was none of the usual warm, compassionate manner so characteristic of his reporting to waiting families.

All Josh could think about was, *What stupid question or remark is this old bastard going to come up with?* There was no "thank you" for saving my son's life, no gratitude whatsoever expressed for his or Luke's efforts to keep Donnie alive.

"I want Dr. Dubonet in Dallas to take over the case," Don said.

"Then you should call him," said Josh as he turned his back to Don and walked away.

"Come back here, young man!" yelled Don, seething, and red-faced. "What makes you think you can just walk off when I'm talking to you? I have rights, you know."

Josh continued to walk toward the door without even glancing back. Don started toward him, but Jeremy restrained him, convinced him to sit in a chair, and hurried after Josh. "Dr. Lehman," Jeremy called out, rushing to block Josh's exit. "Mr. Bradford is upset and naturally concerned about Donnie. Perhaps you could call Dr. Dubonet and explain the details of the situation, and then perhaps Mr. Bradford could talk to Dr. Dubonet over the phone for some reassurance about Donnie's condition."

"Look, Mr. Corbett," said Josh, with fire in his eyes, "I came here and operated on that dopehead son of this old fart and I don't give a shit whether or not any of you are 'reassured.' Furthermore, I don't care, at this point, whether that worthless mass of protoplasm in there lives or dies. You have my permission to do whatever this old bastard of a father wants. My 7:30 case starts in about two hours and I'm going to try to get some sleep. Good-bye, and get lost—all three of you," he added, glaring at Linda. "Now get the hell out of my way!"

With Luke practically dragging him, Josh again turned and walked away.

"You lost it, Josh," said Luke, pulling Josh to a stop after they left the waiting room.

"I'm sorry for your sake, Luke," said Josh. "Otherwise, I don't care. Everyone has a breaking point."

"Josh, you said what I was thinking, but you need to cool it."

"I'm not going back in there, Luke," Josh said.

"Let's try to get Jeremy aside and make some effort to calm the waters," pleaded Luke.

"Whatever you say, Luke," said Josh. "You call the plays. I'm not very good at quarterbacking right now."

"I wouldn't say that," said Luke. "You just threw me a helluva pass. Now that I have the ball, I'm not sure what to do with it, but I'll go back in there and do something. I'll try to make a few more yards," he laughed.

Josh went into the dressing room to change scrubs. He decided to spend the remaining two hours trying to sleep in the surgeons' lounge. He had to stop shaking from anger if he was going to be ready for his first case that morning.

Luke went to the waiting room door and looked in, pausing for a moment to watch Don and Jeremy. Linda was still nestled in a chair in the corner and was not taking part in the conversation. The old man was red-faced, waving his arms and pointing toward the operating room, and yelling some cuss words that Luke wasn't sure he had ever heard before.

They both turned toward Luke when he entered. Luke beckoned for Jeremy to come to the door. He escorted Jeremy to a private consultation room.

"We've got a sensitive situation here, Jeremy," said Luke. "You are aware of the dynamics behind Josh's behavior. He did a beautiful salvaging job in this very complex case. No one could have done better. He saved Donnie's life. Donnie does not need Dr. Dubonet at this time. If Mr. Bradford insists, I can call Dr. Dubonet and request consultation on Josh's behalf."

"Thank you, Dr. Sanders," said Jeremy in a calm, reasonable manner. "I agree with you. I'll see what I can do. In the meantime, we'll keep the two 'battlers' away from each other," he said with a chuckle.

"Then you'll communicate with me if I'm needed," said Luke, handing Jeremy a business card.

"Good plan, Dr. Sanders," he said. "Thanks for your help."

* * * *

Before crashing into one of the recliners in the lounge, Josh went back into the ICU and into Donnie's cubicle for a last minute look. He checked the monitors, the pressure readings, the ventilator settings, the oxygen saturation readings, and the heart rhythm strips. After making minor adjustments, he nodded at the ICU nurse while he reminisced about the many times in the past Linda had been on the other side of the ICU bed in similar cases.

Whatever else had happened, Linda had been an excellent ICU nurse. *What went wrong? Why was this useless pile of horseshit ever placed on this earth?* he asked himself. *He'll probably live through it.* Josh walked out of the cubicle, hating himself. *Have I lost the equanimity that I have enjoyed all of these years as a doctor?* he wondered. "Get some sleep, dude," he said aloud to himself.

* * * *

Josh visited Donnie two or three times daily. He heard no more talk about any outside consultant assuming care of the patient. In fact, old Don was noticeably absent every time Josh made rounds. Josh was thankful for that. Donnie was awake by the next day, but still on the ventilator. With the endotracheal tube in place, he was unable to talk.

When awake, his eyes roved about frantically, seeking some answer to the helpless feeling of not being able to communicate. He fought the hand restraints, trying to reach for the endotracheal tube and jerk it out. Keeping him comfortable was almost impossible. With Donnie's high tolerance for drugs from years of substance abuse, pain control and sedation were constant problems.

With the coaxing of the nurses to take deep breaths, by the fourth day Donnie was making enough voluntary effort in breathing that the endotracheal tube could be removed. Donnie's first words were to demand more pain medicine.

"Pain, pain!" he called out any time he aroused from a somnolent state. "Somebody give me a pain shot! Can't you stupid people see I am in pain?"

"You just had a pain shot, Mr. Bradford," the nurse replied.

"Give me another!" he yelled. "Call my goddamn doctor!"

"We're giving you just what he ordered."

"What the hell does he know? He's not hurting."

"Just try to relax. The pain medicine will help in a few minutes."

"Call my father. Tell him I need another doctor. This dumb-ass doctor doesn't know what he's doing."

"You'll feel better in a while," said the nurse.

"Who the shit is my doctor?" asked Donnie, now a little more alert.

"Dr. Lehman operated on you, Mr. Bradford," she replied. "You're gonna be fine."

"Josh Lehman? Oh my God!" he said and dropped off to sleep again.

With Donnie's resistance to being moved and his pleading to be left alone, it took two nurses—sometimes three—to get him out of bed. The order was: "Up in chair for one hour twice daily."

"Time to get in the chair, Mr. Bradford," said the nurse, trying her best to be cheerful, but knowing what Donnie's response would be.

"Get your ass out of here!" he cried. "I'm not moving to that goddamn chair again."

"You have to move around, Mr. Bradford," she pleaded. "It helps your circulation."

"I don't give a shit about my circulation!" he retorted. "Get me a pain shot!"

"It's not time yet," said the nurse, as she turned to call for assistance in moving him. "First, you have to get out of bed for awhile."

"Leave me alone!" said Donnie. "When I get out of this fuckin' place I'm going to sue everyone of you shit asses."

The same scenario was repeated with each treatment attempt—nursing care, respiratory therapy, or physical therapy. Considering the fact that he had been so near death, Donnie was doing remarkably well. Josh's main concern was his irregular heart rhythm. His blood potassium and magnesium levels were a little low, but not remarkably so. Josh asked Nate McAllister, a cardiologist, to see Donnie in consultation because of his erratic heartbeat. Josh read Nate's written report on the consultation sheet:

The irregular rhythm, characterized by frequent premature ventricular contractions, is likely a manifestation of myocarditis from long standing alcohol and substance abuse in a patient with major chest trauma. His electrolytes—potassium and magnesium—must be monitored closely and any level below normal should be treated.

Josh's visits to Donnie's bedside were strictly professional—a stone-faced, impersonal approach during his examination and while he reviewed the chart. There were never any kind words of encouragement—so foreign to Josh's usual care of his patients.

"Donnie, you've got to cooperate with these people," admonished Josh. "They are just trying to help you."

"Wanta help me? Give me a pain shot and leave me alone."

Josh looked at Donnie with a cold stare for a few moments, said nothing, and turned to walk out of the cubicle.

"Josh! Josh!" he called franticly, a look of terror in his eyes. "Help me!"

An unsmiling Josh paused, glanced back, and then walked away.

*   *   *   *

Fortunately, by making rounds at odd hours—either extremely early or extremely late—Josh had missed crossing paths with Linda, Donnie's father, or Jeremy on his visits. He presumed that they were visiting at regular hours and were being updated on Donnie's progress by the nurses in the unit. Josh had received no phone call inquiries.

On the fifth post-operative day, Josh made rounds later than usual because of an emergency in the early morning hours. He hurried into Donnie's ICU cubicle for the usual check of the monitors and the reports on the chart. He wanted to finish as quickly as possible before Linda or Don Bradford appeared.

Donnie was in bed, asleep, and didn't stir when Josh listened to his chest and went through the ritual of assuring himself that all was well. The nurse in attendance, Janie Reyes, was busy at the bedside table with the patient's morning medication.

Janie was one of Josh's favorite ICU nurses. Always competent, she gave reliable and accurate reports on her patient's status. On the table, Josh noticed a loaded syringe lying beside two empty vials of potassium chloride. Janie noticed Josh glancing at the syringe which was filled with potassium.

"I am just before adding KCL to the fresh I.V. solution bottles, Dr Lehman," said Janie. "Dr. McAllister was just here and left orders for more potassium."

"How is the patient, Janie?" asked Josh.

"Still a few runs of PVC's," she replied. "That's why Dr. McAllister wanted to increase the potassium. Otherwise, Mr. Bradford is very stable. Still complaining that we don't give him enough pain medicine." She laughed. "If we gave him any more we'd have to intubate him again."

"We should be able to remove the chest tube soon," said Josh. "I notice from the record that the drainage has been far less for the last twelve hours."

"Oh, Dr. Lehman, I need a quick break to the bathroom," she said. "Could I make a dash while you're here? I'll finish with the potassium when I return."

"Sure, Janie, take a break," Josh replied. "I'm about finished here. I need to make a few notes in the record before I leave. He'll be all right by himself until you return. I want to leave before I have to talk to him."

"I know," she said, giving Josh a look of understanding.

Everyone in this unit must know about Linda and Donnie and me, thought Josh. *I wish I hadn't said that. I don't want anyone ever to think I'm seeking pity.* He left Donnie's cubicle, then turned to exit through a side door in order to avoid face-to-face contact with either Linda or Don Bradford, Sr. in the event that they might arrive to visit. He just wasn't up to that yet, and would be happy to never have to speak to them again.

Josh had just reached the surgery dressing room to prepare for his first case when the overhead speaker blared: "Code Blue, ICU! Code Blue, ICU!" At the same time, his cell phone vibrated. He whirled to return to the ICU.

By the time he reached Donnie's side, the rescue team had already started resuscitation. A tube had been inserted into the trachea and a respiratory therapy technician was pumping oxygen into Donnie's lungs. A nurse on the team injected stimulants according to the cardiac arrest protocol. Still another nurse managed the defibrillator. Repeated shocks failed to bring about a heart rhythm.

"What happened?" asked Josh. "I just left him; he was fine. Janie?"

"I don't know, Dr. Lehman," said Janie, shaking as though she were about to cry. "It all happened so fast—right after I got back."

"Anything different, Dr. Lehman?" asked the nurse.

"No, just keep trying," said Josh. "I don't understand. You should be able to get some response. Have you increased the voltage?"

"As high as it will go," she answered.

"Something's just not right here," said Josh. "You should get some response from the defibrillator—maybe not a sustained rhythm, but some semblance of a heart-beat. Keep trying."

The team continued their attempts to start a heart rhythm for over thirty minutes, but to no avail.

"Shall we continue, Dr. Lehman?" asked one of the nurses.

Josh hesitated to answer. He knew it was hopeless. He looked up to face the eyes of everyone in the cubicle, saying the same thing without speaking. It was futile to continue.

"No, we can quit. The monitor still shows flat-line. It's useless to go on."

Josh left the ICU and went to surgery to cancel his case. He met Luke in the corridor, hurrying toward the ICU.

"I just got the message!" said Luke. "What is it?"

"Donnie arrested. We couldn't resuscitate him."

"Go straight to my house, Josh," said Luke. "I'll call Jeremy and meet you there in a few minutes—and we'll talk."

"I can't call Donnie's father, Luke."

"We'll talk!" Luke said.

*

Chapter 44

Ann opened the front door and gasped.

"Josh!" she cried. "What's wrong? Are you all right."

"Donnie Bradford just died. Luke is on his way here."

"Come in, Josh," she said, guiding him to a chair. "What happened?"

Josh tried to tell her, but couldn't find words through choking back tears. He sat staring at the floor, speechless, as if in a trance. After a few seconds, he looked up at Ann.

"My conduct, Ann. I was cold, calloused, to the point of cruelty. My behavior sucked, Ann! I blew it with Donnie's father. The nurses on the unit—I see it in their eyes! They are appalled by the way I treated Donnie. Now he's dead. I gave him no hope or encouragement to live. I killed him, Ann!"

"Come off it, Josh!" she said. "You did your best. No one can blame you for your attitude toward him. You are to be admired for what you did for Donnie under those circumstances."

"I don't feel very good right now," said Josh, leaning over, his head cupped in his hands.

"You'll be fine, Josh," said Ann. "Your sensitivity is what makes your patients love you. You'll never lose that."

As Ann massaged Josh's neck muscles, trying to relax him, Luke arrived and went straight to Josh's side. He put his arm across Josh's shoulder and pulled him close.

"It's all right, Josh," said Luke.

"I feel horrible, Luke."

"He feels guilty about the way he treated Donnie," said Ann.

"I know," said Luke. "The nurses keep asking me, 'what's wrong with Dr. Lehman?'"

"What can I do, Luke?" Josh asked. "I don't think I can do another case—ever. I just want to run."

"You've got to stop whipping yourself, Josh," said Luke. "These things happen. It just happened to be Donnie."

Josh sat, with his shoulders drooped and his head hanging low.

"What caused this, Luke?" said Josh. "We couldn't get his heart to start beating. It was as if it were paralyzed."

"Stop thinking about it, Josh. I've already notified your associates that you're going to be off for a few days," said Luke. "Some well needed rest. You can stay here with us or take off for the hills. Whatever. We're not whipped, Josh. It's just half-time. We'll come back and win. It's just a game, Josh. Are you all right with that?"

"I have to be, Luke," he replied. "What am I going to do about talking to old Don Bradford?"

"You have got to talk to him, Josh."

They were both quiet for several moments, Luke waiting for Josh to respond.

"What should I say?"

"The words will come, Josh," answered Luke. "You've been there before."

"Does he already know?"

"I'm sure he does," replied Luke. "I talked to Jeremy."

"Stay close to me, Luke," said Josh, grabbing for Luke's arm.

Luke handed him the number and Josh used his cell phone to make the call. Don's secretary answered and put Josh straight through to Don.

"Mr. Bradford, this is Dr. Lehman," Josh said. "I am so sorry about Donnie. We had great hopes that he was going to make it through."

There was a long pause before Don made any comment. Josh waited, half wishing Don would just hang up.

"What happened, Dr. Lehman?" said Don. Josh winced at the noticeable tone of bitterness in his voice.

"We can't explain it yet, Mr. Bradford. It was probably a pulmonary embolus—a blood clot that went to his lungs."

"I know what a pulmonary embolus is, boy," said Don. "I expect a full investigation of the cause of death."

"Yes, sir," said Josh. "I know this is a tragic loss for you, sir."

"Yes, it is, and I want to know what caused it," he retorted. "I'm holding you accountable."

"Yes, sir," Josh replied. "I understand how you feel."

The phone clicked. That was the end of the conversation.

"You did fine, Josh," said Luke. "Now, go home and pack, mostly leisure clothes. Come back here and spend the night. Jay's visiting Ann's folks. You can sleep in his room. Tomorrow—to the hill country! There is a great lodge near San Antonio. Play some golf and do some physical work-outs. We'll handle things here."

Josh obediently followed Luke's orders. He returned from his condo with a packed bag, took half of one of Ann's tranquilizers, had a glass of wine before dinner and another with dinner, and slept soundly.

Luke left early the next morning, as usual. He left Josh a note with reservation information, telephone numbers, and a message that read: "Relax and refuel. It's time for one of those end-run fake plays you are famous for." Josh knew exactly what he meant and laughed aloud.

✶   ✶   ✶   ✶

Josh did indeed relax in the resort. He ran his usual five miles each morning and played golf each afternoon. In between, he read professional journals, trying to catch up on the latest scientific literature. Of interest was the article about the new Salzman scope that was being used widely in Europe and other foreign countries and was expected to be approved for use in the United States within eighteen months to two years.

Being alone and away from his heavy work load, thoughts of Leah Salzman surfaced from the depths of his brain with more regularity, in spite of his attempts to suppress them. While they were in Geneva, he and Leah had spent some enjoyable hours together, the memories of which could not be totally suppressed. How could he be guilt-free? How could he be judgmental about Linda and Donnie when he allowed himself to be infatuated with Leah while he was still married to Linda? He toyed with the idea of calling Leah, but decided against it. This was no time to get involved.

In spite of his deplorable behavior during the last few days of Donnie's life, Josh was satisfied that his clinical management of Donnie's injury was acceptable, but he was guilt-ridden over the way he had failed to offer Donnie any compassion or reassurance about his condition. Josh was anxious to learn the cause of death—not anxious enough to make a phone call to find out, however.

He found out when he returned to the clubhouse after an afternoon of golf and Luke was waiting for him in the pro shop dressing room, a look of deep despair on his face.

Chapter 45

Mike Garetry grew up in Westlake. After graduating from high school, he enrolled in the police academy. After finishing his training, he joined the Westlake police force as a rookie cop. His father had done the same, years earlier.

Mike's father died from cancer before seeing Mike rise to the top in the force and become a leading detective. The disappointment over his father's premature death was fierce for Mike. He worshipped his father, and his desire to please him was the driving force that took him to the position in the police force that he achieved.

The passage of time didn't erase the bitterness Mike felt about the medical care his father had received—delays in diagnosis, insensitive caregivers, restrictions of choice of treating physicians by the HMO. Mike carried a warped view of all health care providers—including hospitals and physicians—as well as health insurance companies.

The everyday occurrence of crime, especially drug trafficking with Westlake on the main highway from Mexico, created a full agenda for Mike. He simply had no time for anything else. He winced when the chief called him into his office. It was one of those busy days that more than once had sent him scrambling for the Excedrin bottle.

"Mike," said the chief, "I want you to drop everything you're doing. I'm assigning you to a rather unique case. A lot of political clout behind this. I don't think it will take you long to resolve the issues, however."

"My God, Chief!" Mike grumbled. "Do you have any idea the backlog of cases we're working on? Why me?"

"You're well-known, Mike," he answered. "Born and raised in Westlake. Good performance history. Father was a cop. The top echelon in City Hall wants the best. A lot of political pressure. Do this for me, Mike"

"You know I will," replied Mike. "Cut the bullshit and tell me what I'm facing."

"OK, Mike," he laughed. "Here's the story. Don Bradford, Jr., son of multi-billionaire old man Bradford, was injured in an auto accident, had surgery, and five days later died unexpectedly. It appears that he was given an overdose of a drug that stopped his heart—potassium, I think. No one is sure how he got the drug, whether it was hospital error or whether someone deliberately gave it to him. His father owns enough politicians that he can demand and get any investigation he wants."

"Damn, Chief!" said Mike. "People die in hospitals every day. We can't investigate every case. This is foolish."

"I know, Mike," he replied. "There is a lot more to the story. I'll let you unravel it. Thanks, Mike. I knew you'd jump at the chance on this one," said the chief. He laughed and feigned jumping back to escape a body blow.

* * * *

Mike cleared Security at the hospital and went straight to Administration to announce his presence. He presented his court order, allowing him access to Donnie's medical record and was met with a great deal of suspicion regarding his reason for being there. He tried to allay the fears of everyone he met by saying this was a routine investigation.

With the approval of Administration, he established himself in the conference room in the Health Information Management Department and began his review of the contents of Donnie's record, starting with the date of admission to the emergency room.

The only time Mike had ever spent in a hospital was during those last days of his father's terminal illness. Everything about a hospital was a mystery to Mike. He was overwhelmed by the helter-skelter activity, with nurses scurrying about in all directions, seemingly with no organized purpose. The hospital jargon, technical terms mixed with acronyms, left Mike out in the cold.

Now here he was, faced with reviewing a medical record that he couldn't comprehend and most of the time with handwriting that he couldn't decipher. All he wanted was to determine the issues behind the demand for an investigation and the names of individuals responsible for the care of the deceased patient.

The more documents he perused in Donnie's medical records, the more bewildered he became. He was about to call out for help when Darren Johnson came to his rescue. Darren was the director of Risk Management for the hospital. He was alerted whenever there was any likelihood that a patient's hospital stay might lead to litigation of some sort, whether or not there was a valid concern.

At the request of the hospital administrator, Darren already had made an in-depth study of Donnie's case. As soon as he was notified that Mike was looking at Donnie's record, he hurried to the department to be present while the review was taking place.

Darren introduced himself to Mike and explained his role in the hospital.

"I'm here to help you, Mr. Garetry," said Darren. "I'll be here in the department if you should need any information or if you have trouble interpreting what you find in the record."

"I need a lot of help with this right now, Mr. Johnson," Mike replied, stabbing the record with his finger. "First off, I am having trouble making sense out of what I'm seeing here. I guess what's of more importance is that I'm not sure why I'm here."

"Maybe I can help you," said Darren. "This unfortunate young man was the son of a politically powerful individual in the community. I imagine he has demanded this investigation. From what I've been told, he seems to be convinced there was some misadventure that caused his son's death."

Mike put the record down and turned to Darren.

"You seem to be pretty familiar with the circumstances here," said Mike. "Could you just walk me through the sequence of events that occurred from the time Mr. Bradford—Bradford, Jr., I believe—entered the hospital. Any background information about this man would be helpful."

"I'll give you the background first," said Darren. "That is, I'll tell you what I have heard. Don Bradford, Jr.—known as Donnie—was the typical overindulged rich playboy whose sole purpose in life seemed to be seeking pleasurable experiences. As you would expect, that included abuse of alcohol and drugs. He was in great demand at all social events—a 'life of the party' sort of person. That's how he met Dr. Lehman's wife, Linda."

Mike's "antennae" became activated. He sat up straight in his chair.

"Dr. Lehman's wife?"

Darren narrated the entire story of the affair, the pregnancy, the miscarriage, and the divorce. He described Josh's role at the Metcalfe Heart Institute and at Westlake Regional and his reputation as a heart surgeon.

"On the night of his injury," Darren continued, "Donnie was driving a new BMW convertible, under the influence, at a high rate of speed, no seat belt fastened, and crashed into a solid brick wall. He must have been thrown into the top of the windshield. Without the seat belt, in a convertible, the air bags didn't help him.

"He was brought to our emergency room, almost dead, with a severe chest injury—a ruptured pulmonary artery. Dr Sanders, our anesthesia department medical director, happened to be in the building on another case and somehow kept him alive until they could get him to the operating room."

"Dr. Sanders put in a frantic call to Dr. Lehman, the only heart surgeon available, sent an ambulance on a 'red light' run to pick up an unhappy Dr. Lehman and deliver him to the operating room. It was a miracle that they were able to keep Donnie alive."

As Darren talked, Mike made notes and listed the people in the hospital that he wanted to interview. Question after question came to mind as he listened to the story of Josh's behavior and his comments when he reported to Donnie's father following the surgery.

"Could someone else have done the surgery?" asked Mike.

"No," replied Darren. "There was no one else available who was capable of handling an injury that severe. That's why Dr. Sanders insisted that Dr. Lehman come to the hospital. Unfortunately, Dr. Lehman made some remarks over the telephone that were rather shocking to the operating room personnel."

"How could they hear Dr. Lehman's remarks?"

"Dr. Sanders had his hands full trying to keep Donnie alive. He made the call with the speaker phone. Everyone in the O.R. heard both sides of the conversation."

"What did he say that was so shocking?" asked Mike.

"I am told that he said: 'let the son-of-a-bitch die.'"

"OK, let me get this straight," said Mike. "Here's a guy who was screwing the doctor's wife, got her pregnant, caused a divorce, damn near got himself killed, and this same doctor was the only one who could save him. I imagine he was a little bitter. But he came over and did the surgery, right?"

"Yes he did, and did a remarkable job of repairing the artery. The autopsy showed the repaired artery to be intact," answered Darren.

"Can you get me the names of the operating room people?" asked Mike.

"No problem," said Darren.

"And tell me how I can reach Dr. Sanders," Mike added.

"I can arrange for him to come here when you're ready to talk to him."

"Fine," Mike replied. "So they got the patient in and out of the operating room alive. What happened after that?"

"In looking through Donnie's record, it appears that he did remarkably well, considering the severity of the injury," answered Darren. "He was not at all cooperative with the nurses and technicians when they tried to care for him He would refuse to get out of bed or take the respiratory treatments. The doctors were afraid that he would get a blood clot to his lungs. That's what they thought happened to cause his sudden death."

"Also Dr. Lehman was concerned about Donnie's irregular heartbeat and called for a cardiology consultation. The cardiologist warned about the possibility of worsening heart rhythm problems since Donnie was known to be a chronic drug user."

Darren pointed out to Mike the dictated and typed consultation report by Dr. McAllister.

"Do drugs affect the heart enough to cause the heart to stop?" asked Mike.

"Some drugs do," Darren replied. "Potassium is used sometimes to stop the heart momentarily during open-heart surgery, I'm told. You probably ought to ask a cardiologist about the effect of drugs on the heart. I'll give you Dr. McAllister's name and number."

"Yeah, I'll need to talk to him also," said Mike.

Darren stood by and no words were exchanged while Mike made notes on his yellow pad. He finished one page and turned to the next.

"Now, tell me what you know about that last day, specifically the last hour or so."

"This is the confusing part," Darren replied. "It seems that Dr. Lehman made rounds on the ICU and found Donnie asleep. His nurse, Janie Reyes, was preparing to add potassium to a fresh bottle of IV fluid. Potassium has to be diluted with a large amount of IV fluid and given slowly. The cardiologist gave the order for a stronger dose of potassium after he got the blood test report that showed a very low potassium level. Janie's intention was to wait until Dr. Lehman finished his examination of Donnie before hanging the new bottle of fluid."

"She had already loaded the syringe with the potassium and placed it on the bedside table. She asked Dr. Lehman if it would be all right if she went to the restroom while he was there. Dr. Lehman told her to go on, that he would be leaving before she got back, but Donnie was stable enough for her to leave for a short period.

"When she returned, she was met by Linda, Dr. Lehman's wife, coming from Donnie's room, screaming for help. According to ICU nurses, Linda had just arrived and found Donnie in the cardiac arrest state. Of course the arrest was first noticed on the central monitor, so the resuscitation crew was already racing to Donnie's side."

"Where was Dr. Lehman?" asked Mike.

"He had already left. He had announced to Janie that he had an early operation and would be leaving as soon as he made some entries into the chart progress notes. The other ICU nurses reported that he seemed to be rushing when he left the unit. Of course he returned as soon as he was notified."

"Mr. Johnson, can you answer this?" inquired Mike. "Had the new IV bottle been started, and if so was it tested to see if any potassium had been added?"

"First, can you just call me Darren?" he replied. "Next, in answer to your question, the new IV bottle had not been started and our tests showed that no potassium had been added; the loaded syringe that Janie left could not be found, and the autopsy report showed that Donnie had a dangerously high blood potassium level."

"So, Darren, are you telling me that the undiluted drug had to have been pushed directly into the patient and that is what caused his heart to stop?"

"I'm afraid so," he answered.

"Are you trying to defend the hospital, Darren?" asked Mike.

He looked Darren straight in the eye and held the contact while carefully judging Darren's response.

Darren didn't flinch as he returned Mike's fixed stare. He struggled to restrain an outburst of his resentment of this implication that he may not be telling the truth.

"Detective, I'm here to help you compile information on what occurred in this case," he said. "Of course I'm defending the hospital! In my position I am paid to defend the hospital against all sorts of frivolous claims, but I do that by seeking the truth in whatever occurrence I am asked to review. I would think your position would be the same."

"Sure it is, Darren," said Mike, a smirk in his face. "Truth—that's what it's all about, isn't it?"

"I will bring any of the caregivers here for you to interview," said Darren as he stood, gathering together pages of the medical record, and started to leave.

Still skeptical of Darren's narration of events, Mike didn't let up on his interrogation.

"How do you know, Darren," inquired Mike, leaning back and propping his feet on an adjacent chair while keeping up his attack on Darren, "that the nurse—Janie, I believe you said—did not come back from the restroom and mistakenly inject the drug directly into the patient?"

"Every ICU nurse knows better," he replied, trying to hide his irritability.

"But errors do occur, don't they?" asked Mike, tapping his finger on the medical record.

"Sure they do, but..." said Darren, trying to qualify his answer.

"And even the best professionals make mistakes, don't they?"

"Of course they do, but..."

"And if Janie made a mistake, the hospital would be responsible, isn't that right?"

"Yes," he said.

"And your job would be to defend the hospital, would it not?"

"Yes," he replied, then turned toward the conference room door with the medical record in his hands, glanced back and, without saying another word, but with his eyes, shot daggers at Mike before he approached the exit.

"Come back, Darren," said Mike, with a smile. "You know I'm just putting you to test. I really appreciate your help. I haven't reached an opinion, but I could never have gotten this far without you."

"I guess I am a little defensive when my integrity is challenged," said Darren, returning to his chair.

"Darren, do you know of any occasions when Dr. Lehman made any threats directed at Donnie?" Max continued.

"When Linda had the miscarriage, Dr. Lehman was in Switzerland as a consultant for an electronics company. When he was notified about Linda, he came home and went straight to the hospital. He apparently knew the baby was not his; he had heard the rumors of Linda and Donnie's affair. As he approached Linda's room, he ran into Donnie coming out of the room. According to reports of hospital personnel close by he was heard to make remarks like, 'Stay away or I'll kill you.'"

"Are you aware of any physical encounter between the two?" Mike inquired.

"Not that I know of," Darren answered. "Dr. Lehman is known not to be a violent person."

"Darren, I've got a pretty long list of individuals I need to question," said Mike. "Could you help me find these people?"

"Sure," he replied. "Tell me who you want and I will bring them to you."

"Great!" said Mike. "I'd like to start with the anesthesia doctor you told me about—Dr. Sanders, isn't it?"

"Yeah, we will have to catch him between cases."

Luke had a break within a few minutes of Darren's call and came directly to the conference room, without knowing why he was being summoned. Darren tried to explain some of the details of the investigation and then introduced him to Mike.

"Luke Sanders!" Mike said. "I didn't piece it all together. And the Dr. Lehman we've been talking about is Josh Lehman. When I was a small kid in middle school you two guys were football heroes here and in college. What a surprise! You and Josh were my idols. Now look at you—both of you are doctors!"

After they exchanged greetings, Mike explained to Luke why he was making the investigation and the importance of interviewing him to corroborate some of the information he had accumulated. Luke verified the stories about the initial phone call, as well as the reasons for Josh's bitterness and behavior toward Donnie and his father.

"Dr. Sanders, did you ever hear Dr. Lehman make any threats to kill Donnie?" Mike asked.

"Absolutely not!" replied Luke. "Where are you going with this? Josh would never make such a statement or even entertain such thoughts. He is a gentle, peaceful person." Luke stiffened. *Is this cop trying to hang something on Josh?* he wondered.

"I just need to know the facts, Dr. Sanders," replied Mike. "Thanks for coming in."

Luke stood, turned and left without a handshake or a good-bye, but with a scowl directed toward Darren.

Mike interviewed as many of the caregivers as Darren could produce that were in some way involved with Donnie's care from the time he entered the hospital until his demise. Their stories were consistent with what Mike had heard from Darren. A composite picture was gradually coming into focus. Mike waited until last to talk with Janie.

Mike listened closely to Janie Reyes and watched her every move as she talked. She was the key to this puzzle in so many ways. Mike needed to scrutinize her carefully for any sign of deceptiveness or discrepancy in her story. Her voice was so shaky from fright that Mike could hardly understand a word she said. She recoiled in her chair as if she were trying to hide.

"Try to relax, Miss Reyes," said Mike. "I know this is difficult for you. You have nothing to be afraid of. I am just here to try to learn as much as I can about what happened to Donnie. Just relax and tell me in your own words exactly what you remember."

"He was my patient..." she said, tears flowing freely. "I am so scared."

"You don't need to be," said Mike. "I know you must feel badly about losing a patient."

"If I hadn't gone to the restroom..." she sobbed.

"You mustn't feel guilty, Miss Reyes," said Mike. "You did the best you could. Why don't you start with telling me about that period of time before Donnie died?"

Janie dabbed at her eyes and looked up at Mike.

"He was my patient for that shift," she replied. "I had just come on duty and at report the nurse leaving told me that Donnie had a rough night, begging for sedation and pain medicine. She had finally gotten him to sleep."

"She told me about Dr. McAllister giving the order for the increased dose of potassium. The pharmacy had delivered the vials and I filled a syringe and was getting ready to add the potassium to a new IV bottle. Potassium has to be diluted, you know."

"Dr. Lehman came in while I was getting ready to add the potassium, so I waited while he checked Donnie. Donnie never woke up. I stayed in the room with Dr. Lehman until he started writing in the chart, then I asked if it would be all right if I went to the restroom while he was there. I thought it would be a good time to go while he was there."

"Of course," Mike reassured her. "You left him in good hands. Then what happened?"

"He told me not to rush. He said he had to hurry to the operating room and that Donnie was stable and that he would be leaving as soon as he finished writing his progress note."

"So it didn't matter if Donnie was alone for a short period of time?"

"No, patients are being monitored all of the time at the central monitoring station," she answered. "I came back as quickly as I could. I needed to add the potassium to the new IV bottle."

"Was Dr. Lehman still there?"

"No, he had left," Janie said. "Donnie coded before I even got to his side," she added, becoming tearful again. "I met Linda coming out of Donnie's cubicle. She was screaming for a crash cart and a resuscitation team. Linda was an ICU nurse, you know. She knew that he had arrested."

"Linda was, or is, an ICU nurse?"

Janie hesitated for a moment and dropped her head.

"She used to be. She doesn't work any more," said Janie softly.

"Why?" asked Mike.

"Well, after she hooked up with Donnie, she quit doing any shifts at all."

"Was she a good ICU nurse?"

"The best. I wish she hadn't quit."

"What happened to the potassium you were going to give Donnie?"

"I don't know," replied Janie. "I left the filled syringe on the bedside table. I never saw it again. Of course there was a lot of activity going on with the resuscitation efforts."

"So you never added it to the IV fluid?" asked Mike.

"No, I left it on the table. I told Dr. Lehman I would add it when I came back."

"Do you think he added it?"

"No, he knew I was going to do it when I came back," she replied.

"Could Dr. Lehman or anyone else coming into the room tell what was in the syringe?" he asked.

"Oh, yes," she answered. "The pharmacy always labels injectables and places warning notes where they can be easily read."

"So there would be a note and label that identified the medication and a warning. What would the warning say?"

"For potassium, it would warn that it must be diluted before being given," she replied.

"You didn't mistakenly give the potassium, undiluted, directly into Donnie's vein, did you, Miss Reyes?" Mike asked while judging her response.

"No, no!" she cried. "I would never do that. Did someone say that I did that? I would never do that."

"I just needed to hear it from you, Miss Reyes," he said. "We're almost through. I know this hasn't been easy for you. How long had Linda been in the ICU when you saw her?"

"I don't know. I think she had just arrived," said Janie.

"Why do you say that?"

"If she came on the unit and found out that Dr. Lehman was there, she wouldn't have gone in. They don't speak to each other, you know."

"I appreciate your cooperation, Miss Reyes. Please don't discuss our conversation here with others," said Mike as he stood and motioned that Janie could leave.

Darren stood by during the interrogations. After Janie left, he turned to Mike.

"Is there anyone else you need to talk with, Mr. Garetry?"

"I need to question Dr. Sanders again," said Mike. "He was a bit miffed when he left. You people do get offended easily, don't you?"

"You tend to get pretty abrasive at times," replied Darren.

"There's a reason for that." Mike glared at him. "Don't try to withhold anything from me, Darren."

Darren stared back at the detective. Their gazes locked for a few moments while Darren searched for the right words. He decided not to speak, then turned and left to find Luke.

"Can you come back down, Luke?" asked Darren over his cell phone after finding Luke in the middle of a case.

"I've had about as much of that guy as I can stand, Darren," Luke responded.

"I know what you mean," replied Darren. "I want him out of here."

"I'll find someone to cover for me here," said Luke. "I'll be there as soon as I can."

Mike was busy writing his report when Luke arrived. He looked up and motioned for Luke to sit across the table from him.

"Thank you for coming back, Dr. Sanders," he said. "I just need to ask you a couple more questions."

"Please make it quick," said Luke.

"I need to talk to Dr. Lehman," Mike stated with firmness. "I've called his office and his home. He seems to be missing. I thought you might know where I can find him."

"I'm sorry, I can't help you there," replied Luke.

"You mean you *won't* help me," Mike said. "You are not being truthful with me, Dr. Sanders." he added, after noticing the rapid eye blinking and the purposeless movement of Luke's hands—telltale body language that he had long since learned to recognize.

"Either way, I don't feel obligated to tell you where you can find Josh," said Luke.

"Dr. Sanders," said Mike, "let me warn you against interfering with the investigation of an alleged criminal case. I think you know where you can find Dr. Lehman. Let me suggest that you deliver him to the station for questioning within the next twenty-four hours. I would rather not put out a statewide alert and have him brought in with cuffs and then arrest you for obstructing justice. Do I make myself clear?"

"Yes. Is there anything else?" Luke asked as he stood to leave.

"Please sit down," Mike replied. "I have one more question."

Luke remained standing, waiting for the question.

"Dr. Sanders," asked Mike, "if a person is given a large dose of undiluted potassium directly into his vein, how long before his heart would stop beating?"

"Within seconds," said Luke. "Is that all?"

"Thank you, Dr. Sanders," Mike answered and turned to his yellow pad again to finish his report.

Luke arranged for coverage by the other anesthesiologists, updated Ann on the events of the day, filled his car with gasoline, and hit the interstate for the hill country.

Chapter 46

"Luke!" said Josh, as he stepped into the dressing room. "What is it? What's wrong?"

"It's the autopsy report on Donnie—cardiac arrest from a lethal blood level of potassium," replied Luke.

Luke described what he knew, based on a briefing from Darren just before he left Westlake, about the happenings at the hospital with the investigation.

"Don Bradford is adamant about the investigation. He wants criminal charges filed against the hospital, against you, and who knows who else. Darren Johnson says Bradford will likely file wrongful death civil suits against all of us. The police department has assigned the case to Detective Mike Garetry. He has been at the hospital interviewing employees all day. He wants to talk to you at the police station."

"I can be ready to leave in twenty minutes," said Josh, without hesitating. "Old Don wants to bring me down, Luke. He has just the power to do it. Any suggestions?"

"Just like any game, Josh, you can't have good offense without good defense," said Luke, managing to call up a laugh.

"I'll go straight to the police station. Anything else I need to know?"

"Yeah," said Luke, his voice quivering for a moment. "We love you, Josh. We'll be there for you."

"Thanks, Luke."

They first shook hands, followed by a brotherly hug, then parted.

* * * *

On the way back to Westlake, Luke made the decision to call Charles Salzman, without letting Josh know. Early on he had promised Charles that he would keep him informed about any occurrences that might represent a threat to Josh's safety.

Charles had heard about Donnie's death, but nothing of the details. He had even sent condolences to Don Bradford. Charles was upset about this turn of events and asked multiple questions. Luke gave him a rundown of the whole scenario that was evolving.

"I feel responsible for Bradford's action against Josh, Luke," said Charles. "I am sending Tom Weston down. Tom will follow the sequence of happenings and do a little probing on his own. Also, he'll be there with bail in case Josh is charged. I wouldn't put anything past old Don. He has so many political cronies that he controls. He is capable of causing a lot of trouble."

"Thanks for your help, Mr. Salzman," said Luke.

"Just call me Charles, Luke," he said. "I know you feel you are carrying a heavy load right now; but remember, we are there with you."

* * * *

Josh entered the police station amidst uniformed officers ushering handcuffed detainees in and out; some appeared spaced out from drugs, others fighting their restraints and yelling that they were innocent. Josh made his way to what appeared to be a registration desk.

"I was told to come here to see Mr. Garetry," he said to a clerk behind the desk.

She was busy shuffling papers and continued to do so until Josh coughed and cleared his throat. She looked up, finally.

"Mr. Garetry?" she asked, a quizzical look on her face. "Oh, you mean Mike. What is your name?"

"Josh Lehman."

She thumbed through a memo pad, page after page, then stopped, stood and walked through a nearby office door without uttering another word.

Two policemen came from somewhere and Mike came out of the office to stand face to face in front of him. "My God, do they think I'm going to bolt and run?" Josh asked himself.

"Dr. Lehman, I'm Detective Garetry. I have been given the task of investigating the untimely death of Don Bradford, Jr.," said Mike. "I need to ask you some questions. Follow me please."

They went down a long corridor—Mike in front, Josh close behind with a policeman on each side—looking ready to tackle him if he tried to break away. *This is some kind of joke,* thought Josh.

They went into a small room with a table and four chairs. The two police officers remained standing. Mike seated himself and asked Josh to sit down across the table.

"Dr. Lehman, this will be quick," said Mike. "I asked you to come for questioning. The truth is, I have no questions for you. We have a murder on our hands. We know the cause of death, the death weapon, the motive, and the evidence points to you as the perpetrator. Joshua Lehman, you are under arrest for the murder of Don Bradford, Jr."

Mike motioned for the police officers to handcuff Josh while he read him his rights.

Josh offered no comment or resistance and consented to be taken peacefully to a jail cell. As he was being escorted to the confinement section of the building, he passed Luke on his way to Mike Garetry's office. Josh had no need to request a phone call. Luke would handle it from this point on.

Luke wandered around the public area at the police station, trying to get some information on the bail bond process when, to his surprise, he was confronted by Tom Weston.

"Dr. Sanders, I'm Tom Weston," he said. "I think Mr. Salzman mentioned to you that I would be around."

How did he know who I was? Luke wondered.

"Yes, he did," said Luke. "You guys move fast."

"Mr. Salzman expects it," said Tom with a laugh. "Our first task here, Dr. Sanders, is to get Josh out on bond. That might be impossible before tomorrow, but we should try. Mr. Salzman has some strong contacts in the judicial world, so I need to call him as soon as possible. Give me a couple of minutes; I need to update Mr. Salzman on the status here, then I need to talk to you about some plans."

With that Tom streaked off to find a secluded place to call Charles. Within five minutes he was back.

"OK, Dr. Sanders," he said, "everything is in place. Mr. Salzman has our lawyers moving this way. They will try to get the arraignment hearing tonight. We'll post bond and Dr. Lehman will be out. I suggest you go see Dr. Lehman and reassure him that we are moving as fast as possible. I have some preliminary work first—contacting the District Attorney and reviewing the police report—then I'll be down to see Dr. Lehman."

Luke entered the cell under the watchful eye of the jailer. Josh seemed surprisingly calm.

"How's it going, Josh?" asked Luke.

"Oh, great!" he replied with a laugh. "This is just what I needed. Some quiet time to reflect on my career of crime. I'm making a list of potential serial victims. I may take this statewide."

"Get serious, Josh. These people are serious," said Luke. "They want your head on a platter."

"How am I going to get out of here, Luke?"

"Here's what I know: Tom Weston is here and will be here soon to spell out the details for you. Charles Salzman has been updated and has mobilized a team of lawyers. They are on their way. If they can convince the judge to convene for a hearing this late in the day, we can post bond and you'll be out tonight."

"Does Charles know the whole story?" asked Josh.

"Yeah, he does," Luke replied. "I called him, Josh. I thought it best to bring him in the loop."

"If Tom Weston is here, Charles is in the loop big time," said Josh.

"I believe it," Luke answered. "Tom's already started his inquiry, starting with Mike Garetry's report."

"Luke, please do me a favor. Call my dad," said Josh, grimacing at the thought. "He's always had such faith in me. What is he going to think?"

"Sure," said Luke. "I'll handle it. Anything else you need?"

"No, I'm fine, Luke."

Tom appeared, with the jailer leading the way. When they reached Josh's cell, the jailer stopped and blocked Tom from entering.

"One visitor at a time," he announced with a tone that seemed to reflect an enjoyment of this brief moment of authority.

Luke stood, grasped Josh's hand firmly, and left. The jailer stepped aside and allowed Tom to enter.

"I'll let you know how we're progressing, Dr. Sanders," said Tom.

"Let me give you my cell phone number," Luke replied.

"I already have it," said Tom, without blinking an eye.

Tom turned to Josh.

"How are you doing, Dr. Lehman?" he asked. "I shouldn't even ask such a stupid question." He laughed.

"I feel better, seeing you here," answered Josh.

"I'll be brief with this, Dr. Lehman. Anything you don't agree with, just let me know. Our team of attorneys should be here soon. Mr. Salzman is sending them by company plane. They will need some time with you as soon as they arrive."

"Dr. Lehman, from what I see here, I don't predict that there will be any problem with bail. We think the judge will agree to an arraignment hearing this evening. The prosecuting attorneys will present their charges and you plead 'not guilty.'"

"Our attorneys will ask the judge to set bond. The lawyers on both sides will argue about the amount. Whatever is agreed on, Mr. Salzman has said to post it and get you out of here."

"That is the first step. This is a high profile case, Dr. Lehman. The media will go wild. The public likes 'spicy' cases like this. Men will all identify with you. Women will have one of their own ranks to target for condemnation. It's Hollywood stuff. 'See what's happening to the rich and famous.'"

"This is also a high profile case politically. Grant Mankin, the D.A., wants to get re-elected. Other politicians across the state look eagerly to campaign contributions from Bradford, and he is going to put his full, overfed weight toward getting a conviction."

"On top of it all, there is strong public sentiment against the health care industry generally...a lot of talk about patient safety in hospitals, about medication error, about unnecessary operations."

"A doctor accused of killing his patient will stir all sorts of comments. I'm telling you this, Dr. Lehman, to prepare you for some of the unpleasantness that you face. This could get escalated to be on a par with the O.J. Simpson case."

"I appreciate your candor, Tom."

"Now, because of this notoriety," said Tom, "the case will go to the grand jury right away, and assuming there will be an indictment, it will be set for trial within a few days. This is the good news."

"What are my chances, Tom?" he asked.

"From what I see so far, their case is full of holes," he replied. "This looks more and more like a show for Bradford's benefit, with you being center stage. You'll have some good lawyers, Dr. Lehman; don't worry about it right now."

Tom continued. "Mr. Salzman thinks you should stay sequestered with no interviews, no comments, and no public appearances. Let your attorneys make all of the statements to the media. Stay away from your home and office."

"The Salzmans have a large ranch in west Texas, in the Davis Mountains, a very secluded place. The family uses it for 'getaway' occasions. We think you should stay there until this ordeal is over. There is a landing strip there that will accommodate small jets so your attorneys can fly in and out while they are preparing your case."

"Reporters will be trying to follow our lawyers to locate you, but will be out of luck against our private jets, and our pilots will be alerted to that possibility and will know to exercise diversionary tactics."

"The people who live and work on the ranch are all loyal employees, so you will be well protected. Of course the electronic communications system there is just what you would expect Mr. Salzman to have in place."

"Any time you have to make an appearance in court, you will have our security guards as escorts to see that you get in and out without being molested by reporters."

"Oh, one other thing, Dr. Lehman," Tom continued. "Dr. Dubonet sent word that he backs you all the way. He will see that your patients are well cared for. You have a lot of friends out there pulling for you, Dr. Lehman."

"It looks like I'm going to need it," said Josh, as his gaze dropped to the floor. "Tom, I'm getting tired of fighting old Bradford. He's about to grind me down."

"Come on, Dr. Lehman," said Tom. "You're not ready to give up. You're going to win this game."

"Tom, thanks," said Josh. "Can you just call me Josh? I don't even want to hear the word 'doctor.'"

"Sure," Tom replied.

* * * *

After Tom left, Josh lay back on the cot and closed his eyes, trying to clear the cobwebs from his brain. Everything evolved so rapidly, he was having trouble climbing out of a state of shock. What had happened? From Luke's information, someone had administered the potassium to Donnie directly into a venous access line. Who could have done it? Who wanted him dead?

I had nothing to gain by killing him, but the case against me must be strong. I was there. I made some statements that could be construed as a threat. No one else was around. Janie Reyes certainly would not make an error like that.

Josh was tired. The more he tried to unravel all of the tangles, the more exhausted he became. He had dropped off into a light sleep when the unemotional, monotone voice of the jailer announced:

"Your lawyer is here to see you."

Josh sat up and turned toward the door to find Leah Salzman, briefcase in hand, entering.

"Leah!" Josh cried in astonishment.

"My grandmother told me to come here and get you out of jail," she said as she brought out her yellow legal pad, pulled up the one available chair, smiled and gave that tantalizing toss of her head.

"Your grandmother knows I'm in jail?" he asked.

"My grandmother knows everything, dear." Leah laughed. "You know, you didn't have to go to such an extreme to get me to come to you. You could have just whistled."

"You won't believe how close I've come to that."

"Enough light talk," said Leah, unable to control the faint tint of a blush spreading across her face.

"We've got work to do," she continued, after regaining her composure. "Let me tell you how we think this should be handled. I know Tom Weston has briefed you on the bail process and some of the other issues. As for your legal representation, I will be the lead attorney. Backing me up will be two criminal defense attorneys from Dallas, both with excellent credentials. If you disagree with this approach, now is the time to voice it. Just remember, you are not the quarterback in this game. You are more of a spectator."

"I feel like the football being kicked around," he said. "I am grateful that you are going to run the show. I promise…I'll behave."

"And be honest," she said. "Now, first question: did you kill the worthless bum?"

"I did not, Leah," he replied.

"I know you didn't, but I had to ask the question," she said with a grin. "Now all I have to do is convince a jury."

Leah made notes while she questioned him about every detail of the saga—the time Linda first showed an interest in Donnie, Donnie in her, Josh's first suspicion that an affair was brewing. She asked about Linda's drug and alcohol problem, about her treatment in the center. Leah pinned him down on his reactions to the abortion; the emotions he felt on being betrayed.

"Did you ever wish Donnie were dead, Josh?" she asked point-blank.

Josh hesitated several moments before answering.

"I think my feeling was more that I was disgusted that such a person existed at all. I didn't want him dead. I just don't think the world is, or was, any better off because he existed. All he did was 'take' he never 'gave.'"

Leah stopped her interrogation while she made a series of notes. Josh thought to himself, *I must have said the wrong thing.*

"I understand how you feel, Josh," she said. "I know you, Josh Lehman. I know more about you than you think. That's why we decided that I would be the lead attorney. For one thing, I know that regardless of your opinion of Donnie, you lost a patient; and you feel a great deal of remorse. I don't think that's cleared the filtration system in your brain yet. We will not put you on the stand."

Leah walked him through the legal proceedings they would be facing; much the same as Tom had done earlier.

"I like the idea of your staying at the Escondido Ranch. You'll like it there. It's one of my favorite places."

"Why is it called Escondido?" asked Josh.

"The name means 'hidden' in Spanish," she replied. "The ranch is completely surrounded by mountain ranges. It is truly hidden. I wish I could be there with you."

"You mean that is not an option?" He laughed.

"Not now—later," she said, with a toss of her head and one of her enticing smiles.

"I know," he said. "You would be afraid to be around a homicidal maniac."

"I'll take my chances," she said. "Now, switch back into a serious mode. I want to bring out that these charges were instigated by Don Bradford. I think I can do that in cross-examination when the prosecution puts him on the stand to testify about your statements after the surgery. Once I get him in a corner, I think I can agitate him into saying that he has strong political ties and put pressure on politicians to intervene in this case to get a conviction."

"Whatever the outcome of the trial, he is going to file a wrongful death civil suit against you. He wants to destroy you. Before he can file, I will file a defamation of character suit against him. His testimony will be public record and I can use it in a civil suit."

"Leah, I just want my record cleared," said Josh.

"I hear you," she replied, "but remember, I am the quarterback. We can't pass up the chance to use this tactic. Pardon the pun, football hero, but a 'pass' won't work here. We have to run head-on against these people, and we are playing this game in front of millions of spectators."

Chapter 47

The sequence of events evolved just as Tom and Leah had described. After bail bond was set, Josh and his attorneys left the jail and police station to face a crowd of reporters, media people with video cameras, and a multitude of curiosity seekers. Tom's security guards whisked Josh through the crowd, unscathed, into a waiting car. With one of the guards driving and Josh in the back seat, they raced away from the police station, carloads of reporters following. On the adjacent seat, Josh recognized his carryon bag by his initials on the side. The guard looked back in time to notice Josh's astonishment.

"Tom packed a supply of clothes and other essentials for you," said the guard. "He said to let him know if you need anything else."

"How did he do this?" asked Josh.

"You should know Tom by now," laughed the guard.

Tom had arranged for almost all of Josh's clothes and personal belongings to be packed and placed in the car. *How did he get into my home?* Josh wondered, but quickly erased the question from his mind. *Tom just has a way to get things done.*

Josh was taken straight to a private airport, on to the tarmac, and alongside the Salzman jet, dwarfed in size compared to the last jet in which he had been a passenger. The guards stood by while he boarded. The plane was airborne even before the first carload of trailing reporters arrived.

The plane landed in the dark at the Escondido Ranch, on a runway well marked by ground lights and long enough to accommodate the small jet. Josh could see the lights of an approaching vehicle coming towards them. Josh climbed out of the plane, bag in hand, and stepped into a topless Jeep. Even in the subdued light coming from the runway, Josh could see that the driver was a deeply-tanned, rugged-appearing cowboy, wearing high-top boots with jeans tucked inside and a well-worn, deeply creased Stetson hat. A can placed in the console of the front seat told Josh that Ken chewed tobacco.

"You must be Dr. Lehman," he drawled.

"Yes, sir," said Josh.

"Been expecting you. Name's Ken Kincaid."

That was the end of their conversation. By the time Ken turned the Jeep around, the jet shrieked past them for its return trip. In the distance, Josh could see lights that must have been coming from the ranch headquarters. Once at the headquarters compound, Josh was escorted by Ken to his living quarters.

"Know anything about ranching?" asked Ken as they went up the stairs to the bedroom floor of the main house.

"No, sir," he answered.

"This here's a workin' ranch," he replied. "This ain't no dude ranch. Ever rid a horse?"

"No, sir," said Josh.

"Oughta try it."

"Might do that," said Josh, finding that Ken's brogue was infectious.

An evening meal had been set aside for Josh and delivered to his room. Josh picked at the food, then abandoned the effort altogether. He had lost his appetite. All at once, being totally by himself, he felt a wave of intense loneliness. He walked out on the large adjacent balcony. The weather was crisp and cool; he was surrounded by an eerie darkness and a silence that was broken only by the occasional distant howl of a coyote. Never before in his life had he felt so completely isolated. *Can I adjust to this solitude? Maybe this is what prison would be like,* he thought.

Lying in bed, Josh reflected on the happenings of the day and the stark realization flashed before him—he could be found guilty! He recalled the time on the plane when he said to himself that if he ever needed a lawyer, he'd like to have Leah represent him. Little did he know that he would be depending on her now to save his career—save his life! Can she handle it? He found solace in knowing that Charles thought she could. He fell asleep with the comfortable feeling of knowing that he had so many concerned people working on his behalf.

He awakened at daybreak the next morning, dressed, and started exploring the house and grounds. The house, with every amenity imaginable, was more like a resort lodge than a ranch house—Olympic sized swimming pool, a work-out room, and a putting green. The grounds were immaculately kept. Nearby were the barns and the working pens for cattle and horses. In the early morning dawn, with the sun just appearing over the mountain tops, Josh could see some activity in the corrals. He wandered over and climbed up on the fence to watch.

Several cowboys were placing bridles and saddles on their horses. He spotted Ken moving about, stopping at times to examine a horse's hoof or talking to the other men, waving his arm and pointing, as if giving them instructions. *Ken must be the foreman,* Josh surmised. Ken looked up, saw Josh, and motioned for him to climb down and come into the corral. *I must look like some sorta freak to these guys with my open neck shirt, dress pants and shoes,* he thought, as he approached the men.

"Ever seen cattle rounded up?" asked Ken.

"No, sir," Josh replied.

"Wanna go with us?"

"Sure," said Josh, "but I don't know anything about riding horses."

"You'll ride with me in the Jeep," said Ken, a faint smile on his face, as he whistled for his black Labrador retriever to leap into the back.

The mounted horsemen took off toward the pastures, staying together for awhile, then spreading out in different directions. Ken and Josh, in the Jeep, bounced along, some distance behind, until the cowboys were finally out of sight. The sun was in an early morning position as Ken guided the Jeep under a large oak tree, standing alone in the middle of a lush green field, and parked. In the back of the Jeep were containers of coffee and a basket of freshly-made tacquitos.

"Eat before we left?" asked Ken.

"No, sir."

"Better eat something...long time 'fore we git back."

They sat in the Jeep, munching on the egg and potato tacquitos and sipping black coffee. Josh never remembered anything tasting so good. Neither of the two said anything for awhile. Josh finally spoke, after deciding that since he was in the country he had best "do and speak as the country folk do."

"Lived here long?"

"Forty years. Born in Fort Davis."

"Like living in the country?"

"Yep," he replied. "Wouldn't live no place else."

"Married?" asked Josh.

"Yep," he said. "Wife and me been married forty-five years. No kids."

There was a tone of sadness in his voice when he spoke those words. He looked out across the pastures for awhile in silence, then turned to Josh.

"Did you kill that feller?"

"No, sir," said Josh.

"Didn't think so," he replied. "Neither does my wife."

"Thank her for me," said Josh.

"No need to. You operated on her uncle last April…saved his life."

Before Josh could reply or inquire, one of the cowboys came riding up in a fast gallop.

"We got a cow down, Ken!" he yelled. "Looks like she's calving. She's in trouble. I can see a foot."

"Let's go!" said Ken. "Hang on, Dr. Lehman."

They parked the Jeep a few feet away and Ken walked over to examine the cow. She was still, and breathing heavily. With her pains, she groaned and kicked and her belly became taught. A small hoof protruded from her vagina. Ken put on a long glove and inserted his hand almost to his elbow to try to determine the problem.

"Calf's lying cross-wise, head and neck twisted back…she won't be able to push it out," said Ken, looking straight at Josh.

"Can you turn the calf?" asked Josh.

"Too risky," he replied. "Might lose the cow. We'll have to cut the calf out piece by piece. Got to do something quick. She's playing out." Ken turned to Josh with a skeptical look on his face. "What would you do if it was a woman, Dr. Lehman?"

"I'd try to save the baby *and* the mother," said Josh. "I'd sedate the mother to relax her muscles, rotate the baby, and extract it feet first."

Ken stood back and scrutinized Josh from head to foot. Without saying a word, he took off his gloves, went to the Jeep, and returned with a large syringe filled with a clear liquid and attached to a large core needle. He then went to the cow's neck, palpated tissue until he found a vein, inserted the needle and injected the medicine. The cow immediately relaxed every muscle in her body, except the muscles she used in breathing. Ken picked up another pair of long, arm-length sterile gloves and tossed them to Josh.

"Want to try it?"

Josh was astounded. *Do a version and extraction out here in the pasture? Unheard of!* Ken's eyes were fixed on Josh. *He's testing my stamina—my endurance! I am being tested!* thought Josh.

"Give 'em to me," said Josh with a laugh. "I never did like Obstetrics."

The cow was sedated and relaxed. Josh seated himself behind the cow and went to work. He pushed the protruding foot back into the vagina, pushed the calf's head up and out of the pelvis, grabbed both hind legs and pulled them to the outside.

"She gets another shot…that'll wake her up," said Ken, injecting medicine into her neck vein again. "Keep pulling on the legs…in a few seconds she'll start pushing."

Within five minutes, Josh had delivered a large bull calf, feet first. With the last push by the cow, when the head popped out Josh fell back into a pile of fresh manure. Ken cleaned the mucous and fluid from the calf's mouth and he was soon breathing and moving around. Josh looked up to see an audience of three or four cowboys. Not one of them laughed or grinned.

"Ya did it, Dr Lehman!" yelled Ken. The first show of emotion of any kind since Josh had arrived. Ken scraped as much of the manure off Josh's back as he could.

"We have some laundering to do when we get back," laughed Ken.

The cowboys dismounted, gathered around, and greeted Josh with congratulatory comments and handshakes. There was not one remark about the greenish-brown stain from the cow dung across the entire back side of his white shirt. *I feel as exhilarated as if I had just done a coronary by-pass or had just thrown a touchdown pass,* he thought as he silently laughed at himself.

By the time they finished packing the Jeep to leave the scene, the cow was up and sniffing the new calf. The Lab jumped aboard, sniffed Josh once and recoiled into the cargo space in the back of the Jeep. As they drove away, the calf was already on its feet and nursing.

"Not sure if I want you in my Jeep with that cow shit all over you," laughed Ken. "Gonna have to teach you to ride a horse, Josh."

"Please, coach…just let me stay with the Jeep," he replied, with a broad grin.

This was the first time Ken had called him by his first name. From that time forward, Josh never missed a chance to go out with Ken on his pasture rounds. Wearing a pair of working gloves and some old clothes Ken came up with, Josh got up at five-thirty every morning to help Ken. They repaired fences, hung gates, vaccinated cows—every thing imaginable that could be labeled ranch work.

Josh became so engrossed with helping Ken that thoughts of his upcoming trial often were erased from his mind. His shirt from the calving experience in the pasture could never be made white again, but Josh really didn't care. The green stain seemed to be some kind of badge of honor. He was going to enjoy this confinement on the Escondido. *I might just try riding a horse!* he thought.

* * * *

The grand jury returned a capital murder indictment, which came as no surprise. Josh already knew the decision from Internet news, but Leah and one of the criminal defense attorneys still needed to visit him to reassure him that they were working diligently, preparing his defense. Leah and her associate had no sooner landed than Ken met them with the story of Josh's achievement with delivering the calf. Leah cringed on hearing the description of the occurrence.

"Josh!" yelled Leah, after they were together in the conference room. "What in the hell were you doing? We're out there proclaiming you as the top heart surgeon in South Texas and you're out here practicing veterinary medicine?"

"I like it when you're mad," laughed Josh.

"Get serious, Josh!" she admonished. "OK, out here, these people are our people. The media will never know, but…please, Josh. This is no time for theatrics."

"I promise, I'll keep it low key, right after I finish my bronco riding lessons, and after Ken teaches me how to castrate calves." said Josh, trying to suppress laughter.

"Josh, dammit!" Leah retorted. "Keep it low key!"

"I'll do it for you," he replied. "What news have you brought me?"

Leah explained to Josh that the next step was the pretrial hearing—when the prosecution would present their evidence before the court.

"The judge is critical of the strength of the evidence," said Leah, "but he has allowed the case to go on to jury trial. Also, as we predicted, the trial has been set for an early date."

"When will you come back?" asked Josh, as they closed their brief cases in preparation to leave.

"We'll be back from time to time to update you—and to counsel you!" she said. "Please, Josh, behave! I'm glad you and Ken have hit it off, but you have an image to portray. Don't forget that!"

"I'll do my best, Leah," he said in all seriousness, "but you know, this place has a way of making you forget everything else in the world. Everything here is so basic."

"I know what you mean," she replied, "but don't forget that we have some important legal strategy to consider."

"I'll remember, Leah," he answered. "How is your grandmother?"

"Worried sick about you," she said, "Otherwise, she is doing well. We've got to go, Josh," she added, as she bent over to give him a kiss.

"I'm letting you do the worrying," he said.

"I can deal with that," she replied, and with a toss of her head turned to leave.

Leah and the criminal defense lawyers made frequent visits to the ranch to keep Josh apprised of developments. As Tom had warned, every development in the case made front page. Letters to the editor were about fifty percent in Josh's favor. Speculation on where Josh was hiding ran high. There were even rumors that he had skipped the country.

Each evening newscast focused on the case of the heart surgeon who deliberately murdered his patient who, the doctor said, "had wrecked his married life." Josh's whereabouts and mysterious disappearance added to the intrigue and triggered a flood of speculation.

* * * *

Josh stayed in touch with Melba. She couldn't call him and had no idea where he was, but he made a point of talking with her almost every day. She had been through too much with him to be left out entirely.

"Dr. Lehman's office," said Melba.

"Hi, Melba," said Josh. "I know our phone lines are tapped, so we can't say much."

"Oh...Dr. Lehman!" Melba said. "How are you?"

"I'm fine, Melba," he replied. "Any messages I need to know about?"

"Calls, calls, calls...every day," she said. "You have a lot of friends out there, Dr. Lehman...I am so worried. Are you taking care of yourself?"

"I'm fine, Melba."

"The news reports are horrible, Dr. Lehman," said Melba. "All of these reports about your wife and her boyfriend...just horrible!"

"Melba, don't worry about it," said Josh. "Any mail that I need to know about?"

"Yes sir. There's a letter from the hospital...from the administration department."

"Open it, Melba," he said. "Tell me what it says."

"It says you've been suspended from the medical staff. You'll need to re-apply. What does that mean, Dr. Lehman?"

"I just have to invoke the fair-hearing provision of the medical staff bylaws, Melba, as soon as the trial is over. Of course, if I am convicted there'll be no need to fight it."

"Don't talk that way, Dr. Lehman!" she said.

"Anything else?" he asked.

"There's a letter from the Texas Board of Medical Examiners," she replied.

"Don't bother to open it, Melba," said Josh. "I know what it says. I'm sure Mr. Bradford has thrown his political clout around again."

"I've gotten a lot of calls from patients and from doctors in town. They are all concerned about your welfare and want you to know they are pulling for you."

"That's important, Melba," said Josh. "Keep a list for me, Melba. I'll be back some day, and don't worry."

"I can't help it, sir," she said, her voice breaking from the emotional strain. "I don't want anything to happen to you. You are like my child."

"Thanks, Melba," he said. "Knowing you're there for me keeps me going. I care for you, Melba."

Before she hung up the phone, Josh could hear her uncontrolled sobbing.

* * * *

Anticipation of the approaching trial ran high, with questions being raised about whether or not live TV video coverage would be allowed. An in-depth profile of Josh's football career was presented by the media, always colored with statements implying that in whatever situation he found himself, he was driven to win at any cost. Of course every detail of each of his defense attorney's careers was described and dissected.

* * * *

Judge Rupert Blackman glanced at his watch as he climbed the stairs to the third floor of the court house. It was 8:17 a.m. Whatever else could be said about Judge Blackman, he was punctual, and he expected everyone else to be the same. Perhaps he was late today because each day now seemed to lessen his enthusiasm for sitting on the bench, hearing one case after another. Most of the time they were simply repetitions of cases he had heard before.

By the end of the year he would be ready to hang up his robe for the last time and meld into the world of retirement. Then there would be no more schedules or dockets to govern his life. In just a few months, the only decisions he would face would be which lure to use when he went wade fishing in the Laguna Madre flats. With grown children pursuing lives of their own, he and his wife of forty years were ready for leisure living on the Gulf coast—fishing and traveling together and visiting grandchildren.

Judge Blackman checked the docket for the week and shuddered. Coming up was the trial of the doctor accused of killing his ex-wife's lover. He thought he had seen and heard every conceivable case against doctors—charges of negligence, substance abuse, sexual abuse, and other reprehensible aberrancies. This would be a first for Judge Blackman—to hear the case of a doctor charged with murder.

He remembered reading the book about the Houston doctor who killed his wife by neglect. *Thank God that case didn't fall in my court*, he thought. *This case will be bad enough, with the crowds of thrill seekers and the media reporters, all hungry for a few morsels of news of risqué behavior.*

He went into the bathroom, looked at himself in the mirror, and combed the few strands of hair over his receding hairline.

"I should have put on a clean shirt," he said aloud, studying the image he faced looking back at him. "I'll do that tomorrow. Today will just be jury selection. I may even take a nap today." He laughed. "The crowds and the reporters will be here tomorrow."

He straightened his tie and draped his black robe over his shoulders and signaled the bailiff that he was ready to start, exactly at 8:30 a.m.—not at 8:29 a.m. nor at 8:31 a.m.

"All rise!" said the bailiff, as his honor Judge Rupert Blackman, entered the courtroom—without eagerness or vigor—and seated himself at the bench in preparation for swearing in and instructing the panel of prospective jurors.

Selecting a jury was the acid test for attorneys on both sides. Leah was fortunate to have the seasoned criminal defense lawyers by her side during the process.

Each prospective juror was profiled by personality traits, moral and ethical standards, and socio-economic status.

Leah and her associates carefully analyzed each person in deciding whether or not to accept or strike the prospect. By the end of the day they were satisfied that the jury selected was balanced and would be fair.

Chapter 48

On the day of the trial, Josh was flown in from the Escondido Ranch and taken to the courtroom under the protection of the Salzman security guards. The courtroom was packed. The judge forbade cameras in the room, but the sketch artists were busy with their pads and pencils, ready to present their artwork to the media.

The front row of seats was reserved for family and close associates of the defendant on one side and for the victim's family and friends on the other. Luke had arranged for Josh's father and Ann to be present. Since Luke was scheduled to give testimony, he was not allowed to attend.

Likewise, Don, Sr. was not allowed in the court room; however; many of his influential cronies—including Jeremy Corbett—were parked behind the District Attorney and his assistants. Josh glanced across at the prosecution support group. He had never seen so many sober, vindictive-looking people. *This equates to the sixteenth century councils that sentenced witches to be burned at the stake,* he thought.

Josh was seated at the table for the defense, along with Leah and her two consultants. He looked at the jury and did not recognize one single person. He studied each juror, looking for someone with a bit of compassion in their eyes and found no one.

There were six men and six women, all with blank expressions on their faces. Some even appeared frightened; they probably had never been in a courtroom before. The age span was in the forty-to-fifty range. Josh noticed two black men on the panel. Seemingly older than the others, they both appeared to be taking an unusually attentive interest in the proceedings and were the only jurors who ever made eye contact with Josh.

The trial began with attorneys on both sides stipulating one thing or another, leaving Josh completely unaware of what they were talking about. Next on the agenda was the prosecution presenting charges against Josh. The lawyer making the opening statement was Grant Mankin, the district attorney.

The room was eerie, quiet, all eyes on Mankin as he rose from his seat and sauntered to a position in front of the jury box. He stood there before the jury and scanned the group, looking at each juror with a fixed stare, as if he had never seen them before.

"Ladies and gentlemen," he began, "I represent the state in this trial. I represent you. We are faced with a heinous crime—a patient, Don Bradford, Jr., in the Intensive Care Unit, recovering from major chest surgery—was murdered by the injection of a toxic drug that caused his heart to stop beating—a drug that caused his death."

Mankin began pacing back and forth before the jury, his head turned toward the jury every second while he made his presentation.

"We will show that the defendant, Dr. Joshua Lehman, was present at Mr. Bradford's bedside seconds before the signs of cardiac arrest became known. We will show that Dr. Lehman had motives to do away with Mr. Bradford. That Dr. Lehman made statements, overheard by others, that reflected his animosity toward the victim. We will submit evidence that the weapon—the syringe loaded with the toxic drug—was readily available to the accused."

The District Attorney became more dramatic toward the end of his opening statement. He paced the floor in front of the jury and waved his arms like a theatrical performer as he talked. He walked over in front of Josh and ended his presentation by looking straight at the jury while pointing his finger at Josh.

"We will show that this doctor has violated his code of ethics and conduct and premeditatedly has taken the life of an innocent human being, lying in a hospital bed, unable to defend himself."

"All of us have the right to feel safe in a hospital under the care of physicians who work in a hospital. We will present evidence that will prove beyond all reasonable doubt that this doctor is guilty of murder in the first degree of Don Bradford, Jr."

There was a deadly silence throughout the room as the D.A. took his seat at the table for the prosecution. Josh could feel every eye watching his every move—an eerie feeling. He wanted to stand and yell, "I didn't do it!"

The judge beckoned to Leah to respond. She sat still for a few moments, thumbing through papers. She whispered to her defense attorney consultants. Now every eye was on her. *This delay in standing is probably just one of her tactics,* Josh thought.

She calmly stepped in front of the jury box and stood looking at the jurors before speaking. Her demeanor was exactly opposite that of the District Attorney. She flashed one of those Salzman smiles, with a toss of her head that reflected self-confidence, before speaking.

"Mr. Mankin has painted a picture for you of a doctor who goes around killing patients with abandon and a hospital that allows it. That couldn't be further from the truth. Dr. Lehman is a reputable, dedicated surgeon, whose life is devoted to saving patients from death, just as he did for Don Bradford, Jr."

"Mr Mankin also has narrated circumstances that occurred some time before this alleged crime. These were events that stir your emotions and cause you to wonder whether those circumstances played a part in this case."

"I want you to keep that word 'circumstances' in mind throughout this trial. We will show that the prosecution's case is based entirely on circumstantial evidence and that it will leave you with reasonable doubt that Dr. Lehman committed this crime.'

"Thank you for your attention."

She walked back to the defense table and, with a toss of her head, smiled at Josh and took her seat. The judge called for a short recess before hearing witnesses. Leah conferred with the other attorneys, all of them making notes on their yellow pads. Josh wondered if they all wrote the same thing. He was ignored for the most part. Leah finally turned to him.

"Are you doing all right?" she asked.

"Fine," he replied. "What do you think?"

"It's pretty obvious the tack they are taking," she said. "We'll be ready for it."

"I watched the jury when you talked. They hung on every word you spoke."

"I think we have a good jury," she replied. "But you never know."

Judge Blackman returned and the trial resumed. The prosecution began their parade of witnesses, starting with Mike Garetry and his report of his investigation. Mike narrated his findings with the precision of a witness who had been on the stand many times before. When he was passed to the defense attorneys, Leah smelled an opportunity.

"Mr. Garetry, you certainly did a thorough investigation of this case," said Leah. "I'm sure the prosecution will bring other witnesses to verify what you uncovered, so I'm not going into depth in my questions. I am curious…could you tell us how you became assigned to this case?"

"The Chief called me into his office and told me to do it," said Mike, looking a bit astonished at the question and glancing at the D.A., who began whispering to his assistants.

"So the Chief made a special effort to select you for the job. Did he say why he wanted you in particular to take on the task?"

"Well, he said it was a unique case. He used the phrase, 'a lot of political clout' behind it," said Mike, as he squirmed in the chair.

The D.A. jumped up and addressed the judge, "Your honor, is this line of questioning relevant?" he asked.

"I have no more questions, your honor," said Leah, smiling as she returned to her seat.

She hit a sensitive nerve, thought Josh.

Hospital employees, all twenty-five of them, including the nurse caregivers, housekeeping personnel, the pathologist, the director of the laboratory, and the director of the pharmacy, Dr. James Moore, gave their testimony. They told what they saw, what they heard, and what they knew.

Leah declined to cross-examine most of them, except Janie Reyes. Janie was kept on the stand over two hours, giving conflicting stories and becoming more and more apprehensive as Leah bore down on her.

"Janie, I know you are getting tired," said Leah. "But once again, did Dr. Lehman suggest that you take a break while he was there, or did you ask if it would be all right if you left the patient for awhile?"

"I just don't remember," she said, with tears streaming down her face. "If I hadn't left, Mr. Bradford would still be alive," she added with uncontrolled sobbing.

"Janie, one more question," said Leah. "Did you see Linda go into Donnie's room?"

"No", she replied.

"Did you see her come out of Donnie's room?"

"Yes, ma'am," she answered. "She was rushing out, calling for help."

"Did the 'code call' sound before you saw Linda or after you saw Linda come out of the room? I need an honest answer here, Janie."

"After I saw her," she answered.

"Janie, do you remember what Dr. Lehman was wearing when he visited Mr. Bradford?"

"Yes, ma'am," she replied. "He was wearing scrubs. He was on his way to the operating room."

"Was he wearing shoe covers?"

"Not when he made rounds. When he came back after the code call he had shoe covers on," answered Janie.

"Thank you, Janie," said Leah with a smile. "I have no further questions."

Under questioning by the prosecution, the pathologist gave his report, including the lethal level of potassium in the blood and the findings of heart damage characteristic of patients who have used cocaine for long periods of time. Leah had no questions. The witness stepped down and the pharmacist took the stand.

The D.A., after first getting testimony that the intravenous fluid left in Donnie's room was void of potassium, led the pharmacist through the consequences of giving undiluted potassium directly into a person's vein. He passed the witness to Leah.

"Doctor Moore, if potassium is given directly into a patient, I understand from your testimony that the patient would have a cardiac arrest. The heart would stop beating and death would follow?"

"That is correct," he said.

"Is that correctable?" asked Leah.

"It can be, if prompt measures are taken to defibrillate the heart."

"Doctor, the jury may not know what you mean by fibrillation and defibrillation," said Leah. "Would you please explain?"

The pharmacist explained in lay terms what he meant—the heart beating rapidly and irregularly—a rhythm that, with electroshock, often can be converted to normal.

"And can you tell us why Donnie's heart rhythm did not respond to the resuscitation measures?" asked Leah.

"The pathologist or cardiologist could answer that better than I can, but if a person has underlying heart disease, it may not respond to defibrillation."

"And Donnie had underlying disease, didn't he?"

"Yes," he replied.

"Doctor, after a person is given undiluted intravenous potassium, how long before his heart stops?"

"Very quickly," he replied. "But it could vary, depending on the patient's metabolic condition: magnesium level, state of hydration, potassium level."

"What would be the first signs?" asked Leah.

"There would be EKG changes first that would signal the impending arrest."

"And how soon would those changes be noticed?" asked Leah.

"Very soon in most cases, in a matter of one or two seconds," he replied.

"That's all I have, your honor," said Leah. "If the prosecution doesn't object, I would like to reserve the privilege of recalling this witness at a later date."

"Mr. District Attorney, what is your response?" asked the judge.

"I acquiesce, although I cannot imagine what the counselor expects to gain by further questioning of one of my witnesses," said the D.A. "I would like to redirect, your honor, before the witness steps down."

"Dr. Moore," the D.A. began, "is it possible that the adverse effects of the potassium injection on the EKG would take longer than 'seconds'?"

"Oh, yes sir," he answered, "It would be different on each person. It would depend on the condition of the patient."

Chapter 49

The next witness was none other than the great Don Bradford, Sr. Josh looked at Leah, fire in her eyes as she waited. *She can hardly restrain herself from attacking,* thought Josh. *She has a killer instinct!*

With the D.A. leading the interrogation, old Don described Josh's conduct after the surgery, while he was waiting anxiously in the waiting room for a report on Donnie's condition.

He told, with emotion, wiping tears from his eyes, Josh's remark that he didn't care whether Donnie lived or died. Don carried it a step further by saying he had requested consultation with Dr. Dubonet in Dallas, which Josh refused to consider.

"Can you imagine what it was like for a father to be treated like that when his only son's life was hanging by a thread?" the old man added.

The witness was passed and Leah slowly rose to her feet. She had the most angelic look on her face as she approached the witness chair. "My God!" Josh uttered inaudibly, trying to suppress outright laughter. "She's getting ready to attack."

"Mr. Bradford, I am so sorry for your loss," Leah said. "I can't imagine what it would be like to lose someone that close."

"He shouldn't have died," growled Don.

"I don't want to open those wounds, Mr. Bradford. I have only a couple of questions for you."

"I've told everything I know," he said, squirming in his seat, uncrossing and crossing his legs and wiping his brow of the profuse perspiration.

"I know you have," said Leah. "I believe that you pressed charges against Dr. Lehman, is that not true, Mr. Bradford?"

"You damn right I did!" he yelled. "He can't treat me like that and get away with it. I know important people. I've been around a while, you know."

The D.A. again sprang to his feet and addressed the judge.

"Your honor, I object to this line of questioning. It is irrelevant and serves no purpose in this case."

"Sustained," said the Judge Blackman. "Counselors, approach the bench!"

Leah and the D.A. stood before the judge.

"Where are you going with this, Miss Salzman?"

"Your honor, these charges were filed with malice by a disgruntled egomaniac whose objective is to do harm, not achieve justice," said Leah. "If it is your wish, I will refrain from further questioning. However, I request that the witness's answer remain in the record."

"Granted," said the judge. "However, counselor, I do not take lightly your using testimony in my court as building blocks for a civil case, if that is what you're doing. We will have a short recess and then proceed with this trial. We are already in the fifth day, counselors. I would like to wind this up as soon as possible."

"The prosecution rests its case, your honor."

"You may step down, Mr. Bradford," said the judge. "We will recess until nine a.m. in the morning. When we return, the defense will present its case."

"All rise," said the bailiff, as the judge retired to his chambers and the jurypersons to their jury room. Leah and the other two attorneys spent several minutes conferring in whispers, each of them making notes on their yellow pads. Josh felt left out, but didn't dare interrupt. Besides, it gave him time to visit with his dad and with Ann.

Leah finally turned to Josh with a few encouraging remarks and to inform him that arrangements had been made for him to stay in a nearby hotel with around-the-clock security guards. Josh introduced Leah to Ann, after suddenly realizing they had never met.

"You're Jay's mother!" said Leah. "No one is around Josh very long without hearing about Jay." Leah laughed. "And, of course, about Luke and Ann. I am very glad to meet you. Sorry it's under these strained conditions."

"Josh is a part of our family," replied Ann. "We are so worried."

"It's going fine," assured Leah. "Tomorrow will be our test day," she added. "Right now it's hanging in the balance. If all goes well tomorrow, we should be able to swing the pendulum. Oh, by the way, thanks for being here. This kind of family support goes a long way with the jury."

With that brief exchange of words, Josh could tell that so much more was said. Leah showed Ann that she placed high personal priority on the importance of family. She as much as said, "I know Josh; he wants a family just like yours."

* * * *

Early the next morning, Tom Weston and a crew of technicians began moving video equipment into the courtroom. Two large screens were placed high on each side of the room, clearly visible to the jury and to every spectator. In addition, three seventeen-inch LCD flat panel monitors were placed directly in front of the jury box.

Cables, tying the equipment together, led to a central control station placed on a small table. A technician, under Tom's direction, fine-tuned the components of the system. Josh recognized the technician as Kevin Brant from the company plane's communication compartment.

All players arrived and took their respective positions. After a call from the bailiff for everyone to stand, the judge entered, reconvened the trial and summoned the jury. Tom Weston was sworn in as the first witness for the defense. He took the stand and Leah took him through a line of questioning to qualify him as a licensed investigator with credentials that made him an expert witness.

"Mr. Weston, I believe you are familiar with the charges against the defendant, Dr. Lehman, and the issue of whether or not he is guilty of injecting a lethal dose of a drug directly into the victim's vein, causing his heart to stop?"

"Yes, I am," said Tom.

"In this case, the timing of the injection is critical in determining whether Dr. Lehman did indeed inject the drug or whether it could have been injected by someone else," said Leah, addressing the jury. "At the request of the defense, Mr. Weston, have you conducted a time/motion study in this regard?"

"Yes, I have," he replied.

"Could you demonstrate the results of your study for the jury?"

"Yes," said Tom, turning to the jury. "Let me explain the video presentation that you will be viewing. We have used an actor to portray Dr. Lehman's movements, so you can visualize the sequence of events from the time Dr. Lehman left Mr. Bradford's bedside until the emergency code call was sounded."

"However, the EKG telemetry strip that shows the patient's heart beat and rhythm that you will see going across the bottom of your monitor screen is the actual strip that was recorded during those final moments of Mr. Bradford's life. Please keep in mind that you will be watching the actual strip. You will notice that the exact time—the *exact* time—is visible on the strip."

Tom signaled Kevin to start the videotape. Every juror and everyone in the courtroom was spellbound in anticipation of the film. The actor on the screen who represented Josh could be seen writing an order on Donnie's chart. When he finished, he glanced up at the monitor at Donnie's bedside and entered the exact time of his entry as 07:14:04.

The camera zoomed down on the order sheet and portrayed a magnified 07:14:04. The actual telemetry strip from the central monitoring station ran simultaneously with the tape of the actor's movements, and reflected the exact same time. Kevin stopped the tape for a few seconds for the jury to verify the times. After the actor finished writing, he turned and left Donnie's cubicle and walked hurriedly out of the ICU to the operating room suite and to the surgeon's dressing room.

The telemetry tape, running continuously with the video, remained on the monitor for the jury to see, while the camera showed that "Josh" entered the dressing room and placed covers on his shoes. The time, 07:15:53. The telemetry tape then began showing characteristic changes that signaled imminent ventricular fibrillation. This was followed by sustained fibrillation, the quivering motion of a dying heart muscle. The time, 07:16:24. Tom ran the tape on, showing the resuscitation attempts, until the telemetry strip finally showed a "flat-line" appearance.

"So, Mr. Weston, how much time lapsed from the time Dr. Lehman left Donnie's room until the telemetry showed EKG changes indicating the effect of the undiluted intravenous potassium infusion?" asked Leah.

"Dr. Lehman wrote an order at 07:14:04, noted the time on the order sheet, and left to go to the dressing room. The EKG, recorded on the telemetry strip, shows the first signs of change at 07:15:53, almost two minutes from the time he left his patient's side. The sustained fibrillation, the definite lethal effect of the drug, began at 07:16:24, two minutes and twenty seconds after Dr. Lehman left Mr. Bradford's room."

"How would Dr. Lehman have known the exact time to enter for his written order on Donnie's chart?"

"He had to get that specific time from the monitor that was in Mr. Bradford's room that showed the exact time down to the seconds," Tom replied.

"Not from his watch?" asked Leah.

"No," he answered. "His watch would not give him the exact time in hours, minutes, and seconds."

"Mr. Weston, how do you know that the time that appeared on the monitor in Donnie's room was the same as the time that appears on the telemetry strip?" she asked.

"I double-checked with the electronic specialist in the engineering department of the hospital. All times that are displayed on the hospital electronic equipment are calibrated to reflect the exact same time and are checked for accuracy at regular intervals."

"Mr. Weston, would you please run the video presentation again for the jury?"

"No problem," he replied and signaled Kevin to rewind and show again.

"Thank you, Mr. Weston," said Leah. "I would like for you to remain in the courtroom after the prosecution's cross-examination. I will need your testimony on another matter."

The D.A. swaggered up to the witness chair with a cynical expression on his face, as if trying to mimic a cat cornering a mouse.

"That was an impressive movie, Mr. Weston. Was it filmed on a movie set?"

"No, sir," Tom replied without hesitancy and with a confident smile on his face. "It was filmed at the hospital where Mr. Bradford was a patient."

"Who do you work for, Mr. Weston?" asked Mankin, still with that asinine grin.

"I am employed as Director of Security for Salzman Electronics," he replied.

"The attorney for the defense is named Salzman, isn't she?"

"Yes, sir," said Tom.

"So, Miss Salzman and Salzman Electronics instructed you to come up with this ostentatious, theatrical display of electronic equipment to confuse and dazzle the jury into thinking that it was not the defendant who, with premeditation, committed this heinous crime on this defenseless victim," he said, as he walked back and forth in front of the jury box, again waving his arms and pointing to Josh.

"Objection, your honor!" said Leah. "Mr. Weston has been shown to be qualified and certified in his field and is testifying under oath. He was not 'instructed' to do anything. He was engaged to conduct a study on a critical issue in this case."

"Sustained," said Judge Blackman. "Mr. Mankin do you have any direct questions, without innuendos, for this witness?"

"No, your honor," he replied, still with the "cat's got the mouse" grin.

"Do you have more questions for this witness, Miss Salzman?" asked the judge.

"Yes, your honor," she answered. "Would you like for the equipment to be removed from the courtroom first?"

"We will recess while my court is put back in order. We will reconvene in twenty minutes."

With everyone in their places, the judge re-entered with his usual ceremony, seated himself at the bench, and reminded Tom that he was still under oath.

"Proceed with your case, counselor," he said to Leah.

"Mr. Weston," Leah began. "In the course of your investigation in this case, did you ascertain whether or not Don Bradford, Jr. had any life insurance in place on his life at the time of his death?"

"Objection!" screamed the D.A. "Irrelevant and superfluous."

"Counselors, approach," ordered the judge.

"Your honor," said Leah. "The beneficiary or beneficiaries of a large life insurance policy would have motive for committing murder. I simply want to show that as a possibility, thereby casting doubt on the guilt of the defendant."

"Objection overruled," said the judge. "Please show the jury the direction you're taking, Miss Salzman."

"Yes, your honor," she replied, and then resumed her questioning.

"What did you find, Mr. Weston, with regard to life insurance policies?"

"There were two policies taken out six months ago on Mr. Bradford, Jr.'s life through the insurance company that offered coverage to all Bradford employees."

"And what was the death benefit of those policies?"

"Both were for ten million dollars."

"And the beneficiaries?" asked Leah, with the jurors hanging on every word that Tom uttered.

"One was Linda Searcy Lehman and the other was Jeremy Corbett," Tom replied.

An audible murmur was heard to ripple through the courtroom and media reporters began to drift out to report the latest development.

"Both policies were for ten million dollars?" asked Leah, putting emphasis on the dollar amount.

"Yes, ma'am."

"One policy named Linda Searcy Lehman, Dr. Lehman's ex-wife, as beneficiary and the other policy named Jeremy Corbett, an associate of Mr. Bradford, Jr., as beneficiary?" Leah repeated loud and clear for effect on the jury.

"That's correct," said Tom.

"Thank you, Mr. Weston. I have no further questions. Your witness, Mr. Mankin," she said, with that entrancing smile on her face and a toss of her head as she seated herself.

"Mr. Weston, can you tell the jury how and from whom you acquired the information about the insurance policies?"

"I'm sorry, sir, the source is confidential."

"I demand that you reveal your source, Mr. Weston, or I will ask the judge to hold you in contempt."

"Objection!" Leah said. "Your honor, Mr. Weston's code of ethics prohibits his giving information that may be damaging to a source. If your honor wishes, we can recess and call an officer of the insurance company to verify Mr. Weston's finding."

"Objection sustained. Counselors, please move forward in readiness for your closing arguments."

"I have nothing further, your honor," said the D.A.

"The defense rests, your honor," said Leah.

"We will recess until 9:00 a.m. tomorrow and hear the prosecution's closing remarks," said the judge. "I anticipate bringing this trial to a close after the defense's closing tomorrow."

Chapter 50

The room was packed with spectators, some who had arrived at daybreak to contend for a seat, either on the first floor or in the balcony. The judge was adamant about disallowing cameras in his court. As usual, reporters and the media photographers gathered outside.

With the ending of testimony, the courtroom was open to anyone who chose to listen to the attorneys' closings. Luke and Tom Weston were permitted back into the room, and along with Ann and Josh's father were seated behind the defense table. At the bailiff's instruction, everyone stood as the judge entered. He seated himself at the bench and was preparing to summon the jury when the commotion at the entrance to the courtroom began.

"Bailiff, please quell the disturbance, whatever the cause."

The bailiff returned to the judge's side after checking on the noise and whispered, "There's a lady who insists on being admitted to sit with the defendant's family. She won't settle for a seat anywhere else."

"Allow her to enter, bailiff, and escort her to the bench. Miss Salzman, will you please approach?"

"Certainly, your honor," Leah replied with astonishment.

"Only with your permission may we allow this lady's presence during the closings," said the judge.

Leah turned to identify the person.

"Grandmother!" Leah said.

"My granddaughter, she is," Mrs. Salzman said to the judge. "A very bright girl, don't you think?"

"I'm sure she is," said the judge, smiling for the first time since the trial had started. "You have my permission to be seated, Madame."

Mrs. Salzman held her head high, looked at the bailiff as if to say, "I told you so," smiled at Josh, tossed her head, and took a seat beside Ann and Luke. Josh smiled back, thinking, *that's where Leah gets that lovable smile.*

Grant Mankin's closing remarks were, for the most part, a repetition of his opening statement. He stressed the point that Josh was knowledgeable of the effect of undiluted intravenous potassium; that he had the opportunity to administer the drug, being alone with the victim; and that he had motive.

The District Attorney completely changed his demeanor. He was calm and deliberate in his presentation. There was no emotionalism, no dramatic gestures in front of the jury. From somewhere came a high stool that he sat on while talking to the jury. He sat with his shoulders slumped, a saddened facial expression, as if he were about to break down and shed tears.

"No one else was present to push the drug into Mr. Bradford's vein," said the D.A. "The defense has tried to tell you that there were others who could have given the drug. Who else could have done it?"

"You have heard testimony that Linda Searcy Lehman came on the scene to find her Donnie dying and frantically rushed out to summon help. Does that sound like someone who had just injected a deadly drug into someone? Someone that she cared about so strongly that she would conceive his child, would leave her marriage with Dr. Lehman to be with him?

"The defense has tried to cloud the picture with evidence that Linda was the beneficiary of a life insurance policy. All that testimony tells you is this: Donnie thought enough of Linda that he wanted to preserve her way of life in the event of his untimely death—his *untimely* death."

"How many of you have spouses or loved ones who have done the identical thing—made you beneficiary of their life insurance policy? It simply confirms that these two people cared deeply for one another. Would either of the two—so devoted to each other—take the life of the other? I think not."

"In no way am I condoning illicit or immoral entanglements between two parties, but I recognize that in such affairs, the involved persons can develop strong bonds such as we see here. One may very well name the other as a beneficiary. If a bond is that strong, there is little chance that one would hurt the other."

"The other beneficiary, Jeremy Corbett, was Donnie's mentor, his educator. He tutored Donnie in college and groomed him to take over someday the reins of Bradford Holdings, the corporation that employed Jeremy. Jeremy was like a father to Donnie. Jeremy had no motive, was not present, had no knowledge of the effect of potassium."

"Ladies and gentlemen, Dr. Joshua Lehman was there, alone with the patient; he had the opportunity; he was bitter that his wife and Mr. Bradford had developed a meaningful relationship; he made threats that were heard by hospital employees and by the victim's father; and he knew that Mr. Bradford's heart would stop beating from a lethal dose of intravenous potassium and could not be restarted by resuscitation. The temptation was too great for him."

"We have shown beyond all reasonable doubt, and I stress the word 'reasonable', that Dr. Lehman is guilty of murder. You must send this message to the world, and especially to the medical community, that you expect exemplary behavior on the part of all health caregivers. You must find this doctor 'guilty as charged.' Thank you."

He has completely destroyed Leah's case that there could have been someone else that injected the drug, Josh thought. *Why didn't Leah do a personality profile on Linda and show that she is incapable of truly caring for anyone? Linda's sole goal in life is pursuing pleasure.*

Josh looked at Leah. She didn't appear at all concerned—she looked even more confident than ever. The first thing she did was smile reassuringly at Josh, toss her head, and then ask for the stool to be removed as if it were some theatre stage prop.

The courtroom was quiet; all eyes were on Leah. She stood and paced slowly back and forth without speaking, with the jurors in unison following her every movement like spectators watching a tennis match. After what seemed like a lifetime, she stopped and stood directly in front of the jurors. She spoke softly and slowly, keeping her eyes focused on the jurors, shifting from one to the other.

"You remember when we started this trial a few days ago, I asked you to keep in mind the word 'circumstances.' Now you see what I meant," she said. "Other than sketchy pieces of circumstantial evidence, the prosecution has produced absolutely no proof whatsoever that Dr. Lehman is guilty of charges brought against him. Have you heard testimony from any witness who actually saw Dr. Lehman inject the drug into Mr. Bradford? Have you heard any witness testify that they even suspected that Dr. Lehman was guilty? No, you have not!"

"The prosecution has placed Dr. Lehman at the scene; they have shown that the murder weapon was readily available to him; they have contended that he had a motive; but they have produced no one who saw him inject that drug!"

"Let me remind you that the ICU cubicles have glass walls on three sides. Let me remind you that there are twenty to twenty-five nurse caregivers in that unit at any one time—in the open area and in the adjacent cubicles—all curious about Dr. Lehman's and Donnie's strained relationship. Do you not think that some one of those nurses would have noticed any suspicious activity? There have not even been hearsay comments from any of the prosecution's witnesses."

"You have heard Detective Garetry's testimony that he was given the assignment because there was—how did he put it—'political clout behind the investigation.' You've heard Mr. Bradford, Sr. exclaim, when asked if he instigated charges against Dr. Lehman, 'You damn right I did! I know important people.'"

"Did you hear any testimony whatsoever that told you that Mr. Garetry had investigated any other possible suspects? No, you did not. The District Attorney and the investigating detective have made it clear that they want Dr. Lehman convicted, at any cost. You can bet Thursday's paycheck that come election time it will have been costly—to Mr. Bradford."

"What we have shown you by video is that the careful scientific probing by Mr. Weston proved that the onset of clinical signs of the adverse effect of undiluted potassium given intravenously in this case was some two minutes after Dr. Lehman left Mr. Bradford's bedside."

"Dr. Lehman left the ICU, walked to the surgery dressing room, and placed covers on his shoes before the first effect became noticeable on the telemetry strip. You have heard testimony that the effect of this drug becomes evident in seconds. Had Mr. Garetry conducted such a study, he would have stopped and said, 'Whoa! Maybe we had better look for other suspects!' He didn't do that because he was told, 'build a case that will convict Dr. Lehman.'"

"Mr. Mankin has painted an emotionally stirring picture for you of two lovers being so devoted to one another that neither would ever do anything to harm the other. I submit to you that we are talking about two people with a track record of devoting every minute of their existence to seeking personal pleasures for themselves, without regard for their fellowman or for any social consequence. Devoted to each other? Ha! What a joke!"

"Ladies and gentlemen, I tell you this: Dr. Lehman's existence has been and will be always devoted to saving lives, not taking lives. Let him get back to his life's work—building the Heart Institute in this community that may very well some day save your life or my life."

"You must go into that jury room and face the responsibility of deciding whether or not Dr. Lehman is guilty 'beyond all reasonable doubt.' Ladies and gentlemen of the jury, 'reasonable doubt' hangs over this case like a dense, black cloud. Thank you for your attention."

Leah stood motionless for a few awkward moments, then turned to return to her seat. The courtroom was still, an eerie stillness; no one coughed or cleared their throat or even breathed heavily. Mrs. Salzman stood and began clapping, and then turned to the row behind her.

"My granddaughter!" she said, glowing with pride. "Married, she's not. Work, work, work...her life, yet."

The judge slammed down his gavel before she could hardly finish her sentence.

"Madame, I will not tolerate such outbursts in my court!" admonished the judge. "You will remain quiet or you will be asked to leave."

"Oy, vey, that judge!" she said to Ann, loud enough for all to hear. "A kvetcher, yet."

"Madame!" the judge warned.

The judge turned to the jury.

"Ladies and gentlemen, this has been a trying experience for you, sitting there day after day, listening to witnesses, trying to decide if you're hearing truth or untruth. I want to remind you once again. When you go into that room to deliberate, you must remember: for a finding of guilt, your decision must be 'beyond all reasonable doubt.'"

"'Beyond all reasonable doubt' is a state of mind; it is what you feel in your heart to be the truth. All of you might not arrive at the same decision initially, but you must deliberate and arrive at a consensus of opinion before you return and deliver your decision to this court. You will be sequestered until you arrive at a decision."

Chapter 51

At the judge's instruction, the jurors stood and filed out towards the jury room. As they walked away, the two black men both paused and looked back at Josh and smiled.

Leah leaned over to speak to Josh.

"Now we wait, Josh," she said. "There is no way of predicting by the time they stay out what their decision will be. We just have to be ready for anything. We'll wait in the conference room next door for a while."

"What do you think?" asked Josh.

"Can't tell," she replied. "Josh, do you know those two black men on the jury?"

"I never saw them before," he answered.

"They know you some way."

Leah walked over to her grandmother, who was busily engaging everyone around her in some form of dialogue.

"Grandmother, how did you get here?"

"Jackson drove me, of course. I should drive myself, already?"

"Does Uncle Charles know you are here?"

"A keeper I don't need," she replied. "Your speech, beautiful it was! Now you will marry this boy?" she said, loud enough for Josh to hear.

"Grandmother!" said Leah. "You are embarrassing me."

Leah glanced at Josh. He was grinning, ear-to-ear. It was nice to have something to laugh about for a change.

* * * *

An hour dragged by, then two hours. *Why is it taking so long?* Josh wondered. The tension became unbearable. The air was still—knife-cuttingly still—no talking, no joking, very few comments. Even Mrs. Salzman was quiet, sitting close to Leah, holding her hand from time to time.

Luke and Ann sat together, holding onto each other, speechless, but bonded by the same concern for Josh. Josh and his father were side-by-side. *It has taken this tragedy to bring me and my dad this close. I don't want to lose this, whatever the outcome of the trial.* Any semblance of a feeling of fatigue was erased by the apprehension that each person felt, knowing that any minute there would be a knock of the door to summon them to hear the verdict.

Finally, the knock came. They were called back into the courtroom, with the announcement that the jury had reached a verdict. The jurors were seated in their usual places. The expression on their faces told Josh nothing. The judge was already at the bench. He addressed the foreman of the jury.

"Have you reached a verdict in the case of the state versus Joshua Lehman, accused of murder in the first degree?"

"Yes, we have your honor," the foreman, standing, answered.

The bailiff took the paper containing the written words of their decision to the judge. He read the wording, showed no emotion, and returned it to the bailiff, who took it back to the foreman.

"And what say you?"

"We find the defendant—NOT GUILTY!"

The court erupted in a roar of applause. Judge Blackman tried to maintain order by striking his gavel on the table, but soon gave up. Well-wishers in the room surrounded Josh with hugs and congratulatory greetings. Josh made his way to Leah and they fell into each other's arms for a prolonged embrace, tears streaming down their faces.

"A perfect couple they make," said Mrs. Salzman to anyone she could find to listen.

The judge pounded his gavel again to try to regain order. The room was finally quiet. He polled each juror individually, thanked them for doing their duty, congratulated them on their prompt verdict, and dismissed them. For a few minutes, the jurors mingled with the crowd and some consented to interviews by reporters. One of the two black men of the jury made his way to Josh.

"We is happy for yo, Dr. Lehman," he said. "Oh—ole Sam says to tell you howdy. I'se got to call him and tell him yo is all right."

Josh was shocked for a moment that Sam had sent greetings. That explained the smiles from the two black men.

"How do you know Sam?" asked Josh.

"We is all cousins," he answered, nodding toward the other black man who was standing back, reluctant to approach the crowd. "He says yo and Mr. Luke is fine boys," he added with a grin.

"How is Sam?" asked Josh.

"Pretty good," he replied. "The miseries done got him down. He is in a nursing home. Don't get around much or he'd be here."

After getting the name and location of the nursing home, Josh said, "I am going to visit him. I learned a lot from Sam."

"Well, that would be nice, Mr. Josh," he said. "He'd be plumb tickled."

The man turned and joined his cousin and the two left together, busily engaged in what appeared to be lively conversation. Josh debated whether or not he should mention the encounter to Leah. "These two guys, with Sam's help, may have saved my life," he said to himself. He decided to wait, unless Leah asked him again.

Tom appeared with three security guards this time, and along with Josh and Leah plowed their way to the waiting limousine through the throngs of people, including the media reporters and cameramen. Before entering the vehicle, Josh stopped and turned to Leah.

"We've got to answer their questions. It would be discourteous to ignore them now," said Josh.

"Josh Lehman, I would have bet money you would have said that," Leah laughed. "OK, get ready."

They turned to face the cameras and to field the questions.

"Dr. Lehman, do you believe your ex-wife injected the drug?"

"Neither Dr. Lehman nor I have accused Linda Searcy Lehman of any crime," said Leah, before Josh could speak. "I can't speak for the District Attorney."

"How do you feel, Doctor?"

"Relieved that it is finally over," said Josh, with the cameras whirring.

"What are your plans now?"

"I really haven't had time to even think about it," he answered. "I want to get back to my work as soon as I can."

Leah spoke up and made gestures that the interview was over, encouraging Josh to enter the limousine.

"Dr. Lehman will need some time to unwind from the stress he's been under before resuming the stress that's a way of life for him," she said.

With Josh and Leah both in the vehicle and about to close the door, another question was thrown at Leah.

"Miss Salzman, it is rumored that Don Bradford, Sr., will file a 'wrongful death suit.' Can you comment?"

"I suggest you ask Mr. Bradford," replied Leah, closing the door as the limousine carefully crept forward.

Josh and Leah were alone in the back compartment of the car with Tom and the guards in the front section. Separating them was a tinted-glass soundproof partition. It was the first time they had been alone together since the trial had started. They looked at each other and their eyes locked for several awkward moments, as if there were some magnetic force that wouldn't allow them to look away. Leah spoke first.

"Josh, I know what you're thinking. Don't thank me!"

She took his hand in hers and held it with a tender, but firm grip. There were tears in her eyes as she finally turned away without saying another word. They sat side-by-side in silence, each with their own thoughts.

"OK, public enemy number one, where do you want go? Leah chided. "Tell me before I tell you what I think you should do."

"Promise you won't laugh," said Josh.

"Promise."

"I haven't seen Jay in ages."

Leah pushed the intercom button.

"Tom, can we stop by Dr. Sander's house for a minute?"

"Sure, Miss Salzman," he replied.

"Josh will give you the address," she added.

"Thanks, but I have it on file."

Within minutes they were in front of Luke's house. Seeing Luke's car in the driveway reminded Josh that he had not even seen Luke and Ann after the trial. There was so much confusion that he had missed them.

"We'll wait down the street, Miss Salzman, until we see you come out," said Tom over the speaker.

Josh insisted that Leah come with him.

"You're in for a treat," said Josh, with more enthusiasm than Leah had seen for weeks.

"I feel like I am about to meet the Prince of Wales," she laughed, as they approached the front door.

"Did I ever tell you why we call him 'Jay'?" asked Josh.

"No less that ten times," she replied with that Salzman smile.

They were greeted by Luke and Ann with hugs and tears.

"We took your dad home, Josh," said Luke. "One happy man!"

"Thanks, Luke," said Josh. "There were so many people there that I never saw."

"It's over, dude!" said Luke. He grabbed Josh by the shoulders, shook him a couple of times, then gave him a hug. "Hey, keep your act clean! I'm getting too old for this."

"No problem." Josh laughed. "Maybe just a fake play now and then?"

"Just tell me first," said Luke.

"Promise," said Josh.

The thump, thump sound of Jay racing down the stairs, two at a time, let them know, without asking, that Jay was home from school.

"Uncle Josh! Uncle Josh!" he cried as he raced across the room and jumped into Josh's arms.

He held on tightly, with his head buried in Josh's chest. He turned, facing Josh.

"They said at school that you did something bad to that man," he said. "I told them that you helped people; that you didn't hurt them."

"He's been in two fights already at school, Josh," Ann laughed as she pulled Jay away from Josh. "Jay, I want you to meet Miss Salzman. She has been helping Uncle Josh during the trial."

Jay looked at Leah with suspicion and said nothing. Leah gave him one of those warm, captivating smiles and he loosened up a bit. Leah knelt down on her knees to be at Jay's level as she spoke.

"You are right, Jay," she said, her eyes moist as she looked at him with a motherly tenderness. "Uncle Josh would never hurt anyone. It's all over, Jay. You don't need to fight any more. You can tell them at school that the court said that Uncle Josh didn't hurt that man."

Jay moved closer to Leah, hesitated for a moment, then reached out and gave her a hug. Leah was no stranger from that moment on.

As they said their farewells and moved toward the front door, Luke handed Josh a sealed envelope, out of sight and earshot of Leah.

"Nathan Greller gave this to me right after the trial," said Luke. "I have no idea what it is, but he said he wanted you to have it. He made some comment that he couldn't decide whether it would help or hurt your case. He acted a little strange, but I didn't get to talk to him very long. Oh, Ann says she likes Leah," he added.

"Thanks for everything, Luke," said Josh as he placed the envelope in his coat pocket.

*   *   *   *

The minute Josh and Leah stepped out of Luke's house, the limousine pulled up in front for them to enter.

"He's a lovable child, Josh," said Leah. "I can see why you love him so much, and he certainly adores his Uncle Josh."

"Thanks for being so kind to him," said Josh. "Seeing you talk to him made a beautiful picture."

"And it rekindled my remorse over all that's missing in my life," Leah replied.

"Come on!" said Josh. "Look who you're talking to. You have a life ahead of you. And I, for sure, have just gained a life."

"Maybe we can discuss it further," she said.

"I hope so," said Josh.

The limousine seemed to be moving at a greater rate of speed. Leah looked out, trying to get her bearings. She pushed the intercom button.

"Tom, we're not going toward my hotel," she said.

"No, Miss Salzman," she replied. "We are on the way to the airport."

"Why are we going to the airport?"

"Your plane is waiting and ready to take off as soon as you and Dr. Lehman arrive."

"Tom, I have to check out of the hotel and pack my bag. I'm not ready to go home to Dallas," she said with some irritation.

"You're not going to Dallas, Miss Salzman," said Tom, with a tone of cheerfulness to his voice. "You and Dr. Lehman are checked out of your hotels and your bags are packed and in the back of the limousine."

"Tom, what are you doing to us?" she asked.

"I'm just following your grandmother's orders, Miss Salzman," said Tom, with an unprecedented chuckle.

"Tom, you can't do this!" she said. "This is kidnapping. Turn around and take us back!"

"Shall I get your grandmother on the phone for you?" questioned Tom.

Josh laughed during the entire dialogue. Nothing about Leah's grandmother surprised him. Leah looked at him for several seconds and began laughing with him.

"Don't bother, Tom," she said over the speaker and then pushed the "off" button.

Leah and Josh boarded the small jet and took seats facing each other. Without anyone saying, they were sure they were headed for the Escondido Ranch. On the table between them was a wine cooler with a bottle of Chardonnay, uncorked and iced, plus two wine glasses. Attached was a note with a simple five word message: "I love you both—Grandmother."

After a couple of glasses of wine, they relaxed for the first time since the trial had ended. The exhaustion of the last several days had taken its toll. Josh remembered the note from Nathan, and while Leah dozed, he opened it. Fortunately, Leah slept soundly enough that she didn't see the shocked expression on Josh's face as he read Nathan's handwritten note:

Josh, I have been in a sleep-losing dilemma about this. I finally decided you should know. Without an order, I did a DNA test on Donnie's tissue from the autopsy and compared it with the fetus that Linda passed. It didn't match. Donnie was not the father. Also, Josh, Donnie was HIV positive.

"Oh my God!" he said to himself. "I was so wrong."

Thoughts raced through his mind. Who could it have been? Had he known, would he have acted differently? Could there have been a mistake? DNA tests just don't lie. The error rate was less than one in one-hundred thousand. He looked at Leah, still sleeping. Should I keep this from her? He decided this was not the time to cast a damper on their time together.

Josh was intent on putting the past events behind him and try to rebuild his life around his long-range goals. The people who really mattered the most to him were supportive one-hundred percent. Luke and Ann, Leah, Charles Salzman, Dr. Dubonet, Dean Roever, his father, and yes, Grandmother Salzman, were there for him. A warm feeling engulfed him as he drifted off to sleep.

Chapter 52

▼

Josh and Leah both awakened when the plane glided down the runway at the Escondido Ranch. The plane came to a stop, the door opened, and the step platform dropped to the ground. As they prepared to deplane, they looked out to see Ken in his Jeep, his Lab in the front seat, racing toward them, followed by a cloud of dust. Ken jumped from of his Jeep and ran to meet them. He grabbed Josh and smothered him with the traditional Mexican *abrazo*.

"Just saw it on TV, Josh!" he said, his broad grin causing deep creases in his tan, leathery face. "Great news! Glad to see you!"

"Thanks, Ken," replied Josh. "Good to be here again."

"Yeah, I was wondering if I was going to have to go visit you," said Ken, laughing as he placed the baggage in the back. "Oh, good afternoon, Miss Salzman."

"Hello, Ken," she said. "You were worried? We never had a doubt, did we Josh?"

"Never," said Josh. "How are things at the ranch, Ken?"

"Well, we have missed you, and we've been worried about how you were holding up," he answered. "The boys got together and got you a present."

Ken reached down in the floor of the Jeep and brought out a square box—no wrappings, just a box. Josh opened it to find a beautiful pair of Lucchese Boots with his initials embossed on the top.

"Ken, I can't believe this!"

"They said if you were going to be a ranch hand, you gotta dress like one," laughed Ken.

"How did they know my size?"

"They measured a footprint you made down by the creek one day."

"How did they know I wouldn't be in jail?"

"They just knew, Josh…they just knew," he grinned. "Out here in the country, you just know."

"I am speechless, Ken," said Josh. "My throat's choking up."

Josh glanced at Leah, standing by, smiling, but with a sort of devious, evasive look on her face as if avoiding eye contact with him or with Ken.

"You know we're gonna put him to work while he's here, Miss Salzman," chided Ken.

"I'm ready!" laughed Josh.

"Hey, what about me?" said Leah.

"Oh, yes, ma'am, Miss Salzman," he replied, trying to be serious. "Have a job for you too. Girl that gathers the eggs and milks the cow went to visit her mama. Figured you'd help out a couple weeks while she's gone."

"Sure!" Leah responded. "But—two weeks, Ken?"

"Yup," he replied. "Plane won't be back for two weeks. Your grandmother's orders."

"Ken—they're holding us prisoner!" cried Leah. "Josh, do you know anything about this?"

"Not a thing," he answered, trying to conceal his laughter.

"Just joking, Miss Salzman…Mr. Weston said to call when ya'll wanted leave here," said Ken, as they bounced along the road to the lodge. "He will send the plane back when I call him."

Josh and Leah both appeared contemplative as they neared the main house. The weather was beautiful—a sunny sky with a scattering of white, cumulous clouds that seemed bluer that Josh ever remembered. Everything they passed seemed to take on a glow—the grass seemed greener, the trees seemed to open their branches to welcome them. To Josh, the mountain range that surrounded them seemed to be there for the sole purpose of protecting them from the cruel outside world.

"Supper'll be ready in 'bout an hour," Ken said, as they approached the lodge. "Should give ya'll time to unpack and have a drink. Tomorrow the Jeep will be available for you to use if you want to explore the ranch a bit. Be working cattle in a pasture about three miles from here if you wanna join us."

"Which pasture, Ken?" asked Josh.

"Far south end of the valley," replied Ken. "Close to that corral where you and me worked on that loadin' chute—you remember that, don't you, Josh?"

"Yeah, I know where it is," said Josh. "We'll be there."

"Get there by dinner time. Cook'll be there with food then. You know, Josh," he laughed. "When the sun's right over your head."

"I remember, Ken."

"Are you going to make a rancher out of him, Ken?" Leah laughed.

"Gonna try!" Ken said, grinning as he unloaded their bags. "Ain't much to do here except relax and work. Tom said you both need to relax. Cell phone number is by the telephone in your rooms if you need anything. Also printed on the phone in the Jeep. Maids and cook are always excited when we have guests, especially so now with your coming. Been glued to the TV the last few days. Ain't done much else."

Josh and Leah were assigned separate rooms on the second floor. There was no connecting door. However, both rooms opened onto the wide balcony that completely encircled the house. A well-stocked wet bar was located outside in a recessed wall space. Comfortable chairs and adjacent tables were spaced near each bedroom door.

After unpacking and freshening up for dinner, they met on the balcony. Martinis, not too strong, but strong enough, seemed to be just the thing for the occasion. The sun slowly disappeared behind the western rim of the mountains while they sipped their drinks. They were both quiet and exchanged few words, but they saw the feeling of closeness that each felt reflected in the expressions on their faces and in the softness in their eyes. Josh turned to Leah.

"Did you have anything to do with those boots?"

"You'll never know!" she replied, with an impish grin and a toss of her head.

*　　　*　　　*　　　*

Their candlelight dinner was sumptuous and attractively served. The cook could be seen peering around the door from the kitchen to watch their reactions to each course. The waitress did not speak English, so Leah, to Josh's surprise, spoke to her in Spanish and asked for the cook to come out. He hesitated to come forward, but with encouragement, he came close to their table so they could congratulate him on his culinary skills.

After dinner, Josh and Leah sat on the balcony with their after-dinner drinks. They both had been unusually quiet during dinner, and even quieter now while they sat together sipping their drinks. The sky was pitch black, making a contrasting background for the bright sparkle of the stars. The distant mountain ridge was outlined both by the starlight and by some remnant of the setting sun.

Not a sound could be heard, except an occasional coyote call from far away. Leah finally spoke.

"Does this remind you of Geneva?"

"Being together, alone, does," he replied. "I like being with you, Leah."

"Are you getting romantic?"

"Could be," he said. "Are you getting sentimental?"

"Yeah, I like being with you, Josh," she answered.

"Are you going to lock your door tonight?" asked Josh, grinning like a high school boy on his first date.

"I don't think so, but you will have to find out for yourself," she replied with a laugh.

*   *   *   *

They both awakened the next morning, facing each other and only inches away.

"Did you rumple your bed in your room before you crawled in here?" chided Leah.

"Come on," he said. "What kind of early morning greeting is that for two lovers?"

"Are we going to get married, Josh?" she asked.

"Of course!" he replied. "We can't disappoint your grandmother."

"Is that the only reason?"

"I love you, Leah," said Josh.

"I love you, Josh," she said.

With that they fell into each other's arms and pulled the sheet over their bare bodies.

Chapter 53

Jeremy rolled over on his stomach, exhausted as always after Linda drained him of every ounce of energy. He could hear the shower running. Linda ritualistically showered immediately after they had sex, as if she were washing away some symbolism of uncleanliness. He dropped into a stage of deep sleep for a few minutes, and then was awakened to the sound of Linda moving about the bedroom.

He turned on his side to watch the sunrise. From their tenth floor apartment they enjoyed a spectacular view. The walls on two sides of their spacious bedroom were completely windowed. At daybreak, just before sunrise, the horizon often took on a deep orange hue that was reflected in cumulous clouds to portray purple and lavender puffs. It was different each morning, as if an artist had painted a new picture for them for that day.

The Grand Tower, a luxury penthouse apartment leased in the name of Bradford Holdings, was a perk that Jeremy afforded himself. He had managed to hide its existence from everyone else in the company and still have the corporation pay the rent. Of course, after he dropped his bombshell on Bradford Holdings the company wouldn't be able to pay rent on a slum tent.

At the Grand Tower he and Linda could park in the garage and take an express elevator to the tenth floor and not be seen. He would miss the penthouse after they moved, but after getting settled into a new life, he would soon forget the place. He likely would not forget, however, the many exciting trysts with Linda over the last year.

Jeremy climbed out of bed and staggered into the bathroom for his morning toilet. He shut the door and looked at himself in the mirror. "You've got work to do, man; you've got to wind this up today." While he shaved, showered, and made himself ready for the day he reflected on events of the last few weeks.

Neither he nor Linda had openly discussed it yet, but Jeremy knew they both were glad to get Donnie out of the way. How quickly he was out of their minds. They no longer needed to hide or sneak around or make excuses for where they had been to anyone. For the last year, Linda had kept Donnie so looped on alcohol and a combination of drugs that he hardly knew where he was ninety-percent of the time anyway.

Jeremy had almost completed the last compact disc describing the illegal accounting procedures Bradford Holdings had used to defraud the shareholders and the strategy that was used to deceive the government audits. Two packets of CDs, from an anonymous whistleblower, would be delivered—one to the Securities Exchange Commission and the other to the FBI.

He would make another packet for himself and place it in a bank safety deposit box. The original information was secure now. He had coded access so no one except the holders of the CDs would be able to get to the files. He laughed, thinking of the frustration of the company accountants trying to reach the files, with the FBI knocking on the door.

He had almost finished the fund transfers from old Don's personal offshore and Swiss bank accounts. The greatest impact that would rock the financial world was the reinstatement of billions of dollars, plus interest, into the many employee retirement funds Bradford had raided over the years.

Jeremy recalled the hardship that had been inflicted on his mother and father. He thought the final days of his mother's life—her suffering, her bravery, and her final demise. He remembered vividly the days that he had struggled to survive, and the promise he had made to himself. Sweet were the spoils of victory! He leaned back in his chair and stared at the ceiling. Then he closed his eyes, smiled, and said aloud.

"I did it! I did what I set out to do!"

Jeremy had already bled Don's personal accounts down to almost zero and was ready to finalize the process, but then he hesitated when a brief wave of remorse for the old guy swept over him. He transferred $500,000 back into Don's personal account. Don would need a little money to pay legal fees for his defense. Also, he would need some funds to pay off the D.A., plus the other politicians standing in the wings, for their role in the aggressive attempt to convict Dr. Lehman. Then he changed his mind and reduced the amount to $100,000.

With Donnie's death, Jeremy was forced to wind up his scheme to totally erode Bradford Holdings of its liquid assets as quickly as possible. Without Donnie, he no longer had the tool to manipulate funds on a global basis that he'd had before. Even so, he was coming out with an impressive account balance of his own.

Accumulating funds for himself had become a game. *Just another game!* he thought. He would miss the fun, but somewhere down the road he would find another opportunity. It really was not the size of the take; it was the thrill of outwitting auditors—both internal and external. That, plus his determination to avenge the deaths of his parents, were the driving forces that had brought him to this point.

Linda knew nothing about his electronic maneuvers. Her insurance benefit of ten million dollars was safely stored away for her in a Grand Cayman bank. That was all she wanted for her part in doing away with Donnie. Jeremy helped her establish the account and gave her the access information. He warned her over and over again to conceal the code.

Now, I've got to come up with some way to get rid of Linda, he thought, *She has served her purpose.* He toyed with the idea of stripping her offshore account down to nothing. She would self-destruct if she didn't have the resources to call on to support her lifestyle. All he knew was that he wanted to be rid of her. He had to come up with a plan. He was ready to move on, so it had to be soon. He thought of Lennie. No, that would leave a trail.

The answer did come soon. Linda accidentally left her purse open in the bedroom. With little effort, he searched through it and found an airline folder—a one-way ticket to Paris for the next day. She had said nothing to him about her plans. *What a twist,* he thought. *She is leaving me!*

Fully dressed, Jeremy emerged from his dressing room and sat in front of the bank of computers he had had installed in the apartment. He double checked on the items of information he had saved on the CDs to confirm that everything was in order for his next move.

He needed to spend this last day in the office, verifying that he had left no trail behind that could be traced. To conceal that funds were moved to his personal account, he had deleted all of the transfer data from the computer. He placed his new Social Security card with his new number in his billfold. His new passport—with his assumed name, courtesy of one of Lennie's connections—was placed in his jacket pocket so as to be readily available at the customs check.

As per his routine for each day, he moved into the kitchen to start breakfast. He glanced into the bedroom and caught a glimpse of Linda furtively shoving her packed suitcase under the bed before stepping into her dressing area to finish her makeup.

"Linda," he shouted. "I'm fixing breakfast. Anything you want?"

"Whatever you have."

Jeremy loaded his mini-tape recorder, activated it and placed it in his shirt pocket. They sat down across from each for breakfast, both unusually quiet, as if they were in a contemplative state. Jeremy finally spoke.

"Any sad feelings about Donnie?"

"None at all," she replied. "Hey, you made my favorite—egg and potato tacquitos! Thanks. Nah, I'm just glad to get him out of my life."

"Gonna miss having him around?"

"God no!" she said. "He was HIV positive, you know, and was beginning to have symptoms of AIDS—getting sicker by the day. But he wouldn't take treatment. Insisted on keeping it a secret from his dad."

"Why was that?"

"Afraid his dad would find out that he was gay," she replied. "Donnie was going to die anyway. That's why I have no regrets about ending his life. This was the easiest way out for him."

"Why did you ever get so tight with him in the first place?" asked Jeremy while he poured fresh coffee in each of their cups.

"He was fun to be with," she answered. "Except when he would bring in one of his gay friends. Lots of travel and running with a swinging crowd! But his drug habit finally got too hard to control."

"How did he keep his sexuality a secret so long?"

"No one ever suspected it," she replied. "He always brought dates to social events. He was the most eligible bachelor in town. Now, with all the court testimony made public about an affair with me and a pregnancy, no one will ever believe he was gay."

"So, you decided you had had enough?"

"After you managed to get those life insurance policies in place," she answered. "That's when I started planning it. I tried to overdose him several times, but he had too great a tolerance and there never was a real good opportunity."

"While he was in the ICU and had all of those IV lines in place, I knew that was my chance. I carried a syringe and two ampoules of potassium around in my purse every day. What luck to find a loaded syringe right there!" she added, seemingly totally insensitive to the crime she had committed.

"What are you going to do now, Linda?"

"I don't know, probably just hang out with you."

Jeremy smiled over the fact that he got the exact words he wanted on the tape. He stood, cleaned the table, and stacked the dishes in the dishwasher while Linda went back to finish her dressing. "God, I will be glad to get away from this bitch," he said aloud. He made a copy of the tape, added a note that said:

Linda, there is only one other copy of this tape. I am keeping it in a sealed package addressed to the District Attorney, to be delivered if anything happens to me. Have a nice trip to Paris.

* * * *

The next morning, while Linda was showering, Jeremy placed the note and Linda's copy of the tape on her dressing table, along with the tape player. He grabbed his bags and briefcase with the compact discs for the FBI and the SEC, all carefully packed the night before, and quietly stole away to the elevator, thinking *I hope I never see Linda Searcy Lehman again.*

On the way to the airport, he directed the taxi driver to drive past the house where he had lived with his mother. It appeared empty. The grounds were unkempt, and weeds had grown shoulder high. One section of the roof, that he remembered had always leaked when he was a child, now had totally collapsed.

"Stop here for a minute," Jeremy said to the driver.

Memories of those tumultuous days of poverty flashed through his mind. He started to get out of the cab, and then caught himself. He thought of the vows he had made for himself years ago.

"I can put those days behind me now forever," he said.

"I don't understand, sir," said the taxi driver.

"Never mind," replied Jeremy. "Let's go on to the airport."

At the airport, while waiting to board the plane, he found a bar and seated himself so that he had a clear view of everyone who came and went. He saw no one he had ever seen before. With his dark shades, no one would likely remember him. A waitress appeared.

"What'll you have?" an unsmiling waitress asked. *Must be just finishing the night shift,* thought Jeremy.

"Oh, thanks," he answered. "Bring me a martini—with two large stuffed olives."

Jeremy leaned back in his chair and laughed. His flight was called and he got in line for the customs check. He flashed his fake passport, was passed through, and boarded the plane for Brazil. As the jet careened down the runway, he adjusted his first-class compartment seat, smiled, and said aloud, "When I get to

Brazil, the first thing I'm going to do is have another martini with two large stuffed olives."

The End

0-595-31414-7

Printed in the United States
20847LVS00003B/166-168